Catherine Cookson was born in Tyne Dock and the place of her birth provides the background she so vividly creates in many of her novels. Although acclaimed as a regional writer—her novel THE ROUND TOWER won the Winifred Holtby Award for the best regional novel of 1968—her readership spreads throughout the world. Her work has been translated into twelve languages and Corgi alone has over 40,000,000 copies of her novels in print, including those written under the name of Catherine Marchant.

Mrs. Cookson was born the illegitimate daughter of a poverty-stricken woman, Kate, whom she believed to be her older sister. Catherine began work in service but eventually moved south to Hastings where she met and married a local grammer school master. At the age of forty she began writing with great success about the lives of the working class people of the North-East with whom she had grown up, including her intriguing autobiography, OUR KATE. Her many bestselling novels have established her as one of the most popular of contemporary women novelists.

Mrs. Cookson now lives in Northumberland.

Other Books by Catherine Cookson

and published by Corgi Books

THE
BLACK
CANDLE

Catherine Cookson

Crescent
SQUAMISH, BC V0N 3G0

CORGI BOOKS

THE BLACK CANDLE BOOK 0 552 13576 3

Originally published in Great Britain by Bantam Press, a division of
Transworld Publishers Ltd

PRINTING HISTORY
Bantam Press edition published 1989
Corgi edition published 1990
Corgi Canada edition published 1990

Corgi Books are published by Transworld Publishers Ltd., 61–63 Uxbridge
Road, Ealing, London W5 5SA, in Australia by Transworld Publishers
(Australia) Pty. Ltd., 15–23 Helles Avenue, Moorebank, NSW 2170, and in
New Zealand by Transworld Publishers (N.Z.) Ltd., Cnr. Moselle and
Waipareira Avenues, Henderson, Auckland.

Made and printed in Canada

U   0 9 7 6 5 4 3 2 1

To

Dr. Brian Enright,
University Librarian,
Newcastle-upon-Tyne.
My warmest thanks for his help
in my research, particularly that
dealing with the last century.

PART ONE

As It Was In The Beginning
1883

1

It was a Sunday in late September. The heat from the sun was such that the two young men picking blackberries had undone the top buttons of their Sunday coats, loosened their string ties and let the collars of their blue-striped shirts fall open, but still kept their caps on their heads.

The one who looked the elder was thickset; what hair could be seen under the rim of his cap was brown. The other was slim-built and fair; his hair was straight and sticking with sweat to his cheeks, and he now threw a handful of blackberries into the bass-bag that was almost half full of fruit, saying as he did so, 'I'm finished. I'm sweltered. Anyway, there must be six pounds in there.' And to this the other replied, 'I want it full. She always has it full.'

'It's Sunday, man.'

'Is it?'

'Aye, it is; and I'm off.'

'Begod! you're not. Now you get your hand in there again.'

The thickset young man paused and raised his head to where the bramble bush was entangled in the lower branches of one of the sycamore trees that hedged the field and, pressing the brambles aside, he looked to his right towards where the sycamores joined with the woodland from which a horseman was emerging. He had heard the noise of the gallop, but the horse had now fallen into a trot.

His brother, standing close by his side now, was also peering through the bramble. Then, some other movement catching his eye, he looked to the left to where, in the distance and skirting the field, was the figure of a woman, or a girl.

A dig in the ribs made the elder brother turn and look towards the figure, and recognition slowly dawning on him caused his eyes to narrow and his mouth to drop into a gape; but then, gripping his brother by the shoulder, he pulled him down beside him to the ground, for the horse had not only continued to approach but had stopped within a yard or so from them on the other side of the hedge.

When the younger man now mouthed a name his brother doubled his fist in his face; after which they both remained on their hunkers but with their heads poked forward.

Through the tangled brambles they could just discern the gaitered legs of the rider as he walked the horse forward, seemingly to where the girl was standing.

It was the man's voice that came to them first. He was saying, 'Who wrote that note?' But he didn't get an answer for some seconds; then the girl said, 'Me. I did.'

'I didn't know you were so advanced.'

'I can write a bit, an' read.'

'Well, you mustn't write me any more notes. You understand? In fact, you mustn't try to get in touch with me again. You're a silly girl.' Then the man's voice changed as he said, 'No, you're not. You're not a silly girl. You are beautiful, so beautiful, all beautiful.' And then there was a slight laugh as he added, 'Except your hands. Odd about your hands, stained, podgy.'

'Don't touch me!'

'Now, now.'

'I said, don't touch me, not ever again. But what am I

going to do? Me da will put me out. I've nowhere. I won't go to the workhouse, I won't!'

'Sh! Sh! You'll not go to the workhouse. And anyway, all this is your own fault. You should never have been made like you are, dear: you ask for it, you know.'

'I didn't. I didn't. I didn't ask you to touch me. Never wanted it. It was the barn dance, and the beer. I never knew what I was up to.'

'Oh yes, you did. You knew what you were up to all right.'

'I didn't, never! But I do now.'

'You could have been with someone else, my dear.'

'I haven't. I wasn't. You know I wasn't. I mean, you know I hadn't. And that's what you said, you knew I hadn't.'

'Well, what do you want me to do? I can do nothing now. Anyway, you've been refusing me lately.'

'I . . . I want it taken away. I have no money. But I tell you, I won't go into the workhouse, I'll go in the river first!'

'Don't be silly! girl. Don't be silly!'

'I'm not silly. You believe me, I'm not silly.'

'So you want money?'

'Aye. Well, enough to take it away. I'll . . . I'll take money now; I wouldn't afore. Remember that, I wouldn't afore.'

'No. No, you wouldn't, would you? That's something in your favour. How much will you need?'

'I don't know. I'll . . . I'll have to go away some place, into the city, or some place. I . . . I won't go to old Nell's. She takes 'em away all right, oh yes, but she cripples you. I've seen 'em.'

'Oh, you're well versed in this kind of thing, aren't you?'

'No, I ain't. But I know what happens when you ain't married.'

There followed a silence, broken only by the snorting of the horse, and during which the two young men looked at each other questioningly but yet knowledgeably, then turned to look again through the bracken and bramble to hear the man saying, 'Well, that should see you through. And I won't be seeing you again?'

'No, you won't be seein' me again. Never!'

There followed another silence, until the man's voice, this time with a note of regret in it, came to them, saying, 'That's a pity. Yes, Lily, that's a pity. But . . . well, goodbye now.'

The men behind the hedge could see the man bend forward to do something with his stirrup before throwing his leg into the air. They saw the horse being turned and then they heard it galloping away. And when the younger one went to speak, again he was silenced, this time by a wagging finger.

Neither of them could see the girl, but they knew her to be still there because part of her shadow was visible on the grass. And then they were both startled when a hand came groping through from the other side, and they almost fell on their backs from their hunkered positions when they saw the hand feeling around the soil near the root of the tree. They saw the fingers, brown-stained and hardly discernible from the earth, scratching into it, then stop and disappear for a moment, to come back again with a piece of shale or rock, and scrape with this until a hole about six inches deep was made. They watched fascinated and almost breathless as a small leather pouch was pressed into it before being covered by the earth. The hand was withdrawn again but only for a moment. They watched it now placing two pieces of stick, apparently to mark the hole; then it was withdrawn, the brambles were pressed back into place, and a long, low sigh came to their ears.

They allowed a full minute to pass before slowly getting to their feet and looking over the hedge, to see the figure skirting the field again.

'That was Lily Whitmore. Did you see who he was?'

'Aye, I saw who he was.'

'And she's got her belly full. God! wait till this gets . . .'

So quickly did the hands come on his throat that the younger man fell back into the bushes, only to be pulled forward again and shaken. And now he was gasping, 'You gone mad, our Joe?'

'Not as mad as you'll find me if you dare open your slack mouth about this do. D'you hear me?'

'Leave go of me.'

'I'll leave go of you when I'm finished. Now listen to me. You say one bloody word about what's happened over that hedge and you won't know what horse's kicked you. But the first one'll be Andy Davison. You mind Andy Davison? He did six months for you. He did six months that you should have been doin' in Durham because when you were on the run you planted the stuff in his cree. By God! If I'd known as much then as I know now, you would have gone along the line. Well, Andy's still waitin' to find out who did the dirty on him. An' if you live to survive what he'll do to you, then you'll wish he had done the job properly, I can tell you that. Now that's only one thing, for then there's me ma and the insurance money. If she knew about that, you'd be out through the door with a broken skull, as much as she's all for you. And that's not forgettin' Farmer Atkinson's barn.'

'I . . . I didn't do that. Well, I mean . . .'

'You egged daft Davey on to do it, didn't you? And where is he now? In the loony-bin. Why I haven't split on you afore, God alone knows. But I'm tellin' you this time, just one word, just one little whisper in the factory, or anywhere about, and you're for it. You'd have been for it years ago if I hadn't been thinking of Ma.'

'Aye, an' Lily Whitmore. You've always been sweet on her.'

'Well, I'm goin' to tell you somethin': I'm goin' to be more sweet on her; I'm goin' to marry her.'

'*Huh! Marry her?* Me ma wouldn't stand for that.'

'I'm not worried about what Ma's goin' to stand for in the future. I won't be there; you'll be head of the house and lookin' after her.'

'Just because of that?' Fred Skinner pointed down towards the hidden bag, but his brother Joe did not reply directly; he said, 'I don't know what's in there. Whether there's ten or fifty, it would be all the same to me; but we'll find out, shall we? 'Cos I'd only have to leave it there for a matter of minutes and you'd be back, wouldn't you?'

Joe pulled the little bag from the earth, but he didn't open it, he put it straight into his pocket, which brought forth from his brother, and in a tone of disbelief, 'You're not goin' to see how much is there?'

'No; because it doesn't belong to me. But see *that bag there*' – he pointed down to the blackberries – 'you can take that back to Ma, and if you want to open your big mouth you can tell her I've gone a courtin'.'

'*What!* You mean to take her on then? You're kiddin'.'

'You should know me by now, Fred, I never kid; I leave all that to you.'

'You'll be the laughin' stock.'

'Aye, I'll be the laughin' stock if it gets out it isn't mine. But it isn't goin' to get out that it isn't mine, is it, Fred? You understand me? If you don't, I've been wastin' me breath this last five minutes. And you know what I said then; and just as I don't kid I don't break promises.'

After staring at his brother Fred Skinner stooped and grabbed up the basket, and he had taken two steps backwards before he said, 'You think you're a bloody great guy, don't you? There's been no holdin' you since you got that leg-up in the factory.'

Joe answered quietly, 'You've got a tidy way to go; get home.'

'Aye. And you, you've got a tidy way to go an' all. They're right what they're sayin': you're aimin' for manager; but you've got no learnin', even with your night classes, 'cos you're still only about half a step from where you started.'

When Joe took in a long deep breath Fred turned sharply away and walked down the root-encrusted path. His hand in his pocket now gripping the little bag, Joe stood watching his brother until he disappeared, the while thinking: No learnin'. Well, he'd show him. Aye, he would. He'd have learnin'.

As if the thought had acted as a spur, he turned about and ran along by the hedge to where the sycamores met the wood.

Here, the boles of the trees were comparatively clear, which enabled him to pass through to the path on which the horse had emerged only minutes before, and he paused and looked across the field, considering: If he ran would he catch up with her before she reached home? Would she have gone straight home, though? But where else would she go? One place surely she wouldn't go, and that was anywhere near Ponder's Lane, because, being a Sunday and the weather like it was, the lane and the fields beyond would be thick with courting couples and those out to make a start on it, just as the dry-stone walls would be with the lads sitting on them watching the parade of giggling lasses, supposedly going flower-picking. And they did pick flowers, cowslips early on, then buttercups and daisies. The fields around Low Fell and Birtley were stripped on a Sunday. Bairns would take bunches home, but the lasses mostly would scatter theirs or, later, lie on them. That many of them should have been at chapel or church might have been noticeable in the number of empty pews; but not so in the Catholic church. There, they would be packed with the Irish. It wasn't so much fear of God but the fear of the priest with that lot. Lily was Irish; well, at least her stepfather was.

He started to run. What would he say when he got to the house? I want to see Lily? And what would her reaction be? Surprise? If only he could catch up with her before she reached home.

Five minutes later he saw her. She was standing against the wall of the factory, the Mordaunt Black Polish factory where she worked, where they both worked, and which building, with others, bordered the built-up area of Gateshead Fell.

At this end was the unsavoury but sweetly named district of Honeybee Place, four long rows of houses, each named after birds: robin, hawk, finch, and lark, even though the only birds to be seen in this quarter were the gregarious sparrows, except where, in a house, you might find a caged linnet, goldfinch or bullfinch, or, out in the fields beyond, you might startle a lark to rise and then stand watching in wonder as it soared in its singing.

On weekdays this particular area would be swarming with dark-coated and shawled figures, a beehive indeed as horse-driven lorries were loaded with the produce of the factory. Now there was only this young girl.

She had been leaning, head bent, against the wall, but on the approach of footsteps she straightened up quickly, then stopped when she recognised the man coming towards her.

'Hello, Lily,' he said.

'Hello,' she replied, and her hands going nervously to her hat, she straightened it and pulled the sides of her hip-length, dark blue coat together, as if to hide the front of her print dress. Then when she saw the hand come from Joe's pocket and his fingers uncurl to reveal the bag that only a short time before she had buried, she put a hand over her mouth and fell back against the wall, gasping.

''Tis all right. 'Tis all right,' he said. 'This is yours, isn't it?'

She didn't speak, but her head moved from side to side; and now he went on, his voice low, 'I happened to be on the other side pickin' blackberries for me ma. She has them every year. You and he stopped just afore me on the other side of the hedge. There was no time to get away; but then' – he shrugged his shoulders – 'if there had been I still would have stayed . . . Here! take it.' Her hand did not leave her mouth, and he stared at her in silence for a moment before he said, 'I'm going to ask you a question. I know I make me mouth go in there' – he nodded towards the wall – 'I've got to, to keep them up to scratch, but . . . but do you dislike me?'

The hand slid slowly down to her chin, then gripped the top of her coat before she shook her head, saying, 'No. No.'

'Do you like me then?'

There was a pause while her eyes widened and her lips opened and shut without emitting words. And then they came in a low whisper: 'Yes. Yes, I like you all right.'

'Aye, well now' – his head was nodding – 'that's out of the way. Now another question, important this to both of us . . . Will you marry me?'

The hand went across her mouth again, tightly now, pressing out the moist cream skin of her cheeks till they looked like distorted pink balloons.

'Well?'

'You would?' The hand slipped from her mouth and

now she muttered, 'You would? I mean, marry me?'

'That's what I've said.'

She now looked at the small bag that was still in his hand and which was resting against his waist now; and then in a bewildered fashion she said, 'But . . . but I don't know how much is in there.'

'*God in heaven!*' His voice had been almost a yell and now he looked first one way then the other along the building before poking his head towards her and saying, 'An' neither do I. What are you suggestin'? You think because . . . because of this . . . ?' He now threw the bag at her, but her hand didn't go out to catch it and so it fell to the ground.

When she made no move to retrieve it he picked it up again and thrust it into her hand, saying angrily, 'That doesn't say much for what you think of me.'

She was stammering now, 'W . . . w . . . well, I . . . I meant, Joe . . . what . . . what I mean is. Oh, I don't know.' Her head drooped onto her chest and as tears ran down her face and with the side of her forefinger she wiped them off her upper lip and her chin, he said, 'Give over. Give over. But get it into your head, whatever's in that bag's got nothin' to do with it. I've always had a fancy for you . . . well, I mean, over the past two years, since you were sixteen or so. So has many another round about. And yet you seemed to keep yourself to yourself, but apparently not enough.'

Her head was bowed again.

'But I'm not blamin' you, not entirely, because those bastards will get what they want one way or t'other: money talks for them.' He stood for a moment looking down at her bent head; then, his voice changing and a small smile spreading across his lips, he said, 'Anyway, I can't be as bad as the workhouse, can I?'

'Oh, Joe.'

When she raised her head he stood looking into her beautiful tear-filled eyes. He didn't know whether they were grey or green, he only knew they changed with her mood. He'd seen them sparkle with laughter at the antics that some of the lasses got up to, then shed pity, like they had done one day last week when old Fanny Culbert collapsed at her bench and died.

His head now drooped as she said, 'I'll never forget this to my dyin' day, Joe. An' I'll be true to you till the end, however long or short.'

'Aye, well, that's good enough for me. Now, let's get down to brass tacks. You'd better get home and break the news. I'll come along with you but . . . well, I won't go in. I'll give you ten minutes or so, then I'll come and see what reception you've had and we'll take it from there, eh?'

'Aye, Joe. Yes, Joe.'

'Well, come on; leave that wall alone, it's supported itself so far.'

She took a step forward and then, looking down at the bag that she was still clasping in her hand, she said, 'You'd better keep that, because if I go in home with it, I won't come out with it. I know that much.'

'Aye, there's something in that.' He took the bag from her; then dangling it by its string, he said, 'But it would be a good idea if you opened it, wouldn't it?'

'You do it.'

Untying the string, he pulled the top of the chamois-leather bag open, then tipped the coins onto his palm. There were five gold sovereigns, and they both stood looking at them for a moment until he said, 'Well, you'll be needing things later on; but in the meantime I'll do as you say, I'll hang on to it.'

She stood looking at him as he put the coins back into the bag and then placed it in his trouser pocket; but when she still stood as though undecided, he urged her forward saying, 'Well, come on then. Let battle begin.' Which had its effect for she now walked briskly by his side along by the factory wall, then across the dried-mud-ridged front, past the stables where the horses were champing while at their Sunday rest, and so on to the first row of Honeybee Place. And here the stench of the middens hit them with a force engendered by the heat.

The smell did not make them nip their noses or put a hand over their mouths because, through use, they were inured against it. They made their way down between the two-roomed houses, stuck tight together as if for support, and the line of so-called dry lavatories fronting them. One midden was allotted to two houses. Inside would be a rough stone erection stretching across the full width and acting as the frontal support of a stretch of wood with a hole in it. Outside and in the back wall near the bottom would be a hatch which could be lifted up in order to clean the midden.

The idea was for ashes from the coal fires to soak up the effluent; but there never seemed enough ashes to meet the need and so the lane beyond was polluted through the bursting hatches.

It was a disgraceful quarter, the townspeople said, but Honeybee Place, like its counterpart of Bog's End in Fellburn, had been there before the town had come into real existence. Every new mayor was going to make it his business to wipe out the place. But then, of course, the question would arise: where would he propose to house the people until new habitations could be built for them, because they must be near their work?

Joe hated this quarter, and he thanked God he hadn't been brought up here. Yet one minute's walk from the rows was Honeybee Hollow. Only five houses were in the Hollow, and they, too, supported each other. But there was the difference: they were stone-floored, and besides the two rooms downstairs, each had an attic above and a washhouse leading into a backyard. And what added so much to the difference was the tap at the bottom of each yard and next to it the private closet, the same type as the others, but private, almost as great a privilege as the tap. In consequence, the occupants of these five houses had always considered themselves a cut above those in Honeybee Place.

But Lily Whitmore lived in 29 Hawk Row, and as they turned out of Robin Row, Joe stopped and said, 'Look, I'll wait here. I'll give you ten minutes and then I'll come along. What'll you say to them?'

She cast her eyes downwards as she said, 'I'll ... I'll say you want to marry me.'

He gave her a little smile as he said, 'I'd like it better if you said, I want to marry him, or, I'm going to marry him.'

She made an effort to return the smile, then nodded and said, 'Well, I'll say something like that.'

'Does he get rough?'

Her whole body gave a slight shudder before she said, 'He has. He used to, but ... but I've stood up to him lately.'

'That's the way. Well, stand up to him again. And don't forget, I'll be just outside waiting.'

'What'll you say to him?'

'You leave that to me. Well, go on. Don't fret. Everything'll be all right.'

He watched her walk away, zig-zagging between the children playing on the road. She walked good, straight. She was a lovely girl. His want of her had grown over the past months. But so had that of a number of fellas, and they were lads of her own age. Well, he was only twenty-three; what was five years difference? And he'd be more able to take care of her than any of them. But God! what he'd like to do at this minute would be to gallop, as that fella had galloped through that wood, and get him by the throat, and choke the bloody life out of him. Oh, he would love to do that, and take the consequences. Aye, the consequences. But if he took the consequences he wouldn't have Lily, and you couldn't have everything in life.

When she had disappeared through a doorway halfway along the street, he turned his attention to the children playing on the road. One was squawking its head off. It was naked except for a rough calico diaper and it was crawling to where its elders, ranging between three and five, were playing chucks, throwing up a cube-shaped stone while attempting to snatch up smaller stones before it should descend again.

The cries of the children were strident, happy; their faces, dirty and sweat begrimed, were laughing; except for the crawling baby. He watched as one of the bigger girls, definitely all of five years old, screwed round on her knees, thrust out her arms, grabbed up the child and plonked it on her lap with a practised hand. She could have been the mother or the grandmother. His thoughts told him she was learning early in her particular school of life.

He did not possess a watch; he relied for the time on the buzzers from the factory: six o'clock start, eight o'clock break, twelve o'clock break, and five o'clock finish. Some factories kept their employees working till six, or later, and there was no buzzer to signal their release.

When he imagined ten minutes must have elapsed he began to walk slowly down the street, past the women here and there sitting on their doorsteps, most of them flapping their blouses to attract the air. Generally, no notice seemed to be taken of him, except when a voice would call out, 'Why! Hello, Joe. Got lost?' to which he would answer merely by a look. Even before he reached number twenty-nine he knew it was Lily's home by the sound of a man's raucous yelling voice. He couldn't make out the gist of the man's words until he was opposite the door, and then they came to him plainly: 'Begod! you will. I've brought you up, worked for you and you're goin' to walk out now, are you? So you think. Well, let me tell you, miss, you'll walk out when I'm ready an' not afore. Married, you say?'

A woman's voice now broke in, saying, 'Bill! Bill! Stop it! It might be the best thing.'

'Best thing? What d'you mean, woman, best thing?'

There was a pause, and Joe could only imagine that in the room beyond the half-open door the woman and man were staring at each other. And now the man's voice came low, not yelling any more but weighed down with threat: 'By God! If I thought it was right what your ma is tryin' to say, I'd drag you this minute to the church and Father McShea . . . Is it true? Answer me! or I'll throttle you.'

'You lay your hands on me and I'll . . . I'll . . .'

When the trembling voice came to Joe he thrust open the door and, staring back into the infuriated face of Bill Whitmore, he said, 'Aye; you lay your hands on her, just once.'

'What the hell d'you want? . . . Oh! Oh, not you! A bloody Protestant.'

'Aye, me. A bloody Protestant, is intending to marry a bloody Catholic. Now what d'you make of that, big-mouth Bill?'

'You watch it. You watch it else you'll find your gob split from ear to ear.'

'You've always fought with your mouth, Bill; you're known for fightin' with your mouth. Wind an' watter, that's your make-up. Now listen to me—' He now turned towards Annie Whitmore, saying, 'Or perhaps her mother should listen to me. Likely get more sense out of you, missis. But I'm marryin' Lily, and if she wants to be married as a Catholic it's all the same to me. Yet, I don't think she'll bother. For all I care it could be the Baptists or the Methodists. I'm a man of wide tastes, I have no definite opinion, like parsons I could mention who imagine they know what God wants. But if no one of these seems willin' then there's always the Registry Office. So I should imagine within the next couple of weeks or so we should be hitched. But in the meantime she's goin' to come along of me an' stay with me mother, everything above board.'

Annie Whitmore could find nothing to say; all she seemed capable of doing at the moment was to open and shut her mouth while glancing wearily at her husband. That was, until one of the four children in the room, the oldest who looked to be about nine, whimpered, 'Ma,' when she turned and screamed at her, 'Get out of it! Get out of it!' which caused a scrambling of all four children through a door leading into the other room and some measure of decision from herself, for she turned back to her daughter and said quietly, 'You set on this?'

'Aye, Ma. Yes; yes, I am.'

After a moment, the woman, blinking rapidly as she stared at her first-born, whose presence in the house had acted as an irritant since she had married for the second time, said now and still quietly, 'Well, go on and gather your bits of things an' get . . .' to be interrupted by her husband when he cried at her, 'You goin' to let her go like that?'

She faced him squarely and in a flat but firm voice she answered him: 'Aye, I'm goin' to let her go like that, because if her belly's full, what kind of a life is she goin' to have here? An' after all's said'n done, she's mine, an' that bein' as it is, I've got the last word on her.'

'By God! you'll suffer for this, woman.'

'Well, that'll be nothin' new to me, will it, Bill? And, like her, I might take it into me head to say, don't lay your hands on me. Anyway, that's in the future.' She turned now as Lily came out of the bedroom carrying a bundle of clothes in one hand and a long black overall over her other arm and a pair of clogs in her hand.

For a moment she stood looking at her mother; then she said, 'Bye, Ma. I'll see you.' She now looked towards where Joe was standing in the open doorway, but to reach him she would have to pass her stepfather and he was standing at the end of the table, his hands hanging by his sides but his fists doubled. And when Joe saw her hesitate he stepped forward until he was abreast of the man and, reaching out towards her, he said, 'Come on. There's such a thing as overstayin' your welcome.'

As Joe pressed her towards the door Bill Whitmore growled, 'You won't get off with it, you know. I'll get you,' to which Joe reacted by thrusting Lily forward into the street with his flat hand between her shoulders before swinging round to face the enraged man. 'You try anythin' on,' he said. 'You work at t'other Mordaunt's factory, don't you? The candle, isn't it? Well, I've got friends in both fields, the blackin' and the candle, so I'm warnin' you. Just remember there's lots of men round about lookin' for jobs. An' what's more, you can't rely on Lily's pay packet any more, so I'd advise you to think afore you strike out in the dark. Any time in the daylight I'll meet you, coats off, up Ponder's Lane, or the Lodden. But should anything happen to me in the dark, God help you, in all ways.' And with this parting shot he turned around and went out, having to pass now through the small crowd of children who had, as usual, gathered to enjoy a row. One of the girls was saying to Lily, 'You leavin' 'ome, Lily?' and she was answering, 'Yes, Maggie. Yes, I'm leavin' home.'

As he walked her away there was quite an audience along the street, and, without looking at her, he said softly, 'Keep your head up. Don't let anybody pity you. Never do that. So, keep it well up, and don't look back at 'em.'

Five minutes later he pushed open the door of his home and drew Lily into the living-room which, in comparison to the one she had left, could be termed a little palace, so bright and clean and comfortable did it look. But the impression of the room was swept away, indeed obliterated by the look on the face of the woman rising from the rocking-chair.

That the chair had been moving vigorously was evident, for it still swung widely when it was relieved of the small woman's weight.

That his mother had already been given the message by Fred was also evident. Even so, there was still disbelief showing in her face as she looked from her elder son to this girl standing by his side, then back to her son again.

She watched him now throw the bundle that he had been carrying onto a kitchen chair, then take the overall and clogs from the girl's hand and place them by the bundle before saying, 'This is Lily Whitmore, Ma. I suppose Fred has given you my message?'

'Message?' The thin lips were sucked in for a moment before they spurted, 'Rigmarole! Rigmarole! Courtin'. An' what've you brought her here for? She's one of the Whitmore's lot. I know her. I know her. That Catholic scum.'

'*Shut up!*'

'Don't you dare tell me to shut up, I'm your mother.'

'Only too well do I know you're my mother . . . Ma. Well, let me tell you, Ma, I'm your eldest son and since me dad died when I was seven I've been workin' for this house an' you . . . an' him' – he thrust his finger out towards his brother – 'well, that's all finished with; Lily

26

an' me here's goin' to be married, an' we're settin' up house on our own.'

'What!'

'You heard what I said, Ma, you heard. We're settin' up house on our own. There's goin' to be no piggin' in in my life. Now, you've just said Lily comes from that Catholic lot; well, the head of the Catholic lot has just told me his daughter's not goin' to marry a Protestant, so it would appear it's a religious battle. But I've just settled that half an' now I'm settlin' this one, Ma. Do what you like, we'll be married as soon as possible. In the meantime, Lily's stayin' here. She won't mind sleepin' on the saddle over there.' He indicated a wooden couch-like structure, the seat covered with a thin horsehair pad. 'But should you decide to make it uncomfortable for her, an' me an' all, then we'll go out and I'll find a room and . . . we'll live in sin' – he poked his head towards her – 'until we can be wed. Look at it this way, Ma: the longer she stays here the longer your pay packet'll be on the table on a Friday night. But in any case you'll have to get it into your head, it'll only be for a week or two at the longest. An' then your dear boy will have to look after you an' the house. You'll have to see that he gets a full week in, though, won't you, to keep you goin'? But when I'm on, Ma, I'm goin' to tell you what I've thought for a long, long time, and that is, you've sat on your backside far too long. You're forty-one years old and you've never been out to do a day's work for the last twelve years. I've got two women in the tin shop and they're over seventy and they're still goin' strong. You had rheumatics early, but it's never stopped you from slippin' down to the outdoor beer shop. *Oh. Oh. Oh.*' He flapped his hand towards her in unison with his words. 'Don't think you've hood-winked me over the years. An' when you weren't supposed to have a penny left in the house it didn't stop you from layin' your tanner bets, did it?' He drew in a long slow breath, then bent his head for a moment before saying, 'I've said more than I intended. But anyway it had to come out; it's been boilin' in me for years. You never played the game by me, Ma, never. So, I'm startin' a life of me own.'

The small woman bristled. 'Well, you've had your say; now we know where we stand. And I'll tell you where I stand an' what I think. I think there's somethin' fishy behind all this. It's come too quick; you weren't courtin' this time last week. It strikes me as you're bein' had in some way.'

Before he could retort they were all surprised when Lily, almost springing to the chair, grabbed up her belongings, then, turning on the little woman, cried angrily at her, 'I've always said, missis, nothin' would land me in the workhouse. But I'll tell you somethin' now, I'd rather put up with the workhouse than stay another minute with you,' before turning to Joe and saying, 'I've . . . I've got a friend. She'll put me up for as long as I want.'

When he made to protest she shook her head, saying, 'It's no good. You wouldn't get me to stay here if you paid me.'

And on this well-worn saying his mother yelled, 'No! but he'll have to fork out for wherever you go. He's let himself in for somethin', I can see that. I'm the first one to smell a rat.'

Lily had been about to turn away but she paused; then looking over her shoulder at the woman, she said, 'Well, you would do, missis, bein' a close relation to one.'

They were in the street again. She was walking fast and he was by her side, but when the strange noise came from him she stopped and looked at him. His face was slightly contorted, his eyes were wet, and, after a moment of gazing at him, she said, 'I see nowt to laugh at.'

'Oh, Lily. That last shot was a good 'un. I never imagined you to be so quick on the uptake. But you're gettin' tó be a surprise 'cos I've known you as somebody who kept themselves to themselves in the factory, only openin' your mouth when it was necessary. But . . . it might be unnatural for me to say this, but it did me heart good to see me ma bein' met by her match.'

This brought a little smile from her as she turned away, and she walked on more slowly. And now he asked quietly, 'Who is this friend?'

'It's Alice, Alice Quigley.'

'Oh . . . Alice Quigley. Well, I should imagine Alice'll put you up because there's only her and her ma.'

'Yes, I'm sure she will, but . . . but she'll be surprised, sort of, seein' . . . well, I mean, when I tell her you want to marry me.'

'Well, as I see it, there's nothin' strange in that; a lot of fellas would like to marry you, Lily.'

They were beyond the buildings now and crossing an open area cut in two by the almost dried-up bed of a stream and which acted as a boundary or buffer between the factory quarter and the better working-class district of the town.

Being close on five o'clock the area was deserted; everybody would be at their teas, high Sunday tea in most cases. But shortly after six o'clock the place would be thick with strollers. There was a wooden bridge over the stream, and as she went to step on it she stopped and, putting her hand on the weather-beaten post that supported a hand rail, she looked down on to the mud-ridged banks before she asked softly, 'Why are you really doin' this for me?'

'I've . . . well, I thought I'd already told you, Lily.'

'Yes, I know what you said but I can't take it in, sort of. Well, why?'

He now put his hands on her shoulders and looked into

her face; but he found himself unable to put into words why he was doing this. Could he say, 'Because I want you?' which was true enough, he did want her, and he'd wanted her for a long time, all the while imagining her untouched. Now she had been touched; whether just that once or more times, he didn't know. But, likely, if she had come to him clean his feelings of joy would have been, in a way, unbearable, whereas now his emotions were tempered with a feeling of care.

It was she who spoke again, in a low voice, saying, 'You won't take it out of me when once you've got me, will you?'

He seemed to fling his body from one side of the narrow bridge to the other before he barked at her, 'What d'you take me for? Is that your opinion of me?'

She put her hand across her eyes as she muttered, 'Well, they do, you know. Some of them do.'

His hands came on her shoulders again, and now the words that were in his mind came tumbling out: 'I love you, Lily. That's your answer to why, I just love you. And when it's born it'll be as much mine as yours. I promise you that.' Leaning forward now, he placed his mouth gently on hers, that was all; then he took her hand and they crossed the bridge, his mind repeating his own words, 'When it's born it'll be as much mine as yours.' Well, he would have to try to keep to his word, wouldn't he, because it would never be his: male or female it would carry that skunk inside itself.

2

When Bridget Mordaunt dismounted from her horse in the loading bay Mike McGregor, one of the two dray drivers, hurried towards her, saying, 'Good-day to you, Miss Mordaunt. Good-day to you. 'Tis a lovely day you've taken for riding.' Then turning his head, he called, 'You there, Larry? Come and take the miss's horse. And give him a drink, because it's sweatin' he is, the poor beast.'

Looking at the grey-haired man, dressed in thick moleskin trousers and a blue twill shirt covered with a brown leather waistcoat, she said on a laugh, 'He's like his namesake, he has a depressing countenance.'

The man nodded at her as if he understood who the namesake was, and as he walked across the yard by her side, twice he stopped her in order to point out some trifling innovations of which she was already aware. And she smiled to herself at his delaying tactics, for she was already aware that Danny Green had scooted into the factory at the sight of her to warn old George that Miss Bridget was about to appear. She knew that she was addressed as Miss Mordaunt to her face but known as Miss Bridget among themselves, for that was how they would address her when she had accompanied her father on his visits. And as it was half-past four in the afternoon old George was likely in his office, cooling himself with a tankard of frothing beer that one of the lads had been sent out for. But wherever George Fields might be, she knew that the work in the factory would still go on at the same pace and to the same high standard, because Joe would see to that.

It was Joe who came out of the doorway to greet her, saying, 'Good-afternoon, Miss Mordaunt. 'Tis nice to see you. Splendid weather, isn't it?'

'Yes, it is, Joe. But I thought it would have been a bit too hot for you in here.'

Before Joe could give any answer she turned to Mike McGregor, who was now touching his cap as he made to go back across the yard, and she said, 'Oh, by the way, Mike, how is your daughter?'

The man's face brightened and he answered, 'Never better, miss. Never better. This weather suits her down to the ground. 'Tis the damp and the winter that get at her chest. But she's been fine these past weeks. Pray God that such weather lasts.'

'Yes, indeed, Mike. Yes, indeed. Remember me to her.'

'I will, miss. I will indeed. And thank you.'

As they went along the narrow passage leading into the factory, Joe said under his breath, 'I doubt she'll be bothered much longer with either the damp weather or the winter, miss.'

'As bad as that, Joe?'

'Yes, miss, as bad as that. She's on twenty-seven and they usually go with the consumption round about that age.'

She made no reply to this, only made a small motion with her head. Then they were stepping into the factory, and, as always, she wondered how on earth these people stood this atmosphere, with the smell, dust and black, black everywhere, day in and day out, from childhood to old age.

She was walking down between benches occupied mostly by women, some packing the blocks of blacking paste, others dealing with boot-top liquid; still others with

32

heel polish and brown dressing for untanned shoes.

This part of the factory was comparatively clean; it was the workers in the mixing and boiling shop off the main room who, since she was a girl, had caused her to wonder how the men and women stood up to the work day after day until they died, for few of them were fortunate to reach retirement age, as old George had done.

She had early learned the ingredients necessary to make the various polishes, the names had fascinated her, and she had amazed her father by rattling them off like the alphabet: such as Marseilles soap, potassium carbonate, beeswax and water. Mix and boil together to a paste, then add a little at a time, stirring, stirring, powdered rock candy, powdered gum arabic, and ivory black. Stir until homogeneous, then pour, while still hot, into boxes. She had even sung it to a certain tune, that was until she had taken over the business after her father died, when she realised the amount of labour and sweat being constantly expended by the men and women in making the product – and the dirt, especially when soot was required to be used in some processes.

George Fields, wending his way towards her, stopped once to give directions to a young girl standing at the end of a table. It was still part of the pattern to show her that he was attending to his business, seeing that the workers were kept on their toes. And likely that little girl knew as much already about polish making as he did.

'Good-day to you, Miss Mordaunt. Isn't this a pleasure now. Isn't this a pleasure. Has Joe been looking after you? Have you come to look round? Everything's in order, I can assure you. How long is it since your last visit?'

'Oh' – she put her head on one side – 'it might be a month or more. And I'm sure everything's in order, but I happened to be on my way back from Halden Street, so I thought I would just say hello.'

'Oh yes.' The old man pouted his lips for a moment and his head bobbed as he said, 'Halden Street. Candles. Yes, you would have to look up there. Oh yes, I'm sure you would. Thing's goin' wrong?'

The last was said on a hopeful note, and she shook her head as she replied, 'Oh, no, no. They are wanting an extension made and there was a little meeting, you know.' Her voice trailed off. She knew she must not say that the candle business was booming under the management of Bertram King, who was the antithesis of this old man here. One of the new breed of managers. Men who got things done, but were little loved. And although the profits from the candle factory had gone up by thirty per cent in the last two years, she knew which factory she would prefer. No; that wasn't right: she knew which set of people she would prefer to deal with; often when she visited here the girls would be joking and laughing; they made light of life, in spite of everything.

And then there was Joe.

'Would you like to come into the office for a minute? You might like to look through the books yourself. We had two fresh orders in last week. The liquid blackin' is doin' well. An' the tins I ordered came on time . . . Good company that.'

'Oh, that's splendid. And yes, I'd like to come to the office for a moment, but not necessarily to see the books.'

As she continued through the workshop she stopped here and there, saying, 'Hello, Hettie,' or 'How are you, Tommy? And the family?' Then again, 'Harry, you seem to get taller every time I see you. How old are you now? Fifteen? I thought you had been here longer than a year. You have grown.'

So it went on, stopping and starting until she reached the office with the little window, half of which was in frosted glass.

The old man ushered her into his seat behind the long wooden table on which at one end stood a number of tin boxes, and at the other wooden bases in which skewers were stuck, providing a useful and very practical method of having lists to hand simply by piercing them on the skewers. There were also two thick red-leather-backed ledgers on the table.

'Do sit down, George.' She pointed to a wooden chair; but at this suggestion the old man shook his hand vigorously, saying, 'Oh. Oh, no, miss. Don't worry about me being on my pins; I'm used to that.'

'Well, you've been on your pins, as you call them, for many more years than you should have been, and you know that. And last year, when your dear wife was so ill, you thought you would like to give up. Now didn't you?'

'Yes. Yes, I did then, miss, but she's much better, she's much better.'

'Now, George.' She leaned forward with her forearms on top of one of the ledgers and, looking up at him, she said, 'I'm going to be firm with you: you've got to retire. You should have done it, oh, at least five years ago. But you were so valuable that I didn't press you. Now I'm going to. Now, now.' She wagged a finger at him. 'I'll see you're well taken care of, you know that. And I promised you, you can move from where you are now or stay there if you like. But as I said, I promised you you would have a house in Birtley if you wanted, or Chester-le-Street, or perhaps in Gateshead.'

'Eeh! miss, miss, you're so kind. You're just like your dad used to be. There wasn't a better man living than your dad to work for. An' when he went I thought he couldn't be bettered, but you've lived up to his name, miss. You could have been his son in lots of ways. No falderals about you.' He was wagging his finger. 'No disrespect I mean, miss, no disrespect, because there's not a finer figure on a horse than you are. Oh, I've said that all along, I have. I have.'

She smiled as she thought, Yes, you have; but you were the first to nearly drop down with shock when I rode in in breeches. But then she thought, I've got to be very diplomatic in my next move. And so she began. 'I know we'll never get anyone to manage this place like you, George. I'm well aware of that. But I would like your advice on something. Now as you know, there's a different kind of man coming into management. Not that I hold with all their ideas; but nevertheless, times are changing and there they are. A lot of them are called smart alecs. You've said that yourself, and I agree with you. Now, George, you tell me how I'm going to get someone to even try to fill your place, except one of these smart alecs, and he'll likely have no idea of this trade at all. Oh, he'll be all right on the money side, I mean with regard to doing a lot of chat when trying to get orders, you know what I mean. They all are.'

'Yes. Yes, indeed, miss. I know what you mean.' His bottom lip was thrust out now. 'And smart alecs is the right name for them.'

'Well, what are we to do?'

'Well, miss, now I'm a straight man and I'm going to put it straight to you: I'd feel very bad indeed if you stepped out of this factory to find someone to take my place when there's young fellas here who could take over the morrow. There's Johnny McInnis, foreman over stores an' transport. He's been here a long time, longer than Joe Skinner, and he's older. But, to my mind, Joe's got more on top, if you follow me, miss, and he's out to learn, night-school classes an' that. I know he's young, but he's worked with black lead an' blackin' even afore it was ever thought of being used to shine a boot or shoe. But it's up to you, miss, it's up to you.'

She made her eyebrows rise as if in surprise, and she said, 'Joe? Well, he is young.'

'Excuse me interrupting you, miss, he's only young in age, I mean, being twenty-three, but he's got an old head on his shoulders and, you know, he knows this business from A to Z. You'll never do better. I wouldn't rest in me bed, no I wouldn't, an' I'd keep on in this job until I dropped at that desk rather than see it go to upstarts like that King fella. Why on earth, miss . . . excuse me for saying so, but why on earth, miss, you put him in there, I'll never know.'

'Well, I'm sorry, George, but it was either him or no one. We had numbers after the post but no one was experienced enough. And it appears that he had been working in . . .'

'Yes, I know, I know' – he interrupted her again – 'in Hull, for Reckitts. Yes, I know, I know all about that, and his big ideas. Anyway, least said about him the better, for it gets me monkey up just to think about him. So what d'you say, miss, it's either Johnny or Joe? As I said, it's up to you, but if you want my opinion, you'd side on Joe. Aye, you would.'

'Well, if you say so, George. If you say so.'

'I do say so, miss, I do. An' I've said it to meself; not only to meself, I've said it to the missis time and again, the one who should step into me shoes should be young Joe. It'll be a big jump for him mind, because he's only been in the business full-time for nine years.'

Yes, she knew he had been in the business full-time for only nine years. She remembered the day she first saw him. She was on holiday from school and her father was doing his rounds and had taken her with him. And there was this boy. She thought he looked like an imp: he was

37

darting here and there, and he had stopped before her and smiled at her, and she saw that he had the most beautiful eyes.

'Is there something on your mind, miss, about Joe?'

She started slightly before saying, 'No, George; I was just thinking about Father, and I'm sure he would have thought along the same lines as you do.'

'Oh yes, your father. He knew a worker when he saw one.' He leant towards her, saying, 'How would it be, miss, if I sent him in an' you broke the news to him yourself?'

'I would like that very much, George. Yes, that's a good idea of yours.'

Alone in the little office, she looked down at her hands still encased in her riding gloves, and she thought, I'm about to make Joe the manager of a small boot-polish factory. Would it were Palmer's shipyard, or Redhead's, or Armstrong's. Oh yes, would it were.

When the door opened and Joe stood there hesitating on the threshold, she said, 'Come in, Joe. Come in.'

'You wanted to see me, miss?'

'Yes, Joe, I wanted to see you. And I'll come to the point. Mr Fields is long past retiring. He should have done it five, or even ten years ago. But now I'm glad he didn't, because you wouldn't have been ready for the position, I mean, of taking his place.'

When Joe didn't answer her, but stared down into her face, she said, 'You're hesitating. Is there some reason? I know it will be a big change for you. You'll have to train someone into your work; and then there'll be the office.' She now patted the ledger. 'But you can read and write, can't you?'

'Oh yes, miss. Oh yes, I can read and write, and reckon.'

'Yes, yes, I thought you could. Are you still going to the classes?'

'Yes, miss, regularly twice a week; and a lecture when one's on.'

'Good. Good. Well then, what is your answer?'

'Well, miss, it's foregone. I mean, I was a bit stumped. I know old . . . I mean Mr Fields is gettin' on, but he's been here so long . . . well, I thought he wouldn't be leaving till he dropped down dead on the job. An' then there's Johnnie, Johnnie McInnes.'

'Oh, we've been over that.' They exchanged a smile and when she said quietly, 'Mr Fields is really tired and is recognising it. It was he, you know, who recommended you for the position.' Then in a conspiratorial tone, she said, 'I led up to it by asking him if he would like someone like Mr King, you know, from the candle factory.'

'Oh.' Joe's head jerked upwards. 'You put your foot in it there, miss. That name's like a red rag to a bull to him.'

'I thought it might be.'

'He'd rather have taken Danny Green off the dray carts and brought him inside than have anybody like Mr King.'

'Yes, I imagine he would. But he mentioned you; and if he hadn't, I would have done so myself.'

'Oh, thank you, miss. Thank you. You'll not lose by it, I can tell you that; I've got ideas in me head. We could do much better than we do already, you know, miss. Not that, oh no' – his hand was wagging before his face now – 'not that I'm saying a word against Mr Fields's ways. No, they're steady, steady and sure. But I just thought that here and there, there could be a change that I think would bring in more custom. We could do a lot of advertising, like Mrs Martha Simms: Bone manure, charcoal, blackin' and coal dust. You know, her and her lads in Nun's Lane.' He began to laugh, and she with him; and then she said, 'I've seen it. It's done in really beautiful script, too good for the product, I think, but nevertheless, she's an enterprising lady, and we could do worse than copy her and put in an advert mentioning our acid-free boot-top blacking liquid and our special heel polish.'

'Great, miss. Yes, great. An' perhaps you could engage a traveller, sort of.'

'Yes. Yes' – she nodded at him – 'that's a very good idea, too. We must discuss it later, Joe.'

'We will, miss. And thank you very much indeed, yes, indeed. An' you know, it's odd, miss, but I was gonna collar you . . . I mean, I was *goin'* to ask for a word with you on your way out. It's . . . it's about a house.'

'A house, Joe?'

'Aye. Yes. Well, you see, it's like this, miss. I'm for bein' married soon.'

Her lips parted, her head moved, and she repeated, 'Married?' and with the word she experienced a feeling like a smothered blow hitting her ribs.

'Yes. Yes, I know it's sudden, and it's sudden for me an' all. It . . . well, to tell you the truth, miss, an' in private, it was sort of sprung on me, or I sprung it on meself, you could say, yesterday. It's Lily Whitmore.'

'Lily? Oh, she's a very pretty girl, very pretty.'

'Yes, she is, miss, an' nice with it, but . . . but . . . well –' He now looked down towards the desk and, reaching out his hand, he began to draw small circles with his forefinger on the edge of it as he went on, 'I can . . . I can say this to you, miss, because I've always been able to talk to you, haven't I, over the years? Well, it's like this: I've had my eye on her since well, she was sixteen or so. Now she's eighteen. But I've never thought there was much chance for me because, as you said, she is a bonny lass, an' there have been others that had eyes an' all, and this didn't escape them either. So I felt on the sidelines as it were, looking on. And then yesterday I found she was in a fix, an' so . . . You know what I mean, miss, don't you, in a fix? She's . . . she's . . . well' – the circle's increased in size

40

as he directed his gaze down to the table again – 'she's goin' to have a bairn.'

'Oh. Oh. She's . . . ? Oh, I'm sorry.'

'Aye, so am I. But I'm takin' it on me shoulders because, you see, I want her, an' it's a chance I mightn't have got otherwise. At the same time, though, I wish it could have been otherwise, you know.'

She now pushed her riding hat upwards off her brow and pressed a loose strand of hair under it before she said tentatively, 'The father? What . . . what about the father, I mean?'

'Aye. Aye, I know what you mean, miss. But there's as much likelihood of the father marrying her as of –' he was about to say, 'me marryin' you,' but, his mind springing to a nursery rhyme that he remembered since his first and only attendance at Sunday School, he said, 'of the sky fallin'.' The line was mixed up with Henny Penny and Cocky Locky going to tell somebody or other that the sky was going to fall, and so he added, 'That's a line from a rhyme I remember hearing the only time I went to Sunday School.'

'You know who this man is then?'

'Aye, I do, miss.'

'Is he of the –' She couldn't say, gentry, and she couldn't say, class, so she changed to, 'I mean, is he in some kind of high position?'

'Aye, you could say that, miss. Though I don't know what he does for a livin'. I don't think he earns his livin'. None of his type do.'

'Oh. Oh, I see. Well, may I ask if he knows of her . . . condition?'

'Aye. Aye, you may ask, miss, and I can answer, he does. And he tried to pay her off.'

'Are you going to do anything about it?'

'No. No, I'm not, miss, because if I did it would bring

more disgrace on her head. So I'm just goin' to stand the racket. It'll be put on me in any case in most quarters.'

His hand had left the table now. It was rubbing the bottom of his chin and mixing the sweat with the grime from his fingers.

But for a moment there arose in her mind a picture of him dressed in a fine worsted suit, with tan leggings gleaming over highly polished shoes; at his neck a grey silk cravat and, topping his clean-shaven face and fair hair, a high hat. Such a fine figure of a man; and he could have been if only . . . if only . . . yes, if the sky should fall. Odd that he should remember that nursery rhyme since his once and only attendance at Sunday School. The teacher must have been a nice person in that she had deviated from spending the Sunday afternoon stuffing God and the Bible into their little heads.

He was speaking again: 'Well, as I said, miss, what I wanted to ask you was about a house. D'you have . . . or I mean, does your rent men tell you of any to let? I don't mind where, miss. But I don't want Lily to have to start married life in these hovels round here. I can say this to you, miss, because they're not your property; you would never have put up with places like these. An' I don't mind where it is, this side or yon side of Gateshead, Low Fell, Birtley, or anywhere, because we could always get the cart in, at least in the mornings.'

'Oh, I'm sure I can help you there, Joe; there's bound to be a house going empty somewhere. It would be a two up, two down you'd like, would it?'

'Oh yes, miss. That would be simply grand.'

'Well, I'll get in touch with my agent tomorrow and I'll get a message to you.'

'By! you are kind, miss. You are indeed. I've had a lot to thank you for over the years: I knew you had been behind me getting' the gaffer's job; and now you're makin' me manager. Well, there's one thing I can say, miss, I'll never be out of your debt. And, you know, when people say anythin' like that they always end up by sayin', "If there's anythin' ever I can do for you, you've just got to ask." But at this minute I can't see you ever bein' in such a position that you would have to call on me for assistance. Yet, I'll say it, if there's anythin' . . . well' – he grinned now – 'you know the rest. But I mean it.' He took a step back from her and, as a gentleman of rank might have done, he bowed to her from the shoulders, then turned and went out.

If there's anything I can ever do for you . . . Under different circumstances, what he could have done for her! Yes, indeed . . . under different circumstances. She rose from the chair and went out of the office.

George Fields was waiting for her, and he greeted her with, 'He looks like a bairn with a new toy, miss, but he knows only too well it's no new toy. He won't let you down. Don't worry. No, he won't let you down. And I'll show him some more ropes afore I leave. Yes, that's what I'll do.'

They were walking through the factory again and she was nodding in answer to a farewell here and there. Out in the yard, after the old man had called for her horse, she thanked him warmly for suggesting Joe as his successor. Then, as always, she mounted her horse without help; her left foot in the stirrup, she threw her right leg over the animal 'as good as any bloke', as the workers nearly always remarked among themselves, and to raised caps she walked the horse across the yard on to the road, past Honeybee Place, on to Ponder's Lane, deserted at this time of day. Beyond here she turned left and crossed three fields, letting the horse have its head; then at a gentle trot through woodland before skirting farm fields which bordered the outskirts of Low Fell and Birtley; then on to a long bridle path, past the iron gates of Grove House and the Filmore estate. Another half-mile's ride and her horse knowingly turned and trotted between two stone pillars which supported a filigree iron arch in which the words Milton Place were woven.

The drive to the house was comparatively short. It was not, as seemed to be usual, bordered by huge trees but, on both sides, by a neatly clipped beech hedge. On the large stretch of lawn that fronted the ivy-coloured house and standing like sentinels were two enormous blue sitka spruce. Between these, six broad stone steps led down into a terraced rose garden, now ablaze with colour.

She rode into the stable yard, and before she could have dismounted on her own, Danny Croft was holding out one hand to her while taking the reins in his other hand and saying, 'By! miss, you must be sweltered. And he's stewed an' all.'

'Yes, he is somewhat, Danny. Give him a good rub down, but a short drink first.'

'I'll do that, miss, I'll do that this minute.'

She did not go back out of the stable yard to enter the house by the front door, but she made for the kitchen door at the far end of the yard, loosening the buttons of her riding jacket as she went. At the door she pulled off her hat and was fanning herself with it as she entered the kitchen, saying, 'Oh, Peg, you must be stewed in here.'

'Just about, miss; but it doesn't seem to take me fat down, does it?' The cook laughed, then added, 'And you look stewed an' all, miss. A cup of tea, eh?'

'No, no, Peg; something cool from the cellar.'

'A beer?'

'Yes. Yes, a beer; anything wet and cold.'

The cook now turned to a young girl, saying, 'Away with you! Mary, and bring up two bottles.'

As she went up the kitchen she said, 'I'll have it upstairs, Peg. I'm going to change.'

'Very well, miss, very well. It'll be there in a minute.'

Bridget left the kitchen and by way of a short corridor entered the hall. The sun was shining through two long windows flanking a heavy oak door and their light illuminated the whole long room and the staircase rising from the middle of it.

She was about to go up the stairs when Jessie Croft, emerging from the dining-room, said, 'You're back then, miss. You must be roasted alive. What a day?'

'It is pretty hot, Jessie. I've sent Mary down for a beer.' She did not say that cook had suggested the beer and sent Mary down to the cellar.

Jessie, like her husband Danny in the yard, was very conscious of their position in the household, and neither of them was behind in making it felt with the rest of the small staff: they would point out to anybody who was interested that not only did they see to the smooth workings of this house, but also to the other one in Shields. And they would also point out that if they had any choice they knew which one they would prefer to live in; for you couldn't smell the sea so far out in the country, now could you?

'Is Miss Victoria in?'

'Yes; she's up in her room, miss.' And Jessie bent her flesh-endowed body forward and said quietly, 'And she's had a visitor again.'

Bridget's answer was brief: 'Oh,' accompanied by a nod of her head, before she hurried up the stairs, across a narrow balcony and to a broad corridor. And she was about to enter her room when the door opposite opened and Victoria Mordaunt said, 'Oh, you do look hot, Bridget. Why must you ride out on a day like this? Look; I'll get you a drink.'

'There's one coming. I hear you've had a visitor.'

Victoria followed Bridget into her cousin's room, laughing as she remarked, 'Old Mother Shipton's been quick.'

'Yes. Yes, there's nobody as quick as Old Mother Shipton. Do I have to have two guesses as to who your visitor was?'

'No, Bridget, dear, just one . . . Oh!' Victoria now dropped on to Bridget's bed with a plop and pulled up the wide skirt of her dress and petticoats to almost knee height, then spread the ends out across the bed before exclaiming, 'I'm so happy, Bridget. I . . . I could take off, you know, like a bird . . . He's wonderful. And you know what? We are invited to a ball.'

'What ball?'

'Just a ball at Grove House.'

'You are going to the ball, not me.'

'Oh, don't be stuffy, darling, please. Here! let me pull your boots off.'

Victoria now jumped up from the bed and went quickly to where Bridget was sitting and slid down onto her knees and began to pull at one of the riding boots. And as she did so Bridget laughed and said, 'I've told you countless times that's the wrong way. I can manage better myself.'

'Well, I'm not going to turn round and let you stick your foot in my bottom.'

'Oh, well, if you won't, get off your knees and I'll do it myself.'

They were both laughing now as Victoria tugged at the boot and then fell backwards as it finally loosed itself from Bridget's leg.

When there was a tap on the door and the housemaid Florrie McClean entered with a tray bearing two bottles of ale and two tall glasses, Bridget called to her, 'Put them down there, Florrie, and come and pull this other boot off for me else Miss Victoria will have my leg off.'

There was more laughter as the maid, with one good tug, released the other boot and Bridget cried as she nodded at Victoria, 'There! that's how it's done. I told you.'

'Will I pour out for you, miss?'

'No, no, Florrie. I'll see to it. Thank you.'

The room to themselves again, it was Victoria who poured out the beer while Bridget divested herself of her breeches and silk shirt and long stockings, leaving herself still in her corsets, bloomers, and habit shirt while waiting to take the glass of cold beer from Victoria, which she then almost drained at one go, after which she closed her eyes and sighed deeply, saying, 'Nectar!'

'Where've you been all afternoon?'

'You know where I've been, down to the works: I told you I was going.'

'Yes, but you're not usually as long as this.'

'Well, I was held up in the polish factory.' She would never term it 'blacking factory', for she hated the sight of that blacking. 'Old George is having to give up, and not before time. And . . . and Joe, you know, Joe Skinner, he's going to take his place.'

'Joe Skinner? But isn't he young?'

'Not so young. Same age as me, twenty-three, and, at present, I feel as old as the hills.'

'Of course you do, dear, because you won't dress properly. Why must you go round like you do? You could look marvellous in the new styles. You could, you could,' and Victoria bobbed her head to emphasise this.

'Don't be silly. And don't start that again.'

'I will, and I'll keep on, because you go round like a rag bag most of the time. You only look dressed when you're on a horse. And you could look lovely. I know you could. If you'd only let me . . .'

'Look,' Bridget's voice sounded weary, 'this is a subject

I get tired of, you know I do. Have I to point out to you again I am not inclined to be in the fashion, any fashion, never have been, never will be. Now if you could give me a bit of your hips and your bust, and ... and oh yes, your beauty, there might be a chance that I would look presentable. But here I am, just as I heard Jessie once describe me, a line of pipe water, not a curve to be seen, neither back nor front.'

'That's nonsense, and you know it. Now look at Sarah Tweedle. She's thinner than you, much.'

'Well, she doesn't look it, dear. And we know, don't we, why she doesn't look it. But neither you nor any one else is going to get me to wear a bustle and false breasts. What if they slipped? What if they fell out of the bodice and a gentleman had to pick them up?'

They were both sitting on the edge of the bed now, leaning together and rocking with their laughter at the picture her words described.

When their laughter had subsided Victoria touched Bridget's face gently with her fingers, saying quietly, 'You could look lovely, you know: you have high cheek-bones and beautiful eyes.'

'Yes. Yes, I know, dear, and a big mouth, and hair like tow. And I am noted for my brilliant conversation when I am in company.'

'Oh you!' Victoria pushed her cousin into the pillows, saying, 'Yes, you are right, you are really terrible in company. You would think you had never been in a drawing room in your life, the things you say, and mostly to men ... Men don't like to be contradicted, you know. As for the ladies, you come out with terrible things. Remember Kitty Porter?'

'Oh, yes, I remember Kitty Porter.'

'Well, you were terribly rude to her, you know.'

'I wasn't as rude to her as she was cruel to Mrs Forrester,

48

all because not one of her five girls was married.' She began to mimic: 'They're all in the maiden lady stage, but you're going to be well comforted when you're old, dear, aren't you?' Then reverting to her normal voice, she said bitterly, 'She's the type of woman that can smile while cutting your throat.'

'Well, you cut her throat all right that night. She nearly had a fainting fit when you smiled back at her and asked why it was that only dogs were called bitches. Eeh!' Victoria put her hand over her mouth, then exclaimed again, 'Eeh! I thought we would have died, I from choking with suppressed laughter and she from mortification. But she'll never forgive you.'

'That worries me! But there you have the reason I don't want to go to any more balls.'

'Don't be silly.'

'And you stop saying, don't be silly; it's a silly thing to say.'

Again they were pushing at each other like two children, just as they had done since, in fact, they were children, since the day she was ten and her Uncle Sep had arrived on the doorstep with an eight-year-old beautiful, but motherless, little girl. She herself was an only child, and had lost her own mother when she was but six. It was from that time she had become her father's companion, and she had thought she had wanted no other until she saw Victoria, and from that day they had ceased to be cousins and had become like sisters, passionately close.

Bridget got up from the bed and went to the wardrobe, took down a long white lawn petticoat and a blue print dress, and from a chest of drawers took out a pair of white silk stockings. And as she began to dress she said, 'Let's be serious, Victoria: do you really care for him? I mean, is it not just a passing fancy? He's very charming, he's very handsome and naturally attractive, but what

49

does he do for a living? From what I understand, he hunts and shoots, plays cards and also plays at being a farmer, although from what I've seen of it their farm is a very small one and could be run with a couple of men.'

'He works on the estate, too, Bridget. I told you so. He goes to an office in Newcastle. I think they used to be in shipping. He mentioned his father has had a number of losses at sea recently, the latest on the London run from the Tyne, you know, with coal.'

'Oh.' Bridget was pulling her garter over her knee and she twisted it round so that the small silk rosebud should be in the centre as she said, 'If, for instance, you were never to see him again, how would you feel about it? I mean, if he were to tell you he was going to marry someone else?'

When Victoria did not answer she turned and looked at her where she was now sitting on a pink satin upholstered chair. Her eyes were closed and her chin was almost touching the bare flesh above the square neck of her dress and her voice came as a whisper as she said, 'I'm not exaggerating but I think I would want to die if . . . if he became cool to me now.'

'Have . . . have you ever felt like this before, dear? I mean, so intense?'

'No, never. I thought I was in love, you know, with Captain Turner. You remember when he used to come to the house to see Uncle Harry, and remember I cried when I heard he was drowned?'

Yes, and she, too, had cried when she heard he was drowned. And he hadn't come to the house to see her father, he had come to the house to see her. And she might have married him in the end. Yes, she might have, because her father had liked him. Just a fortnight before her father died he had said to her, 'Robert is a fine fellow. He could give you twelve years, but if it were left to me he's the man I would choose to look after you if anything should happen to me.' And it had happened quite suddenly. He had been out to a meeting; and after returning had had a late supper, gone up to bed, and then she had heard him cry out for her; but he was dead before the doctor arrived.

She was just on nineteen when, overnight she became a very rich woman: an inheritor of two factories, both of which had grown from cottage industries and had been making good profits over the last forty years; also the owner of properties in a number of the towns around; maybe only cottages in one, but streets in another. Then there was the interest from various industries carried on along both sides of the river. Yes indeed, she had become a rich young woman. But instead of doing what some ladies would have done after a period of mourning, travelled for a time with a suitable companion, then looked around for an equally suitable husband, what Bridget Mordaunt did was no surprise to her close associates; and it hadn't surprised Andrew Kemp, her father's solicitor, nor the accountant, William Bennett, nor the agent, Arthur Fathers, and least of all, not their two old servants Danny and Jessie Croft, for she stepped into her father's shoes and carried on doing exactly what he had done. Under his tuition she had become conversant with every shade of his businesses, riding or walking side by side with him when he visited the factories or sitting with him in his Newcastle office.

Victoria had rarely accompanied them on any journey because, as her father had laughingly put it, she was more bother than she was worth, for she was always afraid to get her dress soiled. No; Victoria stayed at home and busied herself, as she termed it, with housekeeping. And it showed itself, for it was undeniable that she had a taste for furnishings and how things should be arranged; and she loved dressing up. Whenever she changed her costume in the afternoon Bridget's father would laughingly tease her by saying she was aping the gentry, or preparing herself to run somebody's mansion.

'It's a lovely place.'

'What's a lovely place?'

'Grove House, of course, Lionel's home.'

'Oh, yes, yes. But to my mind it wants a lot doing to it. It's been neglected and will cost a fortune to put it into good order.'

'You can turn the hall and drawing-room into one huge room. Lionel showed me. You wouldn't believe it, that panelling folds back, just like a concertina.'

'Does it now? When did this display happen?'

'Well, I told you, when I visited last week, when he came and picked me up. And you being your stubborn and charming self stated flatly that you had no time to waste.'

'I said that to you, not to him.'

'I know . . . you wouldn't say it to him. Yet' – she pulled a long face – 'you would, if the mood was on you, wouldn't you, dear?'

'Yes, dear, yes' – Bridget's head bobbed – 'I would say it if the mood was on me. Pour me out another glass of that beer; and then I don't know what you're going to do till supper time but I have work to do. I'm going down to the office.'

'Oh! that office. I'd like to set fire to it at times. Why do you want to go there now, I haven't seen you all day.'

'I've got a special letter to write; Joe's going to be married and he wants a house.'

'My! My! Joe Skinner again, your pet protégé. What are you going to give him as a wedding present, the factory?'

'Could do. Could do. I'll have to think about it.'

As Bridget made for the door Victoria ran to her and,

catching her arm, said, 'You will accept the invitation, I mean, to the ball? I can't go on my own. You know I can't.'

Bridget looked into the soft gaze of this girl who was very dear to her, and she sighed now as she said, 'All right, all right.'

'And you'll get a new gown?'

'*No*, I won't get any new gown.' She pulled open the door, with Victoria still hanging on to her arm, tugging at her and saying, 'You will get a new gown. If you won't go into town I'll order half a dozen or so to be sent up for you to choose from.'

'You dare!'

'I dare, because on the last . . . well —' She shook her head and the small ringlets hanging down in front of her ears bobbed on her cheeks as she now cried, 'I'm ashamed for you. Four occasions during the last year you've worn that same old grey thing. I'll tear it up. I will. It makes you look like a . . .'

Bridget was smiling now, and she, too, bobbed her head as she said, 'Yes, I know, a line of pipe water.'

'Well, it's a good description, in that grey thing anyway.'

Bridget was now walking out of the corridor on to the balcony, saying, 'It's good material; it's Italian brocade.'

'I don't care if it's Chinese tapestry from the Ming, Bing, or Bang period.'

Once again they fell about together, making it necessary for Bridget to grab the balustrade of the stairs, and with tears of laughter in her eyes and in a throaty voice, she exclaimed, 'If Miss Rice were here she would say, "Vases, Ming period, Victoria. Vases not vaises."'

As they descended the stairs, Victoria said, 'And I would have piped up, "And couldn't there have been tapestries also, Miss Rice?"' bringing the expected response from

53

Bridget, resuming the deep tone again, '"Sit down, miss. Sit down."'

They were in the hall when Victoria, now really shaking with laughter, said, 'And you remember the day the old cat added, "Your brain, Victoria, is afflicted as is your voice, it's weak."?'

'Oh yes, and you came home crying. She was an old cat. But now, stop your jabbering and go to the kitchen and see what Peg's up to. Nothing hot. Ask her to give us cold soup. Yes, that's an idea, ask her to give us cold soup.'

'She'll have a fit.'

'No doubt, but, nevertheless, ask her. And don't disturb me for the next half hour.'

'Yes, ma'am. Yes, ma'am,' and Victoria dipped her knee twice before turning and skipping towards the kitchen, while Bridget, leaving the hall, went down the corridor and into a room at the far end and which looked part library and part office, for the shelves along one wall held an array of books and those along the other, tin boxes and ledgers. The boxes, all bearing labels, and the ledgers were in sections docketed by a tin label attached to each shelf. It was called an office, and it looked an office except perhaps when you looked at some of the titles on the bookshelves: Brontë, Wilkie Collins, Mrs Gaskell, and in between these Tennyson and Plato's Apologia, while on another shelf, next to Lord Chesterfield's Letters, were volumes of George Eliot and Anthony Trollope.

Whereas the ledgers and tin boxes were meticulously docketed, the books had no order but spoke of a wide and mixed taste in literature.

If Bridget had been questioned about her taste and the jumble of books on the shelves behind her desk, she would have replied, 'Oh well, you must come down to our real home in Shields and there you will see an ordered library.

The books all beautifully bound, all in the same dark red Moroccan leather, their titles engraved on the spines, but so small you can hardly read them. There must be a few thousand books in that library, and they're only distinguishable one from the other by the tone of the leather. You see, in my grandfather's time it was the done thing not just to have a library but to have the books well presented; the bindings must be all similar. The size of the books, too, had to be graded on to different shelves. He would buy books by the dozen, and have them bound by the hundred. But as my father said, to his knowledge he didn't think his father had ever opened one unless there was some indication that it held a map within its pages, because his only interest was in shipping and he studied maps of all kinds.'

Bridget lowered herself into the outsize leather chair which had fitted her father's broad beam but in which she often slid from side to side, especially if she was wearing breeches. From a brass rack to the right side of her she took out a sheet of notepaper. There was a heading to it, saying simply, *Henry Dene Mordaunt*, and underneath, *Manufacturer of Polishes and Candles*. Andrew Kemp had suggested she alter the heading into her own name and she had laughingly said, 'What! *Bridget Dene Mordaunt, Blacking and Candle Manufacturer?*' No, that was her father's heading and it would remain.

She now wrote a letter to her agent in Newcastle, heading it with one word, 'Immediate,' before beginning: 'Dear Mr Fathers.' That name always amused her. She then went on to tell him that he must inform her of those vacant properties in the nearby towns, those at an available distance to the factories being preferable.

Having signed and sealed the letter, she rang a bell, and when Jessie herself answered it, she said, 'Take this letter,

Jessie, and get one of them from the yard to ride to the post office. I want it to catch today's post if possible.'

'Important?'

'Yes, important, Jessie.'

Jessie paused a moment, the letter in her hand; but when her mistress made no further comment she turned and left the room.

Bridget shook her head as she looked towards the closed door. Jessie was ageing rapidly but, as with Danny, such a thing as age must not be mentioned. She couldn't remember ever opening her eyes as a child and not seeing Jessie's face hovering above her and speaking the same words, 'Come on, pet, open up your blinkers.' If there was any way of translating the word loyalty, then both she and Danny exemplified it, for they had been in her grandfather's service. After his death they had then gone on to see to the house for her father and mother. And Jessie had attended her mother through her long illness, the while contriving successfully to be comforter and friend to herself in those early years, especially those prior to Victoria's appearance on the scene with her father, and with his death she had drawn the little girl into her almost motherly warmth, while at the same time condemning her for her dollyfiedness, as she termed it.

And so it had been ever since, except that Bridget knew it was she who held first place in Jessie's affection, as some of her down-to-earth remarks showed when she would say, 'Fancy feathers make peacocks, but you pluck them and see what's left.' The vision of a plucked peacock would always send a gurgle through Bridget's stomach.

Yet Jessie was very much on Victoria's side the day she herself had donned breeches for the first time to ride out: 'Eeh! pet,' she had said, her hands to her cheeks, 'you'll get your name up. If anything'll get your name up that rig-out will. Lass, it's not done. Eeh! the shock of wearin' bloomers on bicycles will be nothin' to you, lass, once you're seen on that road in that rig-out.'

And Jessie's opinion had seemed to be the general one: Dreadful, disgraceful, like a man, so immodest . . . she'll never be married.

That last remark had been made within earshot of her, and she had startled the speaker by going to her shoulder and saying in a soft voice, 'Take off your bustle and I'll take off my breeches and the pattern underneath will be much the same.'

'Dreadful person. Comes out with the most outrageous remarks. She's originally from Shields, you know. Vulgar, but dirty rich. But her sister, or is it her cousin? she's different altogether, quite a young lady.'

Oh, Bridget knew exactly what the opinion of her was among the crowd in which Lionel Filmore moved. And there was something beginning to worry her, too. At first it had amused her, but not any more: the fact that she was considered to be the working partner in the Henry Dene Mordaunt Company. She was the one who saw to the business, while the ladylike one took her rightful place and acted according to her position. Yes, and the niggling thought had now connected itself with the ball and Lionel Filmore. Well, she could do nothing about it at the moment; in any case, perhaps he was only amusing himself. She hoped he wasn't, not with Victoria's feelings being at the height they were. On an earlier stay here, she had heard that he was seeing a lot of Elizabeth Porter, the cat's daughter, as she herself thought of Kitty Porter. Yet, here he was now, pressing his attentions on Victoria, and the word was pressing, because this was his fourth visit within a matter of three weeks. She had mixed feelings about the man. She didn't know if she liked or disliked him, but as Victoria loved him so deeply, then, she told herself, she had better concentrate on his good points and work up a liking.

She pulled a ledger towards her but didn't open it. Her hand flat on the scarred leather, she wondered what it was that directed one's feelings towards another? Was it just the urges of the body? She shook her head at this and her mind answered, No. Yet they were there. Yes, they were there all right. But no; it was something that emanated from the other person. There was no finger that could be put on it. You didn't ask for it or, when it came, welcome it, because such kind of love began with a troublesome feeling: it was based on hopelessness. Yet one couldn't stop it growing, even though in a way despising oneself for the weakness that allowed one to foster such a thought. She had even tried to kill it with ridicule, likening herself to a missionary falling in love with a Zulu who could only communicate by sign language and war dancing. But it hadn't made any difference.

She opened the ledger and got down to the therapy of figures.

3

William Filmore stood with his back to the empty grate. It was a position he took up when the fire was blazing, and it usually blazed during all the winter, spring, and autumn months. So it was a matter of habit, his standing in this position, especially whilst enjoying his after-dinner cigar.

Opposite him, in a deep leather chair, sat his elder son. Lionel was well aware of his assets: he was tall, had an abundance of thick fair hair and a countenance that could only be classed as handsome, whereas his brother, Douglas, a year younger, was short in comparison, being only five-foot-six inches tall, with no manly figure to speak of, being what you would kindly call wiry. Also in contrast to Lionel, he was dark haired. His eyes, too, were dark, deep brown almost black. His face was longish, his chin inclined to jut. His mouth was wide and thin lipped. His disposition, too, was in contrast to his brother's in that he was of a quiet retiring nature and had what the family considered to be strange pursuits, diverse in their choice: he liked chipping stone or whittling wood; and he had a feeling for pigs. Whenever he was not working in one of the big outhouses he had claimed as a workshop, he could be found on the farm looking at the pigs, assessing them, even talking to them, it was said.

Both men were looking at their father now as he said, 'We've got to put on a show, it's important. And you should know that.' He nodded towards Lionel; and Lionel came back with, 'You needn't stress the point, Father. I know it is important, and not only to me.'

'What do you mean by that?' The protruding stomach seemed to expand, the red jowls bristled, and William Filmore, with a backward flick of his hand, knocked the ash off his cigar; then, his arm going forward, the cigar, now glowing between his fingers, was thrust in the direction of his son, and he said, 'This' – the cigar now made a half circle – 'this will be yours before long. What do you intend to do with it? Sell it? Well, I can tell you, if it went on the market it wouldn't cover half the debts. And then there's your way of life. You couldn't live without the hunt, could you? And empty stables out there would be unbearable to you.' The cigar now was pointing towards the long latticed windows at the end of the room; then when it was brought back towards his chest, he said, 'And there is your tailor, and your drink, not forgetting what you lose at cards, because you're the most unlucky bugger on God's earth with a pack of cards in your hand. So –' The cigar was now thrust back between the blue lips, its essence to be savoured for a moment; then, his voice dropping a tone, he said, 'It's a ball we've come to discuss, and at it I hope you'll settle your future. There's no more playing around for you, for slip up here and I'd advise you to take a boat to America and see what you can do with your charm there.'

'You'll need more staff.'

Both the father and brother looked at Douglas. It was as if they had never before heard him speak. And his father's voice was quiet as he said, 'Yes, Doug, you're right, we'll need more staff. So, have you any ideas on the subject?'

'Not really; only I was nineteen when we last had a ball here. That's six years ago, and we had eleven indoors then and eight out.' He looked from one to the other before he ended, 'But things have changed.'

'That's an obvious statement if ever I heard one.' Lionel looked scathingly at his brother; then he added, 'And it can't go down in the annals that you've done much to stop the rot.'

There came a slight tightening of Douglas's jaw, and the chin moved out a bit further, but his voice was level as he said, 'Well, you could say I've been serving my apprenticeship. I sold two pieces last week.'

'*You what!*' It was a joint exclamation, and surprise had caused the father to lay down his cigar on a silver stand that was to his hand on the mantelshelf, and it had brought Lionel screwing round in his chair, asking now, 'You sold your stones, I mean your pieces? Who to? The marble merchant in Gateshead? When was this? What were they?'

'One was the boy fishing, the other was the angel.'

'What did you get for them?' This question came from his father.

'A hundred and twenty for the angel and eighty-five guineas for the boy.'

'Good God!' His father was smiling. 'By! you are a sly cuss. You never let on. We could have drunk to it. What did you do with the money? Have you got it? Was it in cash!'

'Yes, it was in cash, but I've spent it.'

The expressions on the two faces slipped now, and it was Lionel who asked, 'What did you spend it on?'

'On good stone. I've got three more orders.'

Again his father's face was expanding. And now, throwing his big florid and grizzled head back, he seemed to speak to the decorated ceiling as he said, 'I'll be buggered. The runt of the litter earning a living.' Then looking at this second son, for whom he had never had much use, mainly because he looked a weed and, what was more, he had no conversation, and seemingly no interests except as a boy whittling away at wood, then later chiselling stone, and making it apparent that the money being spent on his education was a waste, verified by school reports which were always the same: he didn't work; he was absent-minded; he was a dreamer. Well, by the look of it his dreams had gone into stone and they were actually making money. And more orders ahead, he said. Well, it wasn't a fortune, nothing like what he expected his elder son to capture in order to keep a roof over their heads, but it promised one of them a living. Yes, indeed.

He stared at his son. There was more to this thin, undersized individual than met the eye. Indeed, indeed. He asked now, 'Where are your pieces going to?'

'London, I think. I'm not sure. Anyway, the man does business there. He was a monumental mason himself.'

'Monumental mason! Gravestones and crosses!' His brother's tone was scathing.

'Yes, yes, I suppose so; but he's got a sideline, too. And that, he says, is where I come in. He will take all I can turn out.'

Lionel, pulling himself to his feet, now said, 'A few hundred pounds isn't going to save the city.'

'No, it won't save the city.' Douglas, too, had risen to his feet, and as he passed between his father and his brother he added tersely, 'But it will provide me with a living when this part of the city falls.'

The two men watched the slight figure walk down the room with his loose shambling gait. And when the door banged behind him his father, throwing his half-smoked cigar into the fireplace, remarked, 'There goes a dark horse. But he's right, you know. Oh yes, he's right, because if your deal doesn't come off, how do you think you're going to exist? I've asked you this before. On your wits?

But they won't take you far at cards. And I've said this before an' all. So what is for you? Kitty Porter, you know, won't allow you back into her nest again to pluck her chicken. And so it would mean America. Or you could resort to what some of your type have done before, escorting rich dames around watering places. It's quite the done thing, I hear.'

Facing his father now, Lionel said with some bitterness, 'You don't like me, do you? You've never had any use for me, or for Doug, for that matter. And I'll say this, if there were prizes given for looking after number one, you'd be top of the list. And you know something, the things you don't like about me are what are very prominent in yourself. What pattern did you set for me? Whoring was the first that came to my notice, and under Mama's nose at that. Drink was next; followed by gaming, and that not all straight either, else you wouldn't have had to sell up the London house and resort to this end of the country, which you hate.'

'Get out of my sight!'

'Yes, I'll do that, Father, for the present. But just one more thing: what if I marry her? And oh, I'll marry her all right because she's ripe for the taking. There's no doubt about that. But what if she doesn't want to live here and support your ruin? What if she were to decide we should take up residence in Milton Place? It's a very nice house that, very well kept, not a rambling mausoleum like this. So then what about it?'

'The same about it as if she decided to live here, you'll have control of her money, and I think you'll just be in time because there's a law afoot to give women rights to what's considered their own. So whatever there is I'll expect you to use it in the right way.'

'Well —' Lionel stepped back and as he did so he tweeked each side of his small moustache with his forefinger. 'That remains to be seen, Father,' he said. 'That remains to be seen.'

When he, too, left the room, William Filmore almost groped his way to the leather chair from which he had so recently risen and, dropping into it, he lay back and put his hand to his brow as he asked himself, how was it that one could dislike the flesh and blood that was part of one, that one had made? Well, perhaps he was right, he was part of himself in many ways. But it was too late now for self-recrimination; he hadn't a long time to run; not the way he was feeling now, he hadn't. Then there was Doug. That strip of an individual. All the Filmores had been big-made, burly types. The gallery and the staircase showed them for two hundred years back. There wasn't a fleshless one among them; yet, there he was, the second son, who at twenty-five still had on him a body that made him look like a strip of a boy. And just five-foot six tall. That wasn't his family. But what had he just done? He had shown his big burly handsome brother that he, at least, could earn a living.

Strange that he had never bothered with Douglas; but there had seemed to be nothing to bother with in this undersized Filmore man. For a moment there intruded into his thoughts a deep sense of loss that in his old and shortening age he might have experienced a sense of friendship and perhaps comfort through this unusual descendant in the Filmore clan. But it was too late now.

As he closed his eyes his thoughts took him back to seeing himself standing by the bedside of his dying father, whose last words were, 'Remember, Will, everything in life must be paid for.' And yes, his father had certainly paid, through a crippling and lingering disease, a very high price for what he had called the natural sin of infidelity.

4

'Have you not found out yet how the land lies?'

'Father.' Lionel closed his eyes for a moment and brought his jaws tightly together before he said slowly, 'What do you want me to do? Go to the other one and say, what's her share in all this?'

'I don't see why not. You could put it over in a diplomatic way, because she seems to be the working end of the pair. She seems to make the money and your dear Victoria to spend it, if her dress is anything to go by, which to my mind points to the fact she must have the bigger share in the whole concern. You know, the maids here would turn out better dressed than the other one, flat as a pancake and utterly colourless. Look at her at the last do: not a frill or a bit of ruching to be seen on her anywhere. Putty coloured she was from head to foot, while the other one was decked out like a duchess. Well, it speaks for itself, doesn't it? Have you ever spoken about money to her?'

'Yes, once, and her answer was to laugh and say, "Well, you must know I'm just a poor girl."'

'Poor girl! They were brothers, weren't they, the two fathers?'

'Yes. But it seems her father died when she was quite young; and from the little I can gather they were all living together at the time, the two brothers and their families.'

'Families, you say? Are there any more besides the two women?'

'No. No, they were the only children.'

'Well, all I can say is you should do something before the marriage. You've got two weeks.'

'What do you expect me to do, Father? Go and ask her if she's going to bring a dowry with her? If anything would turn her from the idea of marriage it would be that, I should imagine.'

At this William Filmore turned from where he had been standing near the library table and walked to the end of the room and stood looking out into the deepening twilight of the wet April day. The library was situated at the end of the house and its windows faced across a wide yard to a row of large stone buildings; and looking towards them, he asked, 'Is Doug ready?'

'I don't know. He's likely still over there chipping away. He enjoys being a tradesman,' Lionel answered, to be surprised by his father's response when he swung round from the window and hissed, 'It would be something to your credit if you went and joined him in being a tradesman. At least he's keeping himself and handing a bit into the house at the same time. And it's an art he's following, not bloody blacking and candles. And that's something you want to do as soon as possible, get rid of that blacking factory and the candles and put it into more property where it's already sprinkled along by the river, so I understand.'

'You don't need to tell me, Father, what I'm going to do; I'm no blasted fool.'

William Filmore now walked slowly back down the room, saying, 'No; you're no blasted fool, not in some ways; but in others you're an idiot. Tell me, do you like the girl? I mean, not just like her, want her? Are you for her?'

Lionel did not immediately answer; he ran his hand back over his well pomaded hair, then he said, 'She's very likeable . . . and desirable.'

And it was also some seconds before his father, who was staring hard at him now, said, 'Liking and desirable isn't going to be enough. There's going to be no more of that Lizzie Porter business, I hope. Have you made it plain with her?' for himself now to be surprised by Lionel's answer, who, being further piqued, leaned on the library table and with doubled fist beat out each word: 'Yes! Yes! Yes! I've told you before.'

His father's tone was comparatively calm as he replied, 'Well, it's nice to be reassured. What time is it?' He turned and looked towards the mantelpiece on which stood an ornate French gilt clock presided over, as it were, by the posed lady on its head, and he remarked, 'In an hour's time Alan and Minnie and their five daughters will, as usual, be the first to arrive.' He gave a dry laugh now as he said, 'There's a bevy for you, a nestful of pure chicks and not a cock in sight.' But Lionel was already going out of the door and so he called after him, 'See that Doug's ready,' after which he lowered himself into the chair, pulled out a large red silk handkerchief from the side pocket of his heavily embroidered jacket and mopped his perspiring face and so somewhat smothered the words, which were, 'God in heaven! There'll be some skitting this night. We've reached the depths when the house has got to be saved by a blacking factory. Of all the trades in the world, and most of them can be found in this area, she has to have a blacking factory. Not a brush or comb-maker, or a dyer's, or a cutler's, or a tanner's, or a chain maker's, or a calico printer's, and nothing so lady-like as lace-making, but it has to be a bloody blacking factory. And every one of his friends at the ball here tonight and supposedly celebrating the coming event in a fortnight's time will be smirking, the women behind their fans, the men as they toast the happy couple repeatedly with champagne, or port, or whisky, or rum, or highly laced punch, or sherry. Oh yes, there'll be such a choice, but by two o'clock tomorrow morning there'll be no difference to their bloody fuddled minds; nor to my own . . . nor to my own.'

Among the close friends at the ball were Pat Maybrook, his wife Ann, and their three sons, David, Norman, and Albert, each of these being accompanied by a young lady, David by his fiancée. The Maybrooks' business was the lucrative one of brewers.

Then there was Arthur Porter, his wife Kitty, his son Peter and the notorious daughter Elizabeth. Porter was in the respectable business of shipping.

The Wright family consisted of Stephen, his wife Rosie, and three sons, John, Amos, and James, all confirmed bachelors and so, unattended by ladies. Then there were the Forresters: Alan, his wife Minnie, and their five daughters, the latter all well into their twenties: Jane the eldest at twenty-nine, and, down the line, Mary, Alice, Freda, and Sarah at twenty-two. They were merry girls; at least, they presented a merry front; and they were unescorted except for their parents. However, they knew there would always be John, Amos, and James Wright whom they could fall back on. Just as John, Amos, and James, in their turn, never bothered about escorts, knowing that they would and could pick from the Forrester lasses. And the Wright men being merry souls, there was always a great deal of chaff and laughter whenever the two families met up.

Among the rest of the guests were those invited under the heading of strong acquaintances, men and wives who attended the hunt. They might be farmers, but so-called 'gentlemen' ones.

Altogether, the future groom's guests came to fifty, the future bride's merely nine: Andrew Kemp, Bridget's

solicitor, his wife Jane, and their son Richard, himself a
solicitor; William Bennett, Bridget's accountant, his wife
Nell, daughter Nancy and son Jeff; and lastly Bridget's
agent, Arthur Fathers and his son Philip. Mrs Fathers was
rather unwell.

As was usual the guests had been assembled for about
an hour before supper was announced; and as the table
in the large dining room could accommodate only twenty-
two people, the innovation of smaller tables, each seating
four to six people set around the main board, had been
resorted to. That this arrangement proved difficult for the
serving of the meal went unnoticed as the hired and liveried
waiters were practised in their work and no catastrophe
occurred, much to the annoyance of James Bright, the
butler-cum-footman-cum-valet and anything else that was
required of him in this establishment; and with only four
females under him, the housekeeper Mrs Matilda Pillman,
the cook Rose Jackson, and Kate Swift and Mary Carstairs, who did whatever was required of them, from
assisting the cook to mending their own uniforms and
even washing them at times when the laundress couldn't
cope with what was required of her in one day of
hiring.

Nevertheless, the cook and the three women had, for
the previous week, worked almost eighteen hours a day
preparing for the great do and determining that the supper
spread was going to be something that would be talked
about for some time afterwards, even if it were thought
to be but a prelude to the banquets that would become a
regular feature in this house once Mr Lionel was married
to the beautiful and rich Miss Mordaunt.

They knew that, as engagements went, this one had
been a whirlwind affair, for Mr Lionel had known her for
less than a year and had been engaged to her for a matter
of months only. But there, the sooner the better, for this

house would come alive again, and not before time.

Where the master had got the money from to engage these titivated lackeys and the band of four players, besides all that wine and spirits, the Lord only knew; because they had been lucky to get their half-pay wages last Christmas.

However, to attend to present and future matters: they would all keep their eyes on the leftovers because that lot had arrived in a covered cart, in which Jack Johnson, the yard man, had said were three large wicker baskets, empty ones. And for what did waiters want to carry three big empty wicker baskets along with them, eh?

But now, as the noise and the laughter proclaimed, the guests were leaving the dining-room, the ladies making for the toilet room one way, the gentlemen to a similar room the other way, and, as Kate Swift remarked the while wrinkling her nose, there'd be some cleaning up in the morning in that department, if she knew anything. And not only in the men's room either, for from her experience some of the female gentry weren't as clean as pigs. But let them all away now to that dining room and then make sure what was left on those tables would find its way back to the kitchen . . .

The carpets had been taken up in the hall and from the long drawing-room, and Jimmy Fawcett and Ron Yarrow, the two stablemen, had waxed and bumpered the floor until it shone like glass, so much so that some people were finding it a little dangerous to walk over, especially those ladies wearing the new-fashioned spider heels. But once the dancing started those who could not claim to be dancers of any merit found it easy to glide to the beat of the music, even, in some instances, against it, all, however, with very great enjoyment, as the laughter, chatter, and noise proclaimed.

They had danced mazurkas, minuets, the more boisterous lancers, and then an uproarious attempt at a Scottish reel. There followed a natural and appreciated interval during which more drink and dishes of light sweetmeats were handed round; and more visits made to the ladies' room, and to the gentlemen's, but with less delicacy now than before, for by this time most of the faces were flushed and many stomachs distended.

It was when the leader of the quartet announced that his gentlemen were about to render a waltz by the famous Austrian composer Johann Strauss that Lionel led his future bride on to the floor; and once again Douglas came to Bridget, who was sitting in a cane chair in an alcove near the last window in the drawing-room part of the temporary ballroom. Smiling, he bowed to her, saying, 'Dare I ask you to give me the pleasure of again treading on your toes?'

Bridget now laughed outright; then answering in the same vein, she said, 'Sir, I regret I must deprive you of that pleasure for I have need of my feet. But I would consider it a favour if you would sit with me for a while and we could continue the conversation that the last interval so abruptly interrupted.'

He, too, laughed outright when, pulling a chair forward from the open doors of the conservatory leading out of the drawing-room, he went to place it next to hers but found it wouldn't fit. And when it protruded almost on to the floor he pushed it to one side; then, impulsively taking her hand, he said, 'Come on. Come this way,' and she found herself being drawn round a giggling, waltzing couple and into the conservatory.

The long, narrow, glass-covered room, unlike the main rooms that were lit by gas chandeliers, was illuminated by a number of oil lamps dotted here and there amid the plants, ferns, and other greenery that decorated the slatted shelves.

At the far end, from which the sound of giggles and

laughter was coming, was a group of chattering elderly ladies, all furiously fanning themselves; and so, still holding her hand he muttered, 'We won't join that company, but' – he pointed – 'there's a seat behind here.' And the next moment he had drawn her behind an enormous potted palm.

She could just make out a long wooden bench, and when they both dropped on to it she peered at him, then put her head back and once again gave way to a burst of laughter.

This had been a most surprising evening. From early morning she had been dreading it. She had woken early with a most uneasy feeling on her. In any case it would have highlighted, as it were, the nearness of the impending separation from Victoria, for they had been like sisters, loving caring sisters, and so she would be feeling unhappy; but there was something else worrying her, something on which she couldn't put a finger. Perhaps it was the haste that surrounded this whole business; he had seemed to sweep Victoria off her feet. But then Victoria was only too pleased to be swept off her feet. Her love for this man was, in a way, painful to watch; it was a love, she did not doubt, that would be enduring. She was, in a way, utterly besotted with him. But was he besotted with her? And this she had continually asked herself until she had to admit that she believed he was in love with her. But to what extent?

Much against her will she had let Victoria persuade her to buy a new ball gown, but she had held out firmly against pinks, blues, and greens and plumped for a pale grey; although the style wasn't one she would have chosen, as it had a low neckline and even exposed some part of her shoulders, and a skirt which she had considered to be much too voluminous but which she found was quite flat compared with the gowns of most of the ladies present, both young and old. Her changed appearance, she realised, had been a surprise to the head of the household, but still William Filmore's welcome had not been effusive, although it could be said to have been polite: whereas Victoria's hand was kissed, hers was shaken and only by the tips of her fingers.

But since finding herself, at dinner, seated next to Douglas Filmore, she had, in a strange way, begun to enjoy herself, for she found that this young man had a quiet sense of humour, and it wasn't without a caustic streak when pointing out some foible of one or other of the guests. She had noticed, too, he did not drink much at dinner: not one of his three wine glasses had been refilled.

She'd had a number of dances during the evening, three being with the young man sitting next to her and one with his brother. Lionel, she found, was a much better dancer than Douglas, but not as entertaining a partner. Conversation, too, had been spasmodic and made up of little more than two-syllable words: Was she enjoying herself?

Yes, thank you.

Would she miss Victoria very much?

Of course.

Would she continue to live at Meadow House?

Just for part of the time, when she wanted to attend to business.

Did she prefer the South Shields house?

Yes, she preferred the South Shields house.

Was it necessary to have two houses to carry on the businesses?

She completed a number of dance steps before answering this question while looking him in the face: Yes, she did consider it necessary.

Why?

And to this she had given the simple answer: Because my father thought it necessary . . .

'What are you laughing at? Come on, tell me.'

Before answering him, she took a lace-edged handkerchief from her beaded vanity bag and dabbed her eyes with it; then she said, 'Because it's the first time I've been pulled behind a palm by a young man.'

Now his head, too, was back and their laughter joined, and as his ebbed away he, in turn, peered at her in the dim light, saying, 'You know, you're as refreshing as spring water.'

She did not blush, nor did she come out with some meaningless platitude of denial, but what she did say and quite seriously was, 'You are a very kind man, different from your brother and your father.'

Nor did he make any protest against this statement; instead, he confirmed it by saying, 'Oh yes, I'm well aware of that. I've always been well aware of it, as far as I can remember: I didn't look like Lionel, I didn't act like Lionel, I had none of Lionel's graces. I was, compared with his stature, only half a man. Yet, you know, this never worried me because I didn't want to be like Lionel, or like my father. And, looking back down our family tree, there was no one of them that I wanted to be like. I was an oddity. Yet I knew I liked what I was. Do you think that sounds like the essence of arrogance?'

She shook her head slightly, then said, 'No. It's good to recognise what you are.'

'You recognised what you were a long time ago, didn't you?'

'Well' – she looked away from him and into the palm leaves and the strips of light coming through them. The music had stopped now but the chatter and laughter was louder – 'I can't say that I went in for self-analysis; I just knew what I wanted to do; but more so I knew what I

74

didn't want to do, and that was spend my time in dressing up and sitting for hours in someone else's drawing-room indulging in small chat and gossip, or going into serious debate on the changing fashions, whether your waist should be pushed up under your bust or dragged down onto the top of your hips, all depending, of course, on the tightness of your corsets.'

She now thrust her hand over her mouth and bent forward to still her gurgling, while he once again allowed his head to fall back, though making little sound with his laughter even while his body was shaking, because now they were aware of others coming into the conservatory.

But presently, he caught at her hand and, leaning towards her, he said, 'We may not get the chance again to have a tête-à-tête so I will say to you now, that I've enjoyed this evening solely because of your company.'

His face was quite near and she smiled into it as she said in a low voice, 'I can return the compliment and tell you that I had hated the thought of this evening, but that you have made it a most enjoyable one for me too.'

His smile widened as he whispered, 'You even enjoyed my dancing?'

The smile going from her face now, she shook her head, saying quite primly, 'No, sir; do you expect me to lie? your dancing is atrocious. If it wasn't that my eyesight tells me that you have only two feet I would be led to believe you have an odd one that trips you up at times.'

When he actually pushed her on the arm and she pretended to fall sideways on the form, they were once again shaking with their mirth. Controlling himself, he pointed through the palm leaves, beyond which was coming raucous laughter and spluttering, caused no doubt by some joke. And he made a wild gesture with his hand indicating that they shouldn't go out until the revellers moved on. And so they sat on the form side by side for almost ten minutes, and not a whispered word did they exchange. To Bridget, it was as if they were sitting in utter silence, a silence in which she was experiencing enjoyment. Since losing the companionship of her father she had felt unable to talk to anyone as she had done tonight to this kind man whom she knew to be two years older than herself, yet who looked so much younger, but talked and acted as her father might have done.

The announcement of another dance broke up the raucous group beyond the palm and there followed the rustle of gowns indicating that the ladies from the far end of the conservatory were also returning to the hall. Turning to Bridget now, Douglas said, 'Would you like to go, I mean, really try again?'

'Not particularly. I'd rather sit here, because there is something I'd like to ask you. And you have made it very easy for me. It is just this. Do you think your brother really loves Victoria?'

There was the slightest pause before Douglas answered, but with emphasis, 'Oh, yes. Yes. Apart from everything else, I'm sure he does. But who could resist loving her? She is a very beautiful girl.'

Bridget now took her question a step further by asking, 'Do you think it's only beautiful girls who can be loved?'

'Oh, no, no. But what I meant was, in his case . . . well, she is someone who would be very easy to love. Of course, I am well aware that beauty has only a limited time, unlike character that weathers the years and doesn't fade . . . blossoms, rather.'

'I am very fond of Victoria, you know. We have been like sisters. In fact, much more. Both being without mothers, in a way we acted as substitutes, one for the other.'

'Hello, there.' The voice brought their heads round to look into the palm leaves, for it was as if someone were addressing them from the other side. But then the voice went on thick and fuddled, 'Standing this one out, are you?'

When there was no answer to this, the voice continued, 'You shouldn't have let her dance with Father. He's rocking on his feet.'

'He shouldn't have drunk so much.'

At the sound of this voice Douglas cast a quick glance at Bridget; but she was staring into the palm leaves.

'He drinks very little, does the old man; 'tis rheumatism, his knees buckle.'

'He shouldn't dance then.'

'Felt he had to do his duty. You're lucky, you know, beautiful girl, beautiful.'

'I'm . . . I'm glad you think so.'

'Oh, I do, I do. An' what's more, I think you've turned up trumps. You're a good sort. Changed my opinion. Yes, yes, I have. Don't mind me saying so, changed my opinion.'

'Very kind of you, very kind of you, I'm sure.'

'Well, as I said to the old man, 'tis common knowledge that you're not rolling in it, and here you're gona marry a girl who hasn't a penny.'

Only the music could be heard now and the shuffling of feet and the dimmed laughter and in it Douglas's head was once again turned towards Bridget. Now she was looking back at him. Then when Douglas heard his brother's voice come as a low hiss through the leaves, saying, '*What did you say?*'

'What d'you mean, what did I say? Well, just that . . . well, 'tis good of you to pick her up. Love match. Yes, love match. Now if it had been Miss Brid . . . well, you would have been warm enough all right there.'

'*What are you saying?*'

'Nothing, man. Nothing. Well, Dad doing their business. And 'tis well known Miss Bridget took them in . . . I mean her dad did. Penniless. They were penniless . . . Hi! Hi! Take your hands off me! You should have known. Well, everybody . . . knew, every . . . body . . .'

When the palm swayed towards them Douglas pushed Bridget further along the form out of the way of the falling plant. Then he darted around to where Lionel was thrusting the drunken informant over the tub and onto the swaying plant, and with a surprising show of strength from his thin right arm he brought it up under his brother's wrists and so sent Lionel staggering back. Then pulling the gasping figure upwards from the palm, he said, 'Are you all right, Mr Kemp?'

The man spluttered. 'All right? No, I'm not all right. He's . . . he's a bloody maniac . . . All I said was that she wasn't the one with the cash. Nice party this, attacked . . . Where's my father? I'm off out of here.' The man staggered towards the ballroom door, and Douglas turned to look at his brother, who had now gained some control of himself, and he said to him, almost commanded him, 'Pull yourself together!'

'*Pull myself together?*' The voice was like a hiss. 'Do you know what . . . ?'

'Yes. Yes, I know what. I was sitting behind the palm. And do you know what, too?' Douglas's voice sank to a whisper. 'Miss Bridget was sitting there with me.'

Lionel looked towards the end of the conservatory, then muttered, 'God!'

'Look, it's nearly over, the dance is finishing. Go in there and make the next one the last; then they'll all go, and we can talk.'

'Talk?' Lionel leaned his face, looking unusually pale, closer to his brother's, saying, 'Talk? What is there to talk about? Did you hear him? She . . . she hasn't a penny. *My*

78

God!' He put his hand to the side of his head now and pressed it as if thrusting his thoughts away.

'This has got to be worked out. It's too late now to renege. Go on; do as I say.'

It was, for the moment, as if Douglas were the elder and directing the affairs of the house, for he actually put his hand on his brother's back and pressed him towards the open doors again. But here, Lionel drew in a long breath, squared his shoulders, shrugged off his brother's hand, and walked into the ballroom, leaving Douglas standing now and looking towards the palm lying at such an angle as if it, too, had imbibed over-much on this evening of celebration.

He walked slowly back to where Bridget was standing at the end of the bench, her back against the wall. She appeared to him to be very tall at this moment; and her face looked tight and drawn, the large eyes that had only a short while ago been wet with laughter were now gleaming black and hard through the dimness. He put his hand out to guide her around the palm leaves that were sprawled across the bench, but she refused the gesture, and pressed past him, saying, 'Is this true? He thought she was wealthy?'

He could not look at her; he actually turned from her and, unseeing, gazed down the length of the conservatory before he said, 'I'm afraid so.'

'But she told him. She told me that she had made it plain to him.'

'If that is so, I can't understand it,' he said. 'I recall once her laughingly saying that she was just a poor girl, but rich in so many ways, which, to me, suggested . . . Lionel's love for her.'

'What will he do?'

'I can't say, because I don't know. I can only say, and truthfully, he hasn't got a penny of his own. He depends upon my father; as I did until I started earning a little at my own trade, which I've told you about. But I don't think I have any need to point out to you that my father and the estate are in a very bad way.'

'And Victoria was going to be the saving of it. Is that it?'

He looked away again. 'Yes. Yes, that's it. But' – his head jerked round – 'I'm sure, as I was when I answered your questions, that besides the matter of the money, Lionel is very fond of Victoria. Very.'

She thrust past him to go and stand looking through the open door at the dancing still in progress. And what she said now was, 'I suspected something right from the beginning. The whole thing was too unreal, too like a fairy-tale, too rushed. But I know one thing for sure, this will kill her.'

'Oh –' And Douglas's intervention on behalf of his brother had something of a note of disbelief in it as he went on, 'People don't die these days from unrequited love; the swooning lady's day is over,' but then actually stepped back from the quiet but determined onslaught of her voice as she turned on him, saying, 'What do you know about it? People do die from unrequited love. Not straightaway, no; they just shrivel until there's nothing left of them. And that's what will happen to her. She not only loves that man, she's besotted with him, she adores him and, strangely, she holds him high in honour because she imagined that he was taking in marriage a penniless girl just because he loved her.'

There was silence between them and in it the laughter from those seated around the ballroom shrieked in their ears. Some of it was raucous, the result of some ribaldry or other; some was mere tittering, expressing refined shock. But neither of them moved until the music stopped, when, as if emerging from a deep conclave with herself, she turned to him, saying, still quietly but nevertheless forthrightly, 'Don't do anything. I mean, find him and tell him not to do anything until tomorrow. I'll come over in the morning. I shall be here at half-past nine prompt, and I shall want to see him and his father.'

She went to move away, but his voice saying, 'Bridget!' halted her, and when she looked at him over her shoulder, he said, 'I'm sorry, very sorry.'

She said nothing further, but went on into the ballroom and made her way to where a radiant Victoria was standing fanning herself as she listened to the solicitor's profuse apologies about his dancing.

Addressing the man by his Christian name, as her father had always done, Bridget said, 'Andrew, I want to call on you tomorrow afternoon. Three o'clock?'

'Oh, Miss Bridget, you really are the most . . . you really are. Here I am in the middle of apologising for my feet's atrocious efforts and you are making an appointment . . .'

'Andrew. I am very tired, and Victoria is, too. We are going home now.' She paused and, turning to Victoria, she said, pointedly, 'Say goodbye to . . . Lionel.' She had to make an effort to voice the name.

'But it is just on the last . . .'

'Please! Victoria. As I said, I am very tired. It is near two o'clock in the morning and I have a busy day ahead of me tomorrow . . . Please.'

'Yes. Well. Yes, Bridget.'

As Bridget threaded her way through the dispersing dancers, both Victoria and Mr Andrew Kemp looked after her and Victoria said, 'I've never heard her say she's tired before and she's hardly danced at all. And she looked . . . Oh dear.'

Mr Kemp said nothing but he thought, No, neither have I heard her admit to being tired. And she wants to see me tomorrow at three o'clock. Now what's in the wind? She never does anything without a purpose, does Miss Bridget. She should, to my mind, have been a man. Well, her father nearly made her into one, business-wise anyway.

'Come, my dear.' He held out his arm. 'Let me take you and leave you in the protection of your future husband. I cannot see him here, but we must find him, eh?' Then he added, 'Happy?'

'Oh, yes, Mr Kemp, so very happy. So very, very happy. It's been a wonderful ball.'

And it could have gone on; but Bridget had to bring it to an end . . . Why? And she looked so . . . Dear, dear! She could be very awkward at times.

5

The morning was bright, and from the ridges of a sloping field away to the right of her the sun was drawing up fresh green sprigs. To the left, towering above the high stone wall, the trees were all weighed down with new-born leaves still dripping moisture from the early morning shower.

Hamlet, too, was evidently feeling the pull of Spring because he had the urge to canter, not to walk or trot as he had been bidden to do.

Bridget, deep in thought, was now walking him, for she was nearing the gate of Grove House through which she had only a few hours earlier been driven with a puzzled Victoria by her side, whose thoughts had alternated between the wonders of the evening past and concern for her cousin's changed manner: What was the matter? Had someone said something to her? Having spent most of the evening with Douglas, had he annoyed her? Lionel had said Douglas was a very odd fellow, not caring for company, and when he wasn't chipping away at bits of wood or stone he was tramping the hills.

Bridget had forced herself to answer: No, there was nothing wrong, but she was feeling a little unwell, and she was tired.

And now this morning she had reason to be tired for she had hardly slept. It would have been quite three o'clock before they had gone to bed, and from then her mind had been working and planning the best course to take to assure Victoria's future happiness; she knew, and without a doubt, that as things stood Lionel Filmore would never marry her, and there crept into her mind the thought that perhaps Victoria had withheld the knowledge of her true situation from him. She had twice already questioned her about this and each time had been given the same answer: 'I've told him I'm a poor girl.'

But how had she said that? That was the question. Had she put it over as a joke? Rich people did make a joke of being poor; some even acted as if they were. What about herself? She certainly didn't dress or act the part of a wealthy young woman. And so, thinking along those lines, she felt she was as much to blame as Victoria for the situation that had come about. Going back to the way she dressed: being judged by that, she must have appeared as the working partner.

She wished fervently now that she had done what she was tempted to do when her father died, sold Milton Place and lived permanently in Meadow House, their original home in South Shields: this was the house she had always thought of as home. But, as her father had maintained, Milton Place wasn't a kick in the backside from all that was going on in the business world, particularly in their form of small businesses tucked away under the skirts of the big fellas, the steelworks, the shipyards, the mines, all the grinding businesses that brought men to early death. Theirs, he had laughingly stated, was like a group of little hobbies. But very paying little hobbies, as his father and grandfather before him had made evident in their wills.

She recalled his pet story with regard to the accumulation of pennies. It concerned a man who had done a great service for the king and the king apparently wanted to bestow gold and jewels on him by way of his thanks. But the seemingly humble man had said, 'No, sire. All I would ask of you is to give me a penny and thenceforward each day double the accumulated worth.' A penny! And the king had laughed. This humble man was only asking for a penny and to double its worth each day. But the king laughed no more when within a comparatively short time the man who had asked for a penny to begin with bought his kingdom, leaving him bereft of all he owned.

It was a tall tale, but in 1825 John and Arthur Mordaunt had made their first little batch of blacking, mainly out of soot and fat, and it wasn't a very good or lasting product; but they learnt as they went along. And for them, this start was the equivalent of their penny. It was odd, too, that each of the brothers had two sons, and so this line had followed down to her father and his brother Sep. However, Septimus apparently was the only one of the Mordaunt men who wanted nothing to do with blacking, polishes, or candles; such business was lowly. So he had taken his share, married a beautiful but mindless young girl, whisked her abroad, and there he had gambled in different ways. However, it hadn't been the tables that ruined him but the lure of the goldmines. And, like the prodigal son, he had returned broken in body and also in mind to the house where he had been born, and he and his child had been welcomed with open arms.

It was strange, Bridget thought, if this business of the engagement had taken place in their old home there would have been no mistaking the identity between them, because the story of the two brothers was common knowledge in Shields. It was fresh, not only in the minds of the old, but in those of middle age, and they would have put any stranger straight as to who was the head of the Mordaunt business. And they would have added in their forthright ways, 'She's only got eight fingers but she's got them stuck in all kinds of pies, and she keeps her thumbs bare for testing new ones.'

There was no one about to take her horse, so she tied it to a post, then walked to the front of the house. She had no need to ring the bell because the double doors were open, and she stood looking in to where there was a scurry of activity. Two men were emerging from the long panelled corridor carrying what looked like a china cabinet. The carpets were down on the floor and a maid was arranging chairs, while another's business seemed to be the placing of ornaments here and there. No one seemed to take any notice of her until a man went to pass her. He was carrying a large potted plant which he pressed away from his face as he glimpsed her, then said, 'Oh! Mornin', miss.' Then turning, he called into the hall, 'Mr Bright! There's a young lady here.'

The butler appeared from the region of the drawing room. He was different from the man who last night had announced her and Victoria. Then he had been attired in bright blue livery, as had the other manservants, lending colour to the brilliantly lit rooms. Now the dull grey of his noticeably shabby uniform seemed reflected in his face, and he looked tired. She noticed this, but did not comment on it. What she said to him was, 'I am expected.'

Although he was surprised that she should be visiting at this early hour of twenty-five minutes past nine in the morning, especially so after having left the house only a few hours earlier, he did not, of course, show it but said, 'Oh yes, miss. Come this way. Perhaps you will be good enough to wait in the little sitting-room.' The faintest of smiles touched his lips as he added, 'It is the only room presentable in the house as yet.'

They were passing the foot of the stairs when he exclaimed, 'Oh, here is Master Douglas.'

Bridget looked up towards where Douglas was now descending the broad staircase. He was wearing a plain dark suit and was busy buttoning the coat down from the neck as he approached her, saying simply, 'Good morning.'

'Good morning.'

Douglas turned as though about to lead the way down the corridor, but hesitated and said to Bright, 'Bring in a pot of coffee for four.' This time he placed his hand on Bridget's elbow and steered her along the corridor that was lined, not only with wood, but with enormous oil paintings, which last night had been shown to advantage under the soft glow of hanging oil lamps, but which now seemed to merge into the panelling, only their gilded frames being prominent.

At the end of the corridor another one led off at right angles, and in comparison this one looked denuded for the panelling was bare. Halfway along it, he drew her to a stop, leant forward, pushed a door open and stood aside to allow her to enter. Inside was definitely a sitting-room, and it was bright with sunshine that warmed the chintz covered couch and numerous chairs and lit up one wall of the Chinese patterned wallpaper in such a way that you could believe the figures on it were moving.

Bridget took in the whole room in one roving glance. It was an elegant room, at least the decor was such. Yet, she would have also called it homely, and this impression was furthered by the fact that the chintz covers had definitely seen a lot of wear.

'Do sit down.'

'Thank you, no; I'd rather stand.' She looked at her watch. 'It's turned half-past nine,' she said, and the sound such a remark elicited from him wasn't quite a laugh; but his thin body beneath his coat shook for a moment as he looked downwards while shaking his head slowly from side to side. 'Do you know, we didn't get to bed until nearly four o'clock,' he said, emphasising the earliness rather than the lateness of the hour. 'My father had drunk a great deal but the news that Lionel had to break to him, and not gently, sobered him quite a bit. And I'm sure, like myself, neither of them went to sleep for some while after getting to bed. And now, Miss Bridget, you say it has turned half-past nine. You know' – he was nodding at her now – 'I can remember as a boy, when these occasions of dinners and balls were frequent in this house and my father was much younger than he is today and in much better health, even then, he never rose before the evening after. But now, you have commanded him to be here at half-past nine in the morning. Don't you think you are being a little severe?'

She did not immediately answer, but stared at him; then she said, 'And don't you think, too . . . or should I say, have you asked yourself why I wish to see them at all? Your sense should tell you that I haven't come merely to upbraid, although I shall do plenty of that, let me assure you. But I could have done that through a letter, or through my solicitor. No; I have come because I had already, last night, thought up some kind of solution; not because I want to help your brother, or ease the monetary problem of this house, but simply because I do not want Victoria to die of shame and despair. And please' – she now thrust out her arm, palm upwards – 'don't laugh at that suggestion as you did last night. Just don't.'

After a moment he said, 'I'm not going to laugh at your suggestion, Miss Bridget; I'm only going to say that I think Victoria is a very, very lucky person to have someone like you behind her. It's been my misfortune never to have met anyone, as yet, so concerned for another's welfare and happiness.'

Without making further comment Bridget had turned to look towards the window when the door at the far end of the room opened and Lionel and his father entered.

She forced herself to turn slowly and look at them. They, too, were looking at her, although it would be a better description to say that the expression in Lionel's eyes was more of a fierce glare. But it was his father who spoke first, saying, 'Bloody nice state of affairs you've got us into, miss.'

'The bloody nice state of affairs, as you express it, has in no way been brought about by me, sir, but by your son's conniving. And doubtless with your co-operation, thinking you were both on to a good thing, a small gold mine, in fact. Well, you picked on the wrong digger, didn't you?'

The three men were amazed not only at the stance of this young woman who was the antithesis of anything they would have termed ladylike, but also that she was using phraseology they themselves might have used. It would have been acceptable coming from a man . . . But she was going on: 'This house is in a bad way. It has been going downhill for years and not one of you, nor your forebears, has tried to stop its rot by doing a decent day's work, such as going into commerce. But you were quite willing at this stage of desperation to clutch at the money made out of commerce, even such degrading businesses as boot-blacking and candles. Well, both those industries, together with property and such, made my great-grandfather, my grandfather, then my father, and now me, rich. Even so, had the positions between Victoria and myself been reversed and she was the one with the money, and you' – she was now pointing straight at Lionel – 'had got your hands on it, it still wouldn't have been enough to restore this house to what your father' – she now jerked her head towards the older man – 'would consider its heyday. No, because the man having the right up till now to all his wife owns, it would have been squandered, and although this house would have risen for a time to what you consider its rightful position in your society, its bottom being rotten, it would eventually, and soon, have sunk again. And the money earned from the sweat of the people you despise would have sunk with it.'

The quietness that settled on the room could be described only as the dullness that spreads through a brain after a severe blow. And, as if he had just received that blow, William Filmore sank down on to the couch but without moving his gaze from Bridget who, at this moment, appeared to him neither woman nor man, because no man would have dared stand up in this house and spoken as she had done. And no woman of his acquaintance, right down the years, could have ever thought as this one did.

There was no movement in the room until Douglas gently put a chair to Bridget's side. But this kind gesture was rewarded with a cold stare and a voice equally chilly saying, 'I don't need a chair. What I have to say is better said standing up.'

'Oh, well; that being so, you'll excuse me if I sit.' And at that he moved the chair back to where it had been and sat down. And this left her staring now at Lionel who, like his father, just could not believe that this was happening to him; that this bitch dressed as she was in those breeches and leggings, which in themselves made her into half a man, and that tongue, and the nerve and daring of her, yes, the daring of her . . . At this moment he had the greatest desire to step towards her and bring the flat of his hand across her face, but being made as she was she would likely claw him to bits. How, in the name of God! had she come to be related to such a girl as Victoria.

Oh! Victoria. That puss! And his mind now mimicked her voice, saying, 'Believe me, Lionel, I'm a very poor little girl. Don't laugh. Don't laugh. I am. I am.' And on that occasion he had picked her up, literally, from the ground and he himself had said, 'Well, if that's the case, let me share your poverty. And what we'll do first is sell your wardrobe and some of your jewellery to live on, eh?' This had caused her to laugh gaily and to cling to him and kiss him with a fervour that amazed him and belied her delicate, refined appearance.

'I am asking you a question.' He was brought back to the harsh present to find Bridget looking straight at him. 'As things stand,' she said, 'will you still keep your promise to Victoria and marry her?'

Lionel turned to look at his father, and it was he who, having returned his son's glance, answered Bridget, saying, 'My son is in no position to support a wife. Nor am I in any position to support him.'

'Then what if she were to bring him up for breach of promise?'

It was Lionel now who came back smartly, saying, 'Victoria would never do that: she would never act the rejected woman, she is not that type.'

'How do you know what type of woman she is? You have only seen the engagement side of her, the beautiful, teasing, pleasing side of her. But there is another side, and let me tell you, when you are classifying her, a neighbour of ours in South Shields has just won her case . . . and she a delicate little thing, and against another such as yourself, and, what is more she has *skinned* him.'

The spitting out of the word demanded a silence the while the three men looked at her; then still concentrating on Lionel, she said, 'I have a proposition to put to you. But first of all I will say this. I have never imagined you earning a penny, not even to support yourself, never mind a wife, and I saw Victoria being brought to this house to live in genteel, and not so genteel poverty under the patronage of your father. But I raised no real objections because I knew she would be only too happy to do this. And only God knows why.'

'Woman! you've . . .'

'Be quiet!' This came from Douglas. He was looking hard at his brother now and he said, 'She said she had a proposition to make to you. Hear her out.'

Bridget turned her gaze from Douglas and onto Lionel again, and straightaway she said, 'From the date of your marriage I shall allow you two thousand pounds a year. Half of that would be sufficient to keep you and her in a smaller establishment; but she seems to like the idea of coming here to live, so the extra money should help towards the running of this place.'

She glanced towards William Filmore, who had pulled himself from the back of the couch and was staring at her, his mouth slightly agape. 'But there will be certain conditions attached to this. They will be written out and I shall expect you at my solicitor's at three o'clock on Monday afternoon to sign that you agree with them.'

Two thousand pounds a year. It was as much as he had promised himself out of the income from the factories, et cetera. It was what he had worked out would carry him through until he could sell off the blacking and the candle-wax places. He looked at his father, who was saying, 'That's a very generous offer, Miss Bridget,' and the old man nodded towards her before adding, 'I only hope the conditions attached to the offer won't be too difficult to follow.' He glanced now at his son; but Bridget continued to look at the old man as she said, 'Well, it will be up to him. The offer definitely depends upon the conditions. And the first is that your son finds employment of some kind within the first six months of his marriage. If he doesn't, then the amount will drop by specified hundreds. Should he not have found any kind of employment within a year then the amount will be halved to what I originally thought would be a sufficient sum to provide him to keep a wife in moderate circumstances.'

'God in heaven! Blast you! I'll . . .'

Words choked themselves in Lionel's throat as his father, pulling himself round on the couch, barked at him, 'Shut up! And she's right. My God! It pains me to say this, but she's right.' Then the old man, looking at Bridget again, demanded, 'Are there any more?'

'Yes, one other: that he remain faithful to her. If it can be proved otherwise –' She now turned a sidelong glance on the furious countenance of the man and added quietly, 'In that case I withdraw the whole amount and persuade Victoria to return home.'

Lionel was now supporting himself by gripping the back of the couch. His body was partly bent over it; there was no sound at all coming from him as he listened to her saying, 'There it is. If you agree to the conditions you will be at my solicitor's at three o'clock, as I said, on Monday. It's Andrew Kemp & Sons, Grey Street.' And she turned abruptly now to his father and said to him: 'Good day to you, sir.' And as she walked across the room Douglas rose quickly from the chair and followed her.

After opening the door for her, he walked by her side, down the corridors, across the hall which was now once more a hall with the partition in place, and out on to the gravel drive and to the post where her horse was tethered. And, not until she had put her hands on its bridle did he speak, when he said, 'You are an amazing woman. I could almost say, a dreadful young woman, dreadful in your honesty and in the unusual quality of mind. What you are doing is a very kind thing, but I wonder if it wouldn't have been better to let her suffer for a time, because, you know, there'll be all kinds of suffering ahead for her. Crazy love such as hers which has its foundation really in the attraction of a good-looking face and of a man who looks well on a horse . . . and can gallop it almost to death –' The last word was uttered in low deep bitterness before he added, 'Such love is bound to suffer, because it will wake up one day.'

She had thrown the reins over the horse's neck and was about to put her foot in the stirrup when she hesitated and, looking at him, said, 'I think I've asked this question before, but I say again, how do you happen to belong to this family?'

He smiled at her; then his whole manner changed and he answered in a whisper, 'I'll tell you how I came to know my beginnings. It was Rosie Jackson, the cook, you know' – he pointed across the yard towards the kitchen quarters – 'when I was a skinny little boy, which condition has never altered; well, she told me I was born in Ireland, among the sweet-smelling grass, and was given over to a pixie carrier, who was told to deliver me to a cobbler's family in the centre of the City of Newcastle. He happened to be passing over the cesspool here and the stench was so bad that he dropped me. Fortunately, I hit the bank. And there it was, she said, that she found me her very self and she carried me into the mistress, and the mistress had always wanted a skinny baby, because the one she had was too big and heavy to nurse. And that's how I came to be in this house.'

Bridget couldn't help it: she drooped her head against the horse's flank; she wanted to laugh, she wanted to shake with her laughter but she couldn't allow herself to, this business was too serious, but she turned to him and said, 'Why couldn't Victoria have chosen you?'

He stepped back from her, his face straight, no impish light in his eyes now, and after a moment of looking at her, he said, 'For two reasons. First, she would never have fallen in love with anyone of my build or looks; and secondly, I would never be attracted to anyone of her build and looks . . . Let me give you a hand up.'

She had never needed anyone to give her a hand up

onto a horse, but she allowed him to put his hand under her boot and to hoist her onto Hamlet's back. Then, looking down on him, she said, 'We'll be meeting again ... likely.' And he said, 'Yes, likely.' And at this she rode off whilst he remained watching her until she was lost to his sight when she entered the drive, and the word he muttered to himself was, 'Amazing.'

6

Joe thrust open the door of his old home to see his mother sitting at the uncovered kitchen table, and on it a bread board with the heel of a loaf standing upright. There was no fat on the table, neither dripping, pig fat, nor butter, but there was a brown teapot and a cup and saucer. He did not speak immediately but stood at the corner of the table, scanned it, then on a wry laugh, he said, ''Tis the best display of poverty I've seen for a long time. Are you sure you put tea in the pot, Ma, and it isn't just water?'

'Yes, there's tea in the pot,' she spat back at him; 'but it's been stewed all day. I'm reduced to this.'

He bent forward now, laid his flat hands on the table and growled at her, 'For two pins I'd take my hands and swipe the lot over you. When have you sat down to a table without a cloth on it? And when have you done without your drippin' or your butter? And how much did you lay on with Mickey Tyler the day? Come off it; you sent for me, didn't you, to see this show? Well, it doesn't work, Ma. You should know that by now. I can see through you like a glass window. And come on, say what you've got to say, because I've had a heavy day and I want to get home.'

'Heavy day!' she cried sarcastically, getting to her feet. 'Tell me when a gaffer's had a heavy day. And you want to get home, do you, to your fancy piece?'

'I'm tellin' you, Ma . . .'

'Well, what else is she? Somebody else's rake-off. And

96

who does her bairn take after, eh? Have you recognised him yet? Well, if you haven't now you soon will; lads always show who put them there.'

Slowly he turned from her, for he knew if he looked at her a moment longer he would hit her, and the blow would not be soft. No wonder his father had uttered those strange words, strange to him at the time, when he had said, 'I'm not sorry to go, lad.' But since he himself had then become the sole butt of his mother's tongue and viciousness he had understood why his father should have welcomed release.

He was making for the door when, her voice changing, she said, 'Our Fred's never bought a penny in for on three weeks. You could give him a start. And I can only do part time at the biscuit factory. Me legs won't hold out. And anyway, I don't see why I should be expected to: you're in a position now, you could take him on in the factory or put a word in for him elsewhere.'

He turned to her again. 'I'm not takin' him on, Ma, or puttin' any more words in for him. He's been thrown out of two jobs so far this year. The chain-making was too heavy for him, wasn't it? But it's funny, women have to stick it out. And the tannery men start at six; you might be allowed one sleep-in in a week but not three. Why didn't you drag him out of bed if you're so concerned that he keeps a job? You did me. Oh, aye; you did me long afore I started in the blackin' factory, when I had to do cinder pickin', not so much to bake bread but to keep your idle hands and feet warm. . . .'

He was suddenly pushed to one side by the opening of the door and Fred's coming in, and as he stumbled back Fred said in feigned surprise, 'Oh, I'm very sorry, sir. Did I overbalance you?'

'You'll never overbalance me, lad,' Joe said, glaring at him, and his mother put in, 'No; you won't overbalance the big-head, the upstart that he is, and he's one if ever I saw one: wouldn't give his own kith and kin a chance to earn a livin',' which succeeded in riling Joe further, and he rounded on her, saying, 'He's had every chance to earn a livin'; but he's like you, Ma, he's bone lazy. All he wants is a way to make easy money, and he can't learn there's no way to do it.'

He pulled the door wide again to go out, but he hadn't reached the step before Fred had sprung after him and was now growling under his breath, 'Oh, but there is, lad; there's an easy way to do it. The bairn's come, hasn't it? And it would potch the big event. Oh, aye, it would potch the big event if he wasn't made to co-oper . . .'

Joe had him pinned against the stanchion of the door now, his two hands on the lapels of the jacket had dragged them together, and he was hissing, 'You do! Do that an' I'll do for you. D'you hear? As true as I'm standin' here I'll do for you.'

As he let go of the coat Fred coughed and choked for a moment; then he, in his turn, hissed at him, 'You can't frighten me. You never could and you never will.'

'Well, brother, just you try it on. That's all I'm sayin' to you, just you try it on.' And with this he swung about and marched down the short street, past Mrs McLoughlin, who lived two doors away and was talking to Florrie Burns from the end house. They both looked at him; then, as if in afterthought, Mrs McLoughlin said, 'Nice night, Joe.'

He made no answer to this, not even to cast a glance in her direction, for he knew within the next half-hour everybody in the place would know that the Skinner lads had been at it again.

He had to traverse the whole of Honeybee Place and pass the factory before he could get on the horse bus that would take him to the outskirts of Birtley.

He usually walked the mile and a half distance between the factory and his home, but tonight he couldn't get home quickly enough, not only to see Lily, but also the child. It was her child, yet to all intents and purposes he would be its father from now on. And it was a happy child, it gurgled up at him when he held it, it rarely cried, except when it was hungry. And its mother was happy, yes, its mother was happy. He had made her happy; and she loved him. Strange that, but she did, and she had told him so. Life was good except for . . . oh, yes, there was always an except, for his mother was a mean woman and Fred had her nature. But by God! if he as much as went near that man . . . anyway he, being who he was, could deny the whole affair and have him up for blackmail and perhaps imprisoned. Then where would their happiness go? Lily would be bowed down with shame, as she had been on the day she had been paid off with a bag of five sovereigns. Odd, but he had never used that money, nor had he let her; it was still in the bag in the bottom of the tin box.

Yet if the man should pay up, that, in a way for him and Lily, would be worse than exposure. It might save Lily's face but his own feelings would be such that he really would want to do for Fred, not just threaten him.

He pushed open the back gate and walked up his own back yard, past the water tap, the coalhouse and the closet, and the washhouse, then through the kitchen door into a cosy room in which the fire was burning brightly in a black-leaded stove that had a boiler at one side and an oven at the other; and on the table, spread on a check cloth, were set the implements of a meal for two. But, stooping over a small clothes-rack on which she was hanging napkins, was a big-made, fat, tousled-haired woman, and she greeted him with, 'Oh, there you are then. The water's boilin', there's enough left for your wash; but I had to save it for you, for she's been at the nappies again.' She thumbed up towards the ceiling. 'I've never known anybody so keen on washin' nappies out. 'Tisn't healthy, I've told her. I used to let mine dry on them, the piddle was good for their skin.'

He laughed at her as he said, 'Yes, I bet it was, Mary; and for the sores an' all.'

'Never a sore did they have, not one of mine. A bit skinned in their forks, or on their backsides. 'Tis good for the complexion, is pee. Did you know that? Oh, aye; it's a known thing that rich ladies wash their faces in it.'

He flapped a hand towards her as he made for the far door that led into a passage which gave entrance to a sitting-room and from which a flight of steep stairs led upwards, with Mary's voice following him, crying, 'You know what you'll get if you go up there with them boots on! She's just got off her hands an' knees scrubbin' that lino.'

He stopped and quickly undid the round, thick leather laces of his heavy boots. Then, stepping out of them, he bounded up the stairs and onto the narrow landing; and there, pushing open one of the two doors, he paused for just a second at the sight of the beautiful girl kneeling by the wooden cradle. She had her face turned to him: it was smiling a welcome. Tiptoeing across to her, he said, 'Hello, there.'

'Hello.'

He looked down on the child, saying now, 'Is he all right?'

'Yes. Yes, fine. He was a bit whingey this mornin', but I took him out for a walk in the fields to get some fresh air, but only after I'd fought Mary off, mind. She was bundlin' blankets on me; she said the child would get its death an' it shouldn't have fresh air on its face for three months. Where do they hear such things?'

'Oh, in their own country, across the watter, as they call it, they're full of superstitions an' weird sayings an' tales. And there's so many of them now. Since the famine over there they've flooded the country, and you'd think it was mostly this North-east section. Still, if we've got to go by her they're a warm-hearted, helpful lot.'

'Oh yes; I don't know what I would have done without her.'

No; and he didn't either. The night the child was about to come he had been frantic. The midwife they had booked from Gateshead Fell was as drunk as a noodle, and it took Mary to push her out the door, literally with her toe in the woman's backside. And she had taken over and brought the yelling boy into this world. He would never forget the weird feeling when she had first put the red boiled-looking piece of flesh into his arms. It had been like a wave of heat from one of the kilns. It had not only swept through him, but had enveloped him like a cloud for some moments, during which he could not even make out the tiny figure he was holding.

'I'll carry him down. Will you bring the cradle, Joe? I'm sorry you've got to go through this pantomime every night. If I left him downstairs in the cradle she would have it on the fender and the child kizzened up afore I knew where I was. I don't know how six of hers have survived.'

'Nor me.' He was following her out of the room now, the cradle under his arm. 'Likely they were either only par'-boiled, or just toasted.'

They were laughing together when they entered the kitchen, to be greeted by Mary, saying, 'That child will grow up with rickets if nothin' else. Stuck up in that room that's like an iceberg most of the day. Well, I must be off. 'Tis himself that'll be raisin' Cain because his bite's not bein' put into his mouth. One stone of tatties I've peeled this day; they're in the pot now bein' chased by a rabbit.'

She put her head back and let out a bellow of a laugh, in which both Joe and Lily joined.

The latch of the kitchen door was in her hand when she said, ''Tis a happy family you are. And you'll go on being happy if you keep it low. But once you get past the two, love, as they say, goes up the flue, and from then on 'tis the bones of life you chew.'

When the door closed on her they looked at each other and their exchanged glances held embarrassment, until she put her hand out and laid it lightly on his coat sleeve, saying softly, 'It won't be like that, Joe. I promise you, it won't be like that, not on my part anyway.'

He went to take her in his arms, but then shook his head vigorously, saying, 'I'm mucky; let me get a wash.'

And he had his wash in the scullery, kneeling on the stone floor over a tin bath of hot water. Then he had the full meal of meat pudding, potatoes, and turnip, followed by two cups of tea and a large buttered scone.

While she was nursing the baby, after the table had been cleared and she had washed up the crocks, they would sit before the fire and talk for a while. Then presently, he would turn to the table and either plough his way through an English lesson given to him by the teacher from the Unitarian night class that was held in the Mechanics Hall, or go over books of figures he had brought from the Works. And then it would be supper time, followed by bed.

On Sundays they would take the horse-bus to the outskirts of the town, and from there would walk the moor.

With the arrival of the baby three weeks ago the routine changed. The evenings now centred around the child. But tonight he somewhat surprised her by saying, 'I've got to go out for a while. It's to do with an order.'

'Is it in the town?'

He hesitated before saying, 'Yon side of Gateshead Fell.'

She said, 'Are you goin' to get the train?'

He laughed, then said, 'By the time I walk to the station I could be almost in Newcastle, never mind Gateshead Fell.'

'But it's quite a distance, and you've been on your feet all day.'

He put his hand on the mass of her shining auburn hair, and he looked into her large greenish eyes as he said softly, 'All the love words you could say to me wouldn't touch me like what you've just come out with . . . you've been standin' on your feet all day. Nobody in me life has ever worried about me standin' on me feet, or, years ago, if they were frozen when I went about barefoot; and I've been droppin' on me feet after sixteen hours of goin' from one thing to another. But you're advisin' me to take the train to ease me feet. Oh, Lily.' He leaned forward now and his lips were gentle on hers. And when the tears came into her eyes, in a raised tone, he said to her, 'Why must you always cry when I say . . . well, a civil word?'

'Because . . . because you're such a good man, and I'm lucky. Oh yes, I'm a lucky girl. Life's like a dream in this lovely little house. What am I sayin', little? Four rooms and a backyard and all in it ours.'

'Well, I'll promise you this, lass, before I'm finished there'll be eight rooms, and we'll have a closet inside, aye, and a piano in the front room.'

She fell against him laughing now, and he held her tightly. Then, as he pressed her away, he said, 'You can laugh, but I'm a man of me word. You'll see.'

She watched him take his second best cap and jacket from off the concertinaed clothes-rack that was nailed to the wall to the right of the door, and she wanted to say to him, 'I'll be happy in two rooms in one of the rows as long as you're with me, Joe,' but she refrained because it would bring him back to protest that she would never land up anywhere in Honeybee Place again.

After he had gone out of the door with a warm backward glance towards her, she sat down by the side of the cradle and looked at the child lying peacefully asleep, and her face reflected her sober thoughts: Would he grow up to look like him? Perhaps. Yes, perhaps. Yet, no matter how she tried, she could not visualise the face of the man who had fathered her child. She could see the outline of him, the way he stood, the way he held his head, always a little on the side as if in enquiry. She could hear his laugh, a deep laugh, in a way a thick heavy laugh. Her mind couldn't explain what feelings it created in her. But his face continued to be a blank. Yet the memory of him lingered, seeming to scorn her for this new love, this real love. Yet, she had never spoken the word love to him.

The child, now opening its eyes, seemed to stare at her for a moment, then gave a little grizzling cry and she reacted by picking it up and, unbuttoning her blouse, holding it to her breast; then she sat back in the chair while experiencing a wonderful feeling of contentment and fulfilment . . .

Joe was worried, for he knew that if his brother was hard pushed to follow his twin pursuits of drink and horses he would resort to anything to get the wherewithal to satisfy these needs. He had done it on other occasions, so he wouldn't put it past him from going to that fellow and blackmailing him. No, he wouldn't. Yet, how was he to do it? He wouldn't have the nerve to go up to the house, he'd be shown the door right quick. His only hope, as far as he could see, was to waylay the man, and that could only be done when he was riding back from the hunt or from one of his mad races across the moor. And anyway, he reasoned, if he didn't happen to come across him the night, there would be other nights, other times, because not being at work, he had time to trail the fellow.

He could see no way of stopping him, unless he tipped off Andy Davison about his having potched him. But then, Andy was a bit rough, too rough; he'd likely kick him to death. Oh – he sighed deeply – why was he plagued with a parent like his mother and a brother like Fred? Why couldn't he be left alone as he was now for once in his life?

Before entering the woodland he hesitated. He had been this far only twice since the day of the blackberry picking, but he knew that the path through it was well used as a horse trail before it opened on to a bridle path that ran past two farms before joining the road leading to estates like the Filmores' and houses like Miss Mordaunt's; and it was general news that the day after tomorrow that fellow Filmore was going to marry Miss Mordaunt's cousin, the beautiful Miss Victoria.

Aye, it was general news an' all that the gentry had a licence to whore, and they could pick from their maids in their own household or farmers' daughters, even, if all tales be true, farmers' wives; but they didn't generally get down to factory lasses unless they looked like Lily.

Yes, if anywhere, this is where Fred would be lying in wait for this particular rider; and when he found him, wherever he was, he would tell him, and swear on it, that if he approached the man in any way, he himself would go straight to Andy Davison and tell him who had given him away. It was about the only thing that would make him hold his hand; for, just as he had, so Fred had seen some of Andy's handiwork, and that carried out, too, while he was sober.

He was almost through the wood when he stopped. There was a figure in the distance. He could just glimpse it through the trees. It was a man and he was stooped as if looking on the ground. He moved cautiously forward, but soon realised, by the man's attire, that he certainly wasn't Fred, and he was fingering what looked like a piece of stone that was sticking out of the ground.

He stopped some distance from the man, who turned sharply to look at him, then straightened up, and Joe's first thought was that he was a youth, until the voice belied this by its deep tone, saying, 'Hello there. You out for a walk?'

'Yes, sir.' He moved closer and looked at the stone protruding from the earth, and he said, 'Can . . . can I help you to pull it out?'

'No. No.' The man laughed now. 'This is only the tip of it; you know, like an iceberg, there's quite a big piece in the earth.'

Joe looked puzzled.

'You interested in stones, sir?' he said.

'Well' – there was still laughter in the voice – 'not exactly stones, but stone. I chip away at it, you know.'

'Oh.'

'Cut out figures and things.'

'Oh. Oh, yes, I see, sir, like sculptor men?'

'Yes. Yes, like sculptor men. And' – he now turned away to look along a gully that was bordered by lumps of stone, and indicating it, he said, 'There's a lot of stone there, but most of it's rubbish. This bit though' – he now turned and motioned towards it with his foot – 'could be useful.'

'How will you get it out?'

'Oh, I'll have help. I'll have some of the men from the yard.'

Joe did not enquire which yard.

'This ridge, you know, runs right through the wood. The gully is shallow but the stone must go deep down along it. I shouldn't be surprised –' He seemed now to be talking to himself as he went on, 'I shouldn't be surprised if they start quarrying here some day; and yet they are using bricks now for buildings, because they are less expensive, I suppose. But there's no character in bricks.' He turned and looked at Joe, and Joe smiled as he said, 'They give you good shelter, sir.'

Douglas flexed his shoulders in acknowledgement and said, 'Yes. Yes, you're right there.' Then he looked at Joe more intently. 'Do you live around here?' he asked.

'I used to . . . well, I mean, sir, not so far away. Now I live just outside Birtley . . . in a brick house.'

Their short laughs intermingled, then Joe said, 'Well, good evening to you, sir.'

'Good evening.'

They both inclined their heads; then Joe turned and walked back through the trees, thinking as he went, I should have asked him if he had seen anybody, a fellow, passing; but I suppose that would have sounded funny. He returned to the path and walked on to where it joined the bridle path before turning and making his way back.

The man was still there, but sitting a little further off where the trees had thinned out. He seemed to be perched on a mound of some sort and was looking over the open land edging the wood on that side.

He walked slowly on. He knew he had come out on a fool's errand; it wasn't likely that Fred would tackle a man on a road like this. The presence of the man sitting on the ridge was enough for him to realise that there could be others dotted about the wood. It was only by chance that he had first glimpsed the fellow. Had he not been on the alert, looking, he could easily have passed him. And so there could be others about unseen . . .

As Joe walked along by the line of beech trees, now bursting into full leaf but with their lower trunks still embraced by the tangle of bramble, he, in his turn, was being watched by Fred himself, hidden at the very same spot where they had last year picked the blackberries which had led to the separation in the family. He had seen Joe first coming over the field towards the path, and the sight of his brother had startled him. What he was on the look-out for were the horses that had to come across that field if they wanted to get on to the woodland path. He was waiting for one particular rider, and were he to see him tonight it wouldn't be the first time he had passed him on this very road. It would be truer to say the rider had passed *him*, and at a gallop.

But after he had seen Joe enter the wood he impatiently settled down to await his return, for he could do nothing until his brother was out of the way; even were the fellow to come past now, he wouldn't approach him.

Up till these last few days he had been too afraid even of the idea of approaching the man, knowing what Joe himself would do to him if he found out, and that before he might let on to Andy Davison. But then, his wily rather than intelligent thinking made him call himself a silly bugger, for if he tackled the fellow on the quiet and they came to some agreement, who was to know? Not Joe or anybody else. And the fellow would be bound to want it kept quiet; everyone knew he was to be married in a matter of hours, and that the girl was rich, and he'd get her money, and so he wouldn't want exposure. Now, would he? No. He saw himself as a dim-witted fool not to have taken the chance to bring up the matter with the man before this. And what's more, so he put to himself and, as he thought, cleverly, the threat of exposure would definitely put a stop to his gallop in this form of whoring.

It was almost half an hour later, and he had become weary of waiting, when he saw Joe again. He came walking briskly out of the wood, but instead of continuing along the path by the beech trees, he went straight on to the field, which meant he would be making for the town.

Fred walked up on the inside of the avenue of trees until they ended in the wood; then he pushed through the bramble and onto the path and kept on walking.

The trees were now forming quite a canopy overhead, and further dimmed the light. He didn't like the feeling, and when quite suddenly they thinned out into a kind of glade, he diverted a few steps from the path and stood with his back against a broad trunk and so positioning himself that he could see either way along the woodland.

He had been in this watchful position for but a few minutes when he heard the sound of horses' hooves. Then, there they were, two horses and riders. The horses were bespattered. They had likely been hunting, he thought.

He remained still, and they passed him without noticing him. Unless they had been deliberately looking for him, in this light he must have merged into the dark trunk and the shrubs dotted here and there in the glade. But he quickly realised that the man he was after was not one of them.

He let out a long breath; then once more he was alert, for now there was another horse and rider approaching.

He brought his back from the tree and stood waiting, but again the rider was not the man he was looking for and also passed him without apparently noticing him.

Five minutes later he made up his mind to go back home, having concluded that instead of being out riding the fellow was more likely getting stiff with his pals, as was their custom a night or so before a wedding, when there he was.

Although the twilight was deepening he made him out from a distance. He was a distinct figure, and what was more he was walking his horse, not even trotting it.

As the man neared him and as if he had practised the whole scene, he almost jumped into the middle of the path and put up his hand, calling, 'Stop a minute! Mister.'

Lionel Filmore drew his horse to a halt and looked down on the workman, saying, 'What is it?' The man didn't look a beggar so he didn't bawl at him to get out of the way, but repeated, 'What is it?'

'I'd like a word with you, mister.'

Lionel Filmore's tone now changed, and he cried, 'You get out of the way, and this minute!'

When Fred put up his hand to grab the rein near the bit and saw the whip being lifted and about to come down on him, he cried, 'Don't do that, mister! I'm warnin' you. I want a word with you, and it's about Lily Whitmore. Remember her?'

He watched the man in the saddle stiffen, and feeling he was on the right road, he said, 'You're to be married the morrow, or the next day. Lily's bairn was born a fortnight or so ago.'

'What are you talking about? Get out of my way!'

'There was five pounds in a little washleather bag. It was down the road there behind you; you gave it to her, on a Sunday. Aye, on a Sunday. Well, how would it be if she brings your son up to see Miss Victoria Mordaunt? She's thinkin' about it, but she could be persuaded otherwise. D'you get me meanin', mister?'

It seemed to be minutes before Lionel Filmore slowly brought his leg over the horse's back and stepped down onto the path. Every part of his body was taut. He couldn't believe this was happening to him. He had thought he was all set. He had hated the signing of that paper with that bitch's terms; but two thousand a year was two thousand a year, and on top of this she was still allowing Victoria a dress allowance of five hundred; and she was even paying for the honeymoon in Paris. He had put that to her, standing facing her in that office: 'Is the honeymoon off?' he had said, and had sarcastically added, 'The cost of that will bite deep into my allowance.' If ever he had hated anybody in his life, he had hated her at that moment, and he knew the feeling was returned. But now there was a new hate in him. He felt he wanted to get this fellow by the throat and choke the life out of him because he was threatening his whole existence. Lily Whitmore. He had even forgotten *her existence*. And she had borne a son. My God! He had a son. Bastard or no, he had a son.

Well, he supposed he could have had a son a number of times before, but surely he would have heard about it. But here he was now, hearing about it, and God Almighty! at this time. My God! yes; let that stiff bitch hear of this and there would be no two thousand a year. Even if Victoria would have accepted his infidelity and the fact of the son, that devil in hell would cut off the agreement as if by a stroke of lightning. Oh, he knew her type.

He now glared at the man before leading the horse a few steps into the wood and looping the reins over a branch. He then walked on, still within the trees but keeping to the edge of the clearing. Why he was doing this he didn't ask himself; he only knew he wanted to be well away from the path.

When he stopped he turned to Fred, who had followed him, and was now standing a yard or so away from him. 'You want to bargain, you want money? Is that it?' he asked him.

'Aye, speaking plainly, that's what I want, money. An' . . . an' I'll see she's looked after.'

'I had the faint idea that she had married someone.'

'Aye, she did. That's me brother. But he's not the kind to see to his wife or the bairn. Now me, I like to see justice done.'

'And you've waited until the last moment to see that it's done?'

Fred grinned now, and hunched his shoulders as he said, 'Aye. Aye. You could say I've got me wits about me. I'm not very well in health; I take to me bed quite a bit; but up top' — he tapped his forehead — 'it's in good condition.'

Lionel Filmore was staring unblinking at the face that was becoming less distinct, for he was seeing the fellow as through a red haze, but he let him go on talking and when he heard him say, 'I think we could manage on fifty quid a month,' his mind immediately reckoned up to six hundred pounds a year out of his new windfall. It wasn't to be thought of.

No! No! My God! No! His whole life ruined, finished, ended by this slob.

His hands shot out from his sides, clutched at the shoulders, then grappled towards the fellow's throat; and the attack was so sudden and fierce that Fred had no time to retaliate before he felt himself falling backwards, with his fists that should have struck out in blows, fully opened into widespread fingers to save his fall. His head hitting the root of a tree and the body falling on top of him stunned him for a moment and he became inert. And it was in this moment that Lionel Filmore, loosening one hand away from the throat, groped into an inner pocket of his coat and brought out a small sheath knife that he used for getting stones out of his horse's hooves. It was when the man under him attempted to throw him off while yelling at the same time, that he drove the knife into his neck, and so close was his face to the other's that he saw in the dimness the startled look in the eyes before he himself sprang up.

His hand on the knife covered with blood, he stood gasping as he looked down on the inert figure with the blood spreading from the neck and down the dark coat.

As he took two stumbling steps backwards he became

aware that his hand was held out, the knife still gripped in it, and that both were dripping blood.

Leaning against a tree and using his left hand, he pulled from his pocket a large white handkerchief with which he hastily wiped his hand, but as he did so the knife dropped from it, the point piercing the soil between the roots of the tree, while the blood-stained handkerchief hung slack from his fingers, and immediately the significance and horror of what had happened created in him the urge to get rid of this bloodied thing, but he restrained himself from throwing it to the ground. Then stooping, he grabbed up the knife and was about to put them both back into his inner pocket when he hesitated: the inside of his jacket was lined with grey silk.

He looked wildly about him now as though for a place to throw both the handkerchief and the knife from him. Casting his eyes downwards, he walked halfway round the tree before digging his heel into what looked like a soft patch of soil, then bending with the intention of scraping at the soil with his hand, he again hesitated. He had noticed a thickish twig lying almost at his feet, and with this he scraped at the soil until his efforts were checked by a crossing root.

Almost in panic now he rolled the handkerchief round the knife and aimed to thrust it under the root. But although he could manage to wedge only about an inch of the covered blade under it, his panic was urging him to be rid of these things, and like an automaton that had been wound up to full pitch he frantically kicked the soil over the small hole, pressed it down hard with his heel, then with the side of his foot he raked some loose leaves over the protruding roots.

He now stood for a time, one forearm supporting him against the tree, and as though the automaton was now running down, his movements became slow as he took steps back to where the blood-stained figure was still lying.

He could barely make it out for his gaze was misted with sweat, yet he thought it moved; but as he stared at it he knew it was his imagination. Nevertheless, he skirted it widely in his eagerness to reach the clearing again. Here the twilight seemed like bright daylight compared to the gloom behind him . . .

He untethered his horse, but he found he hadn't the strength as yet to lead him, and he stood leaning against the animal's side for a moment before, taking the reins, he walked with him along the path. But he had gone not more than twenty yards when he was startled so much that he caused the animal to rear its head and step sharply to the side.

Slowly, he turned his head to see Douglas, who had called out, 'Hello there!' coming towards him through the trees.

'What's the matter? Are you hurt?'

He found he had to wet his lips twice before he could speak, saying, 'He . . . he threw me. I . . . I took a gate back there in . . . in the farm field.'

'Good lord! He's never done that before, has he? He's as sure-footed as, well, as a lynx. You've always said so yourself.'

'There's always a . . . a beginning, a first time.'

'You hurt anywhere?'

'No. No, just a bit shaken. He sprang . . . he sprang a shoe. Well, it's a bit loose; I think that must have been the reason. It probably caught on the bar. I . . . I can't blame him.' He tried to smile but found he couldn't stretch his lips when Douglas said, 'No, you'd never blame a horse, no matter who else you blamed. Well' – he laughed – 'what I mean is. Oh, what does it matter? Go on, get yourself home; and I would take a hot bath. Good job it isn't tomorrow, isn't it?'

For answer Lionel drew in a deep breath, made a small motion with his head, gave a light tug on the reins, then walked forward.

Douglas watched him until the path, zig-zagging away, led him out of his sight. And as he turned away the thought occurred to him that Lionel hadn't asked what he was doing alone here in the wood at this time. But then, he wouldn't; he had never taken an interest in anything he had done; and especially not in his stone work that was now providing him with a livelihood, and a good one, so much so that he was contemplating starting a real business. Of course, up till recently the word business would have aroused his father's ire and brought exclamations of open disdain from his brother. But Lionel was now having to change his tune, for business was going to support him for the rest of his life, or at least for as long as he remained in favour with Bridget. My! there was a young woman for you. One had to admire her, if for nothing else, for her business acumen. And, in a strange way, he admired her for more than that. She was such good company. She must be the only woman with whom he had ever been able to hold a conversation made up of words of more than two syllables.

He was on his way back to the gully with the intention of walking along it to see if there might be one or two more pieces of available and suitable stone that, with some manual help from the yard, he could get out of the ground without having to employ diggers. But it would soon be dark, especially where the gully ran through the wood itself. But then there was the clearing. He'd go as far as that, and if there was anything suitable he would come back tomorrow with the men. No; he wouldn't be able to come back tomorrow. It was the eve of the wedding, everybody would be on their toes. Although the reception was to be held at Bridget's house, their yard men would be busy sprucing up the trap and the brake and themselves preparatory to carrying the bridegroom and the staff to the church. On this thought he did not walk back through the woodland but kept to the path that led back to the clearing. And he was halfway across it when he imagined he heard a strange sound like a moan. He stopped. Perhaps an animal had been caught in a trap. Oh, no! he hoped not. There was now a law against traps, but still the devils set them.

He waited, but hearing no further sound he went towards that part of the gully where there were a number of large boulders exposed. These, however, he concluded, would be much too soft for what he required.

It was as he turned away to retrace his steps across the clearing that a sharp wind met him and he turned up the collar of his coat. He didn't like the cold, likely because he had little flesh on his bones. If ever he made enough money he would go and live in a warm country, an island perhaps, one inhabited by kindly natives. And he wouldn't need a house, he could sleep out on the sand, and he would live on fruit and home-made wine, and live to a hundred and one.

Huh! Why did he think such ridiculous thoughts? Who wanted to live to a hundred and one? Who wanted to go on living at all at times? If he reached thirty that would be enough. He had been told that during early childhood his life had been despaired of a number of times; after reaching the age of twelve it would seem he improved somewhat physically but not, his father would have it, emotionally. On one occasion, when deep in his cups, his father had kindly put it that he had shamed him on his first trip when he threw up at the sight of the fox being given its deserts by the dogs; on another: who other than a girl would cry at the sight of kittens being bagged and drowned in the tank?

However, he could recall the great day he had kicked his father and clawed at him when his father, enraged at having been thrown twice in the one day, had tethered his horse in the yard and lashed out at it with his whip. He himself still had the mark down the side of his ear where the whip had been turned on him.

But why was he thinking these old thoughts? All because he had felt cold from that blast of wind and had the silly vision of the warm island again.

He stopped. An animal was just in there to the right of him. Had it earlier been caught by another it would have been dead by now and half eaten. He moved slowly towards the thicket; and then his hand went to his mouth but hardly covered the gape as his mind yelled, Oh my God!

Three steps more and he was bending over a man who had one hand tight to his neck, with his face covered in blood. He bent nearer, saying, 'You're hurt. You've been hurt.'

The wet, blood-laden eyelids lifted, the mouth opened, and the blood dribbled from it. Then the lips came together as the man spoke.

'What is it? Yes?' He couldn't distinguish what the man was saying. It sounded as if he was asking for someone called Billy. Then he made out the words, 'get' and 'go', and he nodded at him, saying, 'Yes. Yes, I'll go. Lie . . . lie still. I'll go and get help.'

As he was about to straighten up the man spoke again. It was a mutter but he made out his own name because he said 'Filmore.' And he answered him, nodding vigorously, saying, 'Yes, I'm Mr Filmore. Now I'll be back as soon as possible. Just stay quiet.'

He shot from the thicket across the glade and onto the wood path. There, he hesitated for one moment. Where was the nearest house? To the right was a farm, but it was very nearly as far as the factories and the town. To the left of him the nearest habitation was his home.

He had always been able to run, but he had never run as quickly as he did now. Yet it took him ten minutes before he arrived, panting, in the yard, there to stand gasping as he called out to Jimmy Fawcett and Ron Yarrow, the stablemen, 'Get the c . . . cart ready! the flat cart. Quick! D'you hear? There's a man bleeding to death in the wood . . . back there.'

'What, sir?' Jimmy Fawcett screwed up his face in enquiry: 'You all right, Mr Douglas?'

'Yes, damn you! Jimmy, I'm all right. I'm telling you, there's a fellow back there bleeding to death. It looks as if he's had his throat cut or something. I don't know.'

'Good God!'

'Where's Johnson?'

''Tis his time off, Mr Douglas.'

'Who else is on?'

'Bill, but he's just gone down to his cottage.'

'Well, get the cart out and I'll go and get Bill to come along with us. Then Ron . . . you take to your heels and go down the road to The Beeches, Doctor Nesbitt is nearly sure to be in at this time. Bring him along to the wood. It's in the clearing.'

'But which wood, Mr Douglas?'

'My God! man, there's only one wood on the road to town.'

'Oh, that one. Oh, all right, all right. I'll do that. Yes, I will.' And with this, he dashed into a stable, swung his coat off a nail and even while putting it on was running out of the yard.

Meanwhile, Douglas almost burst into the groom's cottage, apologising as he gabbled, 'I'm sorry, Bill, but you've got to come along with me. There's a man bleeding to death in the wood. Jimmy's getting the cart ready, Ron's gone for Doctor Nesbitt.' Knowing that this man would follow him, he immediately turned and made for the house.

He now ran through the kitchen quarters, startling Rosie Jackson and the maids. And in the hall, seeing the butler coming out of the dining room he shouted at him, 'Where's Mr Lionel?'

The man's only answer was to turn his face towards the dining-room again, and Douglas, pushing past him, entered the room to see Lionel sitting in a chair at the far end of the table, a glass to his mouth, which he drained as Douglas hurried towards him, saying, 'There's been an accident of some kind, Lionel. I came across a fellow in the wood. It looks as if his throat's been gashed. Will you come and give us a hand?'

'Wh . . . What?'

'Oh, I'm sorry, you're still feeling the effects of your toss. But the poor fellow's likely bled to death by this time.'

Lionel laid the empty glass slowly down on the table and looked at Douglas as he said, 'He's not dead?'

'No, but he likely will be by the time we get there. I've sent Yarrow for Doctor Nesbitt. They're getting the cart ready.'

Looking hard now at his brother, he said, 'Oh, I'm sorry; you're not up to it. It's all right. It's all right,' and he backed from him, flapping his hand and assuring him, 'We'll manage.'

Left alone, Lionel closed his eyes tightly and brought his teeth down onto his lower lip, dragging it inwards on top of his tongue until the pain caused him to desist; then slowly his hand went out towards the decanter, and, as slowly it seemed, he filled the wine glass to its brim. The glass was quickly emptied and once more his head drooped until his chin rested on his chest, and he muttered aloud, 'God Almighty! All that for nothing. And if the fellow was able to speak . . .' and again he said, 'God Almighty!'

7

As Mary Ellen Skinner entered the factory her nose wrinkled and she brought her hasty step to a walk as she looked about her at the dust-laden air. Her narrow glance flitting from one dim figure to another, she stopped at a bench and said to the figure standing there, 'Where's Joe Skinner?'

The worker happened not to be a girl but a married woman, and a mother of five children, but was still known as Susie Fields because she had been Little Susie Fields when she first started in this factory at nine years old. And she had lived in Honeybee Place all her life, and so Mary Ellen Skinner was no stranger to her.

Susie was known to be a bit of a card and no respecter of man or woman of no matter what class, and so, on a laugh, she said, 'Well, the silly bugger was standing in his trousers the last time I saw him.'

The titter ran along the bench but the hands never stopped folding over the squares of blacklead. They all seemed to be working in unison and so fast it seemed that within the blink of an eyelid a block was placed on a piece of paper, the ends of the paper brought together, the sides enveloped and dabbed with glue, then racked. And the process was repeated within almost another blink of the eyelid.

Mary Ellen's lips seemed to be on the point of letting out a loud whistle, but when they parted what she said was, ''Tis a wonder they weren't down then when you were about.'

A lass's hand came out and grabbed Susie's and forced it and the block of blacklead onto the bench again, and from the other side of the bench the man loading a trolley with the wrapped blocks said, 'Well, Susie, you know, you asked for that;' and added, 'Wonder what she's after?'

When Mary Ellen reached the end of the room she asked Johnnie McInnes, 'Where's Joe?' and he replied, 'Oh, hello, Mrs Skinner. You want the gaffer, do you? Oh, well, he's gaffering in the storeroom, I think.' He nodded and jerked his head towards the door.

Mary Ellen peered at him and her head wagged slightly as she said, 'Oh, I thought you were the gaffer, Johnnie, and our Joe the manager? He told me he had bumped you up, seeing you missed getting his job.'

Johnnie McInnes glared after the small sturdy figure as it disappeared into the storeroom and what he muttered under his breath wasn't respectable.

Joe was talking to a cart man. He had a clip-board in his hand and he was checking the small crates being loaded onto the flat dray cart, and he started somewhat when he heard his mother's voice at his elbow, saying, 'I want a word with you.'

He didn't speak but turned and walked out of the loading shed, went through the door into the factory and there, calling Johnnie McInnes forward, he handed him the board, saying, 'Finish that load, will you?' and continued towards the office, and there, before he could ask what had brought her here, she said, 'You want to watch that one. He called you the gaffer and said you were gaffering in there. If you're managing you want to stand on your feet and let them see you're managing.'

'What d'you want? What's the matter?'

She drew in a long breath, before answering. 'Have you see anything of our Fred?'

'I saw him last night. But why should I have seen him since? He knows I won't set him on.'

'He hasn't been home all night. I waited up till nearly three. It's never happened afore.'

'Oh that.' He went behind the desk and sat in the chair before adding, 'He's got to start some place. But then, I thought he was already well versed in that line but would never fork out to stay the night.'

'You're a bitter sod, aren't you?'

'Well, I know where I get it from, Ma. And I've somethin' to be bitter about if I look back over me life, where neither you nor he hasn't. You've both seen to number one first.'

Her head made small movements as she said, 'Who's talkin' about number one? If anybody's seeing to number one it's you: leaving me to fend for meself while you see to your trollop, 'cos that's what she is . . . and you needn't get to your feet 'cos you'll sit and hear me out. I know there's somethin' fishy about her, and our Fred knows a thing or two, but you've threatened him if he opens his mouth.'

He had risen to his feet now, and his voice was dangerously quiet as he said, 'You know more than is good for you, Ma. But don't think you'll get to know anythin' from Fred; he's careful of his skin, is Fred. And remember Andy Davison did time for one of Fred's exploits. But we've been through all this afore, haven't we? Now, Ma, I should go home an' make yourself, as you always do, a good cup of tea. And cook a few griddle cakes an' get the butter out an' treat yourself as you usually do when you're on your own.'

They stared at each other for a moment; then as she turned away from him she said almost under her breath, 'Bad sons always come to rotten ends. And you'll sup sorrow with a big spoon afore you're finished. I know

123

that,' to which his answer was: 'Likely I will, Ma. If you wish it hard enough for me, I certainly will.'

When the door banged behind her he dropped back onto the seat, and a tremor shot through him. It was as if he had been stung by a hornet, and so physical was its effect that he gripped a handful of the front of his coat, and admonished himself. Steady. Steady.

'You don't like it, Joe?'

'Oh, yes, lass, yes. It's fine. I couldn't imagine you makin' a bad meat puddin'.'

'You generally ask for a second do almost afore you've finished your first. There must be somethin' the matter. Now tell me, what is it? Is it your Fred again?'

'Aye; in a way, you could say it's him. But me mother came to the Works the day. He hadn't come home last night. I put it to her, there could be a reason for that, and yet, as far as I can remember, he's never kept a steady lass. But anyway, she went for me. By, she's a bitter pill, is me Ma. The things she said. Well, she's said as much before but it's never affected me like it did the day. It left me with the most odd feeling; I can't describe it. She's not a happy woman, is me Ma, but then she never has been. Me Da used to call her misery guts. Nothin' he ever did seemed to please her: she was always "on . . . the want", he would say.' But then, smiling across the table at Lily, he said, 'Apparently there was a lighter side to her visit, I understand from Bill: as she was passing up the shop she asked Susie where I was, and you know Susie and her mouth, well, she told her the last time she had seen the bugger he was standing in his trousers. But me Ma's not backward in coming forward with her tongue, an' it seemed she sort of insinuated what happens when they come down, which maddened Susie, who was for hittin' her with a block of blacklead. And she would have done, but she was stopped in time by one of the lasses.'

Lily laughed as she said, 'Oh, I can hear Susie. When she opens her mouth somethin' always comes out that you would never hear in Sunday School.'

He was glad to see her laughing and being chirpy, for she had been rather quiet these last few weeks. And he knew why, but the reason wasn't spoken of: it was well-known around the quarter that Miss Bridget's cousin, Miss Victoria, was going to marry the Filmore fella. He himself had never mentioned it, but he knew she would be aware of it even if she never left the house; Mrs Leary was as good as the evening paper. The wedding was to be tomorrow and, from what he understood, quite a big affair: the breakfast at Miss Bridget's house, then a ball at night in the Assembly Rooms in Newcastle.

Well, it would be up to him to think of something to take her mind off it, at least for part of the time. So, as she placed before him the second helping of meat pudding he looked up at her and said, 'How about us havin' a night out the morrow. Mrs Leary would see to him.' He nodded towards the child where he lay in the cradle to the side of the fireplace. 'How about the Empire? I hear there's a couple of blokes on there that bring the house down. They're as daft as a brush, or two brushes.'

She, too, looked towards the cradle, then back at him and smiled, saying, 'Oh, I would like that, Joe. Yes, I would. And I can wear me new hat and coat.'

'Oh lord, that'll mean we'll have to have a box.'

As she pushed him in the shoulder they both turned and looked towards the door that led into the passage from where came the sound of the front door-knocker being rapped.

'Who can this be that uses the knocker?' He pulled a face at her. 'If they're collectin' for owt, I'm not in.'

She was smiling again as she passed him on her way to the passage, and he was about to finish the last few bites from his plate, but stopped, his fork poised halfway to his mouth, his head turned to the side and his ears alert now to the sound of men's voices.

When the door opened and Lily entered, followed by two policemen, he pulled himself quickly to his feet, saying, 'What's up? What's the matter?'

One of the men he recognised straightaway, Constable Salop, and as all policemen were known as slops, so this particular one became Sloppy Salop, who would chase the bairns when they'd be up to some mischief. But they weren't really afraid of Sloppy Salop because the most he did was to shake them by the ear, or wallop it, with an accompanying threat to tell their ma. It was never their da, always their ma.

The other man was a sergeant and it was he who spoke, saying, 'I would like to ask you a few questions, Mr Skinner. But first of all I must tell you that' – he paused – 'your brother is dead.'

Both Joe and Lily now exchanged amazed glances; then Joe muttered, 'Fred?'

'Yes.' The man's voice was very cool. 'He has been murdered. He was alive last night when found in Brook's Wood, but he died in hospital this morning at half past ten. There was no identification on him at the time. And it wasn't until some time later that the mortuary attendant, coming on duty, recognised him.'

'Oh my God! I'll . . . I'll –' He turned again and looked at Lily, saying, 'I'll have to go straight to me ma's.'

The sergeant now seemed to hesitate before he said, 'I . . . I don't think you had better do that. In any case we would like you to come down to the station. There's a few questions we would like to ask you.'

'Questions to ask me? What about?'

'Well as I've just said, your brother was murdered. He died from a stab wound in the throat, and . . . and' — again he paused — 'you have been known to threaten him. Now, now.' He held up his hand, his forefinger wagging. 'You must think before you speak; we'll be taking note of all you say from now on.'

'My God! You can't mean this? Aye, I've threatened him since he was a lad; he was always gettin' into trouble. And I took over after me da died an' I had to keep him steady. Aye . . . aye, I've threatened him. But what are you sayin'? I've murdered him?'

'I would ask you again, Mr Skinner, to come with us.'

Joe now appealed to the constable, saying, 'Mr Salop, you know me. I've never done anythin' in me life to get into the hands of the polis.'

Constable Salop said, 'Well, it was your mother, lad. She said, only last night you had a go at him . . .'

The sergeant's manner became very brisk, and he turned a hard look on his subordinate as he said, 'We'll continue this down at the station.'

Lily was hanging on to Joe's arm, her head was wagging, her mouth opening and shutting; but she uttered no word until he moved from her to take his cap from the rack. Then she turned on the two men, crying, 'He wouldn't! He couldn't do a thing like that. He's . . . he's always looked after him. Gone for him, aye, but kept him out of trouble. His mother's a wicked woman, she is, she is to say such a thing. People have rows, they say all kinds of things in rows . . .'

'It's all right, lass, it's all right. I'll be back. Don't you worry, I'll be back.'

She was clinging onto him so much that he had to force her hands from his arm and his voice had a slight break in it as he said, 'Now be a good lass. You've got the bairn to see to. I'll be back. I tell you, I'll be back.' And with that he walked from the room ahead of the two men; and it was he who opened the front door, there to see what appeared to be the whole street out, with Mary Leary nearest the step. And he turned and said to her, 'Go on in and see to her, will you, Mrs Leary?'

'Aye, lad. Aye, lad. Let that be the least of your worries. What have you done to bring the lousy coppers on to you?'

And that was what Joe was asking himself: What had he done? Nothing. And yet, on his mother's word, it looked as if he was to be accused of murdering Fred. He looked back to the times when he would have liked to do just that and so wipe him out of existence, because he had been a thorn in his flesh since he could crawl . . .

And that's what he kept saying to the two men sitting opposite him across the wooden table. 'Aye, if that's threatening then I've threatened him in all kinds of ways, because as you know yourself, if you look in your books, he's been suspected of this, that, and the other.'

He sat back on the wooden chair, tired. This had been going on for hours now. These were two strange men sitting opposite to him, and one was asking, 'Do you know anyone who has a grudge against him?'

Yes, he knew somebody with a grudge against him, Andy Davison. He pulled himself straight now; even so, he paused before he said, 'Aye, I know somebody with a grudge against him, but . . .' Again he paused. Could he say . . . ? Well, it seemed to be either his neck or somebody else's. And there was Lily and the bairn to think of; and what was more, he was innocent. He said, 'There's a fellow called Andy Davison. He did time for stealin', but . . . but it wasn't him; it was Fred that planted the stuff in his yard. I didn't know till after.'

'And do you know if this man has threatened your brother?'

'No; he didn't know who had set him up. He always swore that . . . well, if he found out, what he would do.'

The men looked at each other; then they left the room, leaving him with the policeman who was standing at the door, and he turned to him and said, ''Tis like a nightmare.' And the policeman replied softly, 'Aye, that's what most of them say when they come in here.'

A few minutes later another policeman came into the room and said to him, 'Come along, lad; you'll be here for the night, at any rate.' And with that he led him out, across the reception area, down a flight of steps, then along a corridor that was lined with heavy knobless doors, each faceless except for a small grid.

The constable opened one of the doors and, pointing to a wooden bench on which there were two folded blankets and a bare pillow, he said not unkindly, 'Make yourself as comfortable as possible, lad. You'll have a mug of cocoa shortly.'

When the door clanged and there was the sound of a key turning in the lock, Joe resorted to an old habit; he put the four fingers of his right hand into his mouth, each nail covering a tooth, and pulled at them as if to loosen the roots.

The following morning he was informed that Andy Davison had been interviewed, and that this had taken place in Newcastle Infirmary where he had, last week, undergone an operation for a shattered kneecap. And so the questioning began again.

As the day wore on, he became not only tired at the unusual pressure of the talking but also very frightened. More so when there came in a man whom he straightaway recognised as the one he had talked to in the wood and, looking at him, said gently, 'Yes; this is the man I spoke to on the night that I found the wounded man.'

When the policeman said, 'Thank you, Mr Filmore,' all Joe could do was gape and repeat the name to himself, 'Filmore.' There was a younger son; he had heard tell of him: first, that he was a bit funny; then that was squashed when next he heard the young fellow had been to a University. But the man he had spoken to in the wood had told him he chipped stone; so he was a sculptor. And this was the brother of the other one. Yet he had been a nice gentleman to talk to. He was still nice, at least from his expression, because he'd looked sort of sad when he'd said he recognised him.

Then the questions started again. What time was it when he had spoken to the gentleman? Where did he go after that?

He went through the town.

Which part? Did he go into any public house?

No.

Did he speak to anybody he knew?

No; because he didn't often go to yon end of Gateshead Fell. But he walked through Low Fell and touched on Fellburn.

Why had he gone so far?

His head was bent when he said, and for what seemed the countless time, 'I was looking for Fred.'

Why was he looking for Fred? came the question; and again for the countless time, 'I . . . I was afraid he might be up to somethin' that might get him into trouble.'

What was this something that would get him into trouble? ' 'Twas a private affair. That's all I'm goin' to say about that, 'twas a private affair.'

'About which you threatened to do for him?'

'That was only a sayin'.'

'Not as your mother expressed it. And she implies, too, that there was something that you didn't wish your brother to do. But she herself knew nothing of it. Now it would help you if you would tell us what this matter was.'

Always at this point he became dumb, stubborn and dumb. He could, of course, say Fred was out to blackmail the real father of his wife's bairn. But Lily had gone through enough. That was one side of it. But there was another side to it: the bloke had, this very day, married Miss Bridget's cousin, and it was well known that those two lasses were closer than sisters and that Miss Bridget had always played mother to the other one, so if he opened his mouth, what would happen? That young lass, Victoria, would be in a state. The scandal would ruin the beginning of her married life. As for Miss Bridget, well, there was nothin' he wouldn't do for Miss Bridget. She had been the one person in his life who had really been kind to him. He was holding the position he was today through her kindness alone. If her father had been still alive, the managing would have gone to Johnnie McInnes. Although he stood well in the eyes of Mr Carter, he knew everybody would expect Mr Carter to suggest Johnnie McInnes for the job. So, on all accounts, he must keep his mouth shut on this because he owed that to Miss Bridget.

Anyway, as he saw it, this had nothing to do with Fred's being polished off. A stab in the neck was likely from some low-down dirty bugger who had it in for him, and perhaps with some justice on his part, Fred having done him down some way . . . But who was he?

He was becoming really frightened now.

8

There was a reason for Bridget's wishing to go down to Meadow House just two days before the wedding. The excuse she openly gave was that she would like to collect all Victoria's things and to pack them ready to be sent to her new home.

Victoria was in the throes of having her wedding apparel adjusted as well as of packing the necessary clothes for her honeymoon. And she had already been made to realise that although dear Bridget was still giving her the dress allowance she wouldn't be able to indulge it all on herself. And so whatever attire she had kept for use in Meadow House would now likely come in useful, especially in the skilful hands of her dressmaker. She therefore offered no objection to Bridget's leaving her at this particular time. What is more, she felt it would do Bridget good to get away by herself for a day. She had been very moody of late, not herself at all; and she'd always felt that she preferred Meadow House to this, their home in the country.

But Bridget had hardly returned to the house and taken off her dustcoat and been hugged by Victoria before she was shocked with the news that Victoria garbled at her.

'My dear, such happenings since you've been away; you would never believe; you would think that you had been away for months. Douglas found a man in Brook's Wood who had been murdered, his throat cut. Did you ever? Did you ever? He dashed back to the house and got the yard men to take a cart; then went with the man to hospital. He had been in the wood . . . . I mean, Douglas had, looking for stones, you know, along that ridge that goes right through . . . Oh dear me! But the worst is, and I'm sure you'll be shocked by this, because you've spoken of him so often and said he was such a good fellow. I've only seen him, myself, a few times but he was nice . . .'

It was at this point that Bridget, now in the drawing-room, pushed Victoria down into a chair, saying sharply, 'Stop rattling on like that! Who's this that I know?'

'The manager. The one you made manager. Joe. You know, he was a kind of protégé of Uncle's, and yours, yes, and yours. Well, he's killed his brother. Murdered him.'

Bridget took a step backwards, her face now looking contorted and her words hardly audible even to herself as she gasped, 'What are you saying? Joe . . . ? Murdered his brother?'

'Yes. Yes, in the wood, Brook's Wood. And today, just this afternoon, Douglas had to go and identify him . . . I don't mean the brother, I mean, Joe, because he had apparently been talking to him just a while before the deed was done.'

'*Never! Never!* Joe would never do a thing like that.'

'Well, Joe had, Joe has, at least that's what everybody's saying. He was in the wood and Douglas said the police say he can't give an account of where he went after that . . . Where are you going?'

'Where do you think I'm going?' The words were snapped out. 'I'm going into Gateshead to see Joe. Is that where they took him?'

'I . . . I don't know. But . . . but is it proper?'

'Proper! What are you talking about? He was the manager of my factory. Proper!' She had almost spat the word at Victoria, who, her lips quivering, almost whimpered, 'You needn't take that attitude with me. And . . . and it's my wedding eve, you know, and I thought . . .'

'Don't remind me! I know it's your wedding eve.'

She was already marching into the hall with Victoria following her and muttering under her breath, 'Why is it . . . why is it you don't like him? What is it? What has he ever done to you? You make me unhappy. You know that, Bridget? You make me unhappy.'

Bridget managed to refrain from retorting, 'You'll be more unhappy before you're finished with that man,' and found herself wondering if it would not have been better to let her pine away, as she would have done. And yet she might not have, human nature being a force unto itself. She had been worried sick these last days about this very matter, and again she questioned herself what would happen if she were to turn on her now and say, 'He's only marrying you because I support him. What do you think of that?'

Oh, the quicker she got out of the house the better; the quicker tomorrow was over the better . . . But Joe. Poor Joe.

'You've just come in; you can't go out again like this. I bet you've had nothing to eat.'

Bridget now ignored Victoria and, turning to where Jessie was standing, she said, 'Tell Danny to get Frank to saddle Hamlet,' and to Victoria stated, 'I'm going up to change.'

As Bridget ran up the stairs Jessie paused for a moment and, looking at Victoria, said under her breath, 'She's heard about Joe then?'

Victoria nodded.

And Jessie, too, nodded as she said, 'Aye, well, I knew that would be her reaction,' then turned and hurried towards the kitchen.

Victoria was waiting for Bridget as she came down the stairs again, and there was a petulant note in her voice when she said, 'I imagined we would have this evening together, my last evening home. You're not behaving nicely, Bridget. I'm going to miss you as much as you'll miss me, but I'm taking it like . . .'

'Be quiet! Victoria.' The words were low and slow and they silenced Victoria and widened her eyes and parted her lips, and left her standing in not a little amazement, watching the young woman who had been not only a sister but also a mother to her for years, as well as a guardian, a shield, a provider for all that was necessary for an easy pleasant life, walk away from her as if she hated her.

The policeman behind the counter recognised the woman who talked like a lady but was dressed like a gentleman in riding habit, but he was certainly surprised when she asked further if she could speak to the man who had been brought in for murder.

'Oh. Oh. Well, I'll have to see . . . You know the . . . Mr Skinner?'

'I have known him since he was a child. He is the manager of my factory.'

'Oh . . . Oh. Well, now, would you like to take a seat, please? I'll be back in a minute.'

She did not take the proffered seat, which was a form attached to the wall, but stood looking at two framed posters on the painted brick wall to the side of her, both dealing with men wanted for burglary and offering a reward of twenty pounds for anyone who would give information that would lead to the conviction of the said man.

A second constable was busying himself turning over the pages of a ledger in between casting furtive glances in her direction. Presently, the first one reappeared, saying, 'Will you come this way, Miss Mordaunt?'

She was led along a corridor and into a room; and there was Joe. Immediately she saw that he looked not only older than the last time she had seen him, but also that there was fear expressed in his face. And that was something new, because she had always looked on him as a strong man, both in his opinions and in his attitude to life, for she knew he had fought against the circumstances in which he had been brought up by trying to educate himself.

There was another policeman in the room, but she turned to the one who had brought her in and asked, 'May we have a private conversation?'

The man hesitated, then said, 'Well, five minutes, miss,' and both policemen went out and closed the door. But as she looked at it she felt that the officers were not very far away, that they were even standing behind it.

Looking at Joe pityingly, she shook her head as she said, 'This is terrible. How has it come about?'

'I . . . I wish I knew, miss. Dear God! I wish I knew. But . . . but I can tell you this, it wasn't by my hand. I never laid a finger on him.'

'I'm . . . I'm sure you didn't. But . . . but have you any idea? Had he enemies?'

'Oh aye, a few. But the one I thought might have done it was a fellow who had been imprisoned for supposed stealin' when he hadn't done the job at all. It was . . . well, it was our Fred. And this fellow always said he would swing for him. But when they found him he was cleared. Oh aye, he was cleared because he was in hospital having an operation.'

'Have you told them where you were that night and what you did?'

'Aye; but it should happen I was in the wood where he was found, and . . . and what's more damning, miss, I was talkin' to a gentleman, Mr Filmore.'

'Mr Filmore?' There was a note of surprise in her voice, 'Mr Lionel Filmore?'

Now she was somewhat surprised at his tone and the stiffening of his body as he said, 'No, not him. Not him, miss, the younger one. But I didn't know who he was. He was looking for stones, he said. We stood chatting for a minute, but it was him who found Fred, and he remembered me talkin' to him. And I ask you, they would put two and two together, wouldn't they, miss? But –' He moved a step nearer and, gripping both hands tightly together in front of his chest, he said, 'Before God and heaven, miss, I didn't do it.'

'*Oh, I believe you, Joe,* I believe you. But what we've got to do now is to find out who did. You must have a solicitor, someone who can defend you.'

'I'll take a lot of defending, miss, because I can't name a soul that I spoke to after that man. And what's more I was so mad at our Fred that I really was out looking for him.'

'You were out looking for him?'

'Aye.'

'But why?'

'Oh, well' – he lowered his head – 'it was a private matter, miss, just atween him and me. He was goin' to do something that was wrong and I was goin' to try and stop him.'

'Oh, well now, if you tell that to the police, or I mean your advocate, it might throw new light on the subject.'

He was looking at her hard now, saying, 'No, miss; I couldn't tell what there was atween us, not to save me life, I couldn't.'

'But why?'

'That's why I can't tell you, miss, why I can't, if you know what I mean. Because there's somebody else could be hurt. Aye, and not only one. But don't you worry, miss. Thank you, though, for comin'. You can do one thing for me.'

'Anything. Anything, Joe. Oh, and I'll work to get you free. Oh, yes, yes, I will. But tell me what you want me to do now?'

'Would you go and see Lily? She's in a state. At least when I left her she was, and she's got few friends. Her people won't have anything to do with her, only abuse her. And there's only Mrs Leary next door.'

'I'll go straightaway and see her tonight. And I'll tell her you'll soon be free.'

'No, miss. I mean, don't build up her hopes. You see, miss, only a few hours before, I had threatened to do practically what has happened. It was at me mother's. And she told them, the polis, and that's what put them on to me.'

'*Oh no!* Your mother did that?'

'Aye, me mother did that. We never got on, you see. We never hit it off. She's a bitter woman and she thought a lot of Fred. I didn't count. And truth to tell, miss, it wasn't the first time I'd said what I'd do to him if he didn't behave.'

As the door opened they both turned and looked at the policeman, and he at them. Thrusting out her hand, she gripped Joe's, saying, 'It'll be all right, Joe. Try not to worry. This thing must be sorted out. I'll see my solicitor tomorrow; he'll set things in motion. But I'll go and see Lily right now.'

'Thank you, miss, thank you. And thank you for comin'.'

She turned hastily from him, went past the policeman, and to the other who was sitting in the corridor she said, 'It's all been a mistake. That man would never kill anyone, particularly his brother. I've . . . I've known him since he was a boy, when he started in my father's factory.'

'Yes. Yes, I know, miss, and he's done well for himself. But ... but these things happen, you know, in families.'

When she turned a look on him as much to say, 'Don't be silly!' he stiffened slightly and it came over in his voice as he said, 'More so in families, miss, than anywhere else. You'd be surprised.'

'Yes. Yes, I would, Constable; I'd be surprised, especially in this case. Good-night.'

'Good-night, miss. Good-night.'

Outside the police station she put her hand in her breeches pocket and brought out a silver coin and handed it to the boy who was holding the reins of her horse. He was surrounded by a number of companions, and when he opened his hand to look at the coin there was a chorus of 'Ooh! Ooh!' And as she mounted, the boy, gripping the coin in his hand, said, 'Hold it any time for you, miss. I'm eleven. I like 'orses, miss. Could do with a job, miss. Could do with a job. Will you remember me, miss. Will you remember me?'

About to turn the horse around, she looked down into the thin dirty face and said, 'Yes, I'll remember you;' then as she put the horse into a trot she heard his high voice calling, 'Me name's ... !' But the name was lost to her, as she knew the memory of him would be, too; there were so many of them. Joe had been like that boy, willing to work, willing to do anything, and that's what had increased her liking for him in the first place; even though she was no older than him, it was his eagerness to better himself.

As the years went on something about him had drawn her irrevocably towards him. However, her inner sense and level-headedness pulled against the attraction and pointed out the impossibility of such an association, and when, following her father's death, she had, in a way, become his master, that had put paid for all time to such day-dreaming. Yet it hadn't obliterated those that would steal on her in the night.

9

The bride having no living male relative, the solicitor and family friend, Andrew Kemp, led her to the altar on his arm. This situation was understandable, but not so that of the bridegroom, whose brother was not standing as his best man. James Wright, the eldest of three bachelor brothers, had accepted this honour.

It could not have gone unnoticed, and it certainly hadn't gone unquestioned: Why was Douglas not taking on this honour? And Lionel's answer had been, Well, Douglas looked so young and being only five-foot-six, and slim with it, he appeared boyish.

That Douglas was in the church at all was due to his reluctance to continue the bawling match he'd had with his father. He was now sitting in the first pew of those on the right-hand side of the church, and vitally aware that to the left of him, and feeling much the same as himself, was Bridget.

When he watched Victoria gazing up in adoration at Lionel as he placed the ring on her finger, he actually felt sick. How was it, he asked himself, that she and Bridget could be full cousins? In spite of her beauty and girlish charm Victoria was nothing but a feather-brained girl. And indeed, girl she was in spite of her twenty-two years; and so, he imagined, she would remain. Yet there was Bridget, not much older, but with a mind of her own and a generosity that she concealed and a beauty that she also contrived to hide. If she had bothered to dress as Victoria did she would have outshone her. He was sure of that.

Yet, she would be the first to deny she had any looks at all. She might not deny her personality, but where looks were concerned he knew she would scorn the suggestion of beauty. It was as if she imagined once she owned up to the latter she would weaken the former. There was a general understanding that brains and beauty rarely accompanied one another, and that if they did the owners of the assets always became notorious in some way. Perhaps it was because certain members of the ruling class, stemming down from Royalty, had set the pattern.

The couple were now kneeling at the altar steps, with the parson standing before them delivering a homily on the sanctity of marriage, of the love that they must share, of the caring in sickness or in health; and finally looking down on them, he blessed them and assured them their marriage would be an example for others to follow.

As Douglas muttered to himself, 'God in heaven!' Bridget, across the aisle, was saying to herself, 'God forbid that anyone should follow his example.' Then, as the organ struck up and the couple rose from their knees and, arm in arm, stepped down into the aisle, she found herself meeting Lionel Filmore's eyes, and the expression in them baffled her. Perhaps, she thought, it was a reflection of that expressed in her own, for she knew she not only disliked this man, she hated him for, through him, she had done something that she knew now she would regret for the rest of her life.

The bride was changing into her going-away costume. Jessie was helping her into the plum velvet coat that matched the dress and the high hat with its single grey feather draping the crown. When, fussily, Jessie went to button the coat, saying, 'There's a keen wind blowing. Now take care, take care,' Victoria checked her hand, saying, 'It's all right, Jessie; I'll do it. But thank you, dear, thank you for being so kind to me over the years.' She bent down and kissed Jessie's plump cheek, then said to her, 'Would you leave us for a minute, I want to have a word with Miss Bridget?'

'Of course, of course, me dear. Naturally you want to have a word, naturally.'

As she turned away, Jessie patted Bridget's arm, then sniffed loudly as she went from the room, leaving the two to look at each other and in silence for a while until Victoria said, 'I'd be the happiest girl in the whole wide world if only I could think you were happy for me.'

'I've always been happy for you, and always shall be.' Bridget now took hold of Victoria's hands, adding, 'You know that.'

'But . . . but why don't you like Lionel? I don't understand; he's . . . he's so wonderful, so kind and thoughtful.'

'Have you ever asked him if he likes me?'

'Yes. Yes, I have, dear.'

'Oh; you have? And what did he say?'

'Well –' Victoria wagged her head a little before she replied, 'It was silly, but he said he looked upon you as if you were my mother because you acted like a mother who doesn't want to lose her daughter; and that's why you . . . you weren't fond of him. He said' – she gave a little laugh now – 'mothers-in-law never like sons-in-law.'

'That's what he said?'

'Well, you've always looked after me. I told him that; and, too, that I didn't know what my life would have been without you. He used to laugh about it at first, but I think now he understands.'

'Yes, I'm sure he does.'

'Wish me happiness, dear.'

'I do. I do. That's all I wish you, ever, is happiness. But . . . but your life is going to be different from now on. You understand that? And when you come back and go to live at the Grove there will be no me, no Jessie, no Peg,

Mary, or Florrie; no Meadow House to run to. Have you thought about all that?'

'Oh yes, yes, of course I have. I know I shall have to get used to their servants and I'll have to learn how to run a house. But, you know, I've had a lot of practice, haven't I? And I haven't done badly in that line, have I now?'

'No. No, you haven't done badly at all. You've done very well in that side of things.'

Victoria laughed happily now as she said, 'Don't you worry, dear. I'll adjust. I know I shall. And anyway, if I get stuck I'll run to Douglas. He's so nice, entirely different from Lionel, but so very nice. Oh dear! listen to that noise downstairs. I . . . I've got to face them all again. His father was very funny, wasn't he, at the breakfast? He didn't drink as much as I thought he would. And, you know, he's been very nice to me. I . . . I didn't care for him at first, but he makes jokes, he makes me laugh.'

'I'm glad of that. Well, come on, button your coat up.'

The next moment they were both enfolded tightly, and after they kissed, Bridget pressed Victoria towards the door, saying, 'Go along. Go along. I'll be down in a minute.'

Now she watched the girl for whom she had cared since she was eight years old move definitely out of her life. She tried to control the choking in her throat, but when she could not blink away the tears she hurried to the dressing table, lifted the china lid off a bowl, picked up the puff and dabbed her face quickly with the scented talcum. Then hastily taking up a piece of soft washleather, she rubbed it vigorously over her cheeks to remove any trace of the powder.

When she reached the hall, a way was quickly made for her among the laughing guests in order that she could reach the door, there to see the groom helping his wife into the open coach to begin the drive into Newcastle, from where they would start the first part of their journey to France. The coach was surrounded by more cheering and waving guests, prominent among whom were the five Forrester girls and, mingling with them, the three Wright men.

Douglas wasn't among them; he was standing on the steps below Bridget, and at this moment he was not thinking of the couple driving off but was remarking to himself about the position of the Wright men's arms about the lively Forrester girls, which, he was sure, portended high jinks when they should all adjourn back to Grove House, and they would likely end up in the barn where the staff would be celebrating. He recalled quite clearly the last time this had happened. It was on Lionel's twenty-first birthday, six years ago. The eventual result of that night had been the taking of long holidays by at least two young ladies.

Well, there was one thing for sure, he wouldn't be there tonight; what was more, he wouldn't be missed. Yet, and he smiled to himself now, Sarah Forrester had for some time looked at him in a certain way, even though he hadn't a penny and would never be able to afford a wife. But that had been before he started selling his chippings; of late her look had become more coy and her lisp more affected than ever.

A large section of the company, the younger ones, were running down the drive after the coach; their elders were returning to the house, some strolling into the drawing-room, others into the dining-room to sample any drinks that were still available.

It was almost two hours later when the last of the guests piled into their carriages and made for Grove House. William Filmore was one of them. He stood before Bridget at the front door. His face was now flushed, and his voice thick as he leant towards her, saying, 'You did her proud,

Miss Bridget, proud. Something to be said for you, you know. Oh, yes, something to be said for you. Will you be dropping in to see me? . . . You don't answer,' he said; then his jowls wagged from side to side as he added, 'Then you know what they say about Mohammed and that mountain,' and his tone now changing, and his whisky-laden breath fanning her face, he muttered, 'Stiff-necked to the end. But by God! I admire your guts. You should have been a man, you know.' He turned from her, laughing, and as he shambled down the steps Douglas came to her side and in a low voice said, 'May I pop in and see you tomorrow?'

'Please do,' she replied, then turned to where the other guests, mainly her own, were preparing to leave. There was the accountant, William Bennett, his wife Nell, his daughter Nancy and son Jeff, and each in turn shook her hand and thanked her. Then there was her agent, Arthur Fathers, and his son Philip. Arthur's wife had died just a month beforehand. Their farewells were solemn, as befitted their recent bereavement. And lastly there was Andrew Kemp, his wife Jane, and their son Richard.

Previously in an aside she had asked Andrew to stay behind, for she would like a word with him. And so now, the door closed on the parting guests, she looked at Mrs Kemp, whom she had never called Jane, yet always called her husband Andrew, thereby keeping to her father's pattern here, and including Richard within the gesture she made with her hand, she said, 'Would you mind waiting just a few minutes? There's something I would like to discuss with Andrew. Jessie here will show you to the breakfast room.' She turned round and beckoned to Jessie, then added, 'It's about the only place in the house that isn't upset at the moment.'

After watching the mother and son follow Jessie down the corridor she turned to her solicitor, saying, 'Will you come upstairs a minute? There's too much going on down here; it'll take them hours to clear away.'

She did not lead him to her bedroom because that had been used as a ladies' room for the guests. But she led him to the end of the corridor, to a deep window seat and, sitting down with a plop, she beckoned him to do the same. And now, looking at him, she said, 'Have I done the right thing, Andrew?'

'Well, Miss Bridget, it was something you wanted to do.'

'No; I didn't want to do it, Andrew, but I felt that the shock would be too much for her; she would never have been able to regain confidence in herself. Let us face it, Andrew. Victoria is not a . . . well, a person who could deal with a calamity. And to lose him at that stage, so near the wedding, would surely have sent her into a decline. True or fancied, it would have been a decline.'

'Oh, I don't know. I can't say I agree with you there, Miss Bridget, because she's always appeared to me a bit of a flibbertigibbet: she thought of nothing but spending money on dress, and your money. She never did anything for it.'

'Oh yes, she did, Andrew. She kept the books and did the housekeeping, and she was quite good at that, you know.'

'Well, all I can say is, she's going to have a job keeping the books and doing the housekeeping where her future lies. And it pains me to think that two thousand pounds of your good money, besides her five hundred, is going to that man, a ne'er-do-well, if ever I've come across one, and I've come across a few in my time.'

'Andrew.'

'Yes? Is there something more? I can tell by your voice, and when you say my name like that I've learned over the years to beware of it. Don't tell me you want to give them more money; for I would really get on my hind legs, I really would.'

'It isn't about them at all, it's about Joe . . . Joe Skinner.'

'Oh, yes.' He hitched himself along the seat towards her. 'I heard about that just this morning. Well, it was in the papers. I really couldn't believe it. He seemed a decent enough fellow, didn't he? You had taken an interest in him and your father did before you. To cut his brother's throat, it seems impossible.'

'It is impossible. He didn't do it.'

'Well now, what makes you so sure of that? Why have they picked him up and named him if there isn't some proof?'

'I've seen him. I went last night. He swore to me that he knew nothing whatever about it. It should happen that he was in the wood that night and whom did he speak to but Mr Filmore.'

'Mr . . . ?'

'No; not the one just gone, but the younger son, Douglas. He's a sculptor. He was examining some stone and Joe spoke to him. It was shortly afterwards that Douglas found the body. No; not the body, for the man wasn't then quite dead. He dashed back to the house and got the men and a cart to take him into hospital. This is what I understand from Douglas and he apparently told the police he saw four horsemen, his brother Lionel, and three others, riding through the wood; but that he also saw this man. But this isn't what caused the police to arrest Joe. It was his mother: she told the police straightaway that Joe had threatened his brother time and again. And Joe admits he was out looking for him to prevent him from doing something; I don't know what and he won't say. But Andrew, everything . . . everything is against him. Yet I know he is innocent, and . . . and what I want you to do is to engage an attorney, the best.'

'Well, well, well. I can understand your worry, but it isn't really up to you to prove him innocent.'

'No, *I can't* prove him innocent, but an advocate or barrister, or whatever, they can get to the bottom of things. Get a man from London.'

'London? Oh. Oh, they don't come cheap.'

'Oh, Andrew, what does the money matter?'

'It matters. It matters, my dear. Somebody's got to keep a hand on the reins where you're concerned. Two thousand, five hundred a year, for how long? How long do you think you'll have to pay that? It's going to take more than half your profits from the factories. And Fathers tells me his rent collectors are having a devil of a job to rake the money in from around Gateshead and Low Fell.'

'Yes, I know that, I know that. But what they lose there is well made up in Jarrow. Jarrow is thriving.'

'Yes, but what did I hear about them thriving? Some of them are buying their own houses through Palmers. Did you know that?'

'Yes, I did know that, and good luck to them. Andrew, stick to the point. The point is, I want you to engage someone to defend Joe. Don't think of the cost; I want the best for him.'

The old man stared at her. He wetted his lips, then nipped the end of his nose between his finger and thumb and said, 'You've always been interested in that fellow since he was a bit of a lad, and you've pushed him on. I remember your father remarking to me that you had got him to go to night-school or some such. And I remember exactly what I said: "What good is that going to do for a man in a blacking factory?" And I've always remembered what your father answered because he was very good at quipping. He said, "She's likely aiming to bring light into his life with a black candle." Now wasn't that quick thinking?'

When she didn't answer he turned from her, bent forward and attempted to press his tight trouser legs further down over his knees; then, getting to his feet, he said, 'Well, I'll do as you say. But of course, I'll have to think about it. And I'll have to take advice on it, because I'm not conversant with London barristers.'

She, too, stood up and, her voice gentle now, she said, 'Thank you, Andrew. But . . . but will you do it as soon as possible?'

He patted her arm as he answered, 'Yes, I'll start yesterday.' Then, his bullet head nodding, he added, 'You know, girl, I'm very fond of you. If I'd had a daughter, I'd have wished her to be made of the same pattern. And you know, I often think of you and wish that soon, quite soon, because age is an illusion and youth flies swiftly, so I repeat, quite soon, you would meet someone that could match your mentality and would be a friend to you as well as a husband. Because that is what is needed in marriage . . . friendship. And that is why there are so many unhappy people in the world, because when love flies up the chimney the heat goes out of the ashes. And love does fly up the chimney, my dear, that love that drives you . . .' He stopped; then inclining his head on one side, he asked, 'Dare I say it to you, you a young lady, that the love that drives you to bed with its first flush fades. It's bound to fade, and then, as I said, if it doesn't leave friendship behind, life becomes a withered thing. I speak from experience, my dear, for I have so many clients that are walking about dead because they didn't prepare for love dying on them.'

'Oh, Andrew, Andrew, you'll have me in tears.' Her eyelids were blinking, yet she smiled as she said, 'I wouldn't dare now contemplate marriage, knowing the pitfalls. You've put me off for life.' And at this she bent forward and in a swift movement kissed him on the cheek, then said softly, 'Who would want a husband when I've got you for a friend?'

He took the compliment in silence but, bending his arm, he held it out to her and she placed her hand in it, and together they walked back along the corridor and down the stairs; and they did not exchange any further words.

10

'Oh, Douglas, if only you hadn't recognised him.'

'But I did, Bridget; I did recognise him, and he recognised me. He admitted it. Don't forget, I was the one who found his brother: when I was questioned I just had to say who had passed that way. I didn't know it was him; I only knew it was a workman. Then, when they asked me to come to court, and I saw the man, I had to say yes, because he recognised me. Anyway, what could you have done if I hadn't recognised him?'

'I could have explained that he couldn't possibly have been there in the wood that night.'

'Oh, Bridget, how on earth could you?'

'I could, I could. I would have got Lily to swear that he hadn't been home, and that her neighbour, Mrs Leary . . . oh, they would have sworn all right.'

'But where on earth could you have said he had been?'

She now thrust her face towards him and she practically ground out the words, 'With me.'

'What! What do you mean, with you?'

'I could say he spent the night with me.'

He looked at her in utter amazement, saying, 'But why would you say that? I mean, you're a lady, he's a working fellow.'

'Well, that's just it; because I'm a lady my word would have been taken.'

'You mean to say you would sully your good name by saying, he . . . he . . . ?'

'Yes, Douglas, I would have sullied this good name for

what it is worth to save a man from going to the gallows.'

He stared at her in silence; then he shook his head slowly as he said, 'There must be more in it than that, Bridget.'

'What are you inferring?'

'I don't rightly know; I'm asking you. Taking the liberty of a friend, I'm asking you.'

She turned slightly away from him as he spoke, and so he couldn't see the expression on her face when she said, 'I've told you before, my father had an interest in him, and I took it from there. I realised that he was intelligent, and under other circumstances he could have made something of himself. And my interest in him deepened when I found he was attending night classes.' She glanced towards him now. 'He used to go to the Unitarian evening school, and the Minister there, who was a friend of my father's, spoke highly of him as a young man: he knew he was supporting his mother who, from what I understood, was a difficult woman, and, at the same time, trying to keep his brother out of mischief.' She paused now, then, looking straight into Douglas's face, she said, 'I admired him.'

Douglas looked hard at this young woman whom he could now call his friend, and could also add he was more than fond of, and he guessed that her admiration for one of her workmen had gone deeper than just interest. These things happened. There was Charlotte Cox. She was never spoken of now. She was a distant relation, second cousin once removed type, and she had been put beyond the pale, buried while still alive, you could say, because she had run off with the baker who had catered for her sister's wedding. And there had been a Bishop at that wedding, a confirmed High Church one. The Cox family had groaned and groaned for years in the agony of this disgrace. Charlotte was now the mother of three children and she herself had grown round and comely in her happy isolation.

Taking Bridget's hand, he moved it gently and his eyes gazed softly at her as he said,

> 'The heart is blind:
> It gropes for a hand,
> Not any hand
> But one whose touch is kind,
> Dove soft;
> It matters not the face
> For the valleys and the mountains of the bones
> Are just a case.
> The heart is blind
> While searching for love.'

Her eyelids were blinking rapidly, and her lips were tightly compressed and it was a moment or so before she spoke when, her voice trembling slightly, she said, 'You are a very good man, Douglas, and I thank you for your understanding. I feel you are a unique person.'

'Odd, more like.'

'Never. What you are is a very human human being.'

However, when he said in a completely changed tone, one that had a brisk business-like note to it, 'But I must say again, Bridget, I think it's unwise of you to attend the court tomorrow. Especially . . . well, under the circumstances,' she withdrew her hand from his and replied as briskly, 'Douglas. Nothing . . . nothing could keep me away from that court tomorrow, for, apart from his wife, I think I must be the only friend he has. And over the past weeks in that prison he has changed. I had thought he would fight, even be aggressive in his own defence, but on the two occasions I have seen him he has appeared already to have accepted the worst. On my last visit I pleaded with him to tell them why he wanted to see his brother, why he had threatened him; and, you know, he just continued to look at me for some time, and then he said, "What has to be will be, miss." He's so changed: the Joe I knew would never have answered like that. That dreadful place has had a nulling effect on him.'

At this point the drawing-room door opened and Victoria appeared, and Bridget said in some surprise, 'I didn't hear the carriage.'

'I didn't come in the carriage, I brought the trap.'

Bridget had risen and as she walked towards Victoria to greet her she said in almost disbelief, 'You brought the trap on your own?'

'Yes, Bridget, on my own,' and the slight terseness in her voice was even more evident when, looking at Douglas, she remarked, 'You here again?'

Douglas gave a slight laugh as he countered, 'Well, if you recognise I'm here again, it must have been one of the times when you, too, were here again. And I wasn't aware that Bridget's house was out of bounds.'

Bridget glanced from one to the other. There was evidently a feeling of animosity between them, which surprised her. She had imagined that when Victoria took up her abode in that house she would find an ally in Douglas. But apparently not.

'Well, I'll be off. See you in the court in the morning, Bridget.'

'Yes, Douglas.'

He gave Victoria no farewell, and when the door closed on him she sat down on the couch and began to arrange her wide taffeta skirt to each side of her knees, her eyes following her hands as she said, 'You see a lot of him, don't you? He can make a nuisance of himself.'

Such a statement would normally have brought forth a corresponding retort from Bridget, but she, already pondering on the relationship between her cousin and Douglas, decided that Victoria must have become jealous of him. She was likely seeing him as a usurper of the position she herself had held in her affection.

She looked more closely at her. There was a petulant expression on her face, more so than she had ever seen before. When she was young she would go into what her father used laughingly to call the pet. 'She's in the pet,' he would say. But as Victoria grew into womanhood such occasions seemed to have become fewer and fewer, when she had gone 'in the pet.'

But she was definitely in the pet now, and it came over in her tone as she said, 'Why must you appear at that trial? You'll get your name up. Mr Filmore said as much. Engaging the best advocate that was to be got from London for the man. It isn't as if he was a relative or anything like that.'

'What's come over you, Victoria? You used to like Joe; at least you appeared to. On the few times you would deign to enter the blacking factory you always remarked on what a pleasant fellow he was.'

'Yes, I might have, but nevertheless he was a common workman.'

Bridget seemed to jump a step backwards from the daintily dressed figure on the couch and she exclaimed harshly, 'And you! don't let us forget, were living well, and dressing well, on the sweat of that common workman and many others like him.' And it was with difficulty she stopped herself from adding, 'You are only living well and dressing well now from the same source.' But she had seen Victoria's head droop and her hand go to her mouth and cover it with a handkerchief as the tears ran down her cheeks, and so she stepped towards her again, saying gently now, 'What is it? What is really the matter? I . . . I thought you were so happy.'

When Victoria's shoulders began to shake Bridget quickly sat down beside her and, taking her hand, coaxed her, 'What is it, dear? What's the matter?'

'I'm . . . I'm going to have . . .' The words trailed away under Victoria's breath and Bridget said, 'What? What did you say?'

Victoria now lifted her head, dried her eyes, then muttered, 'I'm going to have a baby.'

'Oh. Oh, I see. Well now, is . . . is that something to cry about?'

There was silence for a moment; then Victoria, biting on the hem of her handkerchief, murmured, 'Lionel isn't pleased.'

'Why isn't he pleased? I should have thought he would have been over the moon to . . . well, perhaps have an heir. What about his father?'

Victoria turned her head away now and looked down the long room towards the ray of sunlight streaming in through the high windows. And her voice still a mutter, she said, 'He laughed.' Then swinging round quickly towards Bridget again, she almost shouted the words: 'He laughed, Bridget. He laughed so loudly and so long that Lionel had to yell at him . . . Mr Filmore is very crude, Bridget. There . . . there are times when I'm not happy, Bridget. You see, the staff is . . . well, they're different from . . . from what our girls were like. The cook doesn't like me going into the kitchen. And . . . and the house isn't as clean as it should be. I spoke to Douglas about it and asked what he thought I should do, and you know what he said to me?'

Bridget made a small shaking movement with her head and waited. 'He said I had got what I wanted and I had come into it with my eyes open. I used to like Douglas, but he's changed. And he fights with Lionel. They nearly came to fisticuffs recently. Yes, yes, they did.' She nodded vigorously at Bridget's startled look, then went on,

'Douglas called Lionel a leech. Mind you, it was after Lionel had been away for three days in Edinburgh. He was being interviewed for some position to run an estate up in the Highlands, and Douglas accused him of having taken the trip to Edinburgh for a gaming session and said he couldn't manage our own little stint, that's what he called the farm, a stint, so how could he have had the nerve to put in for the post of managing a Scottish estate. It was awful; I ran out of the room. And, you know, it's so unfair of Douglas because Lionel is so good. They're very short of money but he's promised me that every quarter I shall have enough money to meet the ordinary household bills. Of course, I understand I've got to watch out for extravagance from the kitchen, because they order much more than they need. And he left it to me. I know it's going to be difficult, but I must do it. And I've told him I can manage with half of my dress allowance.'

'You'll not; you'll use your dress allowance. If you can manage on half of it then that's all I shall give you.'

'*Oh Bridget, please* don't you start and be awkward. I know it's good of you to continue giving me the allowance, but if I can manage on half . . .'

'If you can manage on half that's all you're going to get.' Bridget sprang up from the couch; then, pointing down to the face that had now taken on a look of indignation, she ordered, 'Say no more! Two hundred and fifty it will be from now on.'

'You're cruel, that's what you are.' Victoria was standing now, her hands nervously buttoning and unbuttoning her tight-fitting grey alpaca coat; they then went to her hair and she began to thrust in a stray curl under the brim of her hat as she repeated, 'You are, you are; there is a cruel streak in you. You've shown it with regard to Lionel ever since the beginning, you have. Yes, you have. It's true what he says about you.'

'And what does he say about me?' The words were flat.

'Doesn't matter. Doesn't matter. Nothing matters any more, because you have changed towards me, all because I love Lionel . . . Frustration and jealousy, that's what he said. Yes, he did; and I think he was right because there you are being talked about: going visiting that murderer in prison, and spending all that money to try and prove he's innocent, when everybody knows he's not, everybody but you. You're getting yourself talked about. Do you hear? Yes, you are.'

There was a note of restrained anger in Bridget's voice as she said, 'This is no longer your home, Victoria, and I would advise you to go back now to the one you have chosen; and when you get there, repeat to your husband exactly what you have said to me, and see what his reaction is. But do not forget to emphasise that I am cutting your allowance.'

'Yes. Yes, I will. As soon as he comes back from London next week, that is the first thing I will greet him with. And I will tell him how right he has been in his estimation of you.'

She was already on her way to the door when Bridget said, 'Do that, dear, do that; and as I said, I'd like you to come back and tell me of his reaction.'

Victoria stopped for a moment and stared back at the once beloved cousin, before flouncing out of the room, leaving Bridget standing gripping the back of a chair as if she were about to lift it from the floor. And being a very human individual, the thought crossed her mind that for two pins she would follow her cousin and really give her something that she could carry back to her new home . . . the truth of the situation. However, be it for two pins or two hundred, she knew she couldn't do it.

11

It wasn't the first time she had been in the Guildhall. The previous visit she recalled had taken place when she was about sixteen. Her father had, at that time, been friends with the then Lord Mayor of Newcastle and he was to meet him in the Guildhall, either to attend a meeting, or following on a meeting; she wasn't quite sure, she only remembered that in the Guildhall she had been horrified by the sight of the courtroom, the details of which the Lord Mayor had so proudly pointed out.

Facing the bench where the judge would sit, but quite some distance from it, and extending into the middle of the courtroom, was a sort of high and square wooden box, made to look fearsome by being topped by pointed iron railings which curved inwards, thus making sure that the prisoner would not attempt to climb out. If found guilty, the prisoner would seem immediately to disappear for he would be hustled from the bottom straight down steps leading to the quayside from where, in earlier years if he were to be deported, he would straightaway be put on a ship, nowadays into the Black Maria that would take him perhaps to Durham jail, there to serve out his sentence. This form of departure ensured that he had no contact with the public seated in rows to the right of him and among whom might have been his relatives, wife, mother, or children.

The witnesses were held in a room that went off a large hall that was part of the courtroom. Here, too, she recalled there was a gruesome contraption. It was really a window-sill, quite narrow, but just able to accommodate three prisoners standing tightly side by side, but hemmed in by an iron gate.

She could recall the feeling of dismay she had experienced when realising that human beings could treat each other in such a barbaric fashion, no matter what they had done. Today that word was inadequate to express the great deep feeling of sickness and apprehension that was enveloping her as she sat amongst the crowd of people thronging the benches.

She could see Joe's head and shoulders and she was willing him to look in her direction, but he was gazing straight ahead at the red-robed and white-wigged figure sitting on the elevated bench.

The well of the court, too, seemed to be swarming with people, among whom she could see Andrew Kemp, his son Richard, and Mr Norman Beale, the advocate who had been commissioned to defend Joe. His opposite number, the prosecutor, was a Mr Pearson. Then there was Judge Hodgson. At the far side of the room and pressed tightly together were the twelve most important people present, the jury.

So far in the proceedings, she felt that if it had been a race, the prosecutor would already have been far ahead of the advocate, for Mr Beale's words and manner seemed not to be as convincing as the prosecutor's, which were already carrying the conviction of guilt.

'You reiterate that you did not kill your brother, but your own words damn you.'

There was an appeal from the advocate, and on it the judge warned the prosecuting counsel to desist from making statements and to return to questioning.

So the prosecutor now said, 'Am I right in thinking your mother was telling the truth when she said that, on the night in question, the night your brother died, you did use words to that effect –' and now the prosecutor leant forward, picked up a piece of paper from his desk and read, '"I'll swing for you one of these days." I ask you, was she speaking the truth?'

'Yes, sir.'

'Speak up, please.'

'Yes, sir. She was speaking the truth. But I had said that to him dozens of times over the . . .'

'Yes, we have heard you make that statement already. Now will you tell the court why you said those words at that particular time. What was the reason?'

'I can't remember.'

'Your memory seems to be particularly vague. You've already said you cannot remember where you went when you left Brook's Wood on that particular night. I fear that if you hadn't been recognised by Mr Filmore you would have denied ever being in the wood. And no doubt you have likely forgotten where you hid the knife.'

Before Mr Beale could again object, Joe's voice rang through the court: '*I had no knife. I've told you. I had no knife. I never carried a knife. Never,*' and the prosecutor, giving a slight shrug towards the jury, said, 'No more questions,' and sat down.

Mr Beale then stood up to question Joe; and as Bridget listened to his smooth, quiet questioning, she cried within herself. 'That isn't the way to do it: that will never impress the jury,' for the man was talking as if he were having a pleasant conversation with someone instead of trying to save him from the gallows.

He was saying, 'You got your brother out of many scrapes, did you not?'

'Yes, sir.'

'Am I right in thinking there is a young man in an asylum now, put there because he set Farmer Brook's haystack on fire? But is it not true that it was your brother who egged him on to do this, in fact, supplied him with the oil and matches?'

'Yes, sir.'

'And is it not true that one Andrew Davison served a term of six months' imprisonment because stolen property was found in his outhouse, whereas the real perpetrator of this crime was your brother who, when he knew the police were looking for the stolen property, placed it in this man's yard?'

There was a slight pause before Joe said, 'Yes, sir.'

'Is it not also true that these are just two instances of your brother's pilfering, and that over the years, you have had to support him by your own work because he could not maintain any employment for longer than a very short time?'

Again there was a pause before Joe said, 'Yes, sir.'

Bridget closed her eyes for a moment. To her, this seemed to be the wrong form of questioning altogether. It would be what the prosecutor might ask, then come back like a shot of a gun, saying, 'So, you had had enough, so you killed him?'

Then almost as if the report of a shot from a gun had brought her head mounting up, she heard the advocate saying, 'Is it true that you are not the father of the child your wife gave birth to some weeks ago, but that she was already pregnant with the child for some months when, out of the goodness of your heart, to save her shame, you married her? And . . .'

'That's got nothin' to do with it. *Nothing. Nothing.*'

'I think it has. Yes, in my opinion I think it has, because it shows you to be a man of good and sympathetic nature and moral heart. We all know how a young woman who gives birth to an illegitimate child is looked upon in this day and age. Especially when her people turn against her, when her only choice, if it can be so called, is the workhouse. And it is known that you have become a very loving husband, a family man. All your neighbours will vouch for this, but more so does your employer who cannot speak more highly of you.' He now turned and looked towards the jury, asking of them, 'Is this the picture of a man who would stab his brother to death and go home and crack a joke with his neighbour, as Mrs Leary has already described –' he coughed twice before continuing, 'then, as she said, pick up the child from its basket-cradle and give it . . . a shuggy, as she amply described, while its mother protested about its being wakened from sleep? Again I ask you, is this the picture of a man who had just murdered his brother? I leave you to answer that question.'

It was at this point that the judge bent and said something to the clerk. The clerk spoke to the usher; then the usher turned and declared, 'The court is adjourned until two-thirty o'clock of this day.' . . .

Bridget made straight for the wash room. She felt she was really going to be sick but, finding the room crowded, she stayed only as long as was necessary.

As she came out she was hailed by Mrs Leary: 'There you are, miss. There you are. How d'you think it's goin'? I put it over right, didn't I? I told him, and I would have done more, only that bloke kept shutting me up. But I got me say in, that I did. Now would a man go and kill his brother, I said, then come home and hold the bairn tight against his decent coat. Not that its nappies had had any time to get wet. I did tell him, didn't I? Spankin' clean, Lily is, and that child is kept as dry as if it never peed. Dear God! they're easily shocked, that lot in there. Queer cards altogether. Even the man who is supposed to be speakin' up for Joe, he wouldn't let me get a word in . . . You're lookin' right peaky, but you'd have a long way to go to reach the colour that Lily is this day. Ill, she is, never away from the closet, her stomach runnin' out of her.'

'Mrs Leary, you'll . . . you'll have to excuse me, my . . . my solicitor and advocate are waiting for me.'

'That's all right, deary. That's all right. We'll be meetin' later on, if God wills, 'cos you'll be goin' to Lily's, won't you?'

'Yes. Yes, I'll call this evening.'

'You're a good lady, a kind lady. God, you are that. Who among the gentry would show concern for a worker like you have. No, begod! not one of them but yourself.'

Bridget walked away with the words, 'show concern for a worker' gyrating round her mind. If it was only known how, in her heart, she held that worker, she'd be the object of scorn, and, yes, from Mrs Leary. She'd be no lady then.

The men were waiting for her in the Merchant's Court. She remembered this room. It was the most beautiful apartment, in which were stored the records of the company of Merchant Adventurers dating back to 1215. It had a magnificent fireplace, and the walls of panelled oak reaching to the moulded ceiling and the panelling holding the coats of arms of all the Lord Mayors. These Merchant Adventurers must have taken upon themselves in some way or another the splendour and dignity of this place when dealing with not only shipping, but all kinds of merchandise that was produced or passed through this ancient city.

However, today none of this touched her. In the crowded room she presently espied Douglas, and, as if he had been waiting to catch her eye, he nodded towards her, but did not make his way to join her or her solicitor, or advocate, because, in a way, his witness would be acting against their cause.

And Douglas was even now worried about something, the while telling himself it was of no consequence and had no bearing on the case. When on the witness stand he had been asked whom else he had seen in the wood that night, he had answered in the same way as he had done up till then; four riders returning from the hunt. He hadn't said he had spoken to one, for the question hadn't been put to him. Another point, the riders were gentlemen. What could they possibly have to do with this sort of case that was dealing with a family feud between two brothers and they working men?

As they walked from the Guildhall to a nearby hotel, Mr Beale said to Bridget, 'It's a great pity that young man who was on the stand chose that evening to select stone.'

'Well, what do you mean?' Bridget slowed in her step and he, looking at her as if she were a young naive girl, said, 'Well, now, what do you really think? Not only has that incident condemned him, but his mother, as far as I can see, has tightened the noose round his neck. My dear. My dear.' He put his hand on her elbow and almost hurried her into the hotel; and he said nothing further until they were seated, when he said, 'If I am able to get for him a term of imprisonment, I shall consider I have won this case; and the only way I can see of achieving this is by continuing the line on which I ended this morning's session: the father of the child.'

'But we don't know who the father of the child is, do we?' Mr Kemp was inclining his head deferentially towards the big man.

'I think I know, sir. And the prisoner's reactions, when I brought up the fact that the child his wife had borne was not his, seemed to confirm my thinking. It was some-body's, wasn't it? and that someone was known by the prisoner. And whom did he know as well as he did . . . his brother?'

Both Bridget and Andrew Kemp stared at the man, and Bridget was crying to herself, 'Oh no;' then, 'Yes, yes. He was keeping silent to shield Lily.' But on another thought she voiced it, saying, 'But if she brought this to light it would condemn him straightaway.'

'I'm aware of that, Miss Mordaunt, very aware of that. But I intend to play on the fact that this man is keeping something silent in order to shield his wife further pain. It will, of course, be put over in such a way that even the dullest of the jury will know why Joseph Skinner killed his brother Frederick. There is no hope it would prove him not guilty, but there is every hope it will enable him to evade the gallows and, instead, do a term of imprisonment. And with the latter judgement he would be left with hope, whereas what can one say about the former? Anyway, as they say, where there's life, there's hope. So let us eat.'

12

Bridget's face was an ashen colour, but her eyes were dry, wide and pain-filled as she looked down at Lily: the child in her arms, she was sitting rocking it backwards and forwards, and had been for the last half hour; and she looked as if she would never stop. She didn't speak for a full twenty minutes after Bridget and Mrs Leary had entered the house, nor had either of them opened their mouths. It must have been Mrs Leary's silence that conveyed the dire sentence to Lily, with the result that she cried out, 'No, no; they wouldn't, not to Joe. He would never do that. Never, never. Would he? Would he?' Then she had lain down the child to do what she had been doing for the past two or three days, run to the closet. When she returned she again picked up the child and from then had sat rocking herself and it.

When Mrs Leary suddenly burst out, 'They're bastards! the lot of them,' then on a quieter note, said, 'I'll make a pot of tea,' Bridget brought her chair as close as she could to the rocking body and placed her hand on the trembling shoulder, and, doing so, she thought that right until the day she died two things would remain in her mind: first, the sound of the judge's voice as he intoned, 'And will be hanged by the neck until . . .' She couldn't bring her mind to finish the words; it skipped them and placed before her the look on Joe's face. And this, too, would remain with her: Joe's face was devoid of colour and seemingly of emotion. It was as if the sentence was no surprise to him;

that he had known from the beginning what the outcome would be.

There had been a great cafuffle outside the court: people of varying opinions standing arguing, reporters rushing for cabs. And then his mother standing facing her in the road just as she was about to step into the carriage and almost whimpering, 'I . . . I didn't think he would get that, I didn't. Prison, aye, but not the other. That'll be two of them now, two of them gone. What's to become of me?'

'You should have thought of that some time ago, Mrs Skinner, and curbed your venom. You're a wicked woman, an unnatural mother.'

It was then she allowed Douglas to help her into the carriage and as he was about to close the door, she leaned towards him, saying softly, 'Come with me, Douglas, please, will you? I've . . . I've got to go to . . . Lily's, and I . . . I don't think I can stand much more today.'

'Yes. Yes, of course.'

After he had taken his seat beside her she had turned for a moment and looked out of the window to where Mr Kemp's advocate was standing outside the Guildhall. Mr Kemp looked very perturbed; his companion's face showed no emotion: he had lost his case and through that a workman would lose his life. It was all in a day's work.

As the carriage had begun to roll away down the uneven road Douglas had caught hold of her hand and held it tightly. He hadn't spoken, nor had she; she had lain against the padded back, her eyes closed. He, too, had lain back and for the most part had remained silent until Danny Croft brought the coach to a stop outside Lily's house, when he had said, 'I won't come in with you.'

'I shall try not to be too long.'

'Take your time, Bridget. Take your time. She'll need comfort,' he had responded.

Bridget was feeling she could take no more at this moment for Lily's grief on top of her own personal feelings was weighing her down. 'Listen Lily,' she said, 'I will be back early tomorrow, and everything will be all right . . . I mean, your future will be. You have nothing to worry about in that way. But I feel I can be of no help to you at the moment, for your grief is too great. Yet Joe would not want you to grieve so. He loves you, very dearly, and you must make an effort and go and see him. You will be allowed to.'

The rocking stopped. Lily turned her agonised gaze on Bridget and she said one word, 'When?'

Bridget didn't know whether she was asking when she could visit Joe or when the fatal day was, so she answered, 'I'll enquire tomorrow morning before I come here.' She did not add, 'Try not to worry, for time is a great healer.' Such words were futile.

She turned now to where Mrs Leary was screwing the black kettle into the heart of the fire and saying, 'It'll be boiled in a jiffy,' and she said to her, 'I'm going now, Mrs Leary. I'll be back in the morning.'

'We'll look forward to it, miss. Yes, that we will. We'll look forward to it.' And now accompanying her to the door, she added, 'You've been a Godsend indeed, for He is like that, God. It's His way: He never bangs a door on you but He pushes another open.'

Under other circumstances Bridget would have laughed, now she just nodded at the woman who opened the front door for her; then she walked across the pavement to where Douglas was standing by the carriage as if he hadn't moved from the time she had left him.

As the carriage bowled away amid a scampering of children and gaping faces from doorways, Douglas asked quietly, 'Was it dreadful?' and she answered, 'Yes. Yes, it was dreadful, Douglas. Yet, this is only the beginning for

170

her: there will come the final day, then the aftermath. God! Why do these things happen?'

He made no answer, for what could he say? Could he answer with a platitude such as, you've got to take the good with the bad, or the rough with the smooth . . . Everything in life must be paid for; it's God's will; and so on? and so on? Platitudes or otherwise, there were no words to ease the agony of living.

The journey was half over when she turned to him and said, 'I'm sorry, Douglas; I've wasted a lot of your time.'

'Now, don't talk nonsense, Bridget. What would I do with my time? I ask you, what have I ever done with my time but sit nicking bits of stone, wondering all the while if it's worth it? Now, if I can do anything to help at all, it will give me a feeling that I'm of some use.'

'That's good of you, Douglas, so good. But . . . but I understand that you are creating a business and . . . and I know from experience . . .' She stopped here, cleared her throat, and then her words were hesitant as she went on, 'As I know from experience that . . . business must be attended to if one is to suc . . . ceed.'

Her voice trailed away as her mind yelled. Succeed! Succeed! She had wanted Joe to succeed. She had been chastising herself for days now . . . no, not for days, particular thoughts such as hers could only be chastised in the night, for it was then she would tell herself she should have done what she had wanted to do when first she had taken over from her father. Joe was still a young fellow then and would have jumped at the chance to go to school, to a real school with the prospect of going on to college, there to be really educated, and, what was equally important, to be polished, to have the rough edges smoothed down, made acceptable to . . . Oh lord. Oh lord. There was a great rough-edged lump rising from her stomach to her throat. It was choking her; and now her gasping breath was breaking the outer shell and there was water spouting from her eyes, nose and mouth, and she was moaning aloud.

Douglas was holding her tightly to him. He wasn't saying, 'There! There! Cry, that's it,' he was saying nothing at all, he just held her shaking body, and his own too was shaking for never before had he embraced a woman like this. He had danced with young ladies, his one hand on their waist, the other outstretched supporting the tips of their fingers, but never had his body as yet been close to that of a woman – he could not even remember the touch of his mother – but here he was holding Bridget tightly to him, cradling her, in fact, and his being was being swamped by a revelation brought into life by her sorrowing for another man.

13

She was standing looking at Joe. There was a table between them. The room was small and there was a policeman standing with his back to the door.

Joe was speaking. He was saying in a strangely ordinary voice, 'I've told Lily, miss, that you said you would look after her, and the bairn. And I told her not to worry; we've all got to go sometime.'

'Oh, Joe.'

'Don't frash yourself. You get used to the idea, you know.'

He now glanced at the policeman standing to the left of him. Then he bowed his head for a moment before placing his hands on the table and bending towards her. He said, with a touch of his old spirit, 'The road would be more bearable, miss, if I had done what I'd said many a time I would do. But I didn't do it. You believe me, miss, I didn't do it?'

'Yes. Yes, Joe, I believe you.'

He straightened up, then glanced at the seemingly immobile policeman again before having to draw spittle into his mouth to enable him to say, 'Will you do somethin' for me, miss?'

'Anything. Anything in the world, Joe.'

'Will you, if you can, try to get to the bottom of it?'

She paused a moment; then answered him with deep emphasis, 'Yes, Joe. I promise you that.'

'It won't do me much good, but . . . but it'll show them I wasn't lying.'

'Yes. Yes, Joe, it'll show them.'

The still figure at the door now stirred and Joe said, 'Well, good-bye, miss.' He held out his hand towards her and she gripped it in both of hers. But she couldn't speak. When she let go of it he moved backwards from the table the two or three steps before turning away and going through the door that the policeman was holding open for him.

She herself was leaning over the table gripping its edge for support when another policeman came in and, with a gentle hand on her arm, brought her upwards and led her from the room, along a passage and into the hallway where Douglas was waiting. He now took her over from the policeman, acknowledging his support by an inclination of his head, then led Bridget out and into the street to the waiting carriage.

After helping her inside, he paused a moment, his foot on the step, saying, 'We won't go home straightaway; we'll stop at an hotel. You must have a drink and I need fortifying, too.' And with that he looked up at Danny and gave him directions to a particular hotel.

In the carriage he immediately placed his arm around her shoulders, saying, 'I should have told you not to go, that you shouldn't go, but I know that would have been fruitless. Could . . . could you tell how he's taking it?'

It was some time before she answered, and there was a note of surprise in her voice as she said, 'Quite . . . quite calmly. It was strange, he was much less disturbed than I was, except . . . except for one moment when he made a request of me.'

'Well, that's to be expected that he would want you to look after Lily.'

'Oh, it wasn't that. I would have done that in any case. I have that all worked out. No; he asked me if I would try to get to the bottom of this, in other words, find out who the real culprit is.'

'Oh, dear, dear, that's a tall order. It would be better all round if the matter were to be dropped now, because just think of the consequences of your finding out who really did kill his brother, if Joe didn't. Everybody, the whole country I should imagine, would be up in arms at the miscarriage of justice. As for the man's family, and I suppose he has some sort of family, the exposure would be unthinkable.'

Bridget made no answer to this, but only thought: Yes, the exposure would be unthinkable.

It was on the last Friday in May that Joe was hanged in Durham jail, and it was on this day, too, that the national newspapers gave front headlines to the event, as they had done on the day that he had been convicted of the murder of his brother. And it was from this date, also, that the unwinding of the tragedy began.

try to get to the bottom of this. In other words, find out who the real culprit is.'

'Oh, dear, dear, that's a bit order. It would be better all round if the matter were to be dropped now, because just think of the consequences of your finding out who really did kill his brother, if Joe didn't. Everybody, the whole country I should imagine, would be up in arms at the miscarriage of justice. As for the man's family, and I suppose he has some sort of family, the exposure would be unthinkable.'

Bridget made no answer to this, but only thought: Yes, the exposure would be unthinkable.

It was on the last Friday in May that Joe was hanged in Durham jail, and it was on this day, too, that the national newspapers gave front headlines to the event, as they had done on the day that he had been convicted of the murder of his brother. And it was from this date, also, that the unmasking of the tragedy began.

PART TWO

A Change of Heart
1884

1

Some days had passed during which Bridget had done a great deal of thinking and life seemed to have fallen back into its old routine: she met her agent; and she saw to business where she thought it was necessary, and part of her business was to visit Lily. She was worried about Lily, for, as Mrs Leary had said to her confidentially, it was unnatural that the girl wasn't crying and had never shed a tear, not to her knowledge.

Then there was Douglas. She had not seen him since he had accompanied her home after her last visit to Joe. Although she was somewhat surprised at this, she again told herself that he, too, was in business and so couldn't spend his days in social visiting.

One good thing, however, had transpired over the past few days. Last evening Victoria had called and apologised for her outburst, the while declaring how much she had missed her, and that Lionel had returned from London the previous day and there seemed to be the promise of an appointment in the offing. It had something to do with shipping, and was connected with cargoes. But he didn't look well, he had a severe cold. And at parting Victoria had put her arms around her and surprisingly said, 'I don't know what I'd do if I hadn't you still to come to.' So things were definitely back to normal, as normal as they would ever be after the past few months.

Today she had gone by train into Newcastle. Danny had driven her from the house to the station, but as she didn't know what time she would return she had told him she would take a cab. And that's what she was now doing, but not to go back home for she was once again making her way to Lily's house, to tell her the plans she had arranged for her future.

After alighting from the cab she asked the cabbie to wait: she could be fifteen minutes or a little more, and the man assured her he would wait as long as she wished. For once she found Lily alone, and of this she was glad, for now she would have no need to say to the kindly but voluble neighbour that she wished to speak to Lily on a matter of some business.

She began as usual by saying, 'How is the baby?' It was no use asking, 'How are you, Lily?' because Lily's face expressed totally how she felt, numb, dead within herself.

And Lily answered as usual, 'He's fine, miss. He's fine.'

'Come and sit down, Lily.' She took the hand of what had been only a short time ago a happy young girl, but who now appeared like a life-weary woman, and she said, 'Sit down. I have something I want to discuss with you. First of all, have you thought about what you are going to do?'

'Yes, miss, go back to the factory.'

'But what about the baby?'

'I'd have to put him out to nurse. Mrs Leary would look after him.'

'Mrs Leary is a very good woman, I know, Lily, but she and her family are of a roughish type and children are very impressionable, even babies, and I'm sure Joe would have wanted the best for your child.'

As she watched Lily's head droop on to her chest, she said softly, 'We must mention his name, Lily. He would want that, he wouldn't want to be forgotten.'

The head came up with a jerk. 'He'll never be forgotten, miss, never! Nor what's happened him.'

'I know. I know. Well, now, I've got a proposal to make

to you. As you know, I've always had Joe's and your welfare at heart, and so what I would like to do is for you to take up a position in my household. It may not be work that you have been used to but I'm sure you would soon learn. Your child would be brought up in a different atmosphere and I would see to his education and . . .'

She almost toppled backwards with her chair, as the table was thrust towards her by the violent movement Lily made in rising from her stool; and now in amazement she watched the young woman turn to the cradle, then grab up her child and stand holding it pressed tightly to her, as she almost yelled, 'In your house at Milton Place! Near him! where he could drop in . . . with your cousin? No! No! No!' Now she swung round and her body seemed almost to bend in two over the child, and she was gasping as she cried, 'I'm sorry. I'm sorry. But no, no way. Thank you, no way.'

Slowly Bridget walked round the table and, stopping in front of Lily, put her arms about her shoulders, so bringing her up straight, and in a low voice she said, 'What did you mean by that, Lily?'

'Nothin', miss. Nothin'. It just came out. Nothin'.'

'Don't tell me "nothing". Look at me. Look at me straight in the face.'

When Lily raised her head and looked her straight in the face they both remained silent while Bridget's mind was actually gabbling, Him! He's the father? Dear God! him . . . And Joe must have known.

When she eventually spoke she could hardly recognise her own voice, such was the fierce anger in its tone: 'Mr Filmore, my cousin's husband, he is the father of your child? And . . . and that's why Joe wouldn't mention him? He told me he knew who it was. Oh, why, why didn't he speak out?'

Compared with her own, Lily's voice sounded calm as

she answered, ''Twouldn't have been any use. 'Twas nothin' to do with it, I mean with what happened to Fred. And . . . and he wanted to save you and Miss Victoria trouble, as she was about to be married. But mostly he didn't want you to be troubled. 'Tis done now, 'tis done. But you see, miss, although I thank you for your concern an' all you've done, I could never go and live with you, no matter what you could do for the boy. Though it would have been a good chance for both of us. But now, miss, I think you must do what Joe did and keep mum, because if you don't there will be more lives spoilt. What happened was as much my fault as anybody's. I was a stupid, ignorant girl, but as I've come to look at it, God works in a strange way because through it I got Joe, even for a short time, I got Joe. Oh, miss – ' She quickly put the child back into the basket and it was now her turn to support Bridget, saying, 'Sit down, miss, sit down.'

Bridget sat down and, leaning her elbow on the table, she cupped her face in her hands. She felt strangely ill, not only at the revelation that Lionel Filmore was the father of the child lying there in the wash basket, but also by the dreadful feeling of hate that was consuming her at the thought of what he had done to a young girl, a young ignorant working girl. What chance would she have had against such as him? Apart from his pseudo charm and power of persuasion, there was his strength.

'Would you like a cup of tea, miss?'

'Yes. Yes, thank you, Lily. I think I would.'

When Lily went into the scullery she turned slowly and looked down on the infant now lying in the cradle again. This was his son. What would happen if she were to confront him with the knowledge and tell him that such knowledge had put paid to their agreement? She knew what would happen: he would likely lead Victoria one hell of a life. But what would Victoria's response be to the knowledge? Would she leave him? She doubted it. She would likely, as so many other women before her had done, come to accept it as part of a man's privilege during his bachelor state. But, on the other hand, what if she decided to leave him and come back to her? Would she want that? *No. No.*

That was strange thinking; but she wouldn't want Victoria back into her life. Her marrying could be likened to the passing of the responsibility of a daughter on to someone else. Her own life was much freer now, and it would have been over the past months too but for the trauma attached to Joe's imprisonment and his final end.

Well, there was one thing sure already in her mind, she could no longer live within visiting distance of Victoria and listen to her prattling about her coming child. And were he to accompany her at times, as very likely he would, she would not be accountable for her own reactions.

Another thought entering her mind begged an explanation; and she put it to Lily, who had just placed the thick china cup of tea in front of her.

'Did . . . did he know about your condition, Lily?'

'Oh, yes, miss, he knew all right. I . . . I wrote him a letter because I was frightened. I felt me da would turn me out in the street an' it would just be the workhouse for me. So, as I said, I wrote him a letter an' told him where I would be one Sunday. He came on his horse and gave me a bag with five sovereigns in it and said that was that. Then he rode off. And I knew I had no place to put the money, in fact I didn't know what was in the bag, so I dug a hole in the hedge an' hid it there. Then, to tell you the truth, miss, I nearly jumped out of me wits when Joe caught up with me near the factory an' he handed me the bag. Him and Fred had been blackberrying on yon side of the hedge and they heard it all.'

'*Never!*'

'Yes; 'tis true, miss.'

'But Fred knew as well?'

'Oh yes, miss, Fred knew.'

Bridget closed her eyes. Fred had known, the dead man had known. She had believed Joe when he said he hadn't killed him.

She opened her eyes again and looked to where Lily was standing staring down into the fire. 'Joe said straightaway he would marry me. I couldn't believe it an' I didn't love him then, 'cos like the idiot that I was, I was still taken with t'other one. But I quickly grew to love him. Oh aye, aye, I did. He was one in a thousand, was Joe, one in a thousand.'

Bridget rose to her feet, saying now, 'I'll . . . I'll have to go now, Lily. The cab man is waiting. But . . . but I would ask you one thing more. Would you come to live with me if I wasn't living at Milton Place? You see, I have another house in Shields. In fact, it is my real home. I was born there, and I love it. But my father bought Milton Place so we could be nearer the Works and such. But were I to live in Shields permanently, would you come?'

Lily turned from the fire, and after a moment of thought she said, ''Tis very kind of you, miss, but I'll be all right where I am. An' you've been through enough worry because of what's happened. I'll always remember your kindness an' how you tried to save Joe. But . . . but I'll be all right.'

'Well, if you change your mind, Lily, I'll be only too willing to have you and the baby. But in the meantime, you will have this house rent free for as long as you care to live in it. And you will receive a pension that would have been owing to Joe if he had' – she paused – 'lived to earn it.'

'Oh, miss.' Now there were tears in Lily's eyes as she murmured, 'You're a good lady. Joe . . . Joe always said this. And, you know, he once told me that when he was a lad he . . . he had a soft spot for you. It was a great liberty, he knew, but he used to look forward to you comin' into the factory. He had a fight with one of the lads one day because they were chipping him about you. But as he grew older, he said he came to honour you. And he was right to honour you.'

She couldn't bear this; she muttered now, 'Good-bye, Lily. I will call again soon.' Then she went out hurriedly, and gave her address to the cabbie; but, as soon as she had taken her seat and the cab had moved off, she covered her mouth tightly with her hand: he had felt the same way about her as she had about him all those years ago. How strange. How strange. How cruel of fate: but for a class barrier they could have come together and he would have been alive today . . . No, no – she shook her head – that was imagining a fairy-tale coming true, and life was no fairy-tale, it was a period of years, long or short, barricaded by rules and regulations according to the womb in which you were thrust and out of which you were born into a so-called class. And although within the bounds of one class there were variations, nevertheless such internal barriers could be crossed, but never, never, between the ruling classes and the working class. Even in the middle class, where she was placed, such a misalliance would be social death for the woman. A man in this class rarely made the mistake of marrying beneath him; he would take, what was called, a mistress; and, of course, this was acceptable.

Joe had loved her, as a boy he had loved her, but then common sense had taken over.

Damn common sense! Blast common sense! To hell with common sense!

Oh dear God! what was the matter with her? She must get home and have a bath. And . . . and she must talk to someone; she was feeling desperate. But to whom could she talk about this?

She could talk to Andrew.

Yes, and what would he say? 'Cut off the allowance immediately.' And then Victoria would suffer. No, she couldn't do that.

There was Douglas.

Don't be stupid! woman; Douglas is his brother.

So she was stuck with her knowledge; and, what was more, her burning hate of that man.

2

'What do you mean? You're selling this place?'

'Just what I said. I'm selling this place, Milton Place.
I'm going back home to live in my real home, Meadow
House. You know it?'

'Don't talk like that, Bridget. Aren't you well?'

'Of course I am well.'

'You can't be. Why should you sell this place and speak
as you did? Do I know our old home! What is wrong with
you?'

'There is nothing wrong with me, Victoria. I am selling this house; in fact, it is already in the agent's
hands.'

'But . . . but all this beautiful furniture and . . .'

'Oh, I have seen to that. I'm taking most of it back with
me and for the time being storing it in the attics until I get
the old stables at the end of Five Acre Field rebuilt.'

'The stables rebuilt? What on earth for?'

'I'm not sure yet, but perhaps I'll turn them into a
house.'

'You've got something on your mind?'

'Yes. Yes, I have Victoria. I'm going to try to persuade
Lily to bring her child there and live with us. I shall find
her a position and help to educate the boy.'

'But . . . but why on earth should you do this? You've
spent a tremendous amount of money already on the case.
Mr Filmore said it must have cost you in the region of five
hundred pounds if a penny.'

'No doubt, no doubt. Well, if Mr Filmore said that he

must have been discussing the case. Did Lionel discuss it, too?'

'No, no, he didn't. He didn't want anything to do with it. He said it was a sordid affair.'

'Oh, he did, did he? And he doesn't like sordid affairs?'

'There is something wrong with you, Bridget. It's nothing new to me that you don't favour Lionel; but I don't know what's caused you to move all of a sudden. And . . . and what am I going to do for help, I mean when the baby comes? And who am I going to visit?'

Bridget's voice was an absolute bark now as she turned from the dressing table where she had been sitting and rounded on Victoria, crying, 'You're married: you've got a home of your own; your husband has friends. Does he not take you to visit them? Do you not have visitors calling? You broke your neck to marry that man, now he should be all in all to you. There should be no need for you to want to visit me or anyone else.'

Victoria took several steps backwards before she spoke; then in a high voice she exclaimed, 'You're jealous! That's what it is, you're jealous. You haven't got a husband; you haven't had a suitor, no one. You're jealous. Lionel was right. From the beginning he's said that you were of a jealous nature.'

'Lionel said that, did he? And much more, I suppose. Now look, Victoria' – Bridget's voice had dropped into a low flat tone – 'I am busy, or I am about to be busy getting dressed for the evening to go out and into Newcastle to have dinner with . . . a suitor. Now go back and tell your dear Lionel that, will you? And as for yourself, my advice to you is: grow up and face the fact that you're a married woman who is about to become a mother. You are also the mistress of a large house, and I should imagine you'd be happier if you learnt to rule your staff instead of whining about them and what they don't do and what they should do. Now, Victoria, have I made my feelings as plain to you as you have made your feelings plain to me? We are both on different footings now. Recognize that. If you wish to visit me in future, I shall be in Shields.'

'I can't believe it. I just can't believe it. You're cruel. Something has changed you . . . someone has changed you. As I've said before, I think you're ill. And as for taking that girl and her baby, I think you must be mad. But then, people thought you must be, going to all the trouble and the fuss in bringing that advocate from London. And all for a workman in a blacking factory. People were made to wonder, you know. People talk. It's been said you always favoured him.'

'Yes. Yes, you're quite right, Victoria, I always favoured him; but I don't consider that a mistake. I do though consider that I made a great mistake over the years in favouring you and spoiling you. What I should have done after Father died was let you work for your living instead of allowing you to dress up like a doll. Now get out of my sight before I say more things that I'll be sorry for, yes, indeed, I'll be sorry for, and you, too. Get out.'

Victoria actually backed towards the door, her eyes wide, and her mouth opened twice as if she were about to say something more but then thought better of it, and now she scrambled from the room leaving the door wide.

Slowly Bridget walked towards it, and, after closing it, she leant against it, and a full minute passed before she drew herself from its support and returned to the dressing table, where she sat staring at herself in the mirror: her face was flushed red, her eyes looked bright and hard, the green standing out prominently in them as it always did when she was angry. They were now demanding of her reflection, Had she ever thought of Victoria as a loving sister? Yes, she had. Had they ever spent happy years together? Yes, they had. Had she ever been jealous of her?

No, never. Then what had come over them? What had come over them, she now told herself, was that Victoria had fallen in love with a waster, a man who had to be bribed in order to carry out his promise of marrying; and from then nothing had gone right.

She rose from the stool and went to the wardrobe to change her dress to go to Newcastle in order to dine with Mr Kemp, when undoubtedly before, during, and after the meal, business would be discussed, and this would include her latest move.

So much for the suitor.

It was a week later and late on a Saturday evening when Jessie, opening the drawing-room door, said, 'Mr Douglas has called, miss. He would like a word with you.'

Bridget had been on the point of going upstairs to bed and she found herself pausing before she said, 'Show him in.' The pause had not been occasioned by the fact that it was late, nor that she was tired and ready for bed, but because, since the day he had seen her home after her last visit to Joe, he had never called; in fact, this particular visit was the first time she had seen him since her outburst in the carriage, whereas she had expected him, knowing the state she had been in and imagining he would be concerned enough for her, to visit her the next day.

He came in hurriedly, saying, 'I'm . . . I'm sorry, Bridget, to be calling so late but I've just arrived back from Allendale, where I've been for the last five days. I went to see a friend who lives up in the hills. Just a little cottage. We don't see much of each other but . . . but she's a dear person.' At this he stopped, drew in a long breath, then said, 'I'm gabbling on, but I thought I should explain my absence.'

'Five days; but it is some time since I last saw you,

Douglas. I thought you must have been very busy with your work.'

He took a step nearer to her and again he drew in a long breath before speaking: 'I wasn't too busy with my work,' he said. 'There was a reason for my not calling, even though I know I should have, for when I last saw you, you were in distress. But there was a reason, I assure you, and I really am sorry I can't give it to you. For that matter I wonder if I ever shall.'

She was not a little puzzled by his answer, and also that he had a friend, in a little cottage and that she was 'a dear'. He was saying now, 'But enough of me. What is this I'm hearing, that you are leaving this house? Why, Bridget?'

She walked away from him and sat down on the seat she had left only moments before, and, pointing to the couch, she said, 'Sit down, Douglas.' And when he was seated, she tried to answer him: 'Like you, I cannot give an honest or full reason for my actions, but I can tell you this much: I want to house Lily and see that her child is well brought up.'

'Oh! Well yes, I can understand that, and yet only in a way because it isn't Joe's child, and you're doing this for . . . for Joe.'

Why was it, he asked himself now, that he always found it difficult to voice that man's name? He had already implied that he understood her feelings for the man, but he still couldn't fully accept the fact that she could have fallen in love with one of her own workmen, one who had apparently worked in the blacking factory since he was a child, because she had a dignity about her. She always appeared to be a superior person, unmistakably class. And so he was surprised now when she said harshly, 'I know it wasn't Joe's child, but it was someone's, wasn't it?'

'Yes, it was someone's. He apparently knew who the father was but he wouldn't say.'

'No, he didn't say because he didn't want to hurt anyone.'

'What do you mean?'

'Just what I say, Douglas: Joe didn't want to hurt anyone. If he had named the man he would indeed have hurt a number of people. As he saw it, and as I thought I also saw it, it wouldn't have done his case any good. Yet, I don't know.'

As she turned from him, he came back at her harshly, saying, 'Well, as I see it now, you know much more about the matter than you did earlier. Has his wife confided in you?'

'Perhaps.'

'Oh, Bridget' – he turned his head to the side – 'she has, or she hasn't; perhaps means she has. But even so, I cannot imagine how the revelation, even if it had come earlier, could have hurt anyone outside . . . well, their own circle.'

'Oh, you can't, can you not? So you think it is impossible for a girl to be seduced by anyone outside, what you call, her own circle? If that's the case you must be very naive about the facts of life.'

He laughed. 'I'm a very naive fellow altogether,' he said. 'I should have thought you had found that out by now: I believe everything I'm told.'

'Oh yes' – she nodded her head vigorously – 'I know that.' Then she went on, 'Well, you can believe this. I'll be very glad to leave this house and this district. I've never felt at home here. My home is in Shields, and that's where I'm going.'

She continued to look at him, waiting for some response, and when none was forthcoming, her manner changing and her voice soft now, she said, 'The only thing I'll miss, Douglas, will be your visits.'

'Oh, shall I not be allowed to visit you in Shields?'

'Of course, of course, but . . . but the distance, it's more than a ten-minute canter.'

'Well, there are still the trains and the horse bus and, lastly, my legs.'

She smiled now at him as she said, 'You'll be very welcome any time, because, of all the people I've met since we've lived here, you are the only one I can call friend.'

'That's good to know, Bridget. But I think you could have made many more friends, at least from our house, if you had given them the chance. Father, you know, is quite fond of you. He admires you tremendously. And Lionel . . . well, I feel he would have been only too pleased to call in with Victoria if . . .'

Not only was he startled by her response but her reaction startled herself, for she actually shouted at him, 'Make a friend of him! Don't you mention his name to me. That man . . . that man! he's the reason . . .' Her hand was on her throat now, checking the flow that had been vehement.

As Douglas in some amazement watched her struggling for breath, his thoughts were leaping back over the conversation that had passed between them since he had entered the room. He knew, of course, and with reason that she didn't like Lionel; and who would, when she had practically to pay him, no, not practically, actually pay him to marry her cousin in order to keep that feather-brained girl happy? But she had scarcely met him since. Yet a moment ago she had been enraged at the mention of his name. Why? As if working at a jigsaw, his mind began picking up pieces of conversation that had passed between them. It ranged over the reasons she had given for leaving the house, and then the defence of that girl and her baby. Then it stopped, as he recalled her attitude when she had suggested that the girl had been seduced not by one of her own class but . . .

She had turned from him, and her head hanging now she muttered an apology, 'I'm sorry. I'm sorry. It's inexcusable. I . . .'

When one hand came on her shoulders and the other lifted up her chin and he said, 'Look at me, Bridget, and go on from where you stopped in your tirade.'

'It was nothing. I didn't mean . . . I just . . . Well, you know I don't care for your . . . your brother.'

'Yes, I know you don't care for him. But dislike and hating are two different things and, coming on top of our conversation, I'm going to ask you a straight question, and it is this: was Lionel responsible for this girl's condition?'

She looked into his eyes. The expression in them was one she hadn't seen before: there was no trace of kindness or humour or the critical enquiry that sometimes accompanied a question; the look in them now made her feel afraid of imparting the truth. Yet, she knew that the truth had already pierced his mind, and so, for answer she muttered, 'Yes, he was.'

He withdrew his hands from her and stepped aside while his gaze still remained on her, then turned away and stood at the head of the couch with his back to her. His body was straight and taut and he appeared to her at this moment to have put inches on to his height. She was suddenly full of concern at the outcome of what she had inadvertently revealed to him. Going quickly to him, she said, 'Please, Douglas, will you consider this just as something between us two? If you don't, there's going to be more unhappiness.'

When he didn't answer, she went on talking, quickly now, almost at a gabble. 'She wouldn't have told me . . . I mean Lily, but I offered to bring her here, and the child, and to take care of them. And her response to this was much the same as mine a few minutes ago: she knew if she were to come and live here she would, some day, come face to face with him. Then there was the child, his child. And you can see now that this is why Joe kept quiet because the revelation would certainly have put an end to Victoria's engagement, as it was then.'

When still he didn't answer, she began to plead: 'Please, Douglas, I don't want to hurt her. We have fallen out. She is really unhappy; she hasn't settled into your home. Please.'

'*All right. All right.*' He was patting her hand in a way that showed his own agitation. And he added now, 'I'll promise you that she won't be hurt; but I must face him with it. And to think' – he now put his hand to his head – 'they discussed it at the table . . . well, at least Father did when the man was hanged. And the conclusion he came to, as did others who were there, was that the child was his brother's, and that's why he had killed him. And everybody thinks the same.'

'Everybody?'

'Well, that was the opinion that was going around during the trial when he wouldn't say who the father of the child was. And then there was that barrister. He led up to it, likely thinking it would create sympathy for the man.' There was a pause in his speaking; then, looking at her intently, he asked, 'Why should he kill his brother if that wasn't the case?'

'He didn't kill him. I'm more sure of that now. At one time I began to think, too, that if it was his brother, there was the reason for his action. But now I know . . . I know he didn't kill him. His last words to me were that he was innocent. He had never done this thing. I told you.'

Douglas walked away from her and picked up his hat which he had laid on a chair, before turning to her again and asking, 'When are you leaving here?'

'A prospective buyer is coming tomorrow to view, but in any case I am taking most of the good furniture down to the other house, and storing it. I have plans for rebuilding some old barns. But until this place is sold, Jessie and Danny will remain to see to things. In the meantime the rest of my small staff will come with me.'

'Oh.' He paused and stared at her for a time, then went on, 'In case I don't see you again before you leave, will you give me your address?'

'Yes. Yes, of course,' she said. 'It is called Meadow House. It is on the Sunderland road out of Shields. Just beyond Harton village there's a bridle path. We're a little way along: there's a sign indicating the house, you can't miss it. You . . . you could get a cab from the station.' She held out her hand to him. 'I hope you will come.'

'Oh, I'll come. Never fear of that, I'll come.' He almost added, 'If it's only to tell you I've killed my brother,' for at the moment that was how he was feeling.

As he turned away from her and went hurriedly from the room and out onto the drive, where he mounted his horse, he asked himself why he should be feeling so furious, for he had always known that Lionel had played around, with little discrimination in his choice. That, of course, was before he became enamoured of Elizabeth Porter, an attachment that had gone on for some time, likely because of the little risk attached to it, as her husband was still in India. He would still have been seeing her when he gave that girl the child. It must have been about that time, too, when he cast his sights on what he imagined was the rich Miss Victoria Mordaunt.

And that fellow Joe had kept quiet about the whole affair in order not to hurt Bridget or her dear cousin, who was then so shortly to be Lionel's bride. However, as Bridget had said, it really had nothing to do with Joe's case.

Of a sudden he pulled his horse to a stop, and the action must have brought his thinking to a similar state, for the thought that had just a moment before presented itself to him had now fled, and the harder he tried to recall it the further it receded into the distance. The only part of it that was left was something to do with a horse. It was as though he had just woken from a dream.

He jerked the reins again and walked his horse for the remainder of the distance to the house.

After stabling it, he was making his way across the yard to his workshop for there, in the presence of the stone, he always felt relaxed and at peace, and he must calm his inner feelings before he met up with his brother; but this was denied him, for there, coming out of the tack room, was Lionel himself.

They would have passed, without greetings, within a few yards of each other, but Douglas looked towards Lionel and said, without preamble, 'I want to speak to you.'

'What?'

'I want to speak to you.'

'Oh, you do, do you?'

As Douglas moved on towards the end of the buildings he felt that Lionel must have remained standing where he was, and so he turned and said, 'This is important.'

'So is my desire for food at the moment; I have been out all day. If you want to speak to me you'll find me in the dining-room,' and Lionel made to turn away, only to be checked by Douglas, retorting, 'I shouldn't think you'd like to hear what I've got to say in the dining-room. Exposures are never pleasant.'

Lionel's head jerked to the side as if he were looking around the yard to make sure there was no one who could have been within hearing distance; then it seemed he had to make an effort to step forward and follow Douglas, although not immediately, into the now dim workshop. He stood within the doorway waiting for his brother to light a lamp. When, presently, the long low room was illuminated he slowly stepped forward and closed the doors behind him, before moving towards where Douglas was standing near a long bench on whose battered top lay a number of mallets and chisels.

He stopped within a couple of yards of him, but he didn't speak. And when Douglas said grimly, 'You are a rotter, a really beastly individual. You know that?' he winced; then his voice scarcely above a whisper, he said, 'What d'you mean to do?' And Douglas answered, 'There's nothing I can do. The girl bore your son, and her husband knew who the father was, but he went to his end keeping silent about it so that Bridget wouldn't be troubled and hurt by the fact that her cousin was marrying his wife's seducer.'

Douglas now watched Lionel's head droop towards his chest and his shoulders actually begin to shake. He saw him glance along the bench towards an upturned box, then go to it and flop down onto it. And when he placed his elbows on the rough bench and dropped his face onto his hands, his whole attitude assuming one of distress, Douglas's feelings towards him almost turned a somersault, and his next words were spoken quietly: 'Well, it's over and done with,' he said; 'Bridget is going to see to her and educate the boy.'

But almost in the next instant his attitude changed again, to amazement now, as Lionel looked up, his face crinkled with laughter, a gurgle in his voice, as he said, 'You are a funny fellow, Doug. You really don't belong in this time. You would do well up in Victoria's court, you would really. So I have a bastard son? My dear fellow – ' He now rose to his feet, and he actually squared his shoulders as he said, 'That's the only one I know of; but the county, in fact the whole country's dotted with 'em. Not mine, of course, not mine.' His row of even white teeth were gleaming in the lamplight, and as Douglas stared at him they seemed to grow longer and become fangs.

He watched him now take a handkerchief and wipe the sweat from his brow, and the smile seeming not to have left his face, he said, 'What's your next move, brother? Do you intend to inform Victoria of my vileness?'

Douglas found he had to force himself to speak. 'No. She'll find that out for herself before long, I'm sure,' he said. 'Likely at the same time as she learns you had to be paid to marry her.'

The smile slowly faded from Lionel's face, and his changed feelings were further emphasised in his voice, low now, as he ground out, 'Well, let me tell you something, brother. I'm having to earn that every day. And I wouldn't care if it was made known to her tomorrow. My God! What I'd like to do at this minute is to knock you flat on your skinny back.'

At this Douglas stepped forward and his voice, too, registered his feelings as he growled, 'Then why don't you try? You'd be in for a surprise, because you're nothing but flab and wind. Your paunch will soon be like Father's. My skinny back, you say. Well, my skinny arms are flint-hard from working with that!' And he thrust his arm out towards a lump of stone. 'So, come on. Have a try. I challenge you. There's nothing more *I'd like to do* at this moment but to drive my fist into your face and my knee into your pot belly.'

'Huh!' There was scorn in the sound, yet Lionel did not attempt to step forward; but it was evident that his brother's remarks had struck home, for he seemed to gain height as he pulled his stomach in and thrust his shoulders back before turning away and marching out of the building.

Douglas stood where he was for a moment; then he

turned and, going to the bench, he lifted up a mallet and began to beat it on the wood, just small taps as if he were applying it to a chisel; and all the while his mind was groping again at that distant something that was troubling him.

When, presently, his groping conjured up his brother's face that only a few minutes before had blanched, he asked himself why it should have when seconds later he had shaken with laughter, and that laughter had conveyed relief. But from what? Had he expected to be accused of something else besides giving the child to that girl?

He laid the mallet aside and slowly walked to the door, but there he stopped. He should go into supper, but he couldn't tolerate the thought of sitting opposite his brother, or listening to his father entertaining Victoria with anecdotes that would become more risqué with each glass of wine he consumed, and listening to Victoria's giggles when she wouldn't really be aware of the meaning of the innuendoes.

However, he knew his absence from the supper table wouldn't be questioned, for he often worked late, and so he took the back staircase that gave on to the end of the gallery, then made for his bedroom. There, he sat by his window for some time, but try as he might he could not get his mind to reveal that something that was troubling him.

3

He dismissed the cabbie at the gates of Meadow House, telling him not to wait as he didn't know what time he would be returning. And he pushed open the iron gates and glanced towards the small lodge to the right of him before going on up the drive. He had walked about forty yards up the slightly curving tree-bordered drive to a sharper curve, almost a bend; and there was the house. It lay beyond a wide lawn, bordered on each side by a grassy bank. The house itself was tall and appeared narrow. There was no symmetry about it. To the right side of it three windows seemed to top each other, the last one disappearing under the eaves; to the left side of the door there was a blankness. The only redeeming feature of the house at this moment seemed to be its stone, which was a creamy-yellow.

There was a wide opening between the end of the house and the grassy bank, and he only just glimpsed that this led into a courtyard. The front door was of plain black oak, with a bell-pull to the side.

He rang the bell twice before he heard a scurrying behind the door. And then it was pulled open, and there was Florrie McLean beaming at him, saying, 'Why! Mr Douglas. How nice to see you. Come on in by. Come on in.'

After saying, 'Good-day, Florrie,' he stepped past her into what appeared a very narrow hallway and waited. Having closed the door, Florrie now pushed open another that was already ajar, and he again passed her and almost stopped in surprise, for he was now in a short panelled corridor which led into a hall. This, too, was panelled, as far as he could make out, from floor to ceiling.

'Oh, come an' take a seat, sir. Look, I'll send for miss. She's down at the old stables. They're doin' them up, you know. Come in the sitting room and bide there. I won't be a minute. She'll be delighted to see you. The fire is ablaze; it's lovely and warm in here.'

Again he was passing her and again he almost stopped in surprise as Florrie pointed down the long room, saying, 'Make yourself comfortable, sir. I'll be back in two shakes of a lamb's tail.'

He was walking up the room now, smiling, and his eyes roaming from side to side. His view of the front of the house had certainly not kindled his imagination to assume the interior might be anything like this. The room was bright with colour, and strangely unfussy. The mantel-shelf, he noticed at once, did not bear a fringed velvet border. There were no antimacassars on the chair backs. The chesterfield fronting the fire was covered with a chintz-patterned cover, as were the two big armchairs set one at each side of the large open fireplace, in which he became immediately interested because the surround was made of carved stone.

He now stood with his back to the fire and gazed about him. The walls were covered in an embossed paper; it was colourful but subdued, as was the carpet. He looked down at the carpet. It may have been a bright red at one time, patterned with bouquets of flowers, but now, like the rest of the room, it was subdued with wear. Right opposite him on the far wall was a Davenport. This writing desk was the only evidence of the usual finicky lady's touch in the room. On each side of it was a china cabinet and by the glint over this distance one was holding coloured glasses. There were a few occasional tables, and a sofa table at the head of the couch, but none was cluttered with knick-knacks. On one was a large bowl of coloured leaves, no flowers among them. He looked towards the door, waiting for her entrance. But after a moment he left the rug and walked further up the room to where the ceiling gave way to a narrow arch supported by columns. Beyond was what looked like a huge alcove, for in it was placed a grand piano and a number of chairs, and beyond these the whole length of the wall was taken up with an enormous window. Slowly now he walked to the window, and his surprise grew, for he was looking on to a set garden, some of the beds still showing late roses, others cleared for the winter. Putting his head closer to the window now he looked along to what appeared to be the real front of the house, and from what he could glimpse it stretched some good distance away.

He started back when the door opened and Bridget's voice said, 'Oh, hello. I'm sorry I wasn't here.' She came forward to him, her hand outstretched, and he took it and the first thing he said was, 'What a remarkable and beautiful home you have here, Bridget.'

'It isn't bad.' She was smiling broadly at him. 'I must show you round. Come and sit down; I've ordered tea. Why didn't you let me know you were coming?'

'Oh, there are many reasons I could give you and all would be lies. But what isn't a lie is, I've been very busy. I've . . . well, I could say' – he now struck a pose – 'I'm a business man. Like yourself, I'm in business: I have taken on a mason, besides the boy I already had. He is a retired man, at least forced into retirement because of lack of employment. But he's a very good man with his hands, and what is more he has got a good head and he has put me wise as to how to go about selling my wares.'

'Oh, I'm so glad, Douglas. And it's wonderful to have an occupation. But come and sit down.'

They were sitting side by side on the couch and she was looking at him, and there was a tender note in her voice as she said, 'Oh, I am pleased to see you, Douglas. It's awful to admit . . . well, not awful, but it's strange for me to say that I have no one to talk to. Yet I am among people all day either in the house or out of it, but having said that I really have no one to whom I can talk.'

He gazed at her in silence for a long moment before he said, 'You don't need to try to explain that feeling to me, Bridget, for I think I was born with it: I cannot remember ever being able to talk to anyone in that house of ours. Right from a child I was told to be polite to the staff, but, and you may not believe this, but my Mama once said to me, "You must not talk to the staff, Douglas, as if they were ordinary people. They are not. God has seen fit to make them lesser mortals. To a degree you are expected to be considerate, but you mustn't talk to them as if they were intelligent beings. All that is required of you is to be polite, correctly polite." '

When Bridget said nothing to this, although her eyes widened and her mouth fell slightly apart, he nodded at her and said, 'Oh, yes, that was Mama. As for Papa and Lionel, and my two uncles who are long since dead, and cousins from my Mama's side who would visit us now and again, should I speak to any of them what was in my mind, as I once did — ' He wagged his head now before, adopting a childish voice, he said, 'I heard a blackbird singing today. It sang four notes of a Beethoven Sonata. This was received by one of my cousins with, "I think you should look out for that one, Will; his brains are as undersized as his body. You'll have trouble there, mark my words. If I had him I know what I would do with him." '

Douglas started to laugh now, saying, 'Oh, yes, I know what Uncle Herbert would have done with me. He had a farm up in Scotland. He couldn't keep his staff, I would have been put to see to the pigs.'

Bridget, too, laughed now as she said, 'Well, don't forget that was what Claudius did before he became Emperor of Rome. Oh, here's tea.'

When Mary Benny came in, pushing a tea trolley, and Florrie carrying a large silver tray, made more heavy with a silver tea service, Douglas rose to his feet and, taking the tray from Florrie, said, 'Where do you want it?'

'It would be a good idea to put it on the table, sir.'

There was laughter all round at this, and the girls were still laughing as they hurried from the room.

It was as Bridget was pouring the tea, she said to him, 'What would your mother have made of that pair?'

'Oh, that the devil had entered into them. He would have been made the culprit, daring them not only to speak as they did, but also to speak before they were spoken to. Out of the gates they would have gone with their bundles, quick march, and without a reference.'

'Well, thank God, times have changed. And they're changing fast in all ways, don't you think?'

'Yes, but not fast enough.' He looked down at the cup and saucer in his hand and into the steaming tea as he said now, 'I wish I was clever. I wish I had brains. I wish I was tall and forceful. I wish all things that are impossible, all those things that would mean I could make myself felt: get into Parliament and force them to right the wrongs that I see every time I go into a town, or pass a factory. But what am I saddled with? A mass of frustrations because I have none of these things that I wish for.'

'Mr Disraeli was a very small man. He had also the disadvantage of being a Jew, yet he was the favourite of the Queen.'

'Oh, Bridget, you are so practical, so down to earth. You are trying to tell me that if I liked I could have risen above my obstacles. But no, dear, I couldn't, because I know my capabilities. I have a grasshopper mind. It only seems to rest, or come to a standstill, when I take a mallet in my hand and beg the stone to show its heart and to guide me to chip out a hand, or the curve of an arm, or better still, the soft cheeks of a child.'

'Here' – she pushed a plate of sandwiches towards him – 'there's fresh salmon in them. Now, while you're eating, let me tell you, Douglas Filmore, that you are a fraud, because you know that you are a highly intelligent individual, you know that you bring poetry out of stone, and not only out of stone, you put it into words, and here you are, sitting there trying to get me to sympathise with you because you're not tall, because you cannot get into Parliament and talk the ears off a donkey and at the end of it will have said nothing.'

Douglas had taken a bite of the sandwich and now he had to press his hand tight across his mouth because he was about to splutter it out. When he finally managed to swallow it his shoulders were shaking and his eyes were wet, and with suppressed laughter still in his voice he was able to say, 'Oh, Bridget, you do me good. And you're so right. I wasn't playing on your sympathy, though, but only trying to make you understand I knew how you felt with regard to feeling alone. I know it's an awful thing to say, but a few years ago I had come to the conclusion that I preferred animals to people; for instance Gippo. I talk and mutter to him by the hour when I'm working.' In answer to the look of enquiry on her face, he explained, 'Gippo's my dog, he's a mongrel, a cross between an Airedale and a Labrador. I don't know which end of him belongs to which. But I'm sure that animal understands every word I say. I know for sure he understands my moods. He is nine now and I dread the time when he'll be no more. He was the runt of a litter and I saved him from the water tank. One of the men was taking him across the yard by the scruff of the neck and he was yelping, and when I stopped him the little beast put its fore paws out and clawed towards me, and that was that.'

They had almost finished their tea when she asked quietly, 'Did you say anything to your brother . . . about the matter we discussed before I moved?'

'Oh, yes, yes, I said something to him all right.'

He was looking towards the fire, and after waiting longer than she could stand for him to enlarge on the something, she said sharply, 'Well, what did he say? What was his reaction?'

He turned and looked at her and replied quietly, 'I don't really know. I'm puzzled by it still. At first when I tackled him he seemed concerned; in fact his face drained of colour. Then when I accused him of taking down an innocent working girl, he almost laughed, and he treated the matter so lightly that I got flaming mad. One thing led to another so that we almost came to blows . . . Oh, don't look so surprised, Bridget; he would have come off second best, I can assure you. My size and slimness is very deceptive, I'm really quite strong. There are, you know, such things as lightweight boxers.' He smiled at her. 'But . . .'

'Yes, but?' She prompted him now.

'Well, I don't know how to put this, but there's something troubling me, something I am trying to recall but yet don't want to recall.'

'Is it anything to do with Joe or Lily, or the baby?'

'I . . . I don't know. And by the way, from what Victoria said yesterday, I understand that you have taken the girl and the baby under your care. She didn't seem at all pleased.'

'No, I know that. But then it's got nothing to do with her.'

'Are they here, in the house?'

'Oh, no, no. They are down in the lodge. You would pass it at the entrance to the drive. It's only a very small place, a kitchen-cum-living-room and two bedrooms. But she's happy to be there. She comes up and helps in the kitchen and brings the baby with her.' She smiled now. 'That was another thing: I had to put it to my small retinue whether they would accept her . . . well, make a place for her among them. They've all been with me for a long time, you know, Jessie, and Danny, and Peggie the cook, and my two merry maids, Mary and Florrie. They work happily together and I didn't want to spoil that. But they were in sympathy with my suggestion, not that she should live in the house but that she should make her quarters down in the lodge. It used to be Jimmy Tierney's quarters. He helps Frank Matthews do the gardens, you know. He also helps Johnnie Moran, who is the yard man. So Jimmy didn't mind moving his quarters to the rooms above the stables. I've made them quite comfortable for him. I told him that he can go back into the lodge later, once I get the old farmhouse and the barn rebuilt. These are some buildings at the bottom of the field. You'd be interested in them, the walls are two feet thick. Once I get them done I'll fit them up for Lily and the child. And you know something, Douglas Filmore . . . that baby boy is your nephew, legitimate or not.'

'Oh, you don't have to remind me of that, Bridget. I've thought of that for some time now and felt something should be done for him and his mother. Yet, what could I do? But then there was you, you were doing everything you possibly could. It was as if the tables were turned and it was your nephew.' He paused before adding, 'And the fact that it wasn't even Joe's child and you're doing all this is something so admirable that I can't find words to express what . . . .'

'Well, don't try, Douglas, just don't try. I don't need any thanks. I don't feel I'm doing anything other than what another thinking person would do for the widow of one of her valued employees. Look at it like that, will you? Well then, have you had enough to eat?'

'More than enough. And now there is something I would like to do.'

'What is that?'

'I would like to see the rest of the house and this old place that has stone that might interest me, as you said.'

'Well, what's stopping us?' She rose from the couch and he with her. 'Where shall we start? By the way – ' She spread out her hand towards the window and the gardens beyond, saying, 'That part is really the front of the house. You come in by the side wall, a very odd arrangement. The entrance isn't attractive at all. Well now' – she was walking into the hall – 'I understand the house was built over a hundred years ago by a shipowner. It was the only one of its kind in this part of the county at that time, and being who he was he had all this mahogany brought in. Hence the hall here and the passages, and the staircase' – she now pointed to the broad spiral staircase – 'were all panelled. Upstairs, too; wherever he could stick wood on the walls that's what he did. The dining-room, also, is panelled. Here it is.' She had turned to her right and was opening a door, and again he felt compelled just to stand and gaze about him; and his voice was full of admiration when he said, 'It's beautiful, really beautiful. And the furniture, too, really beautiful.'

'Yes. Yes, it is; but I find it a little heavy, for it's difficult to bring colour into rooms that are panelled. They all have a certain austereness, a certain dignity that says: Now don't play about with me.'

She smiled at him now before turning and walking out into the hall again. Here, pointing to the end of it, she said, 'That door leads into the kitchen and beyond the kitchen are six rooms in all: Danny's and Jessie's bedroom and sitting room, and the girls' rooms. And, of course, Peggy's. They each have a room to themselves; the other one used to be called the wine cellar. We now use it mainly for storing hams and such. I understand the racks in it were packed from floor to ceiling when the first owner was alive. But Father wasn't a heavy drinker, so our wine cellar was nearly always bare, except for occasions. I'll show you that part later. But over here – ' She now crossed the hall to a corridor and, opening the first door, she said, 'This is the breakfast room. How he missed panelling this one I'll never know. We use it mostly for eating in; in fact, I use it all the time for eating, breakfast, dinner, and supper, because after Father died I found no need to entertain.'

He had gone quickly to the window now and stood viewing another aspect of the garden: 'It's an amazing house,' he said. 'How much land have you?'

'About six acres, that is besides the field where the stables and the old farmhouse stand.'

Out in the corridor again, she opened another door, saying, 'This is my study.'

'Oh yes? Yes, it is a compact library. I'm sure you have more books in here than they have back at the house.'

'Yes, there are a great number, but I'm afraid I've only managed to read a smattering of them here and there. My grandfather, you know, collected books, not I'm afraid for the knowledge or the entertainment they might have afforded him but for the bindings.' She laughed as she pointed to the rows and rows of leather-bound volumes, saying, 'He wanted them to match the panelling.'

He was looking at her desk now and from there to the

two tall wooden filing cabinets set in the wall, one at each side of a fireplace in which a fire was burning brightly, and he said, 'This is where you conduct all your business?'

'No, not really. That is done at the office in Newcastle. I merely keep a finger on it here, and – ' She pulled a small face now, saying, 'I don't always work in here, I must confess, because I find it so relaxing. I often sit there' – she pointed to a big leather armchair – 'And read. Oh' – she again pulled a face – 'and fall asleep and waken up to Jessie's saying, "Now come on out of that and to your bed, miss." '

He hadn't laughed as she mimicked Jessie's voice, but, his face straight and in a quiet tone, he commented, 'You are so fortunate, aren't you? What troubles you have in life you have picked them up, sort of gathered them to yourself, such as Victoria, and Joe, and Lily and her child. Yet, you needn't have done any of these things, you could have stayed happily in this haven and led the life it suggests, peace and tranquillity, entertaining friends, and using your money to spread largesse, sometimes even in a way that wouldn't touch your emotions.'

'You are actually saying, Douglas, that I go out and seek trouble and bring it on myself?'

'Yes, I suppose that's what I'm saying, more or less; and at the same time you are so lucky to have this house, this atmosphere. Yes, that's what I mean, atmosphere, in which to hide and heal your sores.'

'You are not being very kind, Douglas.'

'Oh, my dear Bridget, I am not meaning to be unkind; I'm just trying to tell you that this is a beautiful home. And now I'll add to that by asking why on earth you had to take Milton Place. It was a fine house, oh yes, but so like many others one visits.'

'I didn't take Milton Place, Father did, for reasons I think I've told you before. But I also have a sneaking feeling he thought we girls, as he called us, would have more opportunity of meeting eligible young men in that part of the county, and especially, I think he was more concerned to get Victoria married off than me. He looked upon me as a companion, but I really believe if I had met anyone at that time, and there had been a mutual attraction, he would have made it difficult for me to leave him. He was a lonely man; he had depended on my mother, and then when she died I took her place; then of course' – she paused – 'when he died I was adrift. Yet' – she laughed now – 'I needn't have been, you know, because during that first year I had a number of suitors, mostly gentlemen well set in years who seemed willing to overlook this young, nondescript individual who dressed outrageously when on a horse, and had no sense of fashion when off one; but for each of them I had something that would compensate for all my drawbacks, my coffers were pretty full. Such was my reception of these gentlemen, however, that they thought the game wasn't worth . . . the candle, as they say. After all, they wanted to end their lives in peace.'

He actually put out his hand and pushed her as he laughed and said, 'You are the most ridiculous person, Bridget . . . I mean your ideas of yourself. But at this moment I'm not going to contradict a word you've said, because you'd only pooh-pooh anything that dared suggest a compliment.'

As he stood looking at her he wondered yet again how it was that she had come to love that man Joe. Had it been through pity? Or was it something in the boy that first touched her girlish heart, the boy who'd had to earn his living by scampering round that blacking factory at the beck and call of whoever wanted him? Or was it admiration for how he had worked himself up to the position of second foreman, but not to manager? No; he felt sure it was her love for him that had lifted the man this final step.

If he were to say to her now, 'I love you, Bridget. I'm not going to ask you to marry me because I've got nothing to offer you, but I want you to know I love you,' what would she say? Would she have pity on him? Oh no; he wouldn't want that. No; there was nothing in him that desired the love bred out of pity. He looked at her hair. He imagined it flowing over her shoulders; it was so abundant it must reach her waist. He could see himself putting his hands into it and bringing it to his face.

'What is it? Something on my hair?'

'Oh, no, no. I . . . I was just thinking you . . . you have beautiful hair.'

'Yes. Yes, I know I have, Douglas, and it's about all I do have. And I also know you are the kindest person one could meet in a long day's walk. Father used to use that expression: He's the most honest man you could meet in a long day's walk, he would say. And I repeat, you are the kindest person that one could hope to meet in that long day's walk. And now' – her voice suddenly changed – 'having said that, I'm going to conduct you, Mr Filmore, to see something that I know you admire very much: stone.' She bent slightly towards him before turning and walking out of the room and into the corridor again where she pointed first to one door, saying, 'That room was Victoria's sewing room. She was very good, you know, at making some parts of her attire. And that one' – she now indicated the door opposite – 'is what we used to call the games room. Father and his friends used to play cards there one particular night in the week; on others, he played with Victoria and me. I'll show you round upstairs when we come back because the light will soon be going. Let me put a coat on because it's chilly.' Then turning to him, she remarked, 'You didn't have an overcoat on?'

'No. I rarely feel the cold.' He didn't know why he should lie about this.

'Well, all I can say is you're lucky; I'm a shivery person.'

She went to the side of the staircase now and opened what appeared to be the door of a cupboard and from which she took out a coat with a hood attached; and as he helped her into it she said, 'We'll go through the kitchen way.'

Peggie the cook was standing at the table pounding a large lump of dough and she greeted him with, 'Good-afternoon, sir. An' I would wrap up well, miss. Keep that hood tight; the wind'll go through you.'

He stopped at the table and looked down at the dough, saying, 'I love the smell of yeasty bread. How many loaves will you get out of that?'

Peggie Nixon had stopped her kneading and her face was bright as she answered, 'Four big 'uns, sir, two small and ten buns.'

'All that?'

'Well, sir, when it's risen like it'll be twice its size.'

'Oh, yes, of course, when it rises. Yes, of course.' He looked about him: 'You've got a splendid kitchen.'

Peggie had glanced at Bridget and her smile was broad as she said, 'Aye, sir. An' I've been in it forty-two years come next Saturday. I started when I was eight.'

'Is that a fact?' He looked at Bridget enquiringly now, and she said, 'Yes. Peggie came when mother was a very young woman, before she married. And' – she laughed now – 'when I was born, she was so excited that she almost sent me straightaway into another world. She had brought up a large can of hot water for the nurse and apparently had one eye on me and she tripped, and away she went! and the water and the can just missed me.'

Peggie's whole body was shaking with laughter and it seemed she now thumped the dough as she said, 'The doctor swore at me. And Jessie, who was chambermaid at the time, took me by the scruff of the neck and almost threw me downstairs, an' me twice as big as her, an' older.'

Bridget quite naturally put her hand on Peggie's shoulder as she passed her, and Douglas smiled widely as he said, 'Good-bye, Peggie.'

'Good-bye, sir. Good-bye. 'Tis good to have a laugh, isn't it?'

He paused and looked back at her and agreed: 'Yes, indeed, Peggie, it is good to have a laugh.'

Outside in the courtyard he pointed across to the building, saying, 'That's good stone there, too. You have three horse boxes?'

'Yes, but only two horses. We don't often use the coach. So, there's one for the trap and the other is my Hamlet.'

They walked on down the yard, past a row of outhouses to where a gateway in a stone wall led into a long vegetable garden. After skirting this and passing through a small copse, there before them lay a large field in which the two horses were grazing and at the far side was what looked like a jumble of old buildings. As they crossed the field she remarked, 'Most of this land is only fit for grazing, there's so much stone just under the surface.' She turned her head towards him, saying, 'You would have a field day here digging it all up.'

'Well, it would depend on what kind of stone it is,' he said. But then, as they neared the buildings, he exclaimed, 'If it was anything like that, oh yes.' And standing in front of what had been a large barn he exclaimed, 'Oh, yes, it's beautiful stone. I wonder where this came from. Which is the nearest quarry?'

She made a deprecating sound in her throat as she said, 'Don't ask me, because I have no idea. Stone hasn't been one of my interests. But come inside and see what the men have done.'

Inside the barn she pointed upwards, saying, 'They've re-roofed it in the original style. I got them to do the roofs first to keep the wet out and to get rid of the rotten timbers.'

'Wonderful,' he said. 'And look at the size of it. And this wall' — he now stretched his hands out — 'it's over three feet thick. And the pointing is still good. They certainly knew how to build walls. Do you know the age of this place, then?'

'Yes, I do. Mother's people purchased it after the farmer left during one of the depressions and his name was Mr Price. And, poor man, he was paid a hundred and twenty pounds for his house, this amazing barn and the stables and outhouses attached. This was in eighteen twenty-three. The farm had been built eight years earlier, so the deeds tell us.'

'And what are you going to do with it when it's all renovated?'

'Well, as I told you, I'm hoping to put Lily and her boy into the house. It has only five rooms. It looks much larger than it really is.'

'You didn't tell me why she changed her mind and decided to accept your kind protection.'

'Oh, her father and the priest helped me there. Her father came and upbraided her, saying to the effect, what else could she expect by marrying a Protestant. And he brought the priest who told her that she must return to her religious duties or else she would be damned, or again words to that effect. And the child must be christened in the church; that it had already been christened didn't seem to matter. Nor was her marriage valid, for it had been officiated in a Registry Office, which the Catholic Church didn't recognise. So, in the eyes of the priest she had not only an illegitimate child but she had been living with a man in sin. She was very distressed. She wrote me a note and asked me to go and see her. So there and then I bundled her and the child back here . . . What did you say?'

'I said, God help the boy.'

'Well' – her voice was stiff – 'He will help him, I hope, through me.'

'I don't mean that, Bridget. I mean, in years to come when he learns who sired him and what kind of a man he is.'

'I don't look that far ahead, Douglas. I can only see him having a happy childhood, as far as that is possible, and beyond that, then benefiting from a good education.'

'Well, all I can say to that, my dear Bridget, is, I hope he grows to revere the person who has made all that possible.'

'Oh, come on if you want to see the rest of the place, because the light will soon be gone.'

'Yes,' he said, 'and I'll have to be gone soon, too. I've got to get back to the station.'

'If you will deign to ride in the trap, Danny will take you to the station.'

'Much obliged, ma'am. Much obliged.' He raised his hat slightly at her. And for answer she said, 'Well I'm glad you appreciate the kindness, sir.'

They were in the farmhouse now. What had once been the living room was flagstoned; and, too, there was an open hearth with a rusty spit leaning now drunkenly against one side of the chimney wall, and an equally rusty chain was dangling from somewhere up above.

Bridget pointed to an open door leading into another room, saying, 'That's the sitting-room, but as they say, it's not big enough to swing a cat in. They must have lived close together to keep warm in those days, I think. That's a similar room,' she pointed to another door, 'and two rooms up above. But I shouldn't risk the stairs; one of the workmen has already been through the top stair. But again look at the inner walls, they're the same as the outside ones. If they hadn't made them so thick there would have been much more room to move.'

'Yet it could be quite cosy, I should think.'

'Yes, I suppose so.' She nodded now as she looked around the small room and commented, 'That's if you hadn't many knick-knacks or falderals that you wanted to spread about. Anyway, I imagine Lily will be quite happy to live here. In her spare time she'll be away from everyone, and at the moment, I feel that's what she wants, to be on her own; and it's understandable.'

They were going out into the open now as he said, 'But for how long? She's a very, very pretty woman. What if she decided to marry?'

'Oh, I've thought of that; but it won't be for some time, I should imagine. But if she wanted to and the man was capable of bringing up the boy then I'd be pleased for her; I'd have no objections, not really.'

'Well' – he paused as he smiled at her – 'I can't see, Bridget, that you can have objections in any case, because you have really no claim on the boy, or her, except of gratitude on her part.'

She stopped dead in the middle of the field and, peering at him through the dim light, she said, 'Douglas Filmore, you are the most irritating person: one minute you're flinging compliments about right, left, and centre, the next you are knocking one flat with your logic. Well, let me tell you, I like neither of your ways. As for the latter flattening piece of information, I've already gone into that in my own mind.'

Douglas did not come back as one would have hoped, saying, 'I'm terribly sorry, Bridget,' instead, he said,

'You're down to earth, Miss Bridget, aren't you? You're the matter of fact Miss Mordaunt, you're the speak-your-mind Miss Mordaunt, you are the boss of the factory: "Now you listen to me, sir. I will have it done this way, not that, this way!" That is you, Bridget, isn't it? You are an individualist. But when you meet up with someone who is of like mind, you can't stand it. I thought we were friends and as a friend I was pointing out to you a fact that I imagined you had overlooked. But not you, oh no, not Miss Mordaunt. And let me tell you something more when I'm on. In taking that mother and child, especially the child, under your wing, there may come a time when you wish to God you hadn't. I'm not a fortune teller or a seer, I'm just looking into the future and seeing the progress of my nephew, as you have pointed him out to be; he is Lionel Filmore's illegitimate son, but his mother is a maid, a working woman, and she will rear him, but you propose to educate him, and to what purpose? To inherit Grove House, if there's no other issue? It's happened before that illegitimates have taken their procreators to court to try and claim their rights. What if Victoria turns out to be a breeder and supplies a number of males and females all half-brothers and -sisters of your protégé? Is he going to remain ignorant all his life of who he is? Not on your life, Bridget. And you think of that.'

Bridget stood amazed as she watched the slight boyish figure that hid a strong man march across the field away from her. There was sweeping through her a flood of emotion, indignation and fear, because she knew what he had said to be true, but also surprise that he had voiced it so vehemently; moreover, that he was always surprising her.

She had the very strange and urgent desire to pick up her skirts and run after him and say, 'You're right, Douglas, you're right. But please, don't be annoyed with me, because you are the only real friend I have. Remember what you said in the drawing room a little earlier about being lonely. And I am so lonely, so much so that only yesterday I wished I had Victoria back with me. But that was only a momentary wish. Nevertheless, I wished it. But let me face the fact that I don't want Victoria, I don't want the company of women, I want a man's company. Yes, yes, I do.'

Her head dropped onto her chest. But not any man's company; it would have to be someone like Douglas. Yes, someone like Douglas Filmore.

What had she said to herself last night in bed? That she knew she could have company and in plenty if she took to dressing differently; in fact, that if she followed Victoria's pattern and had her hair dressed and her face creamed and powdered, then she could look presentable, very presentable.

But what had been the outcome of that inner probing? Just that she wouldn't be herself, she would be playing a part, and the men she would attract she would likely despise, and so nothing would come of it. Why then bother to change?

She brought her head up with a jerk and emitted aloud, 'Oh, you!' the words being directed across the field to where Douglas was just disappearing into the copse. And slowly now she, too, made her way across the field.

When she reached the courtyard and saw Jimmy Tierney leading Hamlet into his box she said to him, 'Have you seen Mr Filmore?'

'Aye, miss; he went past a minute ago. He seemed in a hurry. He'll be at the bottom of the drive now, I should imagine. Would you like me to run after . . .?'

'No. No. It's perfectly all right. He's got a train to catch.'

'I could have taken him in, miss.'

'Yes. Yes, you could, Jimmy, but he likes walking.'

He grinned at her, saying, 'He's a fast walker, miss; he was almost at the point of a run.'

As she walked away Jimmy stood holding on to the horse a moment longer as he watched his mistress crossing the yard and going round to the front of the house; and he raised his eyebrows; then turning, he spoke to the horse, saying, 'Well, well, Hamlet. Well, well. A body never knows where a blister might light.'

4

Douglas was very weary. The last part of his journey, after leaving the train, together with his intense thinking on the journey, had tired him.

He approached the house by the back way, which was used mostly by the staff and tradesmen because it was a short cut; and this brought him to the stable yard. The light from the two lanterns hanging from brackets in the wall made it appear like daylight; and Jimmy Fawcett, coming out of a stable carrying yet another lantern, exclaimed, 'You come in the back way, Mr Douglas?'

'Yes, Jimmy. It's been a long walk.'

'You walked from the town?'

'That's it, I've walked from the town, and don't I know it.'

'Why didn't you take a cab, sir?'

'Oh, I wanted exercise, and,' he laughed, 'I got it.'

When from the stable there came the loud neigh of a horse, Jimmy jerked his head back, saying, 'The Admiral's on his high horse, so to speak, Mr Douglas. He's always like that. And he hasn't had enough exercise; and Mr Lionel doesn't like him used too much when he's away. And he won't be pleased either to know he's been to the blacksmith's. When Ron had him out on exercise he sprang a shoe.'

'He always seems to be springing shoes.'

They were walking across the yard now and Jimmy hesitated a moment before saying, 'Oh, no, not The Admiral, Mr Douglas; he wears them down like nobody's business. He's got that kind of hard hoof. I don't know the last time it was he sprang one. Now Prince and Dobbie, oh aye, they're springers all right. By' – he shivered – 'it's goin' to be a cold 'un the night. And you should get somethin' hot into you after that walk, Mr Douglas.'

'I'm on my way to do just that, Jimmy.' And with this he made for the kitchen.

This way took him through the bucket and brush room, then the boot room which led into a big scullery, and from there he pushed open the kitchen door and startled the entire staff, who were sitting round the table. There was the butler James Bright, and Mrs Pullman the housekeeper, Rose Jackson the cook, and Kate Swift and Minnie Carstairs. And it was evident that they had been in deep conclave. He began by saying, 'Oh, I'm sorry. Please don't get up,' and he swept his hand across them to indicate he was meaning them all as they rose from the table; then he went on hurriedly, 'I . . . I came the back way, walked from the station. I'm a bit cold, I wonder, Cook, if I could have a bowl of something hot?'

'Yes, Mr Douglas, of course, of course. You'll have it in a jiffy.' Rose Jackson scurried towards the stove and the butler, assuming the dignity that went with his position, said, 'Could I get you a drink first, sir?'

'Yes. Yes, thank you, Bright. That would be very acceptable.' He walked past them now, nodding and saying, 'I'm sorry I disturbed you.'

In the hall, then going up the stairs, he was wondering what all the conclave could have been about. Likely the young mistress and her interfering. In this respect, at least, he was sorry for Victoria: although he considered her a silly, empty-headed individual, she had tried her best to get the household into shape, but it had been a losing battle from the beginning, for now with five servants expected to do the work of what had at one time been twelve indoor staff, it was a task that would have thwarted even someone much more capable than Victoria . . .

It was half an hour later. He had drunk a glass of port, got through a bowl of soup, then the leg of a chicken and a piece of bacon and egg pie, and was now making his way to the drawing-room. He was actually at the door when it was pulled promptly open and Victoria almost flounced past him on her way to the stairs, and he turned and said, 'Good-evening, Victoria,' but without response until she had her foot on the bottom step when she, too, turned and said, 'It hasn't been such for me.'

'Dear! Dear!' And after entering the drawing-room and seeing his father lounging on the couch and a decanter and glass on the small table to his side, he again said to himself, 'Dear! Dear!' His father in his cups wasn't a pleasant individual. Sober, he was inclined to be a taciturn man, but drunk, his tongue would be loosened and his conversation bawdy. What is more, drunk or sober, he had never been a man to defer to women. And so it was likely Victoria had been the recipient of some of his less nice pleasantries.

'Bloody stupid girl, that! Her belly full but afraid to talk of it. Silly bitches, women. All because I asked her how she thought it got there . . . Where've you been? Haven't clapped eyes on you hardly in days.'

'I have work to do, Father.'

'Work? Oh aye. Two sons working now, and a bloody lot of good they do me. And another thing I'll tell you, her bloody solicitor, Miss starchy Bridget's, he's doling out the money every month. If it's Lionel's, he should have it . . . lump sum, and get the interest. And I'm going to have it out with him an' all, 'cos now he's been taken on at Barnett's, d'you know that? although he knows bugger-all about ships or their cargoes or their victualling. Of course, he'll be no more than office boy, he can't be, yet why are they paying him all that to be an office boy?' He hitched himself up to the end of the couch now by placing his outstretched palm under his stomach to get him there. Then, leaning forward to speak to Douglas, who was standing near the fire, he muttered in a low voice, 'D'you think it would be anything to do with Daisy Barnett? Remember her, blowzy Daisy? She's got through two husbands, and not yet forty. And where's he been these last two or three days, eh? Had to go to Carlisle on business? There's no bloody ships sailing up the main street in Carlisle, is there? But there's an hotel or two there. Oh, aye, on the outskirts an' all. He'll get himself into a bloody jam one of these days with women and he won't be able to get out of it. You'll see, you mark my words. Now if that silly bitch upstairs had any spunk, real spunk, she would make a stand, at least she would smell a rat and wonder where the stink was coming from. But no, it's Lionel this, and Lionel that. And isn't he a clever boy getting such a position. God above! She should twig you don't get a thousand pounds a year for being a glorified errand boy. Some women make me sick . . .'

The room became quiet, not even a crackle from the wood on the fire, until the wind blew a branch against the far window, but it could have been the crack of a gun penetrating the silence, for now William Filmore turned his head sharply towards the window. Then looking back at his son, he said quietly, 'Give me a hand up.' And after Douglas had helped to hoist him to his feet he stood for a moment tugging at both sides of his coat as if aiming to bring them together across the huge mound of his stomach.

His father's next words, however, seemed to Douglas to belie any befuddled state of mind; they made him think that they were being mouthed by a different being, for spoken very quietly now, they were: 'I'm tired of life, Doug. I wake up in the morning and I hate the light; I haven't had a drink then to dull the day ahead. But when I knew that my daughter-in-law was carrying a child, I thought, good, I'll wait until it's born. It's got to be a son. Filmores just breed sons, and once I see it then I can go any time. There's always ways and means. The only thing I hope about the child is that it doesn't take after its father, or its grandfather' – his head was nodding now – 'and has just a little bit of its mother, I would hope.' He now put his hand out and placed it on Douglas's shoulder, saying, 'You know, you don't look a bit like any Filmore that's ever been born. There's not a portrait on that staircase or in the hall that gives you the slightest resemblance. Yet inside, you're a Filmore, more than any of us. You're like my grandfather, not my great-grandfather. No; I remember him dying when I was just a boy. He was another me, somebody who had done nothing with his life except eat, and drink, and whore, and laugh outside while cursing inside. I used to scorn you, you know, Doug – I think I've told you this before – while at the same time having great hopes of my first born, the handsome Lionel. Why did we have him christened that name? Bloody soft name when you think about it, Lionel. It was because your mother's grandfather or some such had been a Lionel. Ah well, I've wined all I'm going to wine for the night; I'm going to bed if I can make the stairs.' His voice changing now, he threw his head back and laughed as he said, 'That's how I'll end, you know, two steps from the top and I'll tumble backwards. That's what it'll be like.'

All that Douglas said to him was, 'Good-night, Father,' and his father answered, 'Good-night, Doug.'

Alone in the room, Douglas now rested his arms on the mantelshelf and let them support his brow. There was a sadness in him that was dragging him into the ground. He had never liked his father. He had despised him because from early on he, too, knew that his parents despised him for not being another sturdy handsome, big-made Lionel. But in this moment his sadness was being woven by strong chords of love brought about at this late stage by an understanding as to why the man had drunk himself into a grotesque shape through an inner want, a loneliness that he recognised because he himself had inherited it. And he knew that had it been possible he would have had Lionel grow up into someone of whom his father could be proud, while he himself would remain despised for his unlikeness to any Filmore, past or present.

He had lain awake for a long time going over the events of the day, beginning with the desire to see Bridget, the desire that he had pressed down hard on for days; then his meeting with her and his pleasure in the house . . . his pleasure in everything that had happened until they went down to that old farmhouse. What had started that row, anyway? And why had he been so vehement? Was it because deep down he knew that her interest in the child and its mother stemmed from her deeper interest in that man, Joe Skinner? The man was dead now and he was indeed sorry that he had come to such an end, but then if you murder someone you've got to expect a form of murder as retribution. She hadn't, though, mentioned the fellow's name now for some time, but likely she was thinking all the more.

And then, his father. Those last few minutes with him this evening had been a revelation. They weren't words of self-pity, but more like confession of guilt, the guilt of having wasted a life and the pity that there was no second chance. You had one and that was all.

He must get to sleep.

As he lay on his back, his hands above his head, his eyes closed, he was in that state between consciousness and the realm of sleep in which irrationality comes into play, mixing the events of the day or the past to form an incomprehensible puzzle. And it now caused him to run alongside a train that was going at speed, then jump onto the footplate and begin shovelling coal into the red heart of the fire. He jumped off and ran across a field and climbed a ladder and began placing stones in gaps in the wall of the big barn he had visited that day. Then Jimmy Fawcett's voice came from the bottom of the ladder, and he looked down at him, and Jimmy was saying, 'Oh, not The Admiral, Mr Douglas. He wears them down like nobody's business.' Then he was at the bottom of the ladder holding Jimmy by the shoulders. But Jimmy's face had turned into his father's and he was yelling at it, 'The Admiral does cast his shoes! He cast one and threw Lionel that night I saw him in the wood.'

Now he was sitting bolt upright in bed, his eyes wide open, staring into the blackness . . . That was the picture he had been trying to recall, that night in the wood when the three riders passed, and then sometime later he saw Lionel walking his horse. The horse wasn't limping but Lionel looked in a state, shaken. Yes. Yes, he had looked shaken and he said he had been thrown because the Admiral had baulked at a gate and had likely caught his shoe on the top of it.

He flung the bedclothes back and now stood gripping the front of his long nightshirt, endeavouring to stop his body shivering, not only with the cold, but with the most dreadful thought that had sprung into his mind. No, not sprung, it had been lying there dormant for a long time; it had been niggling and troubling him.

He groped his way across the room to where he knew a nightrobe was lying across the back of a chair, and after getting into it he groped his way back to the table and lit the bedside lamp. Then standing staring at its glow, he muttered aloud, 'He was shaking like a leaf and he was all dishevelled. It was two nights before his wedding day. But . . . but what reason would he have for killing the man?'

He dropped down on to the side of the bed and his mind started to work backwards. The two dead men were brothers. The man Joe knew who the father of the child was, and if this was so his brother probably held the same knowledge. Now it came out in the court, didn't it, that the brother was of low character. Suppose he had come and tackled Lionel to expose him. It was only suppose, his mind told him. But it also told him there was one thing certain, that on meeting Lionel that night, his condition had immediately surprised him, as did the reason he gave for being thrown from his horse.

He stood up again and began to pace the length of the room.

He couldn't do that, slit a man's throat. He wouldn't do that, slit a man's throat. But then if he hadn't done it, the other man must have, and he had continually stressed his innocence until the day before he was hanged.

Oh God! don't let this happen to the house, for his father would then have no need to fall downstairs to die, he would die of shame. And then there was Victoria and the coming child. He stopped abruptly . . . What was he talking about? He had no proof. A knife had been used and the police had been unable to find the knife: they had seemed to prod and scrape all round the glade. What would a man do with a knife after he had killed someone with it? Bury it? Throw it in the river? Well, there was no river near, and he wouldn't likely stay around and bury it. Hide it somewhere in the house? Yes, he could have done that; there were the attics. But again, what was he talking about? He was condemning him on nothing more than a fancy.

He was pacing again, his mind uttering the words deep

within him: It was no fancy; he had known from that night there was something wrong. Even when he was admitting that he had seen the man Joe and had talked with him in that wood, he had not wanted to admit he had recognised him. And why hadn't he brought to the fore when being cross-examined that he had also spoken to another man, his brother, who had been leading his horse, not galloping with the other three men, as his evidence had suggested? Why? Why had he omitted to say that his brother was in a state? and, if he had been speaking the truth, would have added, in an unusual state for him?

Oh dear lord!

He took off the robe and slowly got into bed again. Tomorrow he would go up into the attics and go through them, through all the old furniture, the boxes, and any place where a knife was likely to be hidden.

What was Mr Douglas doin' scramblin' about in the attics? He had the whole place turned upside down. He said he was lookin' for a map that he remembered bein' used in the schoolroom up there. Well, the boys' books were still scattered on the shelves of the schoolroom. He had described it to Bright, and Bright had described it to Mrs Pullman, and she had passed on the description to the girls, but nobody could remember ever seein' a map that was encased in a hard brown leather-back and fastened with a buckle, and the whole thing no bigger than one's hand. Apparently, there were dotted in it the positions of some old obscure quarries and he wanted the locations to see if there was any decent stone left . . . He was a funny fella, was Mr Douglas. And a bit odd, too, in that he had gone into trade. Nobody in the Filmore family had ever gone into trade. The family had already been goin' down the hill for years, and with this, as Bright said, they had reached bottom.

After two days and the map not having been found, Mr Douglas seemingly gave up his search. But then his mode of work changed. He used to spend nearly all his time in his workshop with his man and boy, but two mornings running now, Joseph Bell, one of the two gardeners, had reported that Mr Douglas had taken to going walks with Gippo. Well, as everybody knew, Gippo was a lazy dog, and it seemed content to lie either inside or outside his workroom all day; and it was getting on and past caring for long walks. It would scamper now and again in the fields after a rabbit, but that was as far as it went. Then yesterday he had the dog out for four hours!

Where did he go?

Joseph didn't know exactly, but probably the town, for he went in the direction of Brook's Wood and that was the shortest way to town. He would have to go through the factory quarter. Not a very nice area. He surely wouldn't have wanted anything there. He had always been a bit odd in his ways, had Mr Douglas. All right in his head, oh aye. Yet, when you come to think of it, it was the head that ordered the ways, wasn't it? . . .

Douglas's head had led him once again to the glade, and as he stood watching the dog sniffing about he told himself of the futility of the search. It wasn't likely, if he had done this terrible deed, that Lionel would have immediately buried his knife; he would have been in too desperate a state to think about it. No; it was more likely that he would take it home and hide it there. He would start on the attics again tomorrow.

But why? Why? It was going to do no good, only cause a lot of pain, even if he could prove anything. And then there was Bridget. What would the effect be on her if her protégé was proved to be innocent and had been hanged for a crime he did not commit? Oh, God in heaven! She would blaze that from one end of the country to the other. Yet, would she, knowing how it would affect Victoria and the coming child? Oh, let him get home. The best thing he could do about all this business, was to forget it. But then he couldn't forget it, *he wouldn't forget it*. If that man was innocent then Lionel must be guilty . . .

'Gippo! Gippo! Come here!'

The dog took no notice, but scampered into the brushwood on the heels of a rabbit, and so Douglas, knowing that the rabbit would have the best of it and would disappear down a hole, waited. But when Gippo didn't return, his mouth open, his tongue lolling as if saying, I gave it a run for its money, he pushed his way around some bushes and there in the near distance he saw the dog scratching at a hole. And when he got up to him he bent down and said, 'It's a fool's game, and you know it. That little lady or gent will have a series of bolt-holes that will reach to the end of the wood. You're wasting your time. Come on.'

As if he had indicated to the dog that a bolt-hole was on the opposite side of the tree the dog now ran round and began to scratch amid thick tangled roots. And Douglas, smiling now, said again, 'You're wasting your time, laddie.'

Sensing this was a game, Gippo again moved part way round the trunk and once more started scratching. And now Douglas cried at him impatiently, 'Come on! Come on! You've had enough,' and, bending down he gripped him by the collar, just as the dog's paw, having caught on something like a piece of paper, pulled it slightly upwards.

'Come on with you!' He took his hand from the dog's collar and slapped it on the hind quarters, pushing it away, and had taken two steps from the tree when he stopped, stood still for a moment, then looked over his shoulder at the dirty piece of paper. Now he was bending over it and, delicately, his finger and thumb touched it and drew it from the ground. His heart racing as if it would leap from his mouth, he pulled at what he saw to be a soiled and stained handkerchief, and as the last part of it left the hole there lay a knife. As if the material had burned him, he lifted his hand quickly away from it, the fingers spread taut; and then the hand was outstretched against the trunk of the tree for support. His eyes were closed and he was saying aloud, 'God Almighty! God Almighty!' while all the time his eyes were staring fixedly on the handkerchief and the knife.

How long he stood there he didn't know, but he had to force himself now to bend and pick up the articles: first, the handkerchief. He held it by the hem, then moved his fingers to a corner, and there, dark-stained but evident were the embroidered initials, L. F. His mother had spent, not only days and weeks, but years with her needle. Everything in the house in the way of linen was embroidered or initialled.

He looked at the knife: the blade was still open, it was rusted. This was the kind of knife that most riders carried.

He now took a handkerchief from his own pocket and carefully wrapped the two things in it. Then looking down on the dog, he said, 'You don't know what you have done this day, Gippo. I could have let it slide while knowing in my heart the guilty one, but not any more.'

5

He stayed late in the workshop. He knew that Lionel had returned home and he knew, as was his wont, he would be sitting drinking in the dining-room after Victoria had gone to bed and the servants, too, had retired. He was often accompanied in this pastime by his father. Well, tonight he hoped his father wouldn't be there. But even if he were, he couldn't keep this to himself any longer. He had been over his approach again and again; he knew exactly what he was going to do. It wasn't, however, what he wanted to do: he wanted to take his brother by the throat and bring him to the same end that he had brought that man. And then there was that poor fellow. He could think of him now as that poor fellow, stressing his innocence all along. And all the while he was imprisoned and then the case going on, his dear brother had got on with his life as though ignorant of it all. He had dared to go to the altar rails and take a wife, a young innocent girl, just hours after he had murdered a man. What kind of an individual was he? A fiend?

He now put out two of the lanterns in the workroom, picked up the third, and went out.

He entered the house by a side door that led into the hall. The drawing-room door was half open and he could see his father shambling towards the couch. As far as he could see there was no one else there, which meant that if Lionel wasn't in the smoking room he had already gone upstairs, likely to pacify his wife for his absence.

Slowly he made his way along the corridor and as slowly

and as quietly opened the door of the smoking room. Lionel was there.

Lionel had turned his head in a lackadaisical fashion to see who had entered the room, and, espying his brother, he said, 'Here comes the workman, one of the busy bees of this world. God has niches for us all, the high and the low and . . .'

'Shut your filthy mouth!'

Lionel brought his head from the back of the hide-covered chair and his large eyes became slits in the high ruddy colour of his face. He stared at the figure standing stiffly in front of him before he said on a kind of tolerant laugh, 'Did I hear aright? Is my little brother once again getting on his moral hind legs? What has he heard this time? Does he want to say, where have you been, you naughty boy? And what naughties have you . . .?'

When his whole body was knocked back tight against the chair and hands came on his throat, his eyes nearly popped out of his head for a moment. And his own hands, gripping Douglas's wrists, took a number of seconds before he could wrestle them from his flesh; yet his release had actually been brought about by Douglas himself: he was again standing taut. And now Lionel growled at him, 'What the hell's got into you?'

For answer, Douglas thrust his hand into his pocket and brought out a clean handkerchief, unfolded it and held it out towards Lionel, allowing the contents to lie between his two palms. And now he watched the colour drain from Lionel's face; then his Adam's apple flutter in his throat, and his chest heave; and only after further swallowing did he draw in a long breath and gasp, 'It . . . it was an accident.'

'You don't cut another man's throat by accident.'

'You don't know anything about it. He was at me, he was blackmailing me. He was . . .'

'Yes, I know what he was about to do, he was going to reveal that your son had just recently been born through a young, innocent girl and that would put a stop to your security, wouldn't it? You wouldn't have minded losing Victoria, but not two thousand a year. Oh, you couldn't bear to think of losing that. You dirty rotten swine, you!'

'It wasn't . . . it wasn't like that. He was . . . Anyway, what are you going to do?'

'What do you think I'm going to do?' And Douglas's anger was such that he couldn't stay the vehement words. 'I'm going to see that the same is done to you as was done to that man Joe Skinner.'

'Begod! you'll not.' Now Lionel was bringing the words out through his clenched teeth. 'I'll do for you first. By God! I will. And give me that here!' As his hand went out to grab the handkerchief and its contents Douglas sprang back, thrust the articles into his pocket, then stood, his slim body went forward, his elbows away from his sides and his fists doubled. So when Lionel came at him, his fists flailing, he was checked by a blow to the stomach and then one to his face. But such was his bulk and height he was only momentarily staggered, and he now almost threw himself bodily on Douglas and with such force that they both toppled to the floor, upsetting a table with a decanter and glasses on it, then they rolled over the rug and towards the fireplace, each aiming for the other's throat, and it was the pressure of the filigreed steel fender against the side of his head that made Douglas aware that the life was being choked out of him. In desperation he twisted and groped for the poker he knew was resting at the end of the fender. Finding it, his immediate reaction was to aim it at Lionel's head.

Into the deepening blackness came a pale light. He could breathe, he heard a voice screaming above him: 'God in heaven! Blazes!' Then he felt himself being lifted from the floor and Bright was saying, 'Come on, sir. Come on.' Bright was dabbing at his neck with a napkin and when he slowly put up his hand to it it was wet. He licked his fingers and they tasted salty. His vision was still blurred, but now he could make out his father standing over Lionel, who was lying back in the chair again as if he had never moved out of it. But the blood was running down the side of his face, and his father was yelling at Bright now, 'Bring a dish of water and some towels, and keep the women out!'

'Yes, sir. Yes, sir.'

The man ran from the room and William Filmore, looking from one to the other, said, 'My God! We've come to something now, out to murder each other.'

'For . . . for a second time.' The mutter came from Douglas.

'What?' His father was leaning towards him. 'What d'you mean, a second time?'

'He . . . he was out to finish me as he did the man in the wood.'

William Filmore straightened his back and it seemed for a moment that even the bulge of his stomach receded, and his voice was a whisper as he said, 'What are you saying, son? What are you saying?'

For answer Douglas put his hand in his pocket and pulled out the handkerchief and, the other hand now letting go of the napkin, he spread the evidence on his palms as he said to his father, 'He . . . he buried these in the wood. The dog unearthed them.'

'No! No! Never. It must be a mistake. He couldn't.' He now turned and glanced to where Lionel was lying back in the chair, his eyes closed, his hand still to the side of his face, and he muttered, 'A man swung for it. A man . . .' He now gripped the back of the chair; then shambling to the front of it he lowered himself slowly down, one hand clutching the edge of the table as if to steady himself, his mouth opening and shutting as if he were gasping for air.

When at this moment Bright came hurrying into the room carrying a dish of water and with a number of hand towels slung over his shoulder, the old man turned his head and looked at him. His mouth remained open for a time and as if he were about to say something, then he pointed towards Lionel, at the same time becoming aware of the female figure standing in the doorway, and in a croaking bawl he cried, 'Get out! Away!'

After the door had banged shut he looked again towards Bright, who was now wiping the blood from Lionel's face; and he cried to him, 'Give me a towel!'

The butler swiftly brought a hand towel and handed it to his master, saying as he did so, 'It's a laceration above the ear, sir,' indicating Lionel with a movement of his hand; 'the hair should be cut,' to which he received for answer only a sharp nod of assent.

William now pulled himself slowly to his feet, went to Douglas and, taking his hand away from his throat, he wiped the blood from his neck and when he saw the oozing jagged line, he said as if with relief, 'It's . . . it's just a surface tear;' then he glanced back to where one of Lionel's hands was lying on the arm of the chair. And now he added, ''Twas his ring. Always said it was like a knuckle-duster.' Then dabbing again at Douglas's neck, he muttered, 'It's all right. It's all right. 'Tisn't serious.'

When Douglas now muttered bitterly, ''Tisn't his fault,' and would have gone on, his father stopped him with a grimace and a slight jerking of his head towards where Bright was still dabbing away at Lionel's wound.

The old man now went over to the butler and, pushing him aside, said, 'Let me see.' And he parted the hair above Lionel's ear, then said abruptly, 'Bring me the scissors.'

After Bright had scurried from the room William stood

back from his sons and, his voice holding a note of sadness, he said, 'This house is fated. Indeed to God! it's fated.'

A minute or so later Bright returned with the scissors, and the hair having been snipped from behind Lionel's ear to reveal the extent of the wound, he said, 'It needs attention, sir, don't you think?' And in answer to this, after a long pause, his master said gruffly, 'Get Mrs Pulman to tear some sheeting and bring some of that carbolic stuff. That'll settle things till tomorrow; then we'll see about a doctor.'

It seemed that the word 'doctor' revived Lionel, for, aiming now to pull himself up in the chair, he said, 'I want no doctor. I'm all right.'

'Aye, begod! you're all right. You've got enough whisky in you to sterilize any cuts, but for how long do you think you're going to be all right after this night's work? And your previous work. My God! I can't believe it. If that comes out, I can't imagine how you'll be able to talk yourself out of it.'

'And he won't!'

At this Lionel's head jerked in the direction of his brother, and he growled at him, 'It's a pity I didn't do for you, too. You bloody sneaking, crawling wasp!'

'*Enough!*'

The door opened again and when Bright appeared with the sheeting and the carbolic, his master said, 'Get rid of all that lot out there. And' – he pointed towards the door now – 'and tell them to mind their tongues. In fact, tie them up. There has been a little quarrel, you understand?'

'Yes, sir. Yes, I understand.'

'Well, lay it on strong. And tell 'em if I hear a word outside, they'll go outside with it.'

The butler just stared at his master for a moment before turning and hurrying out of the room.

William, seemingly now, had to drag himself over to

see to Douglas, who was standing by the side of his chair, his hand still holding the towel to his throat, but when his help was brushed aside by Douglas, saying, 'I'm all right. I'm going to the closet, but I'll be back presently,' his father said, 'Go to bed. I think you should go to bed, son. We'll talk about this in the morning.'

Douglas came back with a growl, 'We'll not talk about this in the morning, Father. We'll talk about this tonight. I have an ultimatum to offer my brother, and he's not going to like either way. But he'll take one or the other, and I'll see that he does, and this very night . . . now! He's not going to get the chance to wriggle out of it by scooting in the morning, because – ' Looking now from his father's face to the white but blazing countenance of his brother, he said, 'I'd have hunted you down. Do you hear? Hunted you down.'

The quietness that immediately descended on the room became eerie, and in it he turned from them and went out.

Lionel, now pulling himself to the edge of the chair and looking at his father, said, 'It's a pity I didn't do for him.'

'God in heaven! I cannot believe my ears.' William's words were now hissing through his teeth. 'You admit then . . .? But what am I talking about? I've seen the evidence. You killed that fellow. Why, in the name of God!'

'He was blackmailing me. He was going to tell that stiff bitch that I was the father of the child just born. His brother had apparently married her to save her face.'

'Well, why in the name of God! didn't you pay up?'

'*Because I hadn't the money.*' The words came out like grit through Lionel's teeth. 'Remember, we were penniless; couldn't even pay for hay.'

It was characteristic, his father thought, that at this moment, he should think of his horse and its feed.

'There was two thousand pounds a year at stake. You

yourself welcomed it, jumped at it, grabbed at it. Was I to lose that? What would you have said? Pay the bugger. That's what you would have said. Keep him quiet. Again I say, with what? And anyway – ' his face twisted into a grimace and he put his hand to the side of his head before adding, 'He was scum, and his brother, too, the one that went. They were all scum, else why should he take her? Yes, why? I've asked myself, and the answer is, I'm sure, both of them had it planned to squeeze me, one or the other.'

His father stared at him. His spirit-befuddled mind was working clearer at this moment than it had done for many a long day. And this showed itself when he said, 'Then why did the man who was hanged not split when he was cross-examined? That would have given his counsel another lead. And, as I see it now, the lead would have been easy to follow. God! I never thought I would say this to my first born, but I regret the night that I put you into your mother. I do indeed. There's been a weakness in you and a nastiness that I wouldn't recognise. I've despised your brother, aye, I have, but if his character had been in your body, you would have been a man. And even now I could say that I wouldn't have been ashamed of you if it had been one of your own class you had killed, and in fair fight. But no; you had to sink so low as to cut the throat of one of the lower orders just for two thousand pounds.'

Lionel was on his feet and it looked as if the nails of the hand that was still pressed against the side of his head were penetrating his skull, for the knuckles were standing up white as he cried, 'Two thousand a year, Father, and five hundred of her own! Two thousand, five hundred! Father, a year!'

William Filmore's nose was actually wrinkling when the door opened and he turned towards it to see Douglas coming back into the room. He had changed his shirt and coat and round his neck was a white scarf, and he now approached his father, saying, 'Will you come into the library, Father? There's a desk there, and there's some writing to be done.'

William said nothing, but just stared into Douglas's face for a moment before turning to Lionel and saying, 'Come along.'

It was full thirty seconds before Lionel put a foot forward to follow his father and brother, half-turned and waiting at the door, out of the room and into the library.

Beyond the long table and under the tall window, which was covered now by the heavy faded embroidered curtains, stood a davenport and, on it, sheets of paper, a brass inkwell, and an ornamental boot made out of the skin of a deer from which were protruding a number of steel pens.

Douglas walked towards the desk, stopped within a yard of it and, pointing to it, said, 'Sit down and write.'

'I'll be damned if I will!'

Douglas seemed to leave the ground as he swung round and cried, 'Listen to me! and I mean every word of this: you'll write what I dictate, else I'll not wait until tomorrow morning but I'll ride into town and tell the authorities that they made a mistake in hanging Joe Skinner. And don't think that you'll be able to stop me in any way, for, let me tell you, if anything happens to me unexpectedly they'll come for you quicker than you could shoot a gun, because I've put it in writing. Oh, yes' – now he turned to his father – 'what I lack in my body I've got in my brain. In this house nobody seemed to recognise that. But knowing what that skunk' – he thumbed towards his brother – 'is capable of doing, I was taking no risks. Now, you have a choice' – he had turned back towards Lionel again – 'and I'm not going to bargain or parley with you.

You sit down *now*!' He had bawled the word, and his father cried, 'For God's sake! Doug, keep your voice down. Please! If you must have retribution, all right, have it, but it'll be no use if this spreads through the house. I could trust Bright, but not one of the other lot, inside or out.'

'Well then, the quicker he sits down and starts writing the better . . . for him.'

William now looked at Lionel, then pointed to the desk. But before Lionel stepped towards it his head drooped onto his chest and his free hand doubled into a fist. Then he was sitting in the round-back swivel chair, and, his hand grabbing up a steel pen, he thrust it into the ink, then held it poised over the paper. But such was his grip on it that the ink dropped in a blob onto the sheet; and his father, who was now standing by his side, whipped it aside before turning and looking towards Douglas.

'Dear Mr Kemp – ' Douglas waited a moment, then went on, 'This is to inform you as from this day, the 12th day of October 1884, I wish you to discontinue the allowance agreed upon on my marrying Miss Victoria Mordaunt.'

'*No, begod!*' Lionel's fist crashed on to the paper and his body was bent far over the desk as if he were about to collapse.

As he slowly raised himself up, his father, who had turned and was staring at Douglas, muttered, 'No. No, Doug; don't go that far. Think what it means.'

'I've thought what it means, Father. He has a choice.'

Lionel's back was straight now; the pen once again in his hand. He waited; Douglas began to dictate again: 'My circumstances have changed and I am now in such a position that I do not require further help. I am, sir, yours truly.'

The scratching noise of the steel nib on the paper seemed

to get louder as Lionel wrote down the last few words, rising even higher as he signed his name. But when he rose from the chair and turned from the desk it was impossible to describe the expression on his face. His father turned from it and to Douglas, who was saying, 'I'll be leaving here tomorrow, Father. I can no longer stay under this roof.'

As William was about to speak, both he and Douglas turned to glance towards the door and the sound of muttered voices; then Bright's voice came clearly, saying, 'No! madam.'

The door was thrust open and there, standing within its frame was Victoria. She was dressed in a blue satin dressing gown. Her hair was hanging about her shoulders. She looked a beautiful picture. She moved up the room now, saying, 'They . . . they were talking on the landing. I was coming out of . . . I understood you had been quarrel . . .' She had been approaching her husband and when she saw the condition of his face she ran to him, crying, 'Oh! my dear. My dear! What has happened? Who has done this?' She now turned to Douglas, saying, 'What is all this about? Why have you been fighting? You are the most disagreeable person these days, Douglas. You are . . .'

'Shut up! woman.'

Her eyes widened, her lips trembled as she looked at her father-in-law, but when Douglas went on, 'You had better get yourself back to bed, madam,' she dared to say, 'I . . . I won't. I won't! I'm not a child, sir. I want to know what all this is about.'

'What it is about, madam, has nothing to do with you.'

'Ev . . . everything that happens to my husband has something to do with me.'

As she went to catch hold of Lionel's arm he thrust her

244

aside and, glaring at Douglas, cried loudly to him, 'Go on! Finish your job. Tell her.'

'*No! No!*' William thrust out an arm towards Douglas as if to stop him; but what Douglas said was, 'It's a matter of money, Victoria, just money.'

'Money?' She was now looking at Lionel. 'What do they mean, a matter of money?'

Lionel looked down into the face of which he had become tired, not only of the face, but of the whole woman, considering her a stupid, empty-headed individual, and blaming her for deceiving him into thinking she was a rich young lady. And oh, he was sure in his mind she had known all along the real situation. And of late he had actually come to hate her, especially during these last few days in Carlisle where, he had told himself, if he had only waited he would have definitely met up with Mrs Daisy Barnett, who was as enamoured of him now as he was of her and who had been the means of getting him a post in the company, which would have promised a bright future ahead, if only he had been unfettered by this silly creature who had been governed by that bitch of a woman. And it was not as much to hit at the bitch as at her that he cried, 'Yes, my dear, as my brother said, it's all a matter of money, because, you see, and prepare yourself for a blow, my dear one, when I discovered just before we were married that you were not the rich young lady you pretended to be, even though saying you were a poor little girl, I was for letting you remain a poor little girl. But the real rich young lady, dear Miss Bridget, bribed me by offering me two thousand a year to marry you. And as I was very hard up at the time, what could I do? But now that I have a position which provides me with a salary of a thousand pounds a year, my dear brother there thought . . . well, it was only right that I refuse the payment I have been receiving for putting up with your presence. So, when he suggested that I should write to Mr Kemp to this effect, we, as you see, had more than words.'

'You cruel swine!'

It was only his father's two arms being thrust out that kept Douglas from springing forward and renewing the fight. The old man cried, 'Enough! Enough!' but now turned to Victoria and said in a much softer voice, 'As for you, my dear, these things happen, these things . . . Oh my God!'

Both he and Douglas rushed forward as Victoria crumpled slowly into a heap, and when Lionel made no move in any direction, Douglas knelt down and lifted Victoria's head. Then looking up at his father, he said, 'Water, a glass of water.'

The old man looked at Lionel, but when he still didn't move he himself hurried as quickly as his cumbersome overweight body allowed and went out of the room. Once the door closed on his father Lionel, looking down on his brother, who was cradling Victoria's head and shoulders in his arms, said in a strangely quiet voice, 'I'll never forgive you, to my dying day. And there'll come the day when you'll be sorry that you ever created this situation. This is a promise, dear brother.' And with this he turned and walked away down the room, there to meet his father coming in, a glass of water in one hand and a decanter in the other. And his father, in a voice that held a plea, said to him, 'Stay and see to your wife, man, because no matter what you do, you can't get over that you married her and she *is* your wife.'

Lionel stared at his father for a moment, then went on past him, and the old man shambled up the room, his body bent.

As he handed the glass of water to Douglas, Victoria opened her eyes, gave a small shake of her head, turned and looked into Douglas's face, then turned sharply away again. And when Douglas said, 'Here, take a drink of water,' she slowly pushed it aside. Then, her palms on the floor on each side of her, she pressed herself from him, got on to her knees, then pulled herself upright. And there she stood a moment looking at her father-in-law before she turned and walked quite steadily down the room.

Left alone, the old man and the young man looked at each other. And it was William who said, 'Well, son, you have unveiled something tonight that is likely to have repercussions for years to come, and you'll have to ask yourself, was it worth it? Aye, that's what you'll have to do, son, ask yourself, was it worth it?' And forthwith, he, too, left the room, leaving Douglas, his hand to his throat again, asking himself the same question. Was it worth it?

6

Bridget stood in the bare drawing-room of Milton Place, bare but for the drapes and the carpets which still remained. The house had been sold but the new owners weren't due to take over legally until January 5th, 1885. There was no seating except on the window sills, and so she paced the room while awaiting Victoria's arrival. In the note she had written to her asking for this meeting she had stated eleven o'clock; now it was almost twenty past.

She was not only worried but somewhat bewildered by the letter she had received from Mr Kemp indicating that he had received instructions from Mr Lionel Filmore to stop the payments as from the date on the letter. And knowing something of the character of Lionel Filmore she could not imagine him rejecting the two thousand a year when it was only because of her offering that sum that he had agreed to go ahead with the marriage.

She had gone to Mr Kemp's office to see if he could throw any light on the matter, but what he had said was merely in line with her own thinking. Lionel Filmore wasn't the kind of man to throw aside two thousand a year even if he had now found employment that was bringing him in a reasonable salary. A man such as he, Mr Kemp had assured her, could never earn enough money to meet his needs.

She had phrased her letter diplomatically to Victoria, saying she would be visiting the factories and, while she was this way, she would like to have a word with her as it was some time since they had met.

Hearing the trap on the gravel drive, she hurried across the empty room and equally empty hall to the front door, and opened it to see her cousin throwing the reins of the horse over the iron horse-post. Victoria had her back to her, but when she turned and made for the front door the change in the beautiful face acted as a shock on Bridget, and she stepped over the threshold to meet her while holding out her hand, saying, 'You look cold,' then added, 'Aren't you well?'

Victoria made no reply. She had not taken the extended hand but she walked past Bridget and into the hall, where she stopped for a moment as if surprised at the emptiness. Then she moved on to the open door of the drawing-room and she had walked to the middle of it before she again stopped and her body gave a visible shudder. And at this, Bridget said, 'Yes, it is cold, isn't it?' She didn't go on to say, 'I'm very cold, too. You're almost half an hour late; I was on the point of going;' instead, she said, 'I'm sorry there are no seats, but come and sit on the window sill.' It was as if she were addressing an acquaintance . . .

'I don't need to sit on the window sill.'

'What is wrong, Victoria? You . . . you look ill.'

'Are you surprised?'

'Yes, I am surprised. And why are you taking that tone with me?'

'My answer to that is, why did you wish to see me?'

'Well, because . . .'

'Please don't bother lying. I know why you wished to see me. You want to know the reason why your solicitor has been informed that the price you offered to get rid of me has now been refused.'

Bridget actually gasped as she stepped back from her, and it was some seconds before she could find words to say. 'Me! get rid of you? What was done was for your happiness, nothing else. If he had turned you down then, like the silly romantic girl you were at that time, you would have pined and gone into decline. You were crazy about him and I couldn't bear to see you unhappy ... Get rid of you? How could you think such a thing!'

'I can think such a thing because, as he said, and he was solid and sober when he said it, not drunk as he was the night before, that I had only to use my sense ... that is if I had any, and ask myself why my cousin would pay a man two thousand a year if it wasn't to get me off her hands. All that business about caring and wanting my happiness was merely a cover, because you could no longer put up with my ... .' She closed her eyes tightly and turned about.

Bridget did not go to her; she did not move; but the words she said now were coated with bitterness: 'And you believed him, after all my years of caring for you? And I wasn't a sister or a cousin to you, I was a mother, and I loved you like a mother. Yes, like a foolish mother I spoiled you. That is the only thing I regret, that I let you go on being a silly girl, with not a serious thought in your head, laughing your way through life.'

'Well, I'm no longer a silly girl.' Victoria had swung round; and her voice was loud and strident now as she cried, 'You can take comfort from that, I've been turned into a woman overnight. I don't think I'll ever laugh again. As for silly thoughts, there'll never be any room in my mind again but for hate. Do you hear that? Because I've been used by you, and him, and because of that I've had to suffer the contempt of servants. What is more, I am carrying a child, and if I could split my stomach open at this moment I would drag it out. Do you hear? Do you?'

Bridget stood open-mouthed. She was astounded. She could not believe with her ears or her eyes that this girl, her cousin whom, as she said, she had mothered and loved dearly, could have changed into this bitter, even vicious-tongued woman. It was impossible to credit. Something terrible must have happened back there in that house to bring on a change like this. It wasn't only the fact of him refusing the money, it was the reason behind it. Why had he refused it? And why had he turned on her and thrown the reason at her for taking it in the first place? Why?

She made her voice remain calm and soft as she said, 'Don't talk like that, Victoria, because no matter what happens you will have the comfort of your child. At the present moment you are ill and I don't know the real cause of it. It can't be just the revelation about the money; there must be something else. What is it? Tell me, what is it?'

For a moment Bridget saw the old Victoria emerge as a puzzled look came on her face and she said, 'I don't know what happened before. They had been fighting in a dreadful way, both bleeding, all cut.'

'Who? You mean, Douglas and him?'

'Yes, Douglas and him.'

'And you don't know what it was about?'

'No.' Her words came slowly now. 'I don't know what it was about. I only know, from the sight of them, they meant to kill each other; and I wish they had. Oh, I wish they had.'

There was the woman back, the new woman. And now Bridget listened to her as she went on, 'You said I'd have the comfort of a child. Who wants the comfort of a child when they're no longer a wife? Spurned, thrown aside, openly, in front of his father and Douglas. But that was when he was drunk.' And now she looked away down the long empty room and, her voice dropping, she said, 'But not the next morning. I have been lonely for months, and I wouldn't believe what my senses were telling me. But he

251

translated my doubts and suspicions into cold facts. And do you know something, Bridget? He wanted to know if I would like to return to the comfort of your protection. He was quite willing that I should. And you know what I told him?' She raised her head now and looked up at the decorated ceiling as she went on, 'I think it was at that point I changed. I practically saw myself change as I said to him words to the effect that he had been paid for me, and if he chose to return the payments that was his business, but I was his wife and although I wouldn't let him lay a hand on me as long as I lived, I would remain in that house and be mistress of it. And he would have to provide for me and the child.' She now looked down at Bridget again as she went on, 'What I should do is put the finishing touches to my bold effort and say, as he had done, I am going to refuse the two hundred and fifty a year you allow me. But the silly girl has gone and the woman knows she'll likely be very glad of that money before life finishes with her.'

Her head now drooped onto her chest, and for a moment Bridget thought she was going to burst into tears, and she was about to step towards her when the voice checked her, saying, 'Don't swamp me with your sympathy, Bridget; I couldn't bear it. I shall try to believe that what you did for me you thought was for the best. Through time I shall likely come to see it that way, but at the present I am bowed low with humiliation. Yet, at the same time I'm filled with a feeling that frightens me. I can't call it courage, or determination, I only know that I want to live in order to retaliate.'

She now lifted her head and stared at Bridget, and Bridget muttered, 'Oh, my dear, my dear Victoria, it is agonising to see you in this state. And you may come back at any time. You know that.'

'I never shall, Bridget. Never. Part of this strange feeling tells me I ... I'll stay in that house until it crumbles around me.'

She now turned and walked towards the hall, and Bridget followed her, but before opening the door to let her out, she said, 'You'll have Douglas. He is a kind man, and ...'

'Douglas left this morning, for good, with three suitcases ...'

'Where has he gone?'

'I don't know.'

Bridget opened the door, but Victoria didn't immediately go through it; she turned and looked around the empty hall, then stepped out onto the terrace and again stopped. And here, looking straight into Bridget's face, she said, 'There is nothing as dead as dead love, for the sad thing is there's nothing left to bury, nothing, when it's been shot into smithereens.'

All the years they had been together they had never had a conversation that reached any depth, nor could she ever remember her making a cryptic remark.

Shot into smithereens.

She watched the *woman* untie the horse, climb into the trap and drive away, all the while looking straight ahead, and into what?

7

It was nearing Christmas, but Bridget asked herself, 'What did it matter?' For the past few weeks she had made herself keep, as near as possible, to routine. On a Wednesday, she had gone by train to Gateshead and visited the blacking and the candle factories. Every Thursday afternoon found her in Newcastle, in the office in Northumberland Street, going over the week's takings with her manager and agent, Arthur Fathers, and discussing with him and the four rent collectors the need for repairs or purchase, or, in some cases, demolition.

Friday, too, she would be in Newcastle seeing Mr Kemp. This part of the business week she usually enjoyed, because he was a fatherly man, and kindly, and he knew all about her, as he had done about Victoria, until recently. These latter visits, however, had been less enjoyable in that her enquiries were centred on the Filmores, and little fresh knowledge of that situation had emerged, only that Lionel Filmore's name was being openly associated with that of Mrs Barnett: they had been seen dining together on several occasions. About Douglas there seemed to be no information. To use Mr Kemp's own words, that young man had apparently entirely disappeared. Probably, he had left the country.

There was a thin sleet forming as, after leaving the station, she made her way to Northumberland Street. She had felt it unnecessary to take a cab from the station for such a short distance, for her destination today was her agent's office. She walked well away from the kerb and close to the shop fronts, because the traffic on the road was thick and consequently the mud was being sprayed onto the pavement. It was as she was passing the door of a tobacconist's shop, her head bent, her eyes directed towards her feet and ankles, the latter well exposed, as she was holding her skirt up away from the wet pavement, that a hand caught at her arm and a voice said, 'Oh, I'm sorry, madam.'

When she looked up at the man who, on leaving the shop, had dunched into her, she said in surprise, 'Oh, hello, Bright.'

'Good afternoon, madam. I'm . . . I'm sorry. I nearly had you over. Pardon me.'

'Oh, I wasn't looking where I was going. I – ' She glanced towards the road now, saying, 'I should have taken a cab but I wanted some fresh air.' And she laughed, 'All I've got is mud.'

She stepped back into the shop porch, saying now, 'You are well out of your way today, Bright, aren't you?'

'Yes, madam, I'm doing a little shopping. I . . . I like a little tobacco' – he turned his head and nodded towards the bottled-glass door of the shop, then added, 'and I purchase a few cigars for the master.' He did not go on to say, 'And such an errand is very humiliating when, at one time, the shop would have been pleased to send them by the box.'

'How are things at . . .?'

Her voice was cut off as a customer pressed between them. And when he had opened the door and another customer emerged from the shop she stepped back onto the street. 'Would you care to have a coffee?' she asked him.

'I should be honoured, madam.'

'There's a good coffee shop further along, let's make for that.' She smiled widely at him, and he, gallantly placing his hand on her elbow and taking up his position on the outer part of the pavement near the kerb, assisted her, as if she were a delicate lady, to ease between the passers-by until they came to the coffee shop. And there, in the warmth and aroma, he pulled out a chair that was placed against a small round table, inviting her to sit before seating himself opposite.

The conversation from then on, at least until they had drunk half the cups of steaming coffee, concerned the merits of coffee and the pleasantness of this room, and how interesting Newcastle was, and had he ever walked through it on a Sunday when it was, or seemed to be, deserted?

It was only after a lull in the small talk that she asked quietly, 'How are things at the house, Bright?'

'Oh, miss – ' The man now took hold of the handle of his cup and began to trace its shape between his finger and thumb before he said further, 'I wouldn't know where to start, miss, to describe the change.'

'My co . . . Mrs Filmore, how is she?'

He was looking straight across the small table and into her face as he said, 'I've witnessed some changes in people in my long career, first a boot boy, then a hall boy, leading to footman, and finally to my present station, and during that time, to use an expression, many people have passed through my hands in that I have helped them off with their outdoor apparel, but never, never have I witnessed such a change as in the young mistress. To put it plainly, Miss Mordaunt, when she came as a bride into that house just a matter of months ago, she appeared a bright, yet shy, reticent young woman. In fact it was the opinion of the staff that she would never learn to rule it because she made so many mistakes. She wanted to take over the housekeeper's post, you know. Apparently she had run your establishment and, I should imagine, well, and I'm sure your own staff obeyed and respected her, but you see, our people have worked under different rules for years, and I won't say they ignored her commands, but they went about things as they always had done. And they have managed very well, too, I would say exceedingly well since the staff was depleted some years ago. So, that was the situation she found, and I don't think it was a happy one for the mistress, but, nevertheless, she still seemed to remain herself. That was up to the night when Master Douglas and Master Lionel indulged in that unfortunate exchange which came to blows, and could have been fatal for one or other of them had the master not intervened. I think it was more than unfortunate that the mistress should hear the maids chattering as they crossed the gallery because she came downstairs and . . . dear, dear! whatever happened in the library caused her to faint. But —' He now lowered his head and remained silent until she said, 'Yes, Bright? Please go on. Tell me all you know.'

The man's voice was low now as he said, 'Well, Miss Mordaunt, the following morning there were words which I overheard. I . . . I sent the maids down from upstairs, but such was the commotion that I could not help but overhear. And I must tell you, miss, I was ashamed of Mr Lionel, but at the same time amazed at the unexpected spirit with which the mistress met his verbal onslaught, for onslaught it was. So, knowing the situation, I fully expected the mistress . . . well, we all, miss, fully expected the mistress to pack up and return to your care. But no; we couldn't have been more surprised in the change in that young girl. And the change, I'm afraid, has not diminished but has increased, so much so that Mrs Pullman has left. She was ready for retirement, I know, but she also knew, unfortunately, she would have no pension. Still, she had been a saving, caring woman, and she was intending to spend the rest of her life with her sister, that was after she herself should decide to go; but ... well, we couldn't believe it when the mistress indicated that the duties of a housekeeper were unnecessary: whatever had to be done in that way, she would see to it. And, dear, dear, dear! she said that Mrs Pullman didn't do any actual work; which, of course, was quite right because as a housekeeper, ordinary work didn't come into her duties: her work was to see to the running of the house; her work was to do with the staff. Of course, again, there are very few staff to control. I think' – he smiled wryly now – 'if it wasn't that I am very necessary to the master I, too, might get my walking orders.'

'Oh, Bright, I am simply amazed, and dreadfully sorry.'

'Oh, you've got nothing to be sorry for, miss. I know, and it won't go any further, of your kindness in financing Mr Lionel. I should imagine it was about that very thing that the brothers fought. There must have been a reason, a good reason, and that, I suppose, was as good a reason as any.'

'Do you hear anything of Mr Douglas? Where he might have gone?'

'Oh yes, I know where he's gone, miss.'

'You do?'

'Yes. But of course I didn't at first. It was when a hired cart came, driven by his mason, and took the stone away that they had been working on. He had to make two journeys and have the help of the yard man to load.'

'Where did they go? I mean, where has he set up his business?'

'Well, as far as I can gather it's in a sort of barn-like place belonging to a farmer yon side of Fellburn. I think the farmer's name is Pearson or Pearman ... no, Pearson. It's odd, but we all agree that we miss Mr Douglas from the house. He was never a one to make demands. I think it was because ... well, as you're not of the family, miss,

I can say this, that he felt he had no right to make demands. It was impressed upon him as a boy, because, you know, he didn't really start growing until he was about fourteen; and then he had an illness and was in bed for some time. It was from then he began to sprout, so to speak ... upwards' — his face went into a little smile now — 'but never sideways, and although he had a real good appetite he never seemed to put on any flesh, not even to this day. Yet I have been amazed at his strength: I have seen him lift a piece of stone that I couldn't even move. Then of course — ' He gave a slight hunch to his shoulder now as he said, 'We both had different training ... in all ways.'

When she looked at her watch he said quickly, 'I am keeping you; but it's been so nice to talk to you.'

'Oh no, Bright, you haven't kept me; I'm so pleased to have met you. Will you do something for me?'

'Anything, anything that I am capable of, miss.'

'Your mistress must be near her time. When the baby comes will you inform me, please?'

'I shall. I shall, miss. But that is another thing that is ... well, not worrying the staff, but causing comment, because when Kate spoke to her about a nurse and asked if they should prepare a room for her, she said, not permanently, just for the confinement. She means to look after the child herself, miss.'

Bridget would have liked to say, 'Well, that isn't a bad thing. Tens of thousands of women are doing that every day.' But such an occupation was, she knew, in this man's eyes attributed only to the lower orders; ladies who lived in houses such as The Grove could not possibly manage without a nurse, besides the wet nurse. Yes, they would indeed be shocked if Victoria decided to feed the child herself.

She now leaned over to one side and took up from the

floor the satchel that she had been carrying together with her leather handbag, and, under the pretext of taking her gloves from the handbag, she slipped out the letter from an envelope that was addressed to her in Shields and, taking a number of sovereigns from the middle pouch of the bag, she placed them in the empty envelope, straightened up and handed it to Bright, explaining, 'That is my address;' and, lowering her voice, added, 'Please accept half the contents for yourself and the rest divide among your staff.'

'Oh, miss, miss.' His hands covered the envelope. 'What can I say?'

She smiled widely at him and when getting to her feet she said, 'Just a happy Christmas.'

He, too, was now standing, and his voice was sincere as he murmured, 'We all wish you that, miss. And . . . and I shall keep you informed about the mistress's condition, and anything else I think you should know.'

'Thank you, Bright. Thank you very much. You have eased my mind. And now, do you think I would be able to get a cab? I was about to go to my agent's office, but I've changed my mind.'

'Oh, I'll see you get a cab, miss.'

And he did. And after he had opened the door and helped her in, he asked, 'What address shall I give him, miss?'

And she looked straight into his face and without any hesitation, she said, 'Mr Pearson's farm, Fellburn.'

And he repeated, 'Pearson's farm, Fellburn. Very good, miss.'

He closed the door on her, shouted the destination to the cabbie, then stood back; and as he watched the cab move away down the muddy road, he said to himself, 'Well! Well! . . . Well! Well!'

* * *

She could see immediately that it was a poor farm. The cabbie had got down from the box and opened the door for her, and now he was saying, 'Want me to wait, miss?'

'Yes. Yes, please.' . . .

It was the farmer's wife who, after weighing her up from top to toe, said, 'Aye, we have a Filmore here. He rents an old barn in Long field. Works the stone, he does. Will you come in and I'll go and send somebody for him?'

'No, thank you.' She didn't like the look of the woman, or the smell of the yard; it had likely permeated the house. 'If you will kindly direct me I will find him.'

'Aye well; that's easy. Along the yard there, past the piggeries, through the gate. But be careful of the planks across the burn, they're slippery. Then you can't miss him.'

She knew that the woman was watching her as she followed her directions.

Before she came to the planks across the burn, she could see what looked like a tumbled-down building to the right of her.

The planks themselves indeed were slippery and after crossing them she found herself impeded by the heels of her shoes sinking into the sodden field. Then she was standing outside the weather-beaten double doors of the barn.

An intermittent sound was coming from behind the doors. It wasn't loud, not loud enough, she thought, to obscure her knocking; but after she had knocked twice and the door hadn't opened she now pressed one side of it forward. It swung easily from her hand and she was looking into a long structure, and she took in immediately not only the man standing with a mallet poised over some stone and the man on his knees rubbing at another piece of stone, but also that the roof at the far end of the structure showed daylight.

Douglas did not immediately come towards her because the sight of her so surprised him she could have been an apparition. When he did make a move it was slow. He laid down the mallet and a chisel onto a bench, then stepping across the roughly paved space, he exclaimed simply, 'Why! Bridget.'

'Hello, Douglas.'

'How on earth did you get here? I mean . . .'

'Yes, I know what you mean. How did I find you? Quite simple; I ran into Bright.'

'Oh, Bright.' He smiled now; then turning to where the man had risen from his knees, he said, 'This is Sam. You remember?'

'Oh yes. Yes, indeed. Hello, Sam.'

Standing up now, Sam touched his forelock and replied, 'Good day to you, ma'am.' Then looking towards Douglas, he added tactfully, 'I'll take time for me bait, sir, and stretch me legs.'

'Yes, do that.'

It wasn't until the man had passed through the barn door and closed it after him that Bridget, continuing to look about her, now allowed her gaze to rest on Douglas as she said, 'Oh! Douglas, what a place. You must be frozen.'

'Not a bit of it. Not a bit of it.' His voice was light. 'Can't you feel a difference from outside? Look.' He pointed to the other end of the room from where the rafters were letting in light. 'That old stove gives out a mighty heat.' He walked towards it, and she followed him; but her eyes weren't so much on the stone as on what lay to the side of a wooden partition: a bench on which stood a spirit lamp, and a pan and some odd bits of crockery; and beyond, an erection that appeared to be a bunk standing four feet off the ground and on which were some neatly folded but coarse-looking blankets.

In utter amazement now she turned to him, and she actually stammered as she said, 'Yo ... you ... you're not ... what I mean, living here? Oh, Douglas!'

'Madam, I'll have you know that my bed is very comfortable. And I am learning a new trade; I might open a restaurant any day.'

'Be quiet! Don't make fun. Why didn't you let me know?'

'Let you know what?' His tone had changed. 'What was there to let you know? That I had fought with Lionel and that life had become unbearable there? And would you please do something about it for me as you always do for everybody you come in contact with?'

His head dropped and he muttered now apologetically, 'I'm sorry. I'm sorry, Bridget.'

After a pause she said, 'So you should be, making me out to be a busybody or do-gooder maiden lady.'

He smiled faintly now as he repeated her words, still muttering: 'Do-gooder maiden lady.'

'May I now ask,' she said, 'what started the trouble at the house? It must have been something drastic to cause him to give up that amount of money.'

He looked away from her as he said, 'Yes, it was quite drastic.'

She waited, then said, 'Well, can't you tell me what it was?'

'No. No, Bridget, I can't. It is something that is best left dead and buried.'

His head gave a little jerk: he was immediately aware of the simile he had come out with, for Joe Skinner was definitely well dead and buried. He'd had nightmares thinking about the poor fellow. One lately had caused him to wake up screaming. In it he had yelled at the poor man, telling him he was going to cut him down. The simile seemed not to have struck Bridget, for she was saying, 'It must have been something pretty bad to have the reaction it did on Victoria. She's an entirely changed person.'

'Well, perhaps that's for the better, because she needed to shed her little girl image.'

'Have you see her since?'

'No.'

'Then, I can assure you, at least to my mind her change isn't for the better, because she has turned into an embittered woman. There seems to be nothing left of her former character.'

He let out a long sigh; then said as though in explanation: 'Our family's fate seems to have hung on money for the last two generations, on money that we have never earned. We have lived in debt for so long: we have eaten in debt, we have been waited on in debt. Yes, many a time I knew those servants hadn't been paid. That's why they left, they weren't dismissed. And all the time I partook of the whole; yet I must admit, with shame at times. But' – he now looked along the length of the old building – 'I am now earning my living, and it has got to keep me and pay a man. And I can sleep easy at nights.' That, he thought, was a stupid thing to say. But it could have been so, for without the knowledge that he had unearthed . . . literally unearthed, this work, and even making this derelict building his home, would certainly have afforded him peaceful sleep.

'You rent this?'

'Yes. Yes, I rent it.'

'They should pay you for occupying it.'

'Oh, not this particular farmer. As Sam says, "That man would skin a louse for its hide." '

'Well, I wouldn't consider that I myself would come into that category with the places that I let. But I do have a building to let.'

'You have?'

'Yes. And you've seen it.'

'Oh, huh!' He wagged his hand at her. 'Now you are playing your lady bountiful. No way, Bridget, no way. Not that I wouldn't like to be working near you, because it's always nice to have someone to fight and argue with at times.' He smiled; but then the smile sliding from his face, he said, 'Thank you all the same, Bridget, but no.'

'You don't believe that it is to be let?'

'No, I don't, dear. You were going to put Lily down there with her child.'

'Yes, I know, and the house is finished. But would she go? No. She said it was too far away. She prefers the lodge, and it's as she says, she has got it very nice. I have spent quite a bit of money on that place, I can tell you, and, being a business woman, I always want results. So, I am letting it, together with a four-acre field as a smallholding. It would be ideal for that. It is now in my agent's hands and I understand he has already one applicant. So you see, I am not playing my lady bountiful. I only made the suggestion because I thought it would be ideal for your requirements, there being a large barn and three other buildings, besides a little house.' She pulled a face now as she said, 'But . . . but I think it's the house that's going to be the drawback. It's rather small for a family, at least for anyone with sufficient money to start that kind of business.'

She knew that his mind was busily working, in fact it had already done a somersault. So she turned away from his awful arrangement for living and walked towards the door, which she had almost reached when, at her side now, he asked quietly, 'What are you asking, by the way, as rent?'

She stopped and glanced upwards as if thinking deeply, then said, 'You know, I can't really remember. It was a bit complicated. There might be the prospective tenant who wanted only the house and buildings, others might only want the field to work. In the last resort it was decided they could be let separately. I even thought if no one wants the field then I could extend the gardens. But in parts it's a bit boggy and it would need drainage. Anyway, I must be off. Oh, Douglas, it's been lovely seeing you; but look' – she leant towards him – 'there's no reason why you can't visit me. What about coming for Sunday dinner?'

'Yes, I would like that. I *would* like that.'

'All right, we will leave it at that.' She did not immediately make for the door now, but turned and looked at the pieces of stone dotted here and there about the room, and she said, 'How's business going really?'

'Oh, pretty well; enough for me to still keep on Sam. The main trouble seems to be the transport. It's difficult to get a cart down here. It's a good job that both Sam and I are as strong as horses, not the dray kind, you know, just the ordinary ones.'

They were smiling broadly now at each other, and she said, 'You always surprise me, Douglas,' at which he threw his head back and said, 'Oh! lady; not as much as you surprise me, not as much as you have always surprised me.'

Following this their hands joined and shook; they exchanged a long glance, and then she was walking through the sodden field again.

When she reached the cab she quickly gave the cabbie directions, and forty minutes later she was standing in her office in Newcastle, talking rapidly to her agent, saying, 'Well, there it is. He may come or he may not, but just say to him what I've said to you. You could add that you were going to take a client out there. Would he, too, like to go and see the place? to which he will likely reply that he knows it. Then let him sign the agreement: eight shillings a week for the house and stables; eleven shillings if he wants the land as well. You can add that he can have access to the main yard, et cetera. You understand?'

'Yes,' Arthur Fathers said; 'yes, I understand, Miss Mordaunt. And I know Mr Douglas . . . well, I've met him on occasions. Very nice gentleman. And I'm sorry to hear he's working under such awful conditions. Leave it to me, Miss Mordaunt. He'll be settled in there before you can say Jack Robinson.'

'Thank you. He may come in today, there's still time, or tomorrow morning. And I will be pleased if you deal with him yourself, and not one of the clerks.'

'Oh, yes, yes, I'll be here all day. And I'll make it my business to be here in the morning, too, just in case.'

'Thank you very much, Mr Fathers. And now we'll get down to the business of the week.'

And as they did so Mr Fathers wondered if she had forgotten it was dinner time. But then she was the boss. Yes, indeed, she was the boss.

It was in the middle of the Sunday dinner that Douglas, looking across the white linen-capped table, checked Bridget's bringing up a spoonful of iced pudding to her mouth with the words, 'Being your new tenant, will I be invited to this every Sunday?' He spread his hand over the table, and Bridget, her mouth still slightly agape, returned the pudding to the plate and forced herself to say, 'What do you mean, Douglas?'

'Well, you gave me all the details and made it clear it was a business deal, so, on consideration, I thought I'd be a fool not to take it up. I hesitated a bit and nearly too long, because it seems your agent was about to show another fellow round.'

'Oh! Douglas, I'm so glad. It'll . . . it'll be wonderful having you down there.'

His voice was low now as he said, 'It'll be wonderful, too, for me, Bridget. You don't know how wonderful.'

'Oh yes, I do.' She was nodding at him. 'After that dreadful place . . . But what about your man, Sam? Is he coming with you?'

'Yes. He lives Hebburn way and he said it'll be the same distance either way. He's a good man, Sam. I'm very lucky to have him. Not only is he good with his hands, but he's good company. He's an intelligent fellow when you get to know him. He hardly opened his mouth to me for the first month I had him, but afterwards I soon learned that he had ideas and opinions.'

He now laid his spoon down by his plate and, his hands placed on each side of it, he stared intently at her as he said, 'It's going to be a new life for me, Bridget, quite a new life for me.'

She controlled the reaction to say, 'For me, too,' for she might have said it fervently: not only did she need company to fill the great hole of loneliness in her but, in a strange way, she knew she needed him, him in particular, and had done for some time, while knowing the thought was ridiculous and as far-fetched, in a way, as had been her feelings for Joe.

268

8

As if she were setting up a new home, she saw to the furnishings of the farmhouse, for it had not been occupied since her father acquired it. Besides the necessary articles she put in a number of small pieces taken from Milton Place.

On first seeing her handiwork Douglas had stood silent for a moment, and then had said, 'This is ridiculous, Bridget. How do you expect me to come and throw myself down onto a couch like that in my stone-powdered clothes?' And she had answered, 'Of course, I wouldn't expect you to throw yourself down onto a couch like that in your stone-powdered clothes; I'd expect you to wash and change beforehand, and cook yourself a meal in your kitchen, as you've refused my offer of eating in the house in the evenings.' And at this he turned on her, suppressed laughter in his face now as he said, 'Well, would you want us to get talked about?'

She would have liked to answer, 'I wouldn't mind in the least,' which would have surprised him just as the thought of it had surprised herself. It was like those other thoughts that had been creeping through the floorboards of her mind and which she had no way of stopping: she had tried pooh-poohing them, even using ridicule, but without effect; and so had answered with, 'Well, if people have nothing better to do but talk about us, then we'll have to be charitable in the thought that while we are suffering others are having a rest.'

'Oh, Bridget. Your capping always amuses me. You are a sharp-tongued young woman, you know.'

'Yes, I'm well aware of that.' And the admission hurt her in a way for she didn't want him to see her as a sharp-tongued young woman; but then, she couldn't see herself changing, she was herself, and that was that . . .

So, Douglas took up his abode, even eagerly, in the stone farmhouse, and a new way of life began, punctuated with protests: she mustn't let the girls come down and clean the place, he could do that himself; she must have a word with her cook and stop her sending pies and cans of soup down for both him and Sam.

He would make one concession. Yes, he would take Sunday dinner with her. And so, here they were, eating together again, and he was remarking on her staff: 'They are all so very excited about Christmas,' he said.

'Yes,' she nodded at him across the table. 'You see, they have a party on Christmas Day, and they invite their friends, and it's high jinks. I have to look in for a time, and you also will have to this year.'

'It's a happy house this, isn't it?'

She did not answer immediately, but when she did her voice was low: 'I've always thought so,' she said, 'simply because I was born here; and our young days were indeed happy, with Victoria flitting about like a butterfly. But,' and the word immediately conveyed a sadness, 'she is no longer a butterfly. I would never in my life have imagined anyone changing so. And she has cut herself off from me entirely. That pains me and worries me because, going back over it all, I feel I am to blame: I should not have bought him and . . . forced him into the marriage in the first place.'

'You did it for the best; there's no vestige of blame to be attached to you. All that has happened stems from my brother. He is utterly selfish. It is as well she has changed, for she would never have been able to exist in that house if she had remained the girl she was. She would have been trampled into the dust by him: by his openly flaunting his women; and probably just as effectively by the way in which he would either ignore her or humiliate her. That started shortly after they returned from the honeymoon, but she didn't recognise it, she always thought he was joking. Come, don't look so sad, my dear. What would you like to do this afternoon?'

'Oh, it's what you would like to do. The sun is shining, and so although it's very frosty, would you like to go for a drive in the carriage?'

He interrupted her here with a flapping of his hand and saying, 'No, I would not like to go for a drive in the carriage, ma'am. What I would like to do is to go into the drawing-room, stretch out and snooze before that big fire. There are two other possibilities, one is to argue with you about something or other, the second is, play you crib.'

'We'll take the latter, sir. But I must warn you, after playing with my father for years I became an expert. And we didn't play for chucks, mind; there was always money on the table, and it was a rare occasion when I didn't gather it up when we finished.'

'I bet that was what the business was built on, the rake-off from your gambling.'

'You're quite right, sir, you're quite right.'

They left the dining-room laughing.

Sunday, she was finding, was a day to look forward to. She was happy or nearly so. Now and again it seemed she still had to have some confirmation, but less and less was she worrying about Victoria; she had become a person who could manage her own affairs. Yet, having agreed on this within herself, there remained the knowledge that Victoria was a very unhappy woman.

Christmas turned out to be a very merry affair. Douglas said he could never remember enjoying himself so much. The highlight was the servants' Christmas party, to which Sam and his wife had also been invited. This pleased Douglas; and he, too, surprised her, for during the limited time she allowed for their visit he had the whole company amused by his whistling of bird songs and then by a very good imitation of a farmyard of animals. Later, both of them muffled up to the eyes against the heavy frost, he escorted her down to what was now his home in order that the party could go on uninhibited. She wanted to know how he came to learn to whistle in such a way, and he told her that it was because he had once, as a boy, been taken to the Empire and had there seen a similar turn, and from then he had practised; on the quiet though, because such a lowly talent wasn't appreciated in the house.

Halfway down the field his grip tightened on her arm and he ran her over the frozen ground, the lantern swinging drunkenly from his other hand, and she laughed as she couldn't remember laughing for a long time. And when they reached the farmhouse door they both turned and lay against the wall for a moment, gasping, and she said, 'You know, there's a mad streak in you, Douglas. It's a good job there are no houses near, else they would think we were wild children on the rampage.'

Inside the house he blew up the damped-down fire into a blaze; then, pointing to the corner of the room to a small decorated Christmas tree, he said, 'Look at that; the girls put it there. Ridiculous, but wasn't that nice of them?'

'It was, indeed,' she said. She recalled Florrie's voice questioning: 'A Christmas tree for Mr Douglas, miss? No! Don't you think he'll laugh at it?'

And to this she had said, 'I don't think so. It will make

him feel at home. And we can hang his presents on it, or lay them around the foot of it.'

Her small staff had included him in their presentation of Christmas presents, a single handkerchief or some such, except Jessie who, quick with her needle, as she said, had looped him off a pair of woollen gloves. She herself had bought him a tie and a fancy waistcoat, neither elaborate nor expensive items. And what had he bought her? An anthology of poetry.

He was saying now, 'Don't take your coat off till the room gets a little warmer.' She had pulled off her fur hood and unloosened the top buttons of her coat, and for a moment his hands went out towards her as if he were about to button up her coat again. Then they dropped to his sides and, now standing before her, he said, 'This kind of life seems too good to be true, Bridget. I'm afraid something will happen, and it will vanish, and I shall find myself back at Farmer Pearson's, having woken up on the bunk and found it all a dream.'

'It is no dream, Douglas, just a new way of life. And I am so happy you are here. It is ... well, it is lovely for me to have your company.'

They were standing looking at each other through the soft light of the oil lamp, then quietly he said, 'Will you do something for me?'

'Anything within my power.'

'Oh, it is within your power: it is just to ask if you will see the New Year in with me in this, my little cosy house?'

'Yes. Yes, of course, Douglas. I'd love to see the New Year in with you,' and only just stopped herself from adding, 'I would like to see the New Year in anywhere with you.'

273

9

They were in the kitchen, Peg Nixon, Mary Benny, Florrie McLean, and of course Jessie and Danny, Jimmy Tierney and Frank Matthews. Johnnie Moran was seeing in the New Year with his family.

It was Florrie who said, 'It'll be funny not drinking the New Year in with the miss. We've always done it and made a wish.'

Jessie looked around the company seated at the long wooden table and she said, 'Well now, the miss has chosen to bring it in with Mr Douglas' – her words were slow and emphatic and full of meaning – 'and when we're bringing in the New Year in the hall I'm going to make a strong wish.' And now she allowed her gaze to pass from one to the other, nodding at each in turn before she ended, 'She's good to us, and if you want to be good to her . . . well, you know what to wish for.'

It was Frank Matthews who asked quietly, 'D'you think she's that way inclined?'

'Aye, Frank, I think she's that way inclined, and had been for a long while but didn't know it. He was a frequent visitor up at the other place. I've heard them arguing the toss, and yet he would come back, and that points in the right direction, doesn't it? And as you know, she keeps busy, nobody busier. Lately she's kept busier than ever.'

Jimmy Tierney was nodding towards Jessie, saying, 'I like him an' all. He's a surprisin' fella: not two pennorth of flesh on him from his scalp to his toes, thin as a rake he is, but you want to see him lift some of them stones of his. And as Sam said to me, he goes on for hours non-stop. Tires him out at times. Surprisin' fella I think, and pleasant. Oh aye, an' pleasant. Not like t'others in his family,' an opinion which started a concerted nodding expressing mutual agreement.

And now Jessie rose to her feet, saying, 'Now one of you fellas go down and bring Lily and the bairn up. Cover him well up. And the table's all set next door, the fire's blazin', but we could do with more wood and coal in there, so I'll leave that to you chaps and we lasses will carry the bottles in. Eh?' which caused high laughter and chaffing and requests from the men to change jobs.

And so they now happily scrambled to add to the last of the preparations for ushering in the New Year of eighteen hundred and eighty-five.

'The house is beautifully warm, you must have had that fire roaring up the chimney all day.'

'Yes, I have, and at what a cost. I sawed wood for nearly two hours.'

'Poor soul.'

'Don't be sarcastic, miss. There's a difference in the work of sawing and that of chipping stone, or carving wood, for that matter.'

'Yes, I'm sure there is.' They smiled at each other now.

As Bridget sat down on the sofa she said, 'Talking of wood, I think you'd better have a porch put on the front of the door. It leads straight into the kitchen, and there's an awful draught there.'

'I don't want any porch put on the door and as a rule I don't sit in the kitchen. Anyway, how often am I in there during the day? And why must you always be wanting to add things, or re-arrange them?'

'Oh, I suppose it's because I've got nothing else to do.'

He sat down beside her, saying, 'Yes, I suppose that's

it. You want something to fill your time, for you live a sort of self-centred life.'

'Yes, you're right; you're always right.'

Again they were smiling at each other; then, pointing over the end of the couch to where a small table was set for a cold meal, a raised pie with other eatables around it, and, squeezed between them, a bottle of wine, he said, 'You haven't noticed my banqueting table.'

'Oh, I noticed it. How could one miss it? You couldn't get much more on it if you tried.'

'That isn't my fault. You speak to Peggie.'

'I certainly shall. My larder must be depleted.'

She now lay back into the cushions at the end of the couch and, her voice and mood changing, she said, 'It's been a strange year. How much longer have we of it?'

He turned and looked at the round-faced clock hanging on the wall at the other side of the room. 'About seven minutes,' he said.

'Don't you think it's been a strange year?'

His tone had changed now as he answered her, saying, 'I would hate to look back on any minute of it if it wasn't that it has led me here. It's only when you look at the picture objectively that you realise that everything seems to have been planned from the beginning. We have no free will as regards the events that shape our lives, only a little bit allowed us within the events ... Do you look back over the things that have happened to you during this year?'

'Oh yes. Yes, I've been doing it all day ...'

'Thinking of Joe?'

She turned and looked at him sharply. 'Yes,' she said. 'Yes, thinking of Joe, but only in connection with Lily's loss and the baby's future and feeling a bit guilty about the promise I made him, to find out who actually did the

276

deed, when I know that I haven't as yet made a start, because I wouldn't know where to start.'

'Best left alone.'

She watched him slip off the couch onto his knees and lift a piece of wood from the basket to the side of the hearth and throw it into the middle of the blazing fire, sending the sparks, not only flying up the broad chimney, but spurting back onto the hearth rug. And as he dabbed them out, she said, 'Do you want to roast us?'

For a moment he remained on his knees looking into the flames; then he got up and, bending over her, held out his hand, saying, 'Come on; it will soon be starting.'

Without a word she rose and they went out of the room and into the kitchen. And there he took her coat and hood from the back of a chair and helped her into them; then from a hook on the door he took down his own coat and buttoned it up to the neck, announcing, 'We'll wait and go out just before they start, because it's bitter out there.'

An oil lamp burned in the middle of the kitchen table and with the glow from the open fire that heated the round oven to the side of it, the room was illuminated with a soft warm light. They stood in this glow and in the silence looking at each other, waiting for the sound of the first hooter. When it came he pulled the door open, took her arm and led her out onto the step.

The sky was high and bright with stars, the frozen field before them appearing like a silver sea. The air hit the back of their throats like old wine and the whole world seemed to be now enveloped in the chorus of ship's fog-horns vying with each other and factory hooters screaming their time signals, all mingled with the sound of church bells, their peals seeming to bound from one star to another, until the very sky itself became a canopy of sound.

They stood shoulder-tight to shoulder until the very last

277

note died away and they were left standing in an echoing silence and seemingly alone in all the world, between the roof of stars and the sea of silver. And such had been the enchantment of the moment that they did not speak as they turned indoors. Not until he had closed the door and dropped the bolt on it and they were standing face to face, did he say in a voice that was thick with emotion, 'Happy New Year, Bridget.' And her answer came almost as a whisper, 'And the same to you, Douglas, the same to you.'

And now he carried out the reason he'd asked her to see the New Year in with him: he put his hands on her shoulders, leant towards her and placed his lips on hers; and he left them there, and when after a moment there was no response and he was about to withdraw, her arms came about him and her mouth answered his and they clung together until they swayed and her shoulders touched the door. Only then did their lips part, but they still held on to each other.

'Oh, Bridget! Bridget!'

She made no answer because she couldn't at this moment when her throat, even her whole body, was choked with unbearable emotion.

The spaces in the floorboards of her mind had widened of late and she'd had to face the fact of her true feelings and what they would mean if given way to, or if they were reciprocated. One of the thoughts pointed out that she would be connected with that family, another that he only saw her as a friend. But now she knew differently.

He was leading her into the sitting-room, gazing at her all the while, and when they once more stood before the fire he again uttered her name, saying, 'Oh, Bridget! Bridget!' but now added, 'Is this true?'

And she could only murmur, 'Yes, Douglas, very true for me.'

'Oh, my love.'

Again they were enfolded, again their lips were together, hard, tight. When they almost tumbled onto the couch, he said, 'Drunk, and without wine.' He now drew her round the couch and to the table, saying, 'Let's drink to this wonderful moment.' And when he had to leave go of her in order to open the bottle of wine, he said, 'I never want to move any further away from you in my life again,' she made no reply: she was finding it difficult to find words to say, in fact she didn't want to speak. This wondrous thing was beyond words, it didn't need words, just actions, to be held, to be kissed as he had kissed her, to hold him in her arms.

They stood, their glasses clinking; then after they had drunk he asked quietly, 'Would you like something to eat, dear?'

She shook her head: 'No. No, thank you,' she said; 'this is enough.' And at that she finished a glass of wine at one go, and he, laughing, followed suit before taking the glass from her and placing them both on the table. Then, his arm about her he led her back to the couch, and there as if both exhausted after some strenuous event, they lay back looking at each other, until he asked softly, 'When did you know?' and she shook her head, saying, 'I can't remember. It seemed to creep up on me, and all the while I was pushing it back. And you?'

'Oh, I can pin-point the very moment. It was in the carriage, when you broke down and I held you. That was the point when the light really dawned. But I think I, too, had been working up to it before, from the night of the dance. You were so different.'

'Oh, I know I was. Victoria emphasised the difference and although, at her command, I got a new dress, it didn't seem to make any difference.'

'Don't be silly.' He tapped her cheek with his fingers. 'Of course you're different. You're intelligent, and you're

279

a girl . . . a woman who is doing something with her life. You were bound to appear different in that company of hunting, shooting, fishing from the male side and frivolity from the women. Not that I don't think some of them were intelligent enough, but they used it mainly in sharpening their tongues and trimming their finger nails into claws. As a boy who didn't seem to matter I was left to listen to their chatter, and as a young man who should, my father thought, be brought out, I was thrust into the men's company, and there, there was still chatter, where you were looked upon as a fine fellow the more bawdy you were. Of course,' he pulled a face now, 'like all groups in all parts of society I must admit they weren't all alike. Pat Maybrook, for instance. I met him the other day and he was genuinely pleased, seemingly, to see me, and to hear that I was doing well. And the Forrester family, the five girls, they were all nice, except' – he now laughed – 'except Freda.'

'Why Freda?'

'She used to chase me. She must have been very hard up, but she did. I was scared of Freda from when I was seventeen or so.'

'I'm glad she didn't catch you.'

'Oh, Bridget. Bridget. I don't know how many times I've said that since this New Year's come in, but I've said it a thousand times in my mind over the past months, especially since I came into this little house. And you know something? I'm going to make my first confession. I planned this night. I thought, I will kiss her. That will give me an opportunity to find out, because everybody kisses everybody, whether drunk or sober, as the New Year comes in. But I told myself, I will kiss her and then I shall know if she has a spark of feeling for me.'

'Oh, my dear, my dearest Douglas.' She was holding his face between her hands. 'You are a schemer, but I forgive you, because I, too, am a schemer, and I have a first confession to make. This place' – she now wagged her head from side to side – 'was never for letting. No cabbie ever raced his horse so hard from that awful farm and shed you were in, to my agent in Newcastle, where I told them what to do. You'd be along, I said, and they had to play it ... well, cagey, as if there was someone else after it.'

His eyes widened, his teeth were now biting his lower lip. He gripped her wrists and pulled her hands from his face, saying, 'You wretch! Oh, you scheming ...'

'Well, what more proof could you have of my love for you?'

'But, Lily and the child, they were coming here?'

'Yes; and so they were, but she would have none of it. Too far away from the house, as I've said, and she had got the Lodge very comfortable. I didn't know then what I was going to do with it, but from the minute I saw you in that place I knew, and ... and oh, my love, I wanted you near me. I did, I did.'

Once more they were enfolded. And now he asked quietly, 'You will marry me?'

'Sir! Sir!' She tried to draw back from him. 'What else?'

'I wish you hadn't any money.'

'But I have, a great deal of money.'

'Well, right from the start I'm going to say this to you. I don't want it spent on me. Do you understand, my dear? I want to work and earn by my working.'

'Oh yes, I understand, and I wouldn't want you to be any other way. But there's one thing I would like to do for you.'

'And what's that, madam?'

'I'd like to have a proper road made from here towards the back gates, so you would have easy access for the transport of the stone, et cetera.'

He fell back from her for a moment, laughing now as she said, 'Here we go! Here we go!'

'That's nothing. It will save the carts getting bogged down in the field. Be sensible.'

'Be sensible.' He had his arms about her again, and hers were about him. And now he said softly, 'There's one thing I haven't told you, and that is, besides you being the most kind and thoughtful creature on this earth, you are also beautiful.'

'Don't. Don't.'

He pulled her more tightly to him. 'You are beautiful. You are a beautiful woman. And I'm going to sculpt you ... not scalp you ... sculpt you from head to foot one day. And I'll make you more beautiful than the head I gave you at Christmas. And that was you, too, you know.'

She became quiet within his hold and when he reached out and lifted her legs across his knees so that she was practically sitting on his lap, she made no move to stop him.

Florrie McLean could not get down the stairs quickly enough; she had to check her legs from running in case the miss's cup of early tea jumped off the tray. And when she burst into the kitchen, Peggie and Jessie both turned from where they were sitting at the table enjoying their early morning cup and demanded, 'What is it? What is it, woman?'

'She's ... she's not there! The bed it's ... it's never been slept in.'

The two women rose slowly from the table and three pairs of eyes exchanged glances. And then the cook sat down and her body began to shake with laughter, and this was taken up by Florrie, but Jessie did not join in. Her head was wagging as she said, 'Well, now, she shouldn't have gone that far. No, she shouldn't. Well, now. And you two' — she was wagging her finger at them — 'don't let this go any further. She'll likely be over in a minute or so. What time is it? Oh' — she looked at the clock — 'quarter to eight. Well, she'll be bound to know by this time that you've taken up her tea. But act ordinary, d'you hear me? Act ordinary as if nothing had . . . well . . . Huh! I was going to say, as if nothing had happened but . . .'

She was biting on her lip now; then her body, too, began to shake, and the three of them now were leaning on the table and Peggie was saying, 'Well, that's that. We know where we stand. But I think we'd better keep it from the men, don't you?'

'Definitely,' Jessie said. 'Definitely, except, that is, if any of them see her coming up over the field.'

'Oh, I don't suppose so,' said Florrie; 'they were all a bit shaky on their feet when they left here, weren't they? And Mr Croft's still in bed, isn't he?'

'Aye, he is,' Jessie said; 'and he'd better stay there for a time. I think he'd be a bit shocked; he wouldn't imagine her being capable of that.'

The word, that, seemed to present a picture again to the three of them, and once more they were leaning against the table and laughing. And they didn't stop until Jessie, taking a pull at herself, said, 'Well, that's set the New Year off for us. I wonder what the end of it will be.'

It was four days later when Victoria received a letter from her cousin Bridget, and when the contents made her hysterical to the point that she laughed uproariously, Bright called Kate Swift upstairs to attend to her, for she was nearing her time and he felt she might do herself an injury. But Kate could not calm her, and when Victoria pushed them aside and shambled out of the bedroom and down the stairs to the smoking room, where she knew she would at least find her father-in-law at this time of the day, Bright and Kate followed her. They watched her thrust open the door, an action which seemed to startle the master, and he turned from where he was sitting, crying, 'Woman! why are you down here?'

'I am down here, sir, to show you this letter.'

William Filmore stared at the woman before him, her stomach protruding like that of a poisoned horse, and he almost snatched the letter from her hands. And after he had read it he looked back at her, saying nothing, which brought the cry from her: 'Well! sir, can't you see the irony of it? Your son married the wrong one in taking me, but your second son is marrying the right one. 'Tis ironic, don't you think? You would have been set and your house in order if he had still lived here, or if your elder son, as you will likely tell him, had had sense and hadn't chosen a pretty face to go with what he imagined was a fortune.' She began to laugh again. 'He is out about his daily business, but if it is possible, when he returns this evening I should like to be present when you tell him the news. Oh, yes, I deserve to be present when you tell him this news, sir.'

'Woman, go to your room.'

'I will go to my room when I am ready, sir.'

His bawl almost lifted her from the ground as he yelled, 'Go to your room! out of my sight.' Then looking to the side and through the open door, he cried, 'Bright! see to it.'

When Bright and Kate came quickly into the room and, one on each side of her, turned Victoria about, she made no protest. Her laughter was ebbing away, driven out by the pains that were starting to catch her breath . . .

Twenty-four hours later Victoria gave birth to a daughter. And it was noted amongst the staff with pity that neither father nor the grandfather asked to see the child, although both of these men were downstairs drinking.

But pity for the mistress had increased in James Bright and also his mind was set on asking questions when he heard his master say to his son, 'Biting you, isn't it, when the runt of the litter has got what you imagined was intended for you? You feel you could do murder again, don't you? It's hard for you to accept that he always had more common sense in his little finger than you had in your whole head. As your wife said, you picked the wrong one. But you were always greedy and . . . bloody stupid. Look what you've sprung on the house now, a female! and our line hasn't thrown off a female in three generations. Always classed ourselves as breeders of men. But I've had to ask meself lately, what kind of men? At least I do when I look at you. The other one is more man than you'll ever be and . . .'

'Shut up! Father. Shut up! I'm warning you. Shut up!'

'You're warning me, of what? I'd be careful, son, be careful with that tongue of yours, for who knows, what one's capable of doing, another can.'

As Bright walked quietly away along the conservatory he told himself that there was something here he didn't understand. The only thing that was clear to him was there was some grave reason behind the fight that had taken place between the two brothers, and it hadn't only to do with money because the lack of that had been a source of trouble in this house for years. No, it was something else. But there was one thing that he was glad of and that was Mr Douglas was going to marry that nice kind Miss Mordaunt. Yet, at the same time, what a pity, he thought, that Mr Douglas hadn't been the elder son, because then Miss Mordaunt would have taken over this house and everything would have become different. Oh, yes, so different.

PART THREE

The Years Between
1896

1

'But, Mam, why have they all of a sudden decided to do this?'

Lily looked at her son and said gently, 'It isn't all of a sudden. The mistress has been talking about if for some time.'

'Well, that's news to me ... and to Amy as well. She doesn't want to go to any boarding school. Anyway, I thought that Mrs Filmore considered Madam Duval's Academy for Young Ladies' – he wrinkled his nose now – 'the very last thing in education. In my opinion it's the very last thing in snobbery.'

'It's about time, Joseph, that you learned to keep your opinions to yourself.'

'Oh, Mam, I do, I do, because I have to. God knows why, and all of a sudden, when for years I've had the run of the place.'

'You've been lucky. Yes, very lucky.' Lily's voice was high and sharp, but her son's was low and there was a puzzled note in it as he said, 'You've been telling me that for years on and off, Mam, and I'd really like to know why. All right, all right, they put me to a good school and now I'm in the Royal Grammar, and they're paying for me. And Mam, let me tell you, I know it, and I feel it, all the time I'm very aware that they're paying for me.'

'Well, that's because of your own make-up. They never mention the matter.'

The boy sighed now, then dropping down again onto the kitchen chair standing by the side of the wooden table, on which there were a number of his books and paper already written upon, he picked up a pencil and stabbed the point into the paper, saying, 'I feel at times that I'm astride a ravine or some such, a foot on either side and the gulf getting wider. There was a time when Amy and I were allowed to scamper from one end of the place to the other, and Mr Filmore treated me like . . . well, as if . . . well, as if I belonged . . . as if I was one of the family. He still does, but . . .'

'Well, that's because he's a kind man an' you've taken advantage.'

'What d'you mean, Mam?' He was up on his feet again, his hand flat on the table leaning towards her to where she had turned now from the oven, a brown dish in her hands. 'Taking advantage? Advantage of what? I've run my heels off for years doing what I was told, keeping my place. But what place? Here we are living in the Lodge, where there's not room to swing a cat, but I've had the run of that house.' He pointed towards the window. 'Since Amy was born, at least from when she could crawl, I've played with her and nobody objected. I've run the woods with her; I've even run by the carriage whenever I could.' He didn't add, 'And Jimmy Tierney would never stop even when Amy yelled at him.' This was another thing that troubled him, the servants. The women were all right, but the men, the older ones who had been in the family for years, they didn't treat him like the master and mistress did, especially Frank Matthews. But of course, he wouldn't because he had been after his mother for years now; and because she wouldn't have him he seemed to hold it against him. He said now, 'Mam, there's something I can't get to the bottom of at times. It worries me.'

'I don't know what you've got to worry about; you've got a good life.'

The boy closed his eyes, turned from the table and

shook his head slowly from side to side as he said, 'Mam, you don't get the point, you never have. You're like a clam and you won't face the fact that I'm not a little boy any longer. I'm twelve years old and I am told that I'm bright. I am almost two years ahead in the mathematics class; they don't know what to do with me. "What are you going to do?" they say. "What are you going to be?" "I don't know," I say.' Now he swung round to her and he repeated loudly, 'I don't know, Mam. There's lots of things I don't know. You won't talk about my father. You won't talk about your people who live in Gateshead. I have a granny there, I understand, and uncles and aunts, but I've never clapped eyes on them; why?'

'Oh, I've told you that until I'm tired. They're rampant Catholics and I committed the sin of marrying a Protestant.'

'Yes. Yes, I've got that far, but that trouble was with your step-father and mother. What about the half-brothers and sisters? You know, I'd like to see somebody that belongs to me.'

She stared at him in silence; then she said, 'I belong to you.'

Her voice was so low and held such a depth of sadness that he almost scrambled round the table and put his arms about her, saying, 'I know, I know, Mam. And I'm grateful. I'm grateful for everything. But there's some things I don't understand, and neither can Amy.'

She immediately pressed herself away from him, and said in some surprise, 'You don't discuss . . . well, I mean, you don't talk about that . . . well . . . ?'

'Yes. Yes, we do. We talk about everything, not just my side, but hers, too. There's her uncle who lives in this big house, married to her mother's cousin and whom she has never seen in her life, either of them, because they never visit. She only knows they've got a daughter called Henrietta who is slightly odd, and they only know this because the butler writes at intervals.'

'How d'you know that?'

'Amy told me. Amy is as anxious to see them as I am to see my granny and uncles or aunts or whatever. But you know what I think, Mam?'

She smiled faintly at him, saying, 'Whether I want to know or not, you'll tell me.'

'Well, it's this. They're sending Amy to boarding school to keep her away from me.'

Lily drew in a deep breath and it was some seconds before she could bring out with any semblance of truth the words, 'Don't be silly. Who d'you think you are that they would go to all that trouble just to stop you and her running around like bits of kids, when you're no longer bits of kids?'

'No. No, she's a grown woman, she's ten and a half.'

'Don't be silly, Joseph. But you know, you worry me at times. You take too much on yourself, you take liberties.'

'Oh God!' He turned away.

And now she cried at him, 'And don't use that expression to me!'

He had turned to face her again and cried back at her, 'Well, I get tired, Mam, of you telling me to know my place and not to take liberties. I . . . I'm not made to bow and scrape. I don't know why it irks me, but it does. And anyway, they've never treated me up there as if I should bow and scrape. They don't expect anybody to bow and scrape to them. It seems it's only you who expects me to bow and scrape.'

'I don't, son, I don't. But it's like this: no matter how nice the master and mistress treat me, I'm still a servant, and . . . and you are, unfortunately, the son of a servant. I say "unfortunately" because you've got a head on your shoulders. Your teachers say you're streets above those of

292

your own age. But it's this way, Joseph, I only want you to see life as it is. It is no fairy-tale. When Miss Amy comes back from the boarding school her ideas will likely be changed and you've got to be prepared for that. She may no longer see you as the boy she played with or the young lad that she argued with. And what is more, she'll be goin' to balls and meeting young men and . . . and I don't want to see you hurt by bein' put on the side and . . .'

'Shut up! Mam. Please, shut up! will you?' The boy now turned away, grabbed up his school cap from a chair and went out. And as the door banged behind him, Lily hurriedly left the kitchen and went up the narrow stairs and into her box of a bedroom. Here, sitting on the edge of the single bed, she folded her arms tightly across her chest and began to sway. The time had almost come, she felt, for what she had daily been dreading for years, the time when he would demand to know why she didn't talk about his father. Once out of the blue he had said to her, 'How did my father die? Was it of the cholera?' and she had taken a fit of coughing that almost choked her. Luckily, in his concern for her state, he hadn't repeated the question, and she had hoped he had forgotten it, but now she knew he hadn't.

After a time she got up and, out of habit, bent down and smoothed out the hollows in the counterpane where she had been sitting. Then she walked to the little window and looked out over the backyard to the stretch of vegetable garden and beyond to the open grassland that led to the copse; suddenly, she put her hand to her throat, for there she saw her son hurrying towards a young girl. She watched them meet and stand for a time as if talking in earnest; then they went towards the wood. And on this she muttered to herself, 'Dear, dear Lord!'

It wasn't so much that they were full cousins, nor was she worrying about Miss Amy, it was her son she was worrying about and the effect on him when he would come to know, as he would some day, how it had come about he was who he was.

Many times she had wished she had never taken up the mistress's offer, and this was one of them.

2

Joseph was tall for his age. His eyes were a deep brown, his nose was largish and his mouth was wide. And there was no fresh blush on his cheeks: his skin looked slightly tanned and over all had a matt appearance. And as Amy looked at him her young heart ached at the thought that after next week and for some months ahead she would not be seeing him.

She couldn't recall a time, except when they had gone on holiday to France last year, that she hadn't seen him every day of which she had been aware in her life: Joseph had appeared to be one of the family; in fact, for her he was the family. She had played with him all her early days. She had fought with him and even scratched his face, then followed him around for days saying she was sorry, until he had yelled at her to shut up, when they had gone at it again. Such was the relationship between them.

He was saying, 'You'll like it when you get there, I suppose.'

'I won't. No, I won't.'

'All right, you won't, but you've got to go and be made into . . . a young lady.' And now there was a cynical twist to his lips as he said, 'Although I don't know how they're going to manage it.'

Immediately she bridled. 'Oh! Don't you? Well, I might be such a young lady that I won't deign to speak to you when I come back.'

His expression darkened, his eyes narrowed, and he said, 'I wouldn't be surprised at all at that because you'll be meeting with a different class of people. Oh, yes.'

'Of course I won't! Why should they be a different class?'

'Don't be stupid, of course they will. And you'll invite them here and they'll look at me and think, Oh, she hobnobs with the servants then?'

She stood back from him. 'What's come over you, Joseph Skinner? I've never heard you talk like that before. You're not the son of a servant; Lily is a friend of Mammy's.'

He poked his head down towards her now, saying, 'Lily is a maid up in the house.'

'Yes, she works there; but it's a different kind of work. Since Jessie died she's a sort of housekeeper, she sees to things. And she and Mammy talk a lot and . . .'

'Yes, and . . . ?'

She could not say, 'Yes, they talk a lot but they don't let me stay with them when they are talking.' One day recently her mammy had been angry with her and accused her of standing outside the door when actually she had been just about to knock. Lily had come out and looked hard at her before turning away.

She said now, 'I was just going to say, well they have known each other a long time, even before you were born, before Mammy and Daddy were married, so they will have things to talk about. Anyway, it proves that she's not that kind of a servant.'

'You're stupid in some ways, you know that?'

'Oh, and you're clever in all ways, aren't you? Just because you can do sums.'

'I don't do just sums. You don't call them sums. I deal with mathematics.'

'Oh' – she wagged her head – 'he deals with mathematics. You're getting too big for your boots, Joseph Skinner, that's what you are getting, and you want to pay attention to that head of yours an' all, it's swelling like nobody's business.'

There was a suspicion of a smile on his lips again as he repeated, 'That's what you are getting ... and like nobody's business. I would recommend, Miss Filmore, that you pay attention to your deliverance in future. Punctuating your speech with colloquialisms does not say much for the teaching at your snooty little school. I think your mother's money's wasted.'

She was biting on her bottom lip now, practically gnawing on it, and a little spray of saliva spluttered from her mouth as she came back at him, crying, 'You are a nasty individual and ... and –' For a moment she was lost for suitable stinging words until she remembered Mary arguing with Johnny Moran in the yard and saying, 'You know where I wish you? I wish you at the bottom of the sea.' And so now she repeated, 'Do you know where I wish you, Joseph Skinner? I wish you right at the bottom of the sea.' And to emphasise her words she thrust her index finger emphatically towards the dead leaves on which they were standing and she finished with a bounce of her head, saying, 'There!' Then turning from him, she scampered through the copse, and his muttered, 'Amy. Amy,' was heard only by himself ...

'Now, what's the matter?'

'He's a pig, Mammy, a pig.'

'Who's a pig?' – as if Bridget didn't know.

'Joseph Skinner. Who else? He's a horrible, horrible individual and I'm never going to speak to him again.'

How often over the years had she heard that, and laughed while hugging her daughter and saying, 'That's right, dear; I wouldn't, not until tomorrow.' But today she did not hug her beloved child to her or comfort her with soft words; she said, 'Come along upstairs,' and, taking her hand, she led her up the stairs, then across the first landing and up again to the nursery floor.

The late afternoon sun was slanting across the wooden table standing in the middle of what had been the schoolroom, at which her daughter and the hated person in question had sat when they were small children and had continually done so for years after starting school; first Joseph and then her, until her daughter's interruptions had become too much and he'd had to resort to his own home in order to get through his homework.

'Sit down.'

'Mammy?'

'I said, sit down.'

As if under duress and she was finding the action painful, Amy slowly lowered herself onto the wooden chair; and her mother, leaning towards her, said, 'You are turned ten and a half years old, and there are times when you act as if you were fourteen or fifteen, but at others, I'm sorry to say, your actions would prove you to be six or seven years old.'

'*Oh Mammy!*'

'Yes, oh Mammy!' Then smiling, Bridget asked, 'What has he done this time?'

Amy sighed, then looked towards the window and brought her hands together on her lap before saying, 'He said, I don't speak correctly; I use colloquial . . . isms.' Her tongue stumbled over the word. 'And he said when I come back from this school I likely won't bother speaking to him because –' Now she was looking straight at her mother. 'You know what he said? I wouldn't speak to him because his mother is a servant.'

'He didn't!'

'He did; but not exactly like that, but . . . well, that's what he . . . yes' – her head was bobbing – 'yes, that's what he meant . . . that's what he said. He said, no matter how you treated Lily, she is a servant.'

Bridget sighed. Deep waters here, deep waters all around. Her voice was low now as she spoke: 'Well, there might be something in what he suggests,' she said, 'because you know, you will meet different people.'

'That's what he said: I'll be meeting all kinds of people, and I won't want to talk to him.'

Bridget sighed again. 'As I've just said, yes, you will meet all kinds of people, but I hope you're not the kind of person who will throw over your old friends.'

'Of course I won't, Mammy. But he's awful; and he always thinks he's right. He talks so clever he makes me mad.'

Bridget rose from the chair and went to the bookshelves and began to rearrange the books. That's what she was fearful of, her daughter getting mad at this young boy who was no longer a young boy, not in his mind anyway. Douglas had said he couldn't imagine from where he had inherited his brain, that it wasn't likely it had come from his mother's side, although of course there could never be any proof of that. And yet, he had maintained that there were no startlingly brilliant members of his own family either.

Her daughter's feeling for this boy, Bridget knew, was something very like her own when she had first seen Joe. But then she had been sixteen and Joe something new on her horizon. Her daughter had been brought up with young Joseph; they had been like brother and sister. But they were not brother and sister.

She had for the first time been forced to bring the matter to the fore by telling Lily they thought it was best that Amy should go to a boarding school. There had been no need to explain why; nor did she explain that it was she who was plumping for the boarding school; Douglas had said, 'Must we do this? In any case, it's calf love and it'll likely peter out; but if it doesn't, would it be so bad?'

And she had answered, 'Not in the ordinary way, but there are so many underlying factors. The boy doesn't know from where he sprang; he thinks he is Joe Skinner's son,' to which Douglas had replied, 'Well, let's face it, my dear, that'll come out some time or other. It's bound to. That boy's got a head on his shoulders and he is not going to be easily fobbed off. And besides my side of the business, there are her people, you know. And up till now she hasn't allowed them to come in contact with him. But . . . well, he'll get about. And there is the future.'

Yes, there was the future, and because of it she wanted to protect her daughter . . . but again, from what? It wasn't only the close relationship, it wasn't only that Lionel Filmore was the boy's father, because as Douglas had already pointed out to her, if there was any bad blood in the boy, then there could be equally as much in Amy, because it all stemmed from the one tree.

'Mammy.'

'Yes, dear?'

'Why must I go to a boarding school? I thought you liked Miss Tripp.'

'Yes, my dear, I do like Miss Tripp, but I think that the teaching there is limited. And Cresswell House has such a good name. Your father has looked into it.'

'I don't think Daddy is all that keen.'

'Oh, he is, he is. He wants your education to be of the best.'

'I could always do things and be sent home.'

They were looking at each other now, and they both laughed, and Bridget said, 'Yes, you could, dear; and I'd send you straight back.'

'You wouldn't!' The child had her arms around Bridget's waist now. Looking up into her mother's face

300

and her mouth wide with laughter, she said, 'Not after the third time, for they wouldn't let me in.'

'Go on; you're an imp.' Bridget pushed her daughter away from her, then watched her run from the schoolroom, crying, 'I'm going to see Daddy.'

Bridget didn't leave the room but walked across to the window and waited. And after a moment or so she saw the small figure emerging from the gardens and running down the field to the workshops, where the little farmhouse was now occupied by Sam and his wife and grandson, Harry, who was fourteen years old and had lived with his grandparents since being orphaned five years ago . . .

Amy burst into the workshop, gasping from her running. And when Sam looked up from his knees, where he had been chipping at the base of what looked like an obelisk, he said, 'Out of puff again, Miss Amy? You'll go up in smoke one of these days with your runnin'.'

'It's only balloons that go up in smoke, Sam.'

'Oh, is it? Oh, we learn somethin' every day.'

'. . . Daddy.' She now tripped to the end of the barn and to where Douglas was bending over a long wooden table on which there were various sheets of paper; and he turned his head and said, 'Hello, trouble.'

'Daddy.'

'Yes, dear?' His attention was on the paper again and the pencil in his hand began to trace a line, but stopped when she said in a small voice, 'I want to talk to you.'

He straightened his back, sighed and said, 'Well, this isn't the place, dear, is it?'

'Well, I don't know of a better one, Daddy, because when you're in the house you're always with Mammy, and what I want to ask you I can't ask you in front of her, because she always . . . well, fobs me off.'

'Well, if the questions are annoying, I'm likely to do the same.'

She came close to his side now and put her hand through his arm, saying, 'They're not annoying, Daddy. Can't we take a walk outside?'

'No, we can't, dear. Look, I am very, very busy. This is an important order and it has to be completed in a certain time.'

When his daughter withdrew her hand from his arm and turned away, he quickly caught her shoulder and said, 'Come around here,' and drew her round to the other side of the table and, sitting down on a long wooden form, he said, 'Well, fire away. What is it you want to ask me?'

'You won't be mad at me?'

'That all depends.'

'Well, I don't care if you are mad at me as long as you answer my question.'

'And that all depends, too, I mean whether I answer your question. But, go on, ask it.'

'Well . . . and' – now she was sticking her finger into his chest – 'I don't listen in to people talking, and I don't do it on purpose; but I have sharp ears . . . well, what I mean is, I can distinguish birds' songs and . . . oh' – she shook her head – 'what I'm going to say is, I heard you and Mammy talking. She had got a letter from the man called Bright, and she told you your father was bedridden.'

He stopped her here, nodding and saying, 'All right, all right, you listened in, and my father's bedridden. Yes, he's been bedridden for a long time. Now what are you going to make of that?'

She looked down towards the grit-covered floor and her voice was small as she said, 'I didn't know until then that I have a grandfather and . . . and I thought it would be nice to see him. Other girls talk of their grandmothers and grandfathers and they seem to like them.' Her head jerked up, an action immediately reminiscent of Bridget, and the look on her face and the sound of her voice could have been Bridget's, as she said, 'Why don't you visit him? Why don't you take me? And, too, I am supposed to have an uncle there who is your brother, and his wife is related to Mammy. It's all very puzzling. People have quarrels and rows in families but they get over them. I . . . I am ten and a half, Daddy, and I've never seen my relations.'

Douglas stood up, reached over the table and drew towards him the piece of paper on which he had been drawing; and it looked as if he was going to take up his pencil again, but instead, he dropped his hand flat onto the table, the fingers spread out, almost as though he was trying to indent the shape of them onto the wood. Then, as if he had come to an unpleasant decision, he muttered, 'I can never promise you, dear, that you will see your grandfather, or your uncle. There are grave reasons for my saying this, very grave reasons, serious reasons. You see, I can never go back to that house again, that house in which I was born; nor can your mother, and for different reasons from mine, one in particular being that her cousin doesn't desire her to visit her. She is an embittered woman, her cousin, and I cannot see anything that is going to change her attitude. Now, my dear –' He turned to her, sat slowly beside her again, took her hand, then said, 'Do something for me. I have never asked you to do anything for me, have I? I have never asked you to promise me anything . . . have I?'

She blinked, then shook her head and said, 'No, Daddy; not that I can remember.'

'Well, then, I'm asking you to promise me something now, and it is that you won't pester your mother by bringing up the subject that we've just discussed. But I can promise you that if in the future there is anything I think I can tell you to explain all this strange behaviour, then I shall do so. It will be when you are older; at least' – he now looked away from her – 'I'll be able to explain in part. But –' He lifted his hand now and cupped her rounded, still babyish chin and, looking into the eyes that were so like his own, while the other features were those inherited from her mother, he said, 'Just remember this, my dear, I love you. I love you very much.' Then he was startled by her next words.

'After Mammy.'

It was a moment or two before he could answer; 'No, not after: on the same lines, but in a different way.

'But what makes you say that, dear? What put that idea into your head?'

'Well' – she glanced again towards the floor, then one shoulder gave a little hunch – 'you . . . you never seem to leave her. I mean, except when you are down here working. And then she comes down and stays with you at times.'

'Well, miss' – he tweaked her nose now – 'how often have your mother and I to go hunting for you? And where do we find you? With Joseph. During the holidays we hardly ever see you.'

'That's different.'

'Oh, I don't see the difference, madam.' He put on an indignant pose now. 'One code of rules for you and another for your mother and me.'

Her head was bent, her lids lowered; and now bending down, his face close to hers, he said, 'My dear, get it into that little probing head of yours that you are very precious to both of us. We love you dearly, so very dearly. You're all we have, but you are all we want.'

Swiftly now she threw her arms around his neck, kissed him, then, turning, fled from the shop.

Douglas stayed by the table for some time, but he didn't resume his work. And when presently he went down the shop Sam, as if talking to the stone, said, 'Queer kettle of fish. Young Harry's all mixed up an' all. 'Tis the times. I can't remember bein' like that in me young days. I think I must have been born when I was about twenty-five.'

Douglas laughed as he said, 'It's a very good age to be born, Sam,' the while thinking that Amy wasn't the only one with good hearing . . .

It was later that night when, lying wrapped in each other's arms, Bridget said, 'What a strange thing for her to say. It isn't as if she has been neglected. In fact, she's been spoilt.'

'She's like her mother, she's very perceptive.'

Bridget did not take this up, but asked, 'If he wasn't there, if he left her or was dead, would you go back to the house?'

'Yes. Yes, I would; but he would have to be one or the other of the things you have just said, left or dead.'

'Well, in that case, my dear, you know what I think and I've thought for a long time.'

'No. What do you think, sweetheart?'

'I think there is something behind the fact that Victoria found out about the money. I feel there is something else that you're withholding from me. I'm right, aren't I?'

It was a good minute before he answered, 'I won't say you're not right, dear, but I can only say this: what there is lies between him and me and I want it to remain like that. And I promise you this, it's the only thing in my life that I shall ever withhold from you.'

'Then I will ask you this. Is what happened to his detriment alone or to . . . the detriment of you both?'

'It is to his detriment alone.'

'Well, that's all I wanted to know. Good night, my love.'

'Good night, my dearest, dearest Bridget.'

3

'She'll have to be put away in the end. If Mr Lionel had had his way she would have gone long since. But it means money. She's never had a tantrum like this for some time. The master heard her and Mr Bright came up to ask me why couldn't I stop her. I mean . . . a daft thing to say.' Katie Swift made an indignant movement with her head, which cook confirmed by bobbing hers, then adding, 'It would take a regiment to calm her down when she starts.'

'D'you know what Ron said?' Katie Swift leant over the table towards cook and, lowering her voice, said, 'He thinks it's mostly because she's almost deaf and gets frustrated because people don't understand what she's sayin'. He says, if they had got proper attention to her from when she was a bairn she could have been improved on. Now what d'you say to that, cook?'

'Well, I don't know.' Rose Jackson sighed. 'There are times when she wanders around like any ordinary bairn, except that she's always swinging her arms about and her legs never seem to be still. Her whole body's at a jangle at times. But she doesn't make any trouble, and once she gets into the vegetable garden she'll stay there for hours. Jimmy gives her a little spade and she digs away. I say, little spade. D'you remember a few months ago when she practically threw it at him and walked into the tool house and picked another one, not a full-sized one but one that Joseph Fable used when he was gardener here? He never liked heavy work, that one. It was a lightish spade. Well, Jimmy said, she went at it like a navvy. And she plants things, any old way and how because there's nobody to show her different. The last odd-job gardener was frightened to death of her, you remember? 'cos she went for him with the shovel. But Jimmy said it was just because he wouldn't show her how to plant. Jimmy's good with her, you know: whenever he's got a spare minute from those two damned horses, he goes down and takes her into the greenhouses and shows her seeds an' things. But as he says himself, what does he know about gardenin'? the nearest he gets to it is the muck.'

Both women now shook with their laughter; then cook, looking at the clock on the mantelpiece, said, 'It's time for the mistress's coffee, although she won't be in her office this mornin', she'll be up in the nursery calming that one down, if not tying her down.'

'Oh, cook, she's never been tied down for a long time. How I used to hate that business 'cos she would look at you from the bed an' her eyes used to be sometimes wild, an' at times they would be sort of pleadin'. I tell you, Minnie an' me have had many a bubble when we've come down those stairs. But that was the fault of old Doctor Ledman; Doctor Curry put a stop to it when he took over. He went for Bright and the mistress. He's not afraid to speak his mind, but you can't understand half he says, him talkin' in thick Scots. And it's queer to see him with her: he talks to her and she mouths words back at him. Anyway, she's had a better life of it since he came on the scene. But what started this last blow-up, I don't know.'

'Did . . . did she see her father?'

'I don't think so. Yet it was just the sight of him that used to set her off into tantrums afore, remember?'

'Remember! I'll never forget that night in the hall. I thought he was goin' to choke her. I think he would have done if the mistress hadn't punched him in the face like she did. Of course, he was as drunk as a noodle. Eeh! that was a night one way or another. Well, there mightn't be much money in this house, but there's certainly plenty of excitement.'

'Here! Take the mistress's tray, an' find out where the youngster is. I've put another cup on the tray in case she's with the mistress, because she likes coffee.'

Katie Swift found that she had to take the tray right up to the nursery, and there she found her mistress sitting on the side of the bed. But her daughter wasn't in the bed, she was sitting on the floor, her back pressed tight against the base of it.

Katie put the tray on a small table, then said, 'Will I pour your coffee out, ma'am?'

'No; leave it. I'll see to it.'

'Yes, ma'am.'

Katie glanced at the girl on the floor, and the girl looked back at her, and the maid who had witnessed her birth thought, as she had done many, many times, Dear God! What a waste of a beautiful face.

The door closed, Victoria bent forward and tapped her daughter on the arm; then, turning her palm upwards, she twice made an upward motion with it. And at this the girl shook her head, to which Victoria's response was to bend over and bring her hand down sharply on the narrow wrist, making her daughter wince before turning slowly onto her knees and rising from the floor and to stand before her mother.

For a girl of eleven years of age she was tall and her body was straight. At first glance she looked to be a normal girl and, as Katie said, a beautiful one. That was until her arms began to jerk and her head to wag as if it was loose on her shoulders. And looking on this for the countless time since she had first witnessed it, Victoria told herself yet again, if she could remain perfectly still for minutes at a time she could stop these antics. Old

Doctor Ledman used to say it was the result of sheer bad temper – he had seen others like it – that was at first, until he had pronounced her deaf. But Doctor Curry had a different diagnosis. He called the temper frustration, and he said she wasn't totally deaf, she could hear certain sounds, even some voices. He had suggested she be sent away to a special school, where she would be taught to talk, at least better than she did now, but also quite well on her hands.

But what had come of that? The school, like everything else meant money, and what was more, she didn't want her sent away. She was the only thing she had in her life on which she could express the little love that remained in her. That it took a hard form at times, didn't matter, nor the fact that often she had to slap her child with slaps verging on blows in retaliation for having herself received similar treatment from both hands and feet.

She had found that if she stood straight in front of her daughter and spoke slowly and mouthed the words there was a gleam in the bright eyes, a gleam, she dared to hope, of understanding.

She didn't know what had created this last outburst, only that it was over, and that it wasn't likely to happen again for some while.

She kept her lips well apart, then mouthed, 'Pour . . . the . . . coffee . . .'

The girl's head dipped slightly with each word her mother spoke; then she made a sound in her throat that was quite unintelligible to Victoria and moved to the table. There, after pouring out two cups of black coffee, she looked at her mother; and when Victoria pointed to herself with her index finger, she lifted up one of the cups and took it to her.

Again mouthing the words, Victoria said, 'Thank . . . you.'

The girl was returning to the table to take up her own cup when there was a tap on the door and Bright entered. He looked to where the young girl was now walking with her cup of coffee towards the chair, and he smiled at her before saying to Victoria, 'The master would like to have a word with you, ma'am, when you have time.'

'I'll be down in a minute.'

There was no, 'Thank you, Bright,' for such preliminaries had been done away with many years ago. These two understood each other, and the man who had despised the silly-headed bride had come to respect and pity the woman she had turned into. It could be said now there was between them an understanding almost verging on friendship. In a way it was akin to that which Bright felt for the old irascible man in the four-poster bed. To himself he likened this three-part association to a triangle, the edges of which were tightly morticed one into the other against the man who treated this house mainly as a lodging.

She now turned to her daughter again and once more began to mouth words: 'Go . . . into . . . the . . . garden . . . for . . . a . . . walk.'

She didn't say, 'Take your spade and go to the vegetable garden,' because that would have indicated her daughter was a menial, but she knew that once her daughter got downstairs and out of the house she would make for the vegetable garden. She was never afraid that she might, instead, go out of the grounds, for she had, as yet, never shown any inclination to wander.

The girl now rose from the chair and almost at a run went past Bright, who was holding the door open. And both he and his mistress stood where they were, listening to her feet pounding the bare boards of the landing, then to the sound of them running down the linoleumed stairs, and not until the sound died away did Victoria speak.

And then she asked, 'What brought on the tantrum, do you know?' and Bright answered, 'It was an encounter, ma'am. Mr Lionel was coming out from the master's room and Miss Henrietta was' – he paused – 'about to enter.'

Miss Henrietta was about to enter. She could see it all, the child's hand raised to knock at the door and he coming out; the exchanged glance of hate, then his arm thrusting out to sweep her aside as usual. Sometimes she would fall, sometimes she would just stagger back. But as she had grown older, there had been other times when she had literally attacked him, the last time tearing at his face and bringing the blood. Then, she had thought he would, in some way, have carried out his threat and had her put away, in spite of his father's opposition. And yet it was really the poverty of the house that had stayed his hand; although his standing in the county had sunk, it wasn't so low that he could risk bringing censure upon himself for putting his daughter into a common asylum.

Victoria made a movement with her head, and Bright turned and went out; and within a moment or so she followed him.

She always tapped on her father-in-law's door before entering the room and if she didn't hear him shout she would go straight in.

William Filmore was propped up in bed. He seemed not to have aged over the years: in fact, his face had a fresh look and the mound of his stomach had definitely decreased. But his voice and manner had apparently remained the same, for he greeted her with, 'Why the hell don't you keep her out of his sight!'

'Tie her up again?'

'No. No; but keep an eye on her.'

She made no reply to this last statement but, standing near the head of the bed, she said, as she always did, 'How are you this morning?'

But instead of his usual reply, 'As you see me, as you see me,' he said, 'Too bloody well for my age. And it's your fault. If it wasn't for this damned leg.' He pointed down the bed to where the bedclothes were arranged over a cage above his legs. 'Your meanness to the cellar hasn't done much for it. And the same applies to the meals: wholesome, yes, but delectable, no.' His expression changing and his voice, too, he said quietly now, 'Sit down, woman, sit down.'

Victoria hesitated a moment before pulling a chair to the side of the bed. Once she was seated he put out a thick blue-veined hand towards her but it reached only the ruffled edge of the counterpane, and this he patted before he said, 'He's at it again . . . the divorce business. A new proposal this time. He'll waive all rights to the child . . . of course, in every other way but one; he's already done that. And he promised you an income almost double his last offer. Of course, you would have to find other quarters so that when I decide to kick the bucket he can bring his fat hog into this house, and her money would renovate it. I asked him why she keeps him on such a short rein now if she's willing to spend a fortune once he marries her, because it's as much as I can do to get that twenty pounds a month out of him. He spends as much on his horses. But he must have his horses. I told him to get rid of one of them at least. I asked him again, too, where he thinks they and the rest of us would have been if it wasn't for your allowance.'

He stopped talking and stared at her. Not one of her features had changed its expression, and there was a deep note of pity in his voice now as he said, 'My dear girl, and, you know, that's how I think of you in my mind. In spite of the structure you've built around yourself over the years, the girl is still there. I upbraid myself many a time, you know, for my manner towards you when you first came. I sometimes think I've passed into a simple-minded dotage, because, lying here most of my days, what can I do but think? Read and think. Yet, on looking back, I don't consider my life ill-spent. I lived it as I was bred to live it.'

He had now looked away from her, and his head was nodding and his gaze directed down towards the counterpane as he said, 'There was enough money in my father's young days, and then in my growing up, to afford us to live like gentlemen. We followed a pattern. All my ancestors had been cosseted from birth to grave: one played a little, one drank, a little or much according to taste, and one gambled and took risks. You know' — he was looking at her again — 'people always associate gambling with cards or dice, even perhaps dominoes; they never associate it with gold mines; the very mention of a gold mine creates a mirage. And when that disappears, what have you? The result of greed: a falling house in which you find it impossible to pull your horns in and to live according to what's left in the coffers. No, that would be too much to ask. So you live on debt until you have to become servile to your grocer.' He now nodded at her as he added, 'You do with sixty pounds a month, my dear, what wasn't achieved with six hundred at one time. Give me your hand.'

She hesitated for a moment before placing her hand in his; and then he gripped it and said, 'You are lonely, my dear. You are lost for companionship of your own kind. Why don't you get in touch with her? She seemed a kindly creature in spite of her stiff make-up. She was good to you for years, and is still good to you. If she wouldn't visit here, you could visit her. What do you say?'

What could she say? How to explain to this old man how she felt? How could she say, she's the last person on earth I want to see. How could she say, at times I'm eaten up with hate of her, because it was she who brought me to this state in paying a man to marry me, a man who would have done anything . . . anything, rather than tie himself to a penniless girl had he been aware of the circumstances beforehand. But what did she do? She offered him two thousand a year. And why? Because she wanted rid of me, for some reason or other she wanted rid of me. But she would have me think it was for my own good because otherwise I would have died for love . . . God in heaven! Died for love of that swine of a man.

She turned her head away and looked towards the end of the room to where the sun was streaming in between the faded brocade curtains onto the equally faded and worn carpet. And she asked herself, as she always did following the increasing tirades in her mind: Had she ever loved him? Was she really, as her cousin had said, besotted with him? No. No, she wouldn't have it; at least, she wasn't so deeply enamoured that she couldn't have got over it if left to herself.

'Don't look so sad, my dear. I only suggested it because I would like you to have . . . well, a little happiness in some way. I can do nothing for you, yet it is strange you do a lot for me, and you have no need, you know . . . I mean, it couldn't be expected of you. Anyway, to get back to the beginning. I told him that the answer would be as before, that you'll stay here as long as I'm alive. And I added that the way you look after me it could be quite a while yet.' He was again nodding down towards the counterpane, and his voice was little above a mutter as he ended, 'And my answer to what he said next was to ask if he intended to finish me like he had . . .' He blinked rapidly, jerked his head upwards and looked towards her.

She was staring at him, but seemed to be waiting for him to go on. And after swallowing a mouthful of spittle

· 314

he went on: 'His horse,' he said. 'Cruel bugger at bottom, cruel bugger.'

She rose from the chair, saying, 'The sun is shining. Are you going to get up today?'

'I'll . . . I'll think about it.'

'I'll tell Bright to come up and see to it.'

As she made towards the door he called brightly, 'What's for dinner today?'

She opened the door and half turned towards him again as she said, 'Vegetable soup, minced veal, French potatoes, and a fruit pudding.'

'Plain and wholesome again,' he said jokingly. 'I'll have no stomach left by the time you finish with me; it's half gone already.'

She closed the door, then walked down the corridor to her own room and as she sat down at the dressing-table she let out a long slow breath and her upper body seemed to collapse. She was staring into the mirror and she spoke to the white taut face, saying, 'Oh God, don't let it happen. Guide me. Please guide me; my child needs me.'

4

Mrs Daisy Barnett's house was situated just beyond the far outskirts of Newcastle. You could say it was where the city was left behind and the country began. It was a small house, comparatively that is, having only twelve rooms, but it was beautifully appointed and if there was a comfort to be had, Lea House possessed it. Its driveway led directly off the main road, and it was surrounded by five acres of its own land.

Over the past ten years Lionel Filmore had looked upon it as home: Daisy Barnett had provided him with the niceties of life and seen to it that even though his position in the shipping company remained still the same as it had been when he first joined, his salary had more than trebled. This, of course, was not shown on the books. That she was older than him by ten years had not at first, nor had since, detracted from his feeling for her; in fact it was her maturity that had at first drawn him to her, together with her intense physical need of him: it would, indeed, have been past his understanding or acceptance to recognise her as a mother figure, a soothing, petting, mother figure, a protective mother figure.

Not that their alliance hadn't been through troubled waters. The excitement of flaunting respectability by taking a young man as a lover when she herself was nearing forty had faded somewhat with the years, and she was now wanting the cloak of respectability. Although she had had two husbands, she desired now the protection of a third, and for reasons known only to herself.

Daisy had two sons, the result of her first marriage. Both men had, from the beginning, looked askance at her association with what they privately termed the waster.

So the bone of Daisy's contention was her dear boy's freedom. She was even willing to pay for his release by providing for the wife and the mad daughter. She would go so far, she said, as even to put it in writing, and this in itself brought home to Lionel how much she wanted his freedom and his name, for over the years he had come to realise that his dearest Daisy was very reluctant to sign anything, as she was also reluctant to discuss business. After ten years strong acquaintance all he knew was that she held fifty per cent of the business and her sons twenty-five per cent each. The business was no longer connected with shipping as such – their last ship had been sold two years ago – but it was now concentrated on chandling and victualling. And that's where he had come in: first, on the victualling side, and then on the chandling side, and although it irked him, even angered him at times, to think that he was no more than a shop assistant in an ironmongery, he had learned a great deal about the business of equipping ships with all they needed.

That he was looked on with suspicion and dislike, both among those above him and those below him, he was well aware. But he was also treated with covert respect, as would be one who was in . . . the owner's pocket; nevertheless, this had not saved him from being twice attacked, once in the daylight and once in the dark. On the latter occasion the attack had taken place, not in the city, where one might expect it from a thug, but within a mile of his own home. And he was convinced he knew who was behind the attacks; one or other of them, anyway. His dear wife . . . and yet from where would she get the money to employ thugs? The other was his brother. He was apparently rolling in it now from his own efforts as well as sitting pretty on his wife's fortune. By God! he would like to throttle him. Above everyone else he'd like to throttle him and, given the chance, he would do it. If he hated anyone in this world it was his brother; and his snipe of a wife came next.

Although nothing further had happened to him in that way over the past two years, his mind was still in the same turmoil, in fact more so. The urge to be free, free from that woman – he had ceased long ago to think of her as a silly girl – had become an obsessive thought, because he knew that if he didn't marry Daisy soon, the atmosphere in that particular house would surely change. Just as he himself was obsessed with one thought, so, he knew, was she: she had turned fifty and the years were showing on her, while he, at forty, was now holding his age extremely well.

He seemed to have spent most of the last year in convincing her that she wouldn't lose him, and for once in his life he meant what he said. If he had ever loved anyone it was this big, even voluptuous, aging woman, for she had given of herself from their first coming together as no one else had or could ever hope to.

He had been wise enough never to have teased her about the other women in his life, but often did about his horses. And strange as it may have seemed, she was jealous of these rivals because she didn't like horses. There was a coach-house in the yard and buildings that could have been turned into further stables, but she wouldn't hear of his bringing his horses here, even though it might have meant spending more time with her than he already did. She herself patronised a particular hostelry, and this would send her a coach or a cab whenever she required one . . .

On this particular fine day he walked up from the quay and into the city to partake of his midday meal. He was well known in the hotel and exchanged greetings here and there in the dining-room. But he had hardly taken his usual seat at the single table near a window when he saw, with some surprise, threading his way towards him down the room, Daisy's gardener and handyman. Lionel found this man a surly individual. He had attempted to be on friendly terms with him, at least as friendly as he would ever allow himself to be with a servant; yet the man had never responded. But Daisy seemed to think a lot of her Rogers. Apparently he had been in her service since her first marriage and he was about the same age as herself.

The man now handed Lionel a letter, saying, 'The mistress sent this. She doesn't need a reply.' And with that he turned about and left the dining-room.

Somewhat surprised at her sending him a letter at this time of the day, he slit open the envelope, then read:

'My dearest boy,
I heard from Bernard this morning that he and Marie are bringing their latest addition for inspection. They will be arriving this afternoon and I cannot say for sure that they will leave tomorrow. I should imagine they will stay another night in order to prepare the poor, delicate creature to face the return journey.'

At the end of this sentence there was drawn a stick figure.

'I will merely exist until Sunday evening. Take care, my dearest . . . I know with whom you will spend the weekend, and if I was near one of them I would surely kick it.
Your very own Daisy,
your little flower of the field.'

At the end of this there was a cross within a circle, which she had explained to him was her being kissed within the circle of his arms.

He wasn't entirely displeased that he had the weekend entirely free. It meant two full days of riding and the thought of it made him attack his meal with relish; at least until he recalled that between times from this evening and over the following two days he would not only have to encounter *her*, but also that other thing, that wild jangling creature. God! he'd have to do something about that one soon for the very sight of her, even from a distance, caused the hairs on his neck to stand up. The fact that any part of him could be active within the creature was abhorrent to him. He didn't know how much longer he could stand it. What was prolonging this endurance was his father — he was the stumbling block, for once he was gone she had promised to leave the house and take her daughter with her so long as provision was made for her. And Daisy would do that, all right.

He had a vision of Daisy installed in the house and it renovated from top to bottom. And she would do that, too. She would make it into a large Lea House and from then on he could see the far past being brought into the present. The county would open its doors again; perhaps not all of them, but enough to make life interesting, variable . . . yes, variable.

He did not see his daughter. He met up with his wife three times but they did not exchange a word. On the Saturday morning he had an early breakfast and rode The Admiral until lunch time. And when he returned he gave orders for a snack lunch, after which he rode Prince until both he and the horse were covered in sweat, which led Ron Yarrow to say later to Mr Bright, 'Those beasts are gettin' on and he'll wind them one of these days and they'll drop down dead under him. He's supposed to care for horse flesh. Funny caring, to my mind. But then, that's him all over.'

He had ordered a hot bath to be got ready, after which he went to the dining-room, where Bright had set a meal for him at the end of the dining-room table. It consisted of soup, braised brisket, and vegetables, followed by a milk pudding which, when Bright placed it in front of him he pushed aside, saying, 'Bring the cheese.' Bright hesitated only a moment before leaving the dining-room and returning with a platter on which was a piece of cheese weighing about a quarter of a pound. Next to it was a pat of butter and two slices of bread.

When he had cleared the board he said to Bright, 'Bring me a jug of coffee, not a cupful,' and poured himself out yet another glass of water from the carafe, the third glassful he had drunk during the meal. He found it almost impossible to eat a meal without the assistance of wine, and for years now this table had been bare of wine, except when he thought to bring a bottle with him. He knew that she allowed his father a bottle in his own room but he told himself that he hadn't yet stooped so low as to go and beg for a glass of wine.

Sunday followed much the same pattern, except that his ride in the afternoon was short, and by four o'clock he was ready to leave the house.

He was standing in his father's bedroom. The old man was propped up in an armchair near the window, his gouty foot resting on a stool. And William Filmore looked up at his son and saw a fine figure of a man dressed in a dark grey suit, his shirt and necktie matching, the patina on his hand-made shoes showing their quality, and he wondered how anything that looked so good on the outside could be so rotten inside, because this son of his was not only a mean man and a cruel one, he was a murderer. He seemed to have forgotten that. It was something that had never been mentioned for years, not even alluded to, but nevertheless it was always to the forefront of his own mind that his son was a murderer. And a low type of murderer, for he hadn't killed one of his own breed in a fair fight, he had done to death a common man. What was more, he was a fornicator of the worst type. Most men were fornicators, but there was a distinctive class among them. There was also a word that seemed to sum him up completely in his own mind: a bastard, not in the real sense of the word, but in the sense that it embodied everything in a man that was no good.

He turned his head to look out of the window as he said, 'She's let you off the lead for a couple of days. What's the reason?'

'No reason. I merely wanted to get a bit of riding in.'

'You'll come one day and those horses won't be there.'

There was silence for a moment; then Lionel's voice came deep and even threatening: 'They'd better still be there, Father. Oh, yes, they'd better still be there.'

The old man's head snapped round now and he said, 'And what would you do if they weren't there, eh? Set fire to the bloody place? Or perhaps you'd do away with her, an' me an' all, eh? That would be easy, wouldn't it? But tell me, if I sold them and this house – and I could sell them: this house is still mine and what stands in it is still mine. And from where do you think I'm going to get the money to pay those down below? Why they stay on here, God alone knows; yet, it's good to know that there's loyalty left somewhere – so what would you do if I sold the horses to pay them, eh?'

'You don't need to sell anything but the land, Father. There's the piece that house builder offered to buy and you wouldn't hear of it.'

'No, I wouldn't at the time, but I changed my mind and now he's got it, at least most of it.'

'What!'

'Yes, you can say what. Now you're going to ask

me why you weren't informed. Are you ever here to be informed of anything? You don't live here any more; your home is with your fat whore. Yes, yes, I sold the land and got five hundred for it. There's still six staff to pay: there are insurances to meet; there is a doctor to pay. Do you think it's all done on your twenty pounds a month? Oh, for God's sake! get out of my sight. We've been through all this before. And let me tell you again, if it wasn't for that girl who is your lawful wife, there wouldn't be any house standing, the bums would have been in long ago. But I wouldn't have been here to see the result of that; there are ways and means to finish a life without cutting a throat . . . What do you say to that?'

When the door had banged the old man lay back and drew in a long shuddering breath. Then after a moment he put his hand along the arm of the chair around which a piece of rope was attached. And when he pulled on it, the other end that was attached to the bed bell-pull rang the bell in the kitchen.

Within a few minutes Bright was standing by his side, and he looked up at him and said, 'Fetch me a drink, Bright. Give me a double dose.'

'But, sir, you know' – he looked towards the swaddled foot – 'the mistress said only one.'

There was no bawling reply from his master, he just said, 'She would understand in this case.'

'Yes, sir.'

Bright went to the dressing-room and there, taking a bottle of whisky from a cupboard, he poured a double measure into a wine glass, and took it back to his master; and after watching him gulp at it and almost empty the glass, he said, 'Would you like to get back to bed, sir?'

'No, Bright, no. It's pleasant here; I can see the gardens, or what used to be the gardens. Even in their wildness they're beautiful . . . Bright.'

'Yes, sir?'

'Why have you stayed all these years with me?'

James Bright remained silent. What could he say?

His master now asked, 'How long have you been in my service?'

'Forty years, sir. I started when I was ten.'

'You are now fifty?'

'Yes, sir.'

'I . . . I must have been twenty-one when you started.'

'You were, sir. There was a great do for your coming-of-age birthday. I had arrived the week before. I can recall the excitement of it. There were a hundred and ten guests and the grounds were hung with lanterns, and the festivities went on for two days . . . and two nights, sir. And all members of the permanent staff down to the cook were each given a golden sovereign, the rest five shillings each; I, being a late arrival, was given a shilling.'

William looked at him in some amazement. 'You remember all that and, here am I, and I can hardly remember a thing about it, Bright. I suppose I was bottled. Was I, Bright?'

'I can't remember that, sir. I only know that you were always able to carry your drink like . . . like a gentleman.'

The old man looked out of the window again. He sniffed loudly twice. Then his voice gruff, he said, 'You still haven't answered my question, Bright. Why have you stayed on here?'

And Bright now answered quietly, 'Because, sir, it was a good house, the staff were always dealt with squarely and looked after in their old age, that was up till . . .'

'Yes, Bright, yes, up till the rot set in. And if I remember rightly now, the rot set in a long time ago.' He was still looking out of the window as he said, slowly now, 'I don't suppose I'll ever say this to you again, Bright. I haven't said it to you before, I know that, but I say now thank you for your loyalty and the care you have taken of me, particularly these last few years for very little reward, in fact for no reward at all.'

When the master continued to look out of the window Bright turned away without speaking; he was unable to speak, for in this moment he felt that if he had never received a penny in wages before, and would never receive a penny in future, what had transpired between him and his master was ample payment for forty years service.

He did not consider that he was a unique breed of man who was born to serve others, and that there was no degradation in doing so; rather, pride in the fact that this position had fallen to his lot in life.

It was about seven o'clock that same evening when Lionel Filmore walked up the drive towards Lea House. As it was still broad daylight he paused before he approached the door because he had noticed that the blinds were drawn, not only in the two long windows that flanked the front door but also in the hall window. He did not stop to question why, but pushed open the door and walked into a surprising dimness.

The hall was little more than a long wide corridor and his surprise turned into something like amazement when he saw, coming from the far end of it, the figures of two men. And not until they were a few yards from him did he recognise Daisy's sons.

Bernard and Simon were men in their late twenties and, in a way, Bernard was his boss, although he rarely saw him; he took his orders from Ralph Gilmore, the manager; and strangely, he had always got on well with Gilmore. And yet there was nothing strange about it when you got down to the reason for this relationship: at Daisy's suggestion he had let Gilmore take the credit for the fresh orders he himself would bring in.

'What's this? What's the matter?'

The two men exchanged a glance. For a moment he imagined they were smiling and this irritated him. 'Look!' he said, his voice taking on a certain note of command, 'why is the house without lights? I mean . . . and why are you here and . . . ?'

'Who has the better right to be here?' This was from Simon, the younger of the two. 'This is our mother's house, isn't it? Well, now that she is no more, who has the better right, I say, to be here?'

'Wh . . . wh . . . what?' There was a stammer now; then again, 'Wh . . . wh . . . what did you say?' the last word ending on a high note; and Bernard, moving past him, said, 'You had better come in here.'

He now followed them into the drawing-room, his drawing-room – he always thought of the whole house as his – and he stared at them open-mouthed as they stood now shoulder to shoulder talking to him, speaking words that his mind kept denying. It couldn't be, it couldn't.

'She had a heart attack on Friday night. It was as well I was here. They took her to hospital but she died within the hour.' There was no regret in the voice; it was as if the man were reading something from a paper. 'She is to be buried on Tuesday.'

Lionel put his hand to his head as he said, 'Oh my God! I can't believe it.'

'No, I don't suppose you can. Anyway, we've packed your things. We've had to loan you two cases; there are three altogether. We haven't packed your overcoats, they are lying on the cases. You will find them out in the coach house.'

'What? What d'you mean?'

It was Simon answering: 'We mean that you no longer have a place in this house. You have lived in it for too long. You have been like a leech on our mother. You have deserted your wife and child and also your ailing father. Oh, we know all about your background, sir, and have done for years.'

'How dare you! I loved your mother, and she me, and . . .'

'You loved this house.' It was the elder son now speaking. 'You loved this house. You loved being a kept man.'

'My God! You . . .' His fists were clenched but he kept them by his sides because the men facing him were not only younger than he but they were as big as him.

'Yes, I would think twice about using your fists. And before you leave we must tell you that we are keeping the gold watch, tie pin, and gold shirt-bands that belonged to our father.'

'They are mine! She gave them to me as a present.'

'If you look inside the watch you will see an initial there, and which is also on the other articles. It is our father's initial. Also there is a gold and diamond pin from the same source. If you want to claim them, sir, you will take us to court.'

Lionel's voice was much quieter now, deep in his throat, a note of fear in it as he said, 'You . . . you can't do this to me. She . . . she was all I had. I mean, there was an arrangement. She promised . . .'

'Yes? What did she promise?'

'Well, to put it plainly' – his voice was rising again – 'that she would always see me right, that she would leave me . . . well, that I needn't worry.'

'It might surprise you, sir, to know that my mother was aware that when she died she would have nothing to leave: her share in the business was hers only for her lifetime. That's why she spent right, left, and centre during it. Our father made this stipulation.'

'I don't believe it. She's bound to . . . I mean, she made a will. She must have made a will.'

'Definitely. Oh, definitely.'

'I want to see it . . . I mean I want to hear it.'

The two men looked at each other and said, 'Well, it will be read after the funeral. You may come and listen, although it will be very embarrassing for you, I'm sure, not to hear your name mentioned.'

'How d'you know my name won't be mentioned?'

'Because we know our mother. And let me tell you something else that we know: you have been trying for a divorce in order to marry her. She likely persuaded you along this line and promised to pay off your wife . . . which she could have done as long as she remained unmarried, but what she didn't tell you was that if she married again, her income, apart from this house, would be practically non-existent. She would be at the mercy of her two sons.' Simon pointed to himself, then to his brother, and went on, 'My father, you see, was a very wise man and he lived long enough to know the woman he had married. She was a very dear creature but she had one fault, she was devious, and I'm afraid, sir, you have been the recipient for some time now not only of her kindness but also of that latter quality. But there, I think she imagined you to be as devious as herself, thinking perhaps that when your father died you were bound to inherit money of some sort; failing which, that you could sell that large property, for whose land, I understand, speculators are even now bidding.'

He was feeling faint, really ill. It was like his marriage all over again, but this time there was no one standing at the side offering him two thousand a year. He turned and he was going slowly towards the door when one of the men said, 'If you don't wish to come to the funeral and hear the reading of the will, we shall understand. If your name is mentioned at all, our solicitor will notify you. That too is understood.'

He passed the elderly maid. She was all in black and

her eyes were red. She did not speak to him but shook her head sadly, and he went out and into the courtyard. The coach-house door was open, Rogers standing just within it. The man had a grim smile on his face as he said, 'You'll need a cab.' He hadn't added, 'sir.'

Lionel looked at the three large cases and the two overcoats lying across them, these topped by two high silk hats and a bowler. He stood looking down at his belongings. He could not believe this was happening to him, not again. He saw his life stretching before him in that big decaying house, meals at the end of a table, no wine . . . There arose in him the desire to scream, to claw at something, to beat his fists into flesh. He turned and looked at Rogers and the man didn't know at this moment how near he was to being attacked; yet he moved quickly aside as Lionel barked at him, 'Yes! I need a cab, and I'll be back.' And with this he stalked out of the coach-house and made his way to the main road, hoping there to pick up an empty cab. And he was fortunate.

Within an hour of walking up the drive to take up his comfortable part-time life again, he was riding out of it for good and all.

It was nine o'clock when the cab drove into the stable yard. And it was Rose Jackson who saw the cabbie dropping the luggage onto the yard, and she exclaimed aloud, 'God Almighty! Look what I'm seeing, cook. He's back for good.' And now she almost screamed at Kate at the other end of the kitchen, 'Go and tell Mr Bright. Quick!'

When the news was given to Bright, he said, 'No! No!'

'Yes. Yes. He'll be in in a minute.'

For once Bright did not tap on his master's door but went swiftly in. And there, looking first at Victoria, who was standing by his master's bed, he almost gabbled, 'He . . . he's come back, sir. I mean, Mr Lionel. For good, it seems. His luggage is in the yard. Came by cab. Something must have happened. I'd better go down.' His head was bobbing. For once Bright had lost his composure, and was it small wonder? For ten years they had been almost rid of him. Now what?

The old man pulled his nightcap well over his ears. His lips were munching one over the other and it was a minute or so before he put his hand out and grasped Victoria's. She seemed to have gone rigid, and he shook her hand, saying, 'Don't worry. Don't worry. He'll do nothing to the child. I'll see to that. And she won't be confined. I promise you, I promise you. Anyway, he won't be here all day, he's got a job. He'll be away most of the time.'

As she looked down on him her voice trembled as she said, 'He'll . . . he'll do her an injury, at least that's what he'll . . .'

'I promise you, he won't. Come here. Bend down.' When her face was close to his, he said, 'Nothing will happen to the child because I've got something on him. You understand what I mean? If he dares to touch the child in any way that'll be the finish of him. Believe me. Believe me. And if he lays a finger on you either. So don't worry.'

He now pushed her away and he actually laughed as he said, 'She's thrown him out. I wonder why she's thrown him out. And hell's cure to him.'

She turned from the bed and went towards the door. What does he mean, hell's cure to him? Funny thing to say. She had never heard that term before, hell's cure to him. But oh, how she wished he was in hell and burning. But he wouldn't be in hell, it was she who would be in hell. But wasn't she in hell now? If only she could pick up Henrietta and fly from this house. Where would she fly to? But the one place her mind suggested as a haven she immediately dismissed, for she saw the land surrounding

330

this entire house as a quagmire into which she would sink dared she step out of it. No; she was tied here until her mind went. But into what? and where? Perhaps into the land where her daughter lived most of her time.

She came to a standstill at the top of the staircase and she looked down into the hall, where three cases were standing and some wearing apparel and hats crowded a hall chair. And at the foot of the stairs there he stood looking up at her, and even over the distance she could see that he looked different: his face was sickly pale as if he were recovering from an illness; only the eyes remained the same.

Who would attempt to ascend or descend the stairs first? She knew that if she did so he would still make his move from the bottom, as had happened before, and even if their clothes were to brush slightly the contact would singe his whole body. She couldn't risk it tonight: she turned and went back across the landing and into her room. And so set the pattern for the years ahead, for the only safety to be found was in avoidance.

PART FOUR

The Reckoning
1903

1

'Why don't you say you love me?'

'Now don't start that again.'

'I will. I'll keep on and on as I have done for years.'

'You talk as if you were an old woman and you've just left school a month.'

'And you talk like an old man and you're still at school, or you're going to school, for what is Cambridge but school?'

He turned from her now and walked towards a tree and pressed a hand against the trunk as if to support himself, and from there he said, 'I may not go to Cambridge.'

She almost sprang to his side.

'Don't be silly! It's all arranged; and Father's so set on your going.'

Yes, her father was set on his going. That man was kindness himself, and so was the mistress, too kind in a way to the son of their maid. But now that maid was ill, seriously ill, and endeavouring to hide it from him. If anything should happen to her when he was away? He shook his head as if to rid himself of the thought . . .

'Is it because Lily's not well?'

He turned to her, his eyes downcast as he said, 'Could be.'

'But she wants you to go. I heard her saying to Mammy it was wonderful and fitting you should go.'

'Why fitting?'

'Well,' she shrugged her shoulders, 'likely because

you've got a lot up top, big head.' She laughed and pushed him with the flat of her hand. 'Mathematical genius. And here's me, I can hardly do my seven times table.'

His manner changing, he smiled at her softly now as he said, 'It's a pity you are so dim. It's a good job you'll never have to work for your living.'

'Oh you!' She was thrusting her hand at him again. 'I can beat you at some things any day. French, German, literature.'

'What about Latin?'

'Oh, Latin.'

'Yes, oh Latin. Your English will be wanting without the knowledge of Latin. I've always said that to you.'

'Yes.' She sighed now before she went on, 'You've always said so many things to me, Joseph, but not the things I want to hear. And why? ... Why? Because you do love me, I know you do.'

He turned sharply away from her, saying, 'Please!'

'Well, you do. And look, Joseph, we are not children any more. I'm not a child nor am I a silly young girl, and I've never been a silly young girl where you're concerned. I'll be eighteen next month. I have finished with schooling. They can no longer send me away or ...'

He swung round on her, crying now, 'There you have it. They can't send *you* away, but I'm going away, not apparently being sent. Oh, and I'm not grumbling, because your people are the kindest couple in the world. But for years now, for some reason or other they have striven to keep us apart. And there must be a reason, because your father is no snob, nor your mother. It isn't just because I'm the son of the maid, because they've done everything to further my position in life, so to speak, for here I am now, ready for Cambridge, and here you are now, left at home, safe out of my presence, and the distance between us will widen ...'

'Oh, Joseph, don't say that. Don't talk like that. But you're right in some ways, I know. And at times, too, I feel that there is something they're withholding from me. What, I don't know. I come upon them talking seriously, and they stop and turn their laughing faces to me. And that's another thing.' Her voice dropped and she half turned from him, and he watched her bite down on the side of her forefinger before she said, 'They're so wrapped up in each other that it's painful sometimes to watch . . . well, at least to me. They tell me that they love me but I feel it's a sort of second-hand love. They've been married now nearly nineteen years and they're oldish. Well, mother is on forty-three, and they act like . . . well, if I was acting like that, even now they would say, "Dear! dear! Don't be silly," or "You've got it bad," or some such comment.'

His voice was low as he now remarked, 'Don't you think it's nice that they still feel like that for each other after all this time?'

'Yes, in a way. But as I see it they're not going to give me a chance to feel like that about you when I'm forty-three.'

His head went back now and he let out a ringing laugh in which she joined, and as it subsided she watched him rubbing his eyes with his fingers as she said, 'You know, that's the first time I've seen you laugh in months.'

He was still smiling when he said, 'You know, in other circumstances you'd be termed a brazen young hussy, chasing a poor young fellow like you do.'

He expected her to come back with some quip to this remark, but when she didn't and her head drooped and she said, 'That isn't all true, Joseph, about the chasing. For years you were as eager for my company as I was for yours. You used to wait for me coming from school. Hide round the side of the lodge or make a nuisance of yourself in Father's workshop while waiting for me coming in . . . When did you change, and why?'

He took a step towards her now and his voice was harsh as he said, 'I don't know when I changed but I know why I changed, if change I did. And we've just been over the reason. What you want to do is to go back and ask your mother, as I have asked myself a lot of late, would she have taken in a working-class girl who was a widow with a small child and bestow much kindness on her if she had known she was going to have a daughter eighteen months or so later? As I see it, in a way she had burnt her boats when she befriended my mother and . . . well, when you came, nothing could be done about it. She couldn't in all faith, turn her out.'

'My mother would never have turned Lily out. She's very fond of Lily, and both she and Father are very fond of you, though you won't recognise it.'

'What I recognise is that they are kind, extremely kind to me, always have been, and this is the question that looms large in my mind: Why are they so kind to me? And why all these years I have never known my mother to look really happy? D'you know that? She never seems happy. It's as if she's carrying a burden of some kind and that burden I feel has brought on this illness that is going to be the finish of her.'

'No, it won't, Joseph. Don't say that. I asked Mammy what was wrong with Lily and she said she had a little stomach trouble, but she was mostly exhausted and tired.'

'Exhausted?'

'Well, that's what she said; but as I see it Lily has only had light things to do, such as sewing and housekeeping, which she took over after Jessie died, and that's years ago.'

'What I fear has exhausted my mother is in her mind.'

338

'You're bent on making a mystery out of this situation, aren't you?'

'No; there's no need, the mystery is already there. And I'd like to get to the bottom of it, but I can see no way, because in the past when I have tried to probe my mother about my father, all I've got out of her over the years is that he died before I was a year old.'

When the sound came to them of a distant handbell being rung, she said, 'Oh, that means they're waiting supper. I'll have to go. Will I see you tomorrow?' He paused before he answered, 'Yes, if you want to. There's three weeks to go yet. I don't leave for Cambridge until the first week in October.' She stepped back from him, repeating, 'If I want to? You know, there are times when I feel humiliated by how I lower myself to you.'

'Well then —' His manner changing abruptly, he cried, 'Don't lower yourself. Oh, I wouldn't want you to lower yourself, not to my level. Oh no, you mustn't do that, never!'

'Oh you! I don't mean that way and you know I don't. You are always twisting things. I mean, within myself I always seem to be crawling.' Her lips were trembling now, her eyes blinking. And when he suddenly caught her hands and pulled her towards him they stared at each other until, with a break in his voice, he muttered, 'Don't . . . don't cry. Please. All right, I'll say it, but there's nothing can come of it. D'you hear? Nothing. But I love you. I've always loved you . . .'

'Oh! Joe.'

'Now, stop it, stop it. Go on, go on' — he pushed her from him — 'because if I were to kiss you . . . that would be that. Go on.' His voice was now rough and she backed from him, her eyes running with tears but her expression soft, illuminated by the light not only of young love but of a love that had seemed to possess her since the day she had looked up into the face of the boy rocking her cradle, which at three years old she still preferred to her cot and would sit in whenever she got the opportunity, in order that he should rock her.

2

'You should just be . . . coming . . . back from your holidays.'

'Well, if that was the case I would just be worn out, sunburnt and blistered all over and still feeling sea-sick. I don't like foreign parts, never have, so stop worrying about that.'

Bridget sat close to Lily's bedside in the narrow room. The lamp was burning on a small table on the opposite side of the bed and Lily, with no vestige of the beauty she once had remaining on her countenance, lay back among the feather pillows as she waited patiently for the end to the torturous pain that was writhing her bowels and which the doctor's potion was now failing to dull. Only the laudanum seemed to have any effect, but that clouded her mind and she wanted that left clear during these last hours of her life.

She said now, 'Is . . . is he still asleep?'

'Yes, dear, he's still asleep.'

'Four nights running; he can't keep it up.'

'Now will you stop worrying about him? He makes up for it during the day.'

'No. No, he doesn't . . . Ma'am.'

'Yes, Lily?'

'After . . . after it's over will you still see to him?'

'*Of course, of course,* my dear, we shall. You know we shall. We . . . we care for him; you know we do. Mr Douglas will always see to him.'

She always referred to her husband as Mr Douglas when

speaking in private to Lily; it hadn't such a possessive and controlling sound, as did 'master'.

The wick of the lamp spluttered and cast a dark shadow over the room for a moment. Then Lily, her voice very low, said, 'He loves her so much and . . . and he's not like the other one.' She turned her deep sunken gaze on Bridget, then ended, 'There's no bad in him.'

As Bridget, with a rapid, agitated movement of her fingers, stroked the hand within hers and said, 'I know. I know, dear,' her mind at the same time was crying, anything bred of Lionel Filmore couldn't wholly escape his character. And what was more, if not recognised by law, in nature young Joe and Amy were full cousins and the coming together of such never bred good.

But she said again, 'Now, Lily, you mustn't worry. Everything will be all right. He's going up to university, he'll be away three years. He'll meet up with all kinds of people. After all, he's young, they are both so young, and as you know, feelings and affections can change. So, don't worry, just know this: We shall always look after him. He will always be our charge, even if he doesn't come back to us, but decides to go on and make a life of his own.'

Lily was looking straight down to the foot of the bed now. 'It isn't fair what the Bible says . . . that the . . . sins of the fathers . . . are visited on the children even to the third . . . an' fourth generation . . . 'tisn't fair.'

When the door opposite the foot of the bed opened and she saw her son enter, she repeated this in a whisper, ' 'Tisn't fair.'

Bridget had stood up now and was saying quietly, 'You were sound asleep ten minutes ago.'

For answer he said, 'Mr Douglas is downstairs waiting for you.'

'Oh, dear, dear, did he wake you?'

'No. No, I was having a wash when he came in.'

Bridget turned to the bed again and, bending over Lily, she said, 'Now rest quiet. I'll be back in a little while.' Then looking at Joseph and, pointing now to the little side table, she muttered, 'In half an hour, the two doses. But anyway, I'll likely be back then.'

'There's no need. I'll be all right. You go to bed.'

She nodded at him, saying quietly, 'We'll see.' And at the door she turned and looked towards Lily and smiled, then she went out closing the door swiftly behind her.

Before Joseph took his seat by the bed he went to the table and from a bowl took the top pad of a number that had been soaked in Eau de Cologne; going back to the bed now he wiped his mother's brow with it. Then taking one hand after the other he wiped her palms before depositing the pad in the china slop pail that stood under the table.

Seated by the bedside now, he again took her hand and held it. But no words passed between them for fully two minutes or more, and then it was Lily who said, 'I . . . I must talk to you,' and at this he said, 'Yes, Mother.'

'First of all, I've got a bit of money put by. The book is in the top drawer there.' She made a motion with her head towards the small chest of drawers. 'I . . . I have saved it with one purpose, that you will know, well . . . a little independence when you go to that place. I've . . . I've never had to buy anything out of my wage except our clothes. We've both been housed and kept by them and also I started with a wage of . . . five shillings a week.' She stopped here and closed her eyes and her fingers now involuntarily tightened on his, and this caused him to turn his head and look back to the table. But now she was going on. 'Then it went up to seven and sixpence, and so for the past almost nineteen years I've been putting it by. So there is over three hundred pounds in the bank. And also I took out a policy that will bring in a hundred pounds, and ... and I reckon after the necessary money is paid out ...'

'*Mother, please!*' He had his head bent on his chest now and Lily, bringing her other hand onto his head, said, 'Listen, please, my dear, these things have to be talked about. Time is runnin' out. Now, now, now, look at me.' When he raised his white strained face, she said, 'That is all that need be said about money. But there is something else more important and I have been fightin' with meself for a long time whether I should tell you or not. But if I don't, I feel that it will come to you sometime or other in your life.'

She now took her hand from his head and lay back in the pillows and, her breath coming in painful gasps, she remained silent for some minutes, and then hesitantly, she began, 'You, I know, have been aware of something ... not quite right. But before I tell you anything I want your promise.' She turned her head and looked into his face and repeated, 'Your promise, a solemn promise, that whatever I say you will not let on ... well, I mean, divulge it to them. Well, not to anybody, but not to the mistress ... or to Mr Douglas, because there is a reason why they have wanted to keep you and Amy apart. You are known as Joseph Skinner. That is not your name. My dear Joseph was not your father. I wish to God he had been, for he was the best and kindest man that ever walked this ... earth. Your name should have been Carter. I was known as Lily Whitmore, but that was my ... step-father's name. I was working in Miss Bridget's, I mean ma'am's blacking factory when I became pregnant. I had misbehaved. I'm making no excuses, no, none at all; all I can say he was a gentleman, a man of the world and I was a silly, stupid, ignorant girl, and when I was on three months pregnant –' she stopped here and her head drooped and again she was

344

gasping for breath before she could go on, 'Joe Skinner, who was foreman in the factory, saved me from having to go into the Workhouse. He married me and I grew to love him. In the few months we had together I grew to love him and I have never stopped to this very minute. Nor has one day passed from that day on which he died but that I have thought of him.'

When once more her head fell back onto the pillow and she closed her eyes, he brought his face close to hers and even he himself could not hear the words that came from his mouth in a thin whisper, so that he had to repeat them, 'My father? Who was he, then?'

She opened her eyes and looked deep into his and she said now, 'Your promise? Your promise?'

'Yes. Yes, Mother, I promise.'

'You'll . . . you'll not let on that . . . that you know?'

He was bewildered, puzzled, but he muttered, 'Yes, yes, I mean no, I won't let on. I promise.'

'His brother.'

He withdrew slightly back from her, his face twisted in bewilderment, repeating, 'His brother! Whose?'

'Mr Douglas's.'

He shook his head, then sat well back in the chair now and stared at her. She was lying with her eyes closed, her chest heaving the bedclothes into billows. 'His brother? Mr Douglas's brother, the master's brother? God! No, because that would mean . . .' He closed his eyes tightly and put his double fist on his brow as if to steady his racing mind. Then after a long moment he made a sound like a sigh. He had imagined that made him and her half-brother and sister, but it just meant they were cousins.

And that's what it had all been about. They were cousins. And that man, the one who had a bad reputation, the one who had deserted his wife and mental child for years, until the woman he was living with died and he returned to the house. He had heard nothing of them for years, not even their name mentioned.

'I'm . . . I'm sorry. I shouldn't have told you.'

'*Oh, you should, you should.*' He was holding both her hands now, reassuring her. 'I . . . I only wish you had told me earlier and then I would have understood their reaction towards me.'

'They . . . they have been good to you.'

'Yes. Yes, I know, I know, and I've always wondered why? But he . . . he in a way is my uncle?'

'Yes.' She made a slow movement with her head. 'In a way, yes. But . . . but never claim it. You . . . you won't, will you?'

He paused just a moment before saying, 'No. No, I won't. Rest easy.'

'In . . . in the bottom drawer' – her head was moving again – 'there is a tin box. Fetch it.'

When he laid the small round tin box on the bed he noticed the writing on the rim: 'Doctor J. C. Murray's Ozonized Snuff'. It showed a pestle and mortar in the middle and in between them the words, 'Trade Mark'.

'Open it.'

When he opened it he saw a small, grey-looking chamois leather bag. It was stiff to the touch and after Lily made a signal to him to open it, he did so.

He did not tip out the coins but handed the bag to her and it was she who, turning his hand over, poured the five sovereigns on to his palm.

He stared at them for a moment before lifting his eyes to her and saying, 'What do they mean? What do they stand for?'

'That's . . . that's what was paid for you.'

'Paid for me?'

'Yes. Pu . . . pu . . . put them back and . . . and never use them. But remember the price . . .'

She stopped now and gritted her teeth, and at this he roughly bundled the sovereigns and the tin to the foot of the bed; then he went to the table and poured out first a dose of the doctor's medicine and then a measure of laudanum into another glass. When he took them to the bed she almost grabbed both glasses from him and one after the other she swallowed their contents. Then, as her hands dropped onto the counterpane, still holding the glasses, she let out a long slow sigh, and smiled wearily at him as she said, 'Everything will be all right now.'

He took the glasses from the counterpane, after which he put the money back into the bag and returned it to the tin box, which he replaced in the drawer. He didn't fully understand her last words about the payment; but he wouldn't trouble her any more tonight. She would go to sleep now.

He arranged her pillows, and once more wiped her face and hands with a dampened Eau de Cologne pad; then he was about to take his seat when she held out her arms to him and, drawing his head down to hers, she kissed him, and, her voice quite light-sounding, she said, 'I want you to remember something, and it's this. I've never regretted havin' you from the minute you were born, and, if it is possible, each day I've become prouder of you.'

He laid his cheek gently against hers for a moment but he could utter no words. He was choking with heart-breaking emotion, for the only thing he possessed in the world was about to leave him. From now on he would have nothing, no one of his own. Those up there, even Amy, who had all become suddenly related to him, they were strangers. And the father he had found, what of him? He glanced towards the chest of drawers. That money, those five sovereigns. She had said, 'That's what was paid for you.' Was that what he had paid her for his pleasure?

If that was so he would one day ram them down his throat.

He started slightly when she said, 'Good-night, Joe.'

She never called him Joe, always Joseph, but he answered her, saying, 'Good-night, dear.'

'I'll sleep well tonight.'

'That's good.' He leant forward and gently arranged the bedclothes around her shoulders, and then he sat back and waited . . .

It was five o'clock the next morning. He was in the kitchen making up the fire when the door opened and Douglas came in and he said immediately, 'I'm sorry, Joseph. Mrs Filmore lay down for what she promised herself would just be an hour. I was to waken her. But I fell asleep, too. I'm terribly sorry. How is she?'

'She died at a quarter past three.'

'Oh God!' Douglas put his hand to his head. 'And you alone here. Oh, I'm sorry; and there's been one or other of us here for the past week.'

'Don't worry. There was nothing you could do. Anyway, it was as I would wish it. She went in her sleep.'

'Look, come on up to the house. I'll get the girls to come down and do what is necessary.'

'It's all done.'

'What!'

'I've seen to her.'

Douglas's face was screwed up, expressing a mixture of disbelief and astonishment, as he said, 'Oh, you shouldn't! It . . . well, I mean, it . . .'

'She's my mother. I've tended her for weeks, haven't I?'

Douglas now stared at the young man who had somehow suddenly become strange and distant in his manner. But that's what shock and bereavement did to people, so he said, 'Well, anyway, come up and have some breakfast.'

'Thank you, but I'm not at all hungry.'

'Oh, very well. But . . . but there'll be things to see to, the undertaker and . . .'

'Yes. Yes, there will. But there's plenty of time.'

'Of course, of course . . . Well, Mrs Filmore will be down shortly.' . . .

Douglas was walking slowly up the drive as he told himself that shock played havoc with some people, but of course he knew it was coming, didn't he? In fact she had lingered on longer than any of them thought she would. Yet the young fellow seemed strange, aloof, as if he were on the defensive. But what about?

He stopped dead. Had she told him? No. He shook his head. If she had, his attitude would have been entirely different. He could have imagined that he would have been pleased at the relationship; the fact that he was a full cousin to Amy wouldn't have deterred him, no matter how it was deterring both Bridget and himself, Bridget even more than himself for she had always looked for traits of Lionel in him. He himself could honestly say that he had never glimpsed any. Yet, as Bridget said, you did not know what went on in another's mind. But, oh, he'd be glad when the young fellow got himself away to Cambridge. That kind of life would likely blow the cobwebs off him and also obliterate his young love. Well, he hoped so, indeed he did. But then, thinking like that, what about Amy? What about her cobwebs? There was a great deal of Bridget in Amy, the determination to get to the bottom of anything, whatever the cost. Oh, dear, dear. And now there was the funeral to see to, although he would like to bet, from that young gentleman's manner this morning, he would see to that, too, himself. Dear, dear! life was trying at times. It would be much easier if one didn't have offspring, just a wife, a wife like his dearest Bridget.

And then the question arose again, weighing him down:

should he, or should he not have told her? He had thought if he could be alone with her just before she died then he would say to her, 'You are right, Lily, your husband was innocent. My brother was the guilty man. But it was no use exposing him, because the man ... your dearest husband, was already dead ...' But he had been unable to do so; the chance to be alone with her before she died had been denied him, for not once had he sat by her bedside: that vigil had been shared between her son and Bridget, relieved during the day by one of the maids. So, he shouldn't blame himself because another factor to this business might have ensued: if she had had strength enough to respond to such news she might have passed the knowledge on to Joseph, and then what would have happened? He felt he knew: she would divulge his parentage.

Well, hadn't that to come out sometime? But who was to tell him?

It was as Douglas looked into the grave that there swept over him, as in a wave of heat, a sense of regret so deep that it brought beads of perspiration out onto his brow, and in his mind he was shouting down to the elaborate brass-bound coffin: Oh, Lily, Lily, I'm sorry. I should have told you in order to make up for the years you've lived in sadness, merely existing. Over the past few days I've come to know how you must have felt for him. You suffered all your life for loving as I myself do. Yes I do, for love is a suffering because it's threaded with fear, fear for your loved one, fear of being deprived of the fear itself. Oh, Lily, forgive me.

The clods were falling on the coffin. The people were moving away. Bridget was crying bitterly. As he took her arm he saw his daughter come and stand close to Joseph, and he stretched out his other hand and gently turned her about, leaving the young man standing alone by the grave . . .

Joseph's eyes were dry. He had shed no tears over his mother's going, because all his emotions seemed to have gathered into a block inside his chest and become frozen, emitting a feeling that could only be compared with that of a winter chill.

As he turned from the grave and walked amidst the headstones to the path, he could see in the distance the carriage and the group around it. They were waiting for him, but he wished they weren't; he wanted to be on his own.

As he stepped onto the path a man, who had been standing on the grass verge, approached him and, stopping in front said, 'Hello, lad.'

Joseph looked at him in some surprise, not because the man had spoken, but because of his way of address. When he went on to say, 'You don't know me, but I was your ma's half-brother. Me name is Mick Whitmore . . . Never heard of me?'

Joseph shook his head. 'No,' he said. 'No, I'm sorry.'

'No need to be sorry, lad. She always kept herself to herself. I can remember the day she left home to marry your dad. I was seven at the time. I can even recall that I missed her. We all missed her, me two sisters and me other brother. He was only three, and he died afore he was five. Me two sisters . . . well, they might be living in Timbuktoo for all I see of them, but that doesn't worry me. They are both married and comfortable down in Yorkshire somewhere, and I'm married meself, and comfortable. Many's the time I thought I'd look her up, but then she cut adrift and she was carrying her burden and I didn't want to push in, nor me wife. It was a great pity about your dad because most people had a good word for him, apart from his mother. By! she was an old bitch. Well, she swore his life away, didn't she? He would never have swung if it hadn't been for her. But she's got her deserts. She's in the Gateshead Workhouse now, I hear, and . . .'

'What did you say about being . . . swung . . . ?'

'Well, you know, your dad. He'd only married Lily a matter of months . . . well, you know,' – the man's head was nodding now – 'he killed his brother. You must know . . .' His voice trailed off and he said, 'Oh! God Almighty! She never told you?'

Joseph made no sign, he just stared at the man who had suddenly become related to him.

'Why? Oh, she should have told you that. But it's a wonder somebody hasn't thrown it at you, lad, knowin' what people are. Well, you know, as I said, your dad was hung for killin' his brother and his mother stood up in court and said that she had heard him threaten him. Of course, I was only a bairn when this happened, but I heard it so often from me mother over the years that it could have happened yesterday, and you know, it was the people who took Lily in, at least, the man Mr Filmore, who found the brother in the wood and he had just been talkin' to your dad a short while before. 'Twas all a funny business. Eeh! lad, I wouldn't have spoken about it if I had thought you hadn't have known. It seems impossible, you know, that you didn't, 'cos the owner of the factory where Joe worked, she married Mr Filmore, didn't she? I mean, well what I understand is, you live in their lodge . . . and you mean to say they've never let on?'

The words came out slowly now as he said, 'No, they've never let on.'

'Eeh! lad, that's funny, odd if you ask me. But mind, lad, there's a lot of people, me ma included among them, who stood by the fact that your da had nowt to do with that business. It was one of Andy Davison's lot, they said. 'Twasn't him himsel' because he was in hospital at the time, so I understand, but he had a lot of cronies, an' they knew that your da's brother had potched them from time to time. It was a nasty business. But oh lad, I'm sorry.' His head now wagged. 'And . . . and you don't mind me makin' meself known to you?'

'Oh no. No, of course not.'

He had a father to whom he could make no claim, but now he had an uncle, or a step-uncle, who was holding out his hand to him. He took it, and the man said, 'Look, I don't want to push, never have, but if you feel like droppin' in for a cup of tea anytime, we live at thirty-six Mount Pleasant Road, Birtley. I've got no family: there's just me and the wife, but you'll be more than welcome, lad.'

'Thank you. Thank you. I'll remember.'

They nodded at each other, and then the man stood aside and let him walk up the path to the square, where Douglas was standing by the coach.

Douglas did not enquire who the sympathiser was, nor did Joseph volunteer any information. He got into the coach and took his seat beside Bridget, opposite to Amy and her father, who was also his uncle, and he wanted to lean forward and say to him, 'Why didn't you tell me that my father was hanged for murdering a man?' Then there sprang into his pain-ridden mind the thought: But he wasn't my father; he was someone called Joseph Skinner, someone his mother had loved.

He lay back against the leather-padded seat and closed his eyes. Well, at least he wouldn't have that on his mind, too. But why hadn't they told me? The whole thing was like a spider's web, and there in the middle was the spider and the spider was his father. He must see him. He must look on him even if it be only from a distance.

353

3

They were in the kitchen of the Lodge when Amy asked, 'Where are you going?'

'I'm going to visit my new-found step-uncle.'

'Oh. The man who you were talking to in the cemetery?'

'Yes.'

'Where does he live?'

'In Birtley.'

'How long will you be away?'

Joseph looked into the large brown eyes, thinking, Strange, but I'm really on an equal footing to you, class-wise now, even if I am really a bastard. Your father is my uncle. No step here. You are my full cousin. This being so, you would have thought, now that we are coming out of the dark ages of dear old Victoria, that they would see the situation in an enlightened fashion. But no, we are still in the status quo.

He answered her now, 'I don't know.'

'There's only a week before you go up to Cambridge.'

'Yes, that's true, only a week.'

She took a step towards him, saying quietly, 'I know how you must be feeling, but . . . but don't push me out.'

'Please, Amy.'

'There you are, you see.' She tossed her head to the side. 'That's what I mean. That's all we've got out of you, any of us, for days now, two words: Thank you. No, thank you. Yes, perhaps. And now it's, Please, Amy. As I said, I know how you feel in losing Lily, but the way you're going on you'll lose everybody. Yes. Yes, you will.' She was shouting now. 'And me!'

Her statement seemed to have shocked her into immobility, for she stood stiffly, her mouth half open, staring at him, and as he stared back at her he was saying loudly in his mind, Oh, no! Amy. No! I won't lose you. But there are things I must do, things I must get to the bottom of before I let myself go where you're concerned.

Why should he suddenly feel old? A few weeks ago he had been looking forward to the time when he would go to Cambridge and enter a new way of life; that was before he realised the seriousness of his mother's illness. Even then, there was still the light shining in the distance; but not any more; the feeling in him now was that there would be no more school of any kind for him.

Amy's turning away brought him back to the situation, and he said, although now more out of politeness than of interest, 'Where are you going?'

She was at the door now and she turned round and snapped, 'Not the same place as you're going finally, and that's nowhere and achieving nothing. And I'll tell you something more: I'm finished throwing myself at your feet. If there's any kneeling to be done in the future it won't be coming from me.'

The door was closed with such a bang that for a moment he screwed up his eyes against the sound. Then he sat down in the wooden chair by the table on which his breakfast things still remained and, holding his head between his hands, he swore aloud . . .

When Amy entered the hall it was to see her father and mother going up the stairs, and they both turned and looked down at her. 'You were talking about going for a few days to Harrogate,' she said, and Bridget answered, 'Yes, dear, we were.'

'All right.'

'You would like to go?'

'Well, what am I saying? Yes! Yes, I would like to go.'

Another time Douglas would have retorted quickly, saying, 'Remember to whom you are speaking!' But a tight grip on his arm turned him about, and they proceeded up the stairs and not until they were in their bedroom did Bridget speak, when she said, 'Chastising will not help at this stage. He'll be gone next week and she'll have weeks to cool down. We'll have to arrange theatres and trips and . . .'

'I think he should be told, at least what is necessary at the moment.'

At this, two thoughts clashed in her mind: the first that the road would then be open to him; he would no longer class himself as inferior, the son of a servant. He would see himself as Amy's equal, in status anyway; that his mother had been a servant would no longer carry any weight. Then the second: why did Douglas always seem to suggest that there was something more than the boy's parentage to divulge? Right from the time of his nightmare she had felt there was something worrying him at the back of his mind, especially so when he had called out Joe's name.

However, her main concern now was her daughter and her happiness. She could see no happiness for her married to the son of Lionel Filmore; and Douglas was of the same mind. This she knew, but here he was saying that he was going to tell Joseph of their true relationship.

She said quietly, 'I . . . I would leave it for a time. It might be too much coming on top of Lily's going.'

Douglas thought for a moment, then nodded at her, saying, 'Yes. Yes, it might, but it should be soon because it's beginning to worry me and the fact that we've kept it from him for so long. It will be no use telling him that Lily wanted it that way.' He then asked, 'How long do you intend we should stay in Harrogate?'

'Well, we have the weekend and perhaps we could return on Tuesday or Wednesday.'

'Better make it Tuesday at the latest. There's quite a lot of work in and . . .'

'Oh! you and your work.' She went to him and put her arms around his neck and as she did so he said, 'And you, too, missis, you and your work, opening another polish factory. I've never heard of such a thing.'

'It's going to be modern, right up-to-date. I've told you, you should come through and see the sight and . . .'

'You know what I feel about factories of any kind. Why don't you sell the lot?'

'Oh' – she pushed him away from her – 'd'you want to break my heart? What would I do with my days when you're stuck down there with your lumps of stone? I do finish at a decent hour and some days I don't work at all; but you, it's seven days a week with you. So, don't you tell me, sir, to sell my pet hobby.'

He put his head back now as he laughed and repeated, 'Pet hobby, and you competing with some of the big names in the city. D'you know you are actually feared in some quarters?'

'Oh, yes, yes, I know that, and that's how I want it.'

'Oh my dear.' His voice dropping to a lower tone, she turned and looked at him as he went on, 'Nobody would believe there are two distinct women inside you.' She moved towards him and again she had her arms around him and his around her, and she said, and also softly, 'And no one would believe that it's only because I live with a wonderful man who makes me feel, as I never felt before in my life until I met him, like a girl.' Her head dropped back and she laughed, adding, 'That's why I daren't look in the mirror very often, because it would give the lie . . .'

Her words were cut off by his lips tracing each feature of her face, and when they came to her mouth she returned his kiss as passionately as when their mouths had first met on that New Year's morning.

4

He had taken the train from Shields to Gateshead. He had
been in the town a number of times before when, together
with Amy, he had accompanied her mother on a tour of
the two factories. The first visit had been when he was
quite a young boy and the impression it had left on him
was that of a dark, dusty and dirty place. It wasn't until
he was in his teens that he became critical in his mind of
the conditions under which the people worked. He was
given to understand that there had been great improve-
ments made over the nine years in both the machinery in
the factories and the conditions of the workers. It must
be two years ago since he last visited the polish works
with Amy and her mother, and what became evident to
him on that occasion was there were two Mrs Filmores:
one who talked business like a man, he imagined; the
other the doting wife and mother and lady of the house.
Now, as he passed Honeybee Place, he noticed that some
of the houses were being knocked down, and not before
time, he thought.

When he skirted the iron railings that now bordered the
factory premises he stopped and looked about him. He
knew that Mrs Filmore had once lived within a couple of
miles of the factory in a house called Milton Place, and
he also knew Mr Filmore had been born quite near there.
He didn't know the name of the house, but from what he
had picked up from the servants in the kitchen he knew
that Mr Filmore's brother still lived there and was married
to Mrs Filmore's cousin.

When he had asked his mother about it and why the two ladies never visited each other, she had said she didn't know. It was family business and he wasn't to question Miss Amy about it. It was up to them to mind their own business. Now did he understand?

And such had been her tone and manner that he had said, yes, he understood, even though he didn't; he only knew it was something that hadn't to be talked about.

There was a man passing and he stopped him and asked, 'Could you please direct me to a house called Milton Place?'

The man didn't answer for a moment. He turned his head to one side, rubbed his tongue around his front teeth, then said, 'Milton Place? Now, now let me see.' And he looked about him; then seeming to come to a decision, he pointed to a narrow path, saying, 'The bridle path leads you into the fields, then into a wood, and people use it as a short cut to I don't know where. But you want Milton Place.'

His tongue made another journey over his teeth before he pointed to the left of him, saying, 'Your best bet, I think, is to take the straight road, though it might seem round about to you, 'cos I imagine it would be a good mile or more. And if I were you' – he looked upwards now and pointed to the sky – 'I'd put your best foot forward because we're in for rain, an' if it's anything like yesterday's lot you'll be drenched. And you're without a mackintosh, lad.'

Joseph smiled at the man. He felt inclined to laugh, for he had made a pantomime out of directing him; but he said, 'Thank you very much, sir.'

'You're welcome, lad, you're welcome. But do as I say and act like spring-heeled-Jack, or else you're goin' to be sodden.'

Joseph actually did laugh now and he nodded to his

informant before hurrying across the open space and taking the road the man had indicated.

Who was spring-heeled-Jack? And he would be sodden . . . What a character. And there were so many like him, kind and humorous men; and yet they seemed to be only among the workers.

At school in Newcastle he had met the fathers of two or three of the boys, but they seemed to be all of a pattern; doctors, solicitors, business men, all correctly dressed, all speaking the same language; polite, dry, condescending to youth.

But that man was right, the sky was darkening; it was now almost like deep twilight and it was only one o'clock.

He was walking through a built-up area and he noticed that the front doors were all painted in different colours, as were those of many of the houses in the streets in South Shields. But quite suddenly the houses gave way to fields and now he was walking along a narrow road bordered by a dry stone wall, and it seemed never ending. But it was as it eventually joined up with a rough main road that the rain started in earnest.

He stood peering first one way then the other while the rain poured down his face, but he could see no sign of shelter or habitation. So now, choosing the road to the left he did actually run, and quickly, but the road seemed endless.

He stopped; he was out of breath. The rain was now coming down in sheets and he couldn't see more than a couple of yards in front of him; and he was aware that it had penetrated through to his shirt and vest. Head down into the rain, he walked on, asking himself why had he been such a fool as to follow that man's instructions, because he hadn't himself really known where the place was. Anything amusing about the encounter was dismissed from his mind for he knew that he was actually lost, and what was more he had to make the return journey. So why keep walking straight on?

It was just at this moment of decision to turn around that the cottage loomed up. It almost seemed to him that it had sprung out of the ground, for there it was set back behind what appeared, through his rain-washed gaze, to be a low white fence.

He stumbled through the gate and groped at the black-iron knocker on the door, and it seemed to him that the door was opened as quickly as the cottage had appeared.

'Yes? Oh dear! Oh dear! You are wet, aren't you?'

'I'm . . . I think I'm lost. I wonder if . . . if you could tell me how to get to . . . well, I just mean, back to the town?'

'Come away in, unless you want to get your death standing there.'

'I'm . . . I'm very wet.'

'Of course you're wet, lad. Come away in.' A hand came out and gripped his arm and none too gently he was pulled over the threshold into a lamplit room, then pushed aside so the small dumpy woman could bang the door closed.

'My! My! You are in a pickle. You're wet enough to be wrung out.' She laughed up into his face now, adding, 'I could put you through the mangle. Give us your coat here.' Her movements, like the grip on his arm, were rough as she helped to pull the coat from him. Then she exclaimed, 'My! you're wet to the skin. What brought you out on a day like this without a top-coat?'

'It . . . it was quite fine when I left home.'

'Well, 'tisn't fine now and hasn't been for days up here. Yesterday we had a flood and it looks like another one the day, because it's in for it.' She thumbed towards the window to the side of the door now, then said, 'Where you makin' for?'

362

'I . . . I was looking for a certain house and . . .'

She cut off his voice saying, 'You're makin' a pool on me mat. Take your boots off, then get to the fire.' When she saw him hesitate, she said, 'Well, d'you want to get dry or not?'

'Oh yes. Yes, please.'

'Well, get yourself to the fire.'

He had taken off his hat as soon as he entered the room; she now helped to divest him of his waistcoat, which he laid on a wooden chair to the side of the door, only for her to whip it up, saying, 'I'll put them out the back. I've had the boiler on in the wash-house. I cook the hen and duck crowdie in it, you know. Anyway, it's warm in there and they'll dry off.'

He watched her now scurry across the room and disappear through a door; then he walked to the fire. It was an open range and it was heaped high with blazing coal; a kettle was sizzling on the hob. He looked at the basket chair that was set to one side of the fireplace. It had a padded seat and a head cushion pinned to its high back. He looked to the other side where, at right angles to the fireplace, was a short settle. It, too, had a padded seat.

He stood with his back to the fire and surveyed the room. It was a largish kitchen and the table in the middle of it was covered with a green chenille cloth trimmed with bobbles. A black oak delft rack stood against the wall and in the far corner of the room he could make out a whatnot, the wood of its shelves almost hidden by the pieces of china standing on them. The floor of the room was made of stone slabs but covered here and there with what his mother had called clippy mats. The ceiling was low and black-beamed and from it hung various shapes he thought must be small hams, and in between them bunches of herbs. It was like a farm kitchen. Perhaps it was a farm.

'Oh, my stars! You're steamin' all over, lad. Now that'll

bring on somethin'; give you your death. Take off your shirt and vest.'

'It'll soon dr . . .'

'Take them off! There's nothin' that a man has that I haven't seen. But anyway, you'll have linings on; and look, I'll get you a cover of sorts. In the meantime, get them off.'

She now went along the kitchen and opened a door and to his surprise he heard her mounting some stairs, then the sound of her footsteps overhead, and he looked upwards as he thought, What a surprising little woman. In a way she was like the man who had put him on the wrong road.

Slowly he pulled off his shirt and vest and, more slowly still, stepped out of his trousers. He was wearing knee-length linings and they were dry round the hips but wet towards his knees.

He was standing holding his trousers out towards the fire when she came back into the room again, and he swung round to face her as she approached him, holding out a garment.

'It's a kind of dressin' gown thing. My lad used to wear it. It's a bit threadbare in parts and many's the time I've been goin' to cut it up for the mat. I don't know why I didn't; but now' – she grinned at him – 'I see I've been keepin' it for you. Put it on. How's your pants?'

'Oh, they're almost dry. Thank you.'

'Here, give me your other togs. I'll stick them round the boiler. Oh . . . but' – she paused – 'I don't think I can get them all round. Better still, I'll bring the fireguard in and hang them over the side here. Eh?' Once more she was grinning at him, but he could say nothing in reply.

Left alone again, he felt for a moment that he had walked into a dream, and more so, when she returned with the fireguard and said, 'You haven't taken your socks off. Get them off and put them over the end of the guard, then plonk yourself down.' She pointed to the settle and he obeyed her.

'Now, Charlie, get a move on.'

He realised in amazement she was talking to the kettle as she ground its black bottom into the blazing coals. Then, turning to him while thumbing towards the kettle, she said, 'He'll be knockin' steam out of that spout within five minutes and then we'll have a good cup of tea, eh?'

There was a gurgle rising from his stomach. He forgot entirely for a moment, and for the first time since he had sat at her bedside, that his mother was dead, and he put his head back and laughed out loud. When he brought it forward the little woman was standing by his knees and she, too, was laughing as she said, 'Me talkin' to Charlie, you find that funny? Well, you know, when you live on your own you get like that. But I'm only funny in parts, lad, so don't worry.'

As he wiped his eyes he watched her go to the table, take off the chenille cloth, fold it up and put it to one side; then go to a drawer and bring out a tablecloth and put it on the table; after which she laid out two cups and saucers and two plates, and from a larder that appeared to be situated partly under the stairs, she brought out various items of food: a loaf of bread on a board, a lump of butter in a dish, a plate of scones, and a glass dish of some preserve. After she had cut some slices of bread, she put them on a plate and carried them to the settle and, laying the plate beside him, she pointed to a long brass toasting fork hanging on a nail to the side of the fireplace, and she said, 'Get a hold of that and toast some bread. Push the guard out of the way for a minute.'

He did as he was bidden. Six slices he toasted, during which time she had buttered each slice of toast as it was done, mashed the tea in a brown earthenware teapot, put a woollen tea-cosy over it, placed it on a tray with a bowl of sugar and a jug of milk and set it on the side of the table, before saying, 'Well now, come on and sit up.'

When he found himself sitting on a wooden straight-backed chair facing her, she said, 'Tuck in. There it is, help yourself. I've set it all out but I'm not goin' to put it into your mouth.' Her face was one large grin again and he grinned back at her. But before he reached out to take a piece of toast he leant towards her and, his voice quiet, he said, 'May I know your name, please?' And she said, 'Yes, lad, you may. It's Bertha Hanratty.'

And now he repeated, 'Mrs Bertha Hanratty. Well, Mrs Hanratty, will you tell me, please, if this is a dream or am I awake?'

Now it was her turn to throw her head back and let out a laugh that belied her small stature. Then after a moment she said, 'Aw, lad, you find me queer, do you?'

'No, not at all queer, only extremely kind and . . .' When he paused she put in, 'And?'

'Well, this is a very odd thing for me to say now, but it's as if you had been expecting me, such was your welcome.'

He watched the smile slide slowly from her face; and she picked up a slice of toast and began to cut it in two as she said, 'No, lad, I wasn't expectin' you, but I was very glad to see you. I get few visitors and all them I know. The occasional tramp comes along. They have their roads, you know, and they leave signs where one following on will get a bite. And then there's a man or two now and again on the road looking for work. They're nearly always the result of some war or other. But . . . but you were different, and this is a special kind of day because it's me birthday. I'm sixty-two.'

'Oh, many happy returns.'

'Thank you, lad, an' I may say you're as good as a

birthday present. In fact, I think I'll look upon you like that.'

'Have you any family?'

'Yes. Yes. I've got a family, lad, or I had a family. But I've never seen them for years. My son, James, he's in Australia, forty-three he is. I hear from him about once a year, if that. Then me daughter's in Jersey, the island, you know, Jersey. Lena's forty, she's got two bairns. I've never seen her or the bairns, not in years. But it didn't matter so much as long as I had my Willie, that was me husband. He's been dead these eight years. Still, life must go on, mustn't it?'

He couldn't say, 'Yes. Yes, it must;' he only knew of a sudden that he was in the company of an old and lonely little woman who oozed kindness.

'Well, come on, keep eatin'; an' by the way, now I've given you my life story, what about yours? What're you doin' round here? Because I can see from your clothes that you're neither beggin' nor lookin' for work.'

'No, I . . . I was looking for a house where a friend of mine used to live, called Milton Place.'

'Oh, Milton Place. Well! Well! But you're on the wrong road for Milton Place. That's the Thompsons' house. Are they friends of yours?'

'Oh no. I . . . I only know someone who used to live there before, Mrs Filmore; but she was called Mordaunt then.'

'Oh! Oh!' Her face was stretching now. 'Well! Well! She's been left there years ago and she married a Filmore, didn't she? and his brother lives along the road not a mile away in Grove House.'

He heard himself say, 'Does he?'

'Oh yes. Oh my! There's a family for you. Talk about the mighty fallin'. Eeh! I can remember back as far as when I was ten, when I used to work for Colonel Taggard over at The Brambles. They were friends of the Filmores, backwards and forwards they were. Then there were the Maybrooks, who had breweries, and Porter, they were in shipping, and there used to be some goin's on, especially at the hunt time. Eeh! but if you were to see them now, I mean the Filmores, well, the one that's still livin' in The Grove. Have you met any of them?'

'No. No, never.'

'Oh, well then, I can't be givin' anythin' away. Well, with one thing and another it's like a madhouse there. And they've got a poor lass who's not all right in the head. Some say she's just deaf and gets into tempers when she would scratch your eyes out. But there's one thing she has done, they say, and that is made the kitchen garden like nobody has in years. She spends her days there, 'tis said. She's cleared up paths and hedges and bits of the rose garden. So, to my mind she's still got a bit up top. But inside the house, they say, it's like Paddy's market. Well, Mr Bright, he's been the butler there for years, he's an old fellow himself and he still tends the master, and to all accounts he's been bedridden, really bedridden for the last three or four years. The last thing I heard was they had had three different fellows there givin' him a hand, but they didn't reign long, not one of them. And the young mistress, well, she was young when she went there, but she had a life of it. He left her, you know, the son . . . the eldest son, and lived openly with a woman in Newcastle. For years that went on, then she goes and dies on him, so it was said, and back he comes. Well, from all I hear he's been in one job after another. He victuals ships, so I'm told, or works for people who do. And they've only got one man now in the yard because there's only a single horse left. I used to have a crack with him' – she nodded at Joseph now – 'the yard man, but I haven't seen him for God knows how long. The last time he told me about the mistress there, the one that went there when young an' is now in her middle years, well she had a heart attack or some such, and not a bit of wonder by all accounts. Funny how a family can reach rock bottom, isn't it? But there, that's life. It lifts some up and tosses others down. Anyway, young man' – she now poked her head towards him – 'I've given you all me news and that of the district and you haven't had to buy a newspaper, and the odd thing is, I don't even know your name. What do they call you?'

What did they call him? Joseph Skinner. Or should he rightly go by his mother's name, Whitmore? But then, that wasn't her name, it was her step-father's. Her name was Carter, so she had told him. Well, according to law, he supposed, that's the name he should be known under. Again he looked at the old woman and just as he had thought before, so he said to himself now. She's lonely. But like most lonely people, once they get going their tongues wag. Yet whom could she connect Joseph Skinner with? Nevertheless, he heard himself say, 'My name's Carter, Joseph Carter.'

'Joseph Carter. 'Tis a plain name, a kind that one remembers. Well now, while you finish up that toast' – she pointed to the plate now – 'I'll go and turn your clothes on the boiler . . .'

She turned his clothes on the boiler. She washed up her crocks in a tin dish that was standing in a shallow, brown-glazed stone sink. Then she sat opposite him and regaled him with more history of her life and that of her husband's, from the time when this house was the toll house and her father-in-law the toll keeper. But when she married Willie and her family began to arrive, he built on two rooms to the side. So now she had three bedrooms, where one was all she needed. But she was kept busy with fourteen hens, twelve ducks, six geese and a gander, besides four pigs, two in litter.

When, at half-past four in the afternoon it was raining as hard as ever and the twilight seemed to have deepened, she looked out of the door and exclaimed, 'Lad, if you make for Gateshead in that, you're goin' to get wetter than when you came; and what's more, there's not a light on the road until you come to the big house. The first one will be The Grove and I shouldn't imagine they'll bother with the light on the outside gates. There will be on the Thompsons', but that's a good step further on. Then you've got some way to go to get into the town. So, lad, what about it? You're welcome to stay the night, more than welcome.'

He did not hesitate in his acceptance of her offer; he couldn't face the thought of being wet through again, nor groping his way along dark roads, only to be lost yet again. But what was more, he felt comfortable here, and she had blotted out his own thoughts and the reason that had brought him to this part in the first place.

She was saying now, 'The bed in the room above this won't be damp because the chimney runs up by the wall. But it's not big, you can hardly swing a cat in it. Still, I don't suppose that'll trouble you.' Then she put in, 'By the way, I've never asked you what's your trade?'

What was his trade? Could he say, 'I was about to go up to university in a few days time, but now I don't know'? What he said was, 'I . . . I haven't really made up my mind. I would like to teach.'

'Oh well, if you can afford to wait to make up your mind, that's all right. Your people must be well off.'

'They are dead.'

'Oh, I'm sorry. Where d'you live, and who with?'

'I . . . I've been living with friends. My home is in South Shields.'

'My! You've come a step out of your way, lad, haven't you?'

He had got used to the habit of her head being poked towards him, and here it was once again as she said, 'I'm a nosey parker, that's what you're thinkin', isn't it, I'm a nosey parker?'

'No, not at all, not at all. I'm thinking you're a very kind lady.'

'Aw, well, that's nice of you, lad. But to tell you the truth, the good turn I've done is nothing to what you've done to me, because I don't mind admitting I get lonely at times.' And on a laugh she pointed to the kettle, saying, 'I can't get Charlie to answer me back.'

They were both laughing together again; and so it went on until she showed him up the stairs to the narrow room that could hold only a single iron bed, a wooden chest, and a chair, and when she pointed to a frayed hand-worked text above the bed and, leaning forward, he read,

> 'Cast thy bread upon the waters
> And hope to get a baker's shop back.'

Once more their laughter joined and she said, 'I've left it there. This was my lad's room. Well, he went to Australia, as I told you, but I don't know whether he got his baker's shop because he never sends me any of his bread.' For a full moment the smile left her face; then she said, 'Good-night, lad. You'll sleep well.'

He did sleep well, and was woken in the morning with a cup of strong tea and his clothes laid ready on the one chair. When, later in the kitchen, he sat down to a break-fast of two eggs and two thick slices of ham reposing on pieces of fried bread, he ate it all.

Before he left she took him out the back way and showed him her smallholding, from which she derived a livelihood; then she was standing at the gate with him looking up to the sky and saying, 'By! that sun's got a nerve to come out after yesterday, hasn't he?'

He made no rejoinder to this, but he took both her hands in his and shook them gently, as he said, 'These last hours will stay with me for a long time, Mrs Hanratty, and as I promised you, I shall come back and see you; because you won't take payment for your kindness, I'll always feel in your debt, and that's the only way I'll be able to repay you.'

The little woman now made no reply, but her head kept nodding, and as he walked away from her down the road he knew that her eyes were still on him, as was the weight of her loneliness, caused mostly, he thought, by the neglect of her family. Life was strange. Some people were deprived of love, others were surrounded by it. He himself had been surrounded by it and he had accepted it as normal, even at times being irritated by it and its demands.

He had been walking smartly for about twenty minutes along a road that lay between open farmland; but abruptly the landscape changed, for to the left of him began grounds bordered by railings, some lying drunkenly on the brush-wood, while spiderly trees struggled up between the branches of larger ones. He now felt the beat of his heart quicken as he realised that he was nearing the house he had come purposely to see.

It was some distance further before he came to the iron gates. One was open, permanently so, because he noted that the grass was growing high into the filigreed iron-work. He stood, his hand gripping the cold edge of the other gate. The drive ahead disappeared into the darkness of overgrown trees. He turned his head to the right to where stood the lodge. That, too, was set among long grass and was definitely uninhabited.

Should he walk up that drive and to the house? What then could he say? 'Can I see my real father, please?'

Huh! Did he *want* to see his real father who, by all accounts, was a no-good reprobate?

It was on this thought that he turned away and walked along by a stone wall. Here, too, there was evidence of neglect, for some of the top copings were lying where they had fallen on the verge of the road. Further along, the wall ended abruptly, and there again were two iron gates; but both of these were wide open, and the drive that went through them showed it was used and he could see clearly for some good way along it. Would he be able to catch a glimpse of the house from the far end?

He wasn't really aware that the thought had urged him forward, until he was brought to a stop by the beginning of another stone wall running at right angles away from him and there, beyond the wall, he saw a great stretch of well-kept garden and in the far distance a figure bending over. It was a woman; she had her back to him. Then, when the figure straightened up and turned in his direction, even from this distance he knew now he was looking at a girl . . . the girl, the one whom Mrs Hanratty had said was wrong in the head, and who, yes, if it was she, would be his half-sister. The thought made his whole body quiver.

He had stepped over a narrow ditch and was walking between neat rows of vegetables, and he was more than half-way towards her when she moved, not backwards away from him but towards him.

He was the first to stop. He was now standing to the side of a row of cabbages and she had come to a halt about three yards distance, and he was simply astonished by the look of her. She was tall and her head was without covering and her auburn hair was in two plaits, the one hanging over her shoulder almost reaching her waist. But it was her face he was concentrating on. It was so beautiful that he told himself she must be normal; this couldn't be the daughter who was considered mental.

'Good-morning,' he said.

When she made no reply he thought, with further amazement, it must be her. He was about to speak again, to say that he was sorry that he had disturbed her, when she opened her mouth wide and let out a sound. It wasn't a scream nor yet a cry, yet it was high and the only way he could translate it was by the word, 'Wong'. When she emitted it again she turned her head to the side and in the direction of a long greenhouse. And now he saw a man come hurriedly out of it and towards them, and at his approach she began to wave her arms and her head wagged, and she made a number of, to him, unintelligible sounds. But the man seemed to understand her, for he now nodded his head at her, saying, 'Yes. Yes. All right, Miss Henrietta. All right.' Then, approaching Joseph and with his back to the young girl, he said, 'You needn't be scared: she's all right, she's only deaf.'

'I'm not scared.'

'You're early.'

Joseph's eyes widened and he made a small movement with his head; then the man said, 'How did you get here? Did you walk from the town? Because you're not from round about, are you?'

'No. No, I'm not from round about.'

The man now stepped back a space and looked him up and down, saying, 'You're not the usual sort that answers for the job, an' you don't look as if you'll be much use at liftin' or helpin' either, and it stated that plainly in the paper. Where've you come from?'

He could answer this; he said, 'I've . . . I've spent the night with Mrs Hanratty.'

'Oh, old Bertha. Oh, well, why didn't you say? She put you on to it, did she?' He laughed now and made a movement with his hand as if he were about to punch Joseph on the shoulder as he said, 'I bet you couldn't get a word in. She's better than the *News Of The World*, but she's a good sort. I haven't seen her for some time. How is she?'

'She seems very well.'

Now the man narrowed his eyes as he said, 'Are you related? You're not her grandson from Australia, are you?'

'No. No, I'm not.'

'Ah well, that's a pity. She just lives to hear or see one of 'em. Lonely she is, but with a heart of gold. Well, then, I think you had better come and see Mr Bright, 'cos you'll be workin' with him. By the way, I'm Ron Yarrow.' He now turned to the girl who had moved to his side and, his mouth forming the words slowly and widely, he said, 'New fella for to help your grandpa.'

The girl now glanced at Joseph, then turned back to Ron Yarrow, who laughed and mouthed the words, 'Don't . . . go . . . by . . . looks, Miss Henrietta. He's . . . young . . . an' . . . likely . . . as . . . strong . . . as . . . a . . . bull.'

The girl smiled at him and shook her head, and now she was mouthing words which sounded to Joseph like, 'Fairy tin bule,' causing Ron Yarrow to laugh again and to look towards Joseph and explain, 'She says you're a very thin bull. But come on.'

When Joseph made no move, Ron Yarrow said, 'What's the matter? You're not frightened of her, are you?'

'No. No, of course not.'

'Well then, come on.'

While sitting in the kitchen last night with Mrs Hanratty he thought he had stepped into a dream; now he imagined he must be continuing it, and when he moved it was as if he were being pulled forward, for he kept telling himself he must not go into that house, because he didn't know what his reactions would be if he saw the man.

He was following Ron now past two further greenhouses, both in a very bad state of repair; then through an arched way in a high wall and so into a big yard, lined on one side with horse boxes, a barn and other buildings. And they were halfway across it when Ron Yarrow stopped and, turning to Joseph, looked him up and down, saying, 'You're well put on, lad, an' you don't speak the local twang. You must be hard set for a job to take this on;' then he let out a slow breath, and concluded, 'Well, you're here, so you'd better see what you're in for afore you skip out the gate quicker than you came in.' And at this he hurried forward, opened the door, and entered the kitchen; and when Joseph, following him, remained on the threshold, he turned and almost barked at him, 'Well! come in. There's nobody goin' to bite you.'

Rose Jackson, who was now well into her sixties, was sitting on a high stool before the kitchen table chopping vegetables: her plump hand holding a sharp-pointed knife that was dicing a carrot with machine precision. But she stopped in the process and looked at Ron Yarrow as he, pointing to Joseph, said, 'This is another one of 'em, cook. He's not half as old as the last one, and not half as big either, but beggars can't be choosers.'

He now turned to address the other occupant of the kitchen, Katie Swift. The years were piled on her, too, and he said, 'You'd better go and get Mr Bright, that's if he's finished with the first clean-up. Is Minnie up there with him?'

'Yes; he's got to have help of some sort.' She was looking at Joseph as she spoke. 'And Minnie would welcome the devil if he'd offer to give a hand.'

As Joseph watched Katie Swift walk up the kitchen he was overcome by a feeling of panic and he turned to the man and said hurriedly, 'I don't think . . . you see . . . well, it should happen that . . .'

Rose Jackson slid her plump body off the stool, looked at him and said quietly, 'Give it a try, lad. They're in hard straights up there. It's fifteen shillings a week and your grub. That's a good wage, I can tell you, an' more than can be afforded. But they're desperate for help. He's not a bad fellow when you get to know him. A bit fractious at times, does a bit of yellin', but his bark's worse then his bite, and he's at the end of his days. It's just to relieve Mr Bright an' keep the master clean an' turn him, an' things like that.'

Joseph stared at her. The woman was talking about the man who was really his grandfather and she was pleading with him, and when he wet his lips and swallowed deeply, she said, 'Have a cup of tea an' take a seat.' She pointed to a settle, which stood in a similar position to the one in Mrs Hanratty's kitchen but was twice as long, and as if he were a child he obeyed her.

Sitting on the settle, he now watched her brew the tea, all the while talking to the man who had brought him in, and as he listened to them it was only their voices that registered, not what they were saying, because his mind was racing ahead. If he were to stay here . . . If *he were*, then what would he say to Mr Douglas and the missis? And there was Amy. They would be home on Monday or Tuesday. If he were to tell them he was staying here he would have to tell them the reason why, that he now knew who he was. No, he couldn't do that: that would cause more trouble and he had promised his mother not to divulge what she had told him. He couldn't tell them. But what he must do is go back and collect some clothes and leave a letter. But what would he say? Where could he say he had gone? Not to university, because when he didn't turn up there, somebody would likely enquire why. No; he would tell them that he felt he had to get away for a time; and then he would write to the university and say . . . what would he say to them? He was ill and would come up later? Because if the man upstairs was so old and

377

near his end, there would be no need for him to stay, would there? And he could leave then and resume his life.

Don't talk so damned silly, man! . . . He almost spoke the words aloud. Resume what life? His life would never be the same again. *He* would never be the same again. This part of the dream he had stepped into was stark reality. Whatever happened now would change his life forever. He knew that, and even before he met the servant called Bright or the old man, his grandfather, who was near death, he knew he would stay here.

'Drink it up while it's hot.'

He had just taken a sip of the tea when he saw the gardener man go quickly down the room to meet an elderly man who had just come in the far door, and after a low and hurried conversation they came towards him, where he was now standing awaiting them.

James Bright stared at the tall young man who was staring back at him, and he did not speak immediately, for he was racking his brains as to where he had seen him before or someone like him. Over the years he had had a lot of young men through his hands and this one reminded him of someone he had known in the past. So it was a moment before he spoke, when he asked Joseph, 'What is your name?'

'Joseph Carter.'

'Are you from these parts?'

'Yon side of Gateshead.' Well, that was true, Shields was yon side of Gateshead, although quite some way.

'Have you been in this kind of work before?'

'I . . . I don't know what kind of work is expected of me.'

'You would see the advert?'

It was Ron who now put in in a low voice, 'He just heard of the post from Mrs Hanratty. He's a friend of hers.'

378

'Oh. Oh.' Bright nodded, then added, 'Well, you had better come along and see what your duties are. By the way, what kind of work have you been doing?'

Joseph swallowed deeply, then said, 'Sort of clerical, but I wanted a change.'

'Clerical?' Bright's heavy eyebrows moved upwards; then he sighed before saying, 'Well, come along.'

When Joseph entered the hall his steps slowed for a moment as he gazed about him. Two shafts of sunlight from the tall windows, one each side of a huge oak door, streamed across a carpet and partly up the panelled walls, seeming to show up and emphasise the shabbiness of the rest of this large room. He now slowly climbed the stairs, slowly because he was keeping in time with Bright's step.

On the landing Joseph again paused as his eyes took in the gallery and the two broad corridors going off. It was as they entered the left one that a door halfway along opened and a woman came out. Her step, too, was slow. She was wearing what looked like a loose dressing-gown. Her hair looked slightly tousled, and she stopped at their approach and drew the collar of her garment closer round her neck. Then she was looking at the tall young man as Bright explained his presence. But she didn't speak to him, nor did Joseph utter a word.

So this was the cousin Victoria. She was still, in a way, beautiful, but it was a dim, faded beauty, like the reflection of her daughter's through a mist.

As they walked on Bright said under his breath, 'That is the mistress. She hasn't been well of late . . . fine lady.' Then he pushed open a door and entered a room. But Joseph did not immediately follow him: he not only paused, he came to a standstill on the threshold. He was looking into a large room and right opposite to him was a huge four-poster bed. There were no drapes on it except at the head and these were of some heavy faded material, and in the bed was a figure, the body half-propped up against a pile of pillows. The rest of the room seemed cluttered with furniture, large and small. But what hit him forcibly after the sight of the old man was the odour that emanated from the room. It was hot and thick with a body smell.

A middle-aged woman was standing at the far side of the bed, and when a voice from the bed, said, 'Who's that, Minnie?' she peered at the newcomer and said, ''Tis a visitor, master.'

There came a yell: 'Visitor? I want no bloody visitors . . . Bright!'

'Yes, sir?' Bright moved to the bed now. 'It's not that kind of visitor, sir; it's . . . it's a young man who has come to assist me.'

'Assist you . . . again? You never keep the blasted fellows, so why do you pick 'em? Dolts, all of them. Big-fisted, muddle-headed dolts. Bloody idiots.'

Joseph had now walked further into the room where he could see, over the foot of the bed, the white straggly-haired, bony and flushed face of this old man. He watched the tongue flick in and out of the wet lips; then the mouth opened and in an extraordinary loud voice that belied his age, the man said, 'Don't stand there like a stook, man! Come up here where I can see you. I want to know who's going to handle me, not lay me out before me time. Donkeys could do better than some of 'em. I'm telling you, Bright.' He had turned again to Bright, who now beckoned Joseph to come towards him; and when Joseph complied he stood aside to allow him to get near enough to his patient for scrutiny.

But when Joseph stood by the head of the bed and looked down into the rheumy blue eyes, he found them staring hard back at him, and in silence, until Bright said, 'This is a young man . . .'

'I'm not bloody-well blind. No matter what else is wrong I've still got me sight and me mind, I keep telling you, Bright . . . Who is this?'

It was now that Joseph spoke for the first time. 'My name is Joseph Carter, sir,' he said.

The scrutiny continued, and then the old man said, 'You're nothing but a lad.'

'I'm . . . I'm in my twentieth year, sir.' That sounded older than nineteen and a half.

'Where . . . where do you hail from?'

'Beyond Gateshead, sir.'

There was more scrutiny; then, 'Don't talk local.' Turning to Bright now, the old man demanded of him, 'Hoist me up!'

Bright pushed Joseph aside, then nodded to Minnie Carstairs, and at this the woman ran round to the other side of the bed again and, almost lying across half of it, she put her hands under her master's armpits while Bright, with his arm around the old man's waist, gave an unseen signal and then both of them lifted the recumbent form together, causing a long groan to come from the old man and his head to fall back onto the pillows for a moment as he drew in a long breath. Then, taking a white handkerchief that was tucked into the side of his pillow, he slowly wiped his eyes, before once again peering at Joseph. He did not speak to him but turned to Bright, saying, 'Get rid of them, I want a word with you.' And at this, Bright motioned to the maid to take Joseph out, while saying, 'Wait downstairs for me.' But before they reached the door it was unceremoniously thrust open and the girl appeared, and as she ran towards the figure in the bed she cast a smiling glance at Joseph; then almost in a light leap, she was sitting on the bed leaning over the old man, holding his hand and talking in her own fashion.

After a moment, the old man answered her, saying,

'Yes, yes, all right, my dear. We'll see, we'll see. Go along now and ... and tell your mama, I ... I want to see her ... Understand?'

She made one deep obeisance with her head; then, scrambling from the bed, she ran from the room, past the maid and Joseph, and again unceremoniously at a run into her mother's room, while Joseph, not a little amazed at finding himself in this weird position, followed Minnie downstairs.

Back in the bedroom the old man, looking at Bright, said, 'Give me a drop, Bright.'

'But sir, the doctor said, nothing before ...'

'Bright, does it really matter what he says? Between you and me, I ask you, does it matter?' And to this Bright answered, 'No, sir. After all, no.'

'Then get me a drop.'

As he had done countless times before, Bright went out of the room and into the adjoining dressing-room to pour out for his master a slightly adulterated whisky. And awaiting his return William Filmore closed his eyes and looked back into the past.

'Drink it slowly, sir.'

And as if doing what he was told the old man sipped at the whisky. Then he asked Bright a question.

'Does that fellow remind you of anybody, Bright?'

'I ... I thought he did, sir. I was looking back over the staff who I have had through my hands over the years, but their faces eluded me. Yet, in some strange way he seemed familiar, and he is well spoken. I don't know why he should want a position such as this ... pardon my saying so, sir.'

'Yes, I pardon your saying so, Bright. He says his name's Carter. Does that ring a bell?'

'Not in the least, sir.'

'And he's from Gateshead somewhere.'

'Yes, that's what he says, sir.'

'Why has he taken up this line?'

'He . . . he says he was tired of clerking, sir.'

'Clerking? Well –' The white head moved backwards and forwards on the pillow; then on a sigh he said, 'We'll see. We'll see.'

As Bright arranged the already tidy eiderdown over his master's limbs, William Filmore now asked quietly, 'Where's the other one?'

Such was the relationship between these two men now that the master of the house could refer to his son as 'the other one'. And Bright answered, 'He left for town early this morning, sir, as he's done for a number of mornings. I think he may have another position.'

'For how long this time?'

'Well, that is to be seen, sir.'

'Have you seen the mistress this morning?'

'Yes. She is up and about, sir.'

'I'm worried, Bright. She's not good at all, is she?'

'She's going through a difficult time, sir.'

'Difficult time? You file words down, Bright, until they lose their meaning. Difficult time? She's a sick woman. She should be in bed with proper nursing. If I feel guilty about anything in my life it's about her. Do you know that, Bright? Do you know that?'

'Yes. Yes, I'm well aware of that, sir.'

'Oh, go on with you, get out; you're well aware of too damned much. Anyway, see that that young fellow stays on. He'll be something different to look at. Do you know what Miss Henrietta said?'

'No, sir.'

'She said, he was nice . . . and young. Dear God! 'Tis awful that child never sees anyone of her own age. This house is full of the dying and decrepit, or aging individuals. And you're one of 'em, Bright. Go on, get out.'

James Bright went out, shaking his head and smiling. His master had had a good night: he was talking volubly again without every word being a curse or a reprimand. Down in the kitchen once more, he said to Joseph, 'The wage is fifteen shillings a week and your meals; and you could sleep above the stables if you so wish. The accommodation is basic, a bed and the necessary . . .'

'I'll lodge at Mrs Hanratty's.'

'Oh yes, yes. That would certainly be more comfortable. And it's merely a good walk away. When can you begin your duties?'

The answer was prompt, 'Say, tomorrow?'

'Very well. Your hours will be from 7.30 in the morning till 6.00 in the evening.'

The movement of the butler's head now indicated to Joseph that he was dismissed: and so, looking in turn from the maid to the cook, he said, 'Goodbye, and . . . and thanks for the tea.'

'You didn't drink it, lad.'

He smiled apologetically at the cook and went out, there to meet Ron Yarrow in the yard, and Ron said, 'Well, you goin' to give it a try?'

'Yes. Yes, I am. I'll start tomorrow.'

'Good. Good.'

As he now made his way towards the arch through which he had entered the yard Ron stopped him with, 'If you're goin' back to Mrs Hanratty's, take the driveway. That'll knock a bit off the journey.' And he pointed to the other end of the yard, adding, 'Cross over the front, the drive goes off it.'

'Thanks. Thanks.' He turned about and went in the direction Ron had indicated.

He was passing the front of the house. It looked huge, gaunt, uninhabited. It could have been empty for years.

At the end of the drive he stood pondering. Should he

make straight for home, pack up some things and leave a letter, then come back? Or should he ask Mrs Hanratty if she would have him as a lodger? Although he felt sure she would jump at the possibility, he also felt that he should ask her first, and so he made his way back, at a run now, towards the cottage.

Bertha was attending her livestock family by cleaning out her henhouse, and when he called to her from the back gate, she turned and stood stiffly, watching him for a moment before she threw down the rake and hurried towards him.

Smiling broadly at her, he said, 'Do you want a lodger?'

'A lodger? You?'

'Yes, me.'

'What's happened to bring this about? You've had an afterthought or something? I thought you would have reached your home by now.'

'I haven't been very far. I'm going to take the job on.'

Her face puckered up until all her features seemed to converge together and she almost spluttered, 'Down there! at The Grove? You? How . . . how's this come about? You'll never last there. Dear! Oh, goodness gracious me! Look, come in and have . . .'

'No. No, Mrs Hanratty. I . . . I must hurry back home now. I want to pack up some things. But . . . but I'll tell you how it came about when I get back.'

'Oh, lad, lad.' She followed him round the side of the cottage and onto the road. Her face beaming, she said, 'What a couple of days this has been. Talk about things bein' washed up by the rain. Look' – her head was bobbing now – 'I'll get the other room ready for you, air the mattress an' that, it's twice as big as the one you were in last night.'

She pointed now to the side of the house. 'It's that one, the one my Willie built on.'

'That'll be nice. Thank you.' He was backing away from her and when she brought her elbow into her waist and wagged her fingers at him, he laughed and waved back in return . . .

5

'Where do you think he's gone?'

'I haven't the faintest idea, but it's certainly not Cambridge, by what he says in his letter. I'd better write to his college, although he says he's informed them. But he's certainly got something definite in mind because as he says here' — he now tapped the letter — 'he doesn't know exactly how long he'll be away. It may be a matter of weeks. Dear! Dear!'

Douglas flopped down onto a chair and, looking at Bridget, who was standing by a side table, her hand beating out a quick tattoo on its edge, he said, 'I feel more and more that I should have had a talk with him immediately after Lily died. For him to know the truth then could no longer have hurt her.'

'Don't blame yourself for that, dear. Anyway, I don't agree with you on that point. Ask yourself, what would have been the result? Discovering that you were his uncle and your brother was his father, would likely have had a very adverse effect. He would have considered he had been kept in the dark all these years and that our interest and kindness to him had merely been because of the relationship, illegal even as it is.'

'Oh, it isn't illegal, dear. He was illegitimate but it isn't illegal.'

'I see it as illegal because he couldn't be recognised and he would have been hurt by the stigma. As Joe's son he would have at least felt he had a father, no matter how lowly. Just imagine if he had made his way to that house and confronted Lionel. The outcome of that is unthinkable.'

'Well, dear, does that mean he must never know?'

'Oh, dear me!' Bridget now went and sat on the couch and, holding her hands out to the blaze of the fire, she murmured, 'I still have it on my mind that I am the instigator of all this trouble.'

He now rose and went and sat beside her and, putting his arm round her shoulder, he laughed gently as he said, 'Are you meaning to say you had something to do with his birth?'

'Oh, Douglas.' She nudged him with her elbow and he went on, 'The boy was born before Victoria married. The only thing, as I see it, that you've got to regret, is your generosity in the first place. And it has gone on. How much did you send Bright last time?'

She jerked her head, saying, 'None of your business.'

The door opened and they both turned to look at Amy as she came up the room towards them, and Bridget, glancing at the letter in her hand, said, 'What did he say to you, dear?'

For answer, Amy held out the letter, saying, 'There! read it. It's a really passionate epistle.'

Bridget took the letter from her daughter, unfolded the sheet, then read:

Dear Amy,
   I'm having to be away for a short time, but I'll be back. What happens then remains to be seen.
                    Joseph.

As Bridget handed the letter back to her daughter, the young girl looked at her father, saying, 'Have you any idea at all where he has gone, Daddy?'

'None whatever, my dear. You know as much about

where he's likely to be as I do. In fact, as you know much more about him than I do, I would leave you to guess.'

'He could have gone to his new-found step-uncle that he met the day Lily was buried.'

At this both Bridget and Douglas exchanged glances; then it was Bridget who said, 'I shouldn't think that he would visit them with the idea of staying; and from the letter he seems to propose that he will be away for some time. Anyway, I think it is very thoughtless of him to go off like this. But then he's always been a law unto himself, strong-headed and . . .'

'You have never liked him. Why don't you say it?'

'Amy, please, don't say such a thing. I'm very, very fond of Joseph and always have been. I've had his welfare at heart since he was a child. Yes, before you came on the scene.'

'Now, now, dear, don't get upset.'

Amy watched her father put his arms around her mother's shoulders and the tenderness of the action made her want to cry out as if from some loss within herself, and she checked the embrace by crying, 'I'll find him. Yes, I will! And I'll marry him. You won't like that, will you, Mammy? But I will.'

Bridget rose from the couch and walked slowly towards her daughter and, standing before her, she said, 'What has come over you, Amy? All I want in life now is your happiness and . . .'

'And that's what I want, too, Mammy, and I'll only get it by spending the rest of my life with Joseph. I've . . . I've known from the beginning. I'm no child in spite of the fact that you've tried to keep me one. I love Joseph and I know he loves me. I do, I do.'

Bridget now turned and looked at Douglas, who was standing just a few feet away from her and, her voice low, she said, 'I think this is the time for explaining. What do you say?'

He looked steadily at her for a moment before he answered, 'Yes. Yes, I think you're right,' he said. Then, putting his hand out to Amy, he said, 'Come, my dear. We have something to tell you.' And now he led her back to the couch, and they sat, one on each side of her, and Douglas, nodding across at Bridget, said, 'I'll leave the beginning to you. . . .'

It was ten minutes later: Douglas had taken up the thread of the story, and he was ending, 'So you see, you are cousins. He is my nephew, the son of my brother, my only brother' – and his voice now took on a bitter note – 'who's anything but an honourable man.' And when he added, 'There are things that even your mother doesn't know about him,' Bridget's eyes widened and her mouth opened, but she didn't speak.

Nodding now towards her, Douglas said, 'Yes, there are things you don't know about him, dear; nothing to his credit, more's the pity.' Then turning his attention back to his daughter, he finally ended, 'I have always been reluctant to reveal to Joseph his real beginnings because he will have nothing to be proud of in that quarter, and in another I'm sure he would be shocked to know that his step-father was hanged for murder, a murder that both your mother and I firmly believe he never committed.' He shook his head now. 'Oh, yes, we firmly believe he was hanged for another man's crime. So, now do you understand our attitude?'

Amy was lying back on the couch, her head turning from her father to her mother, and when she bit down on her lower lip and her whole face trembled they both embraced her, and through her tears she now muttered, 'I'm sorry. I'm sorry. I've been stupid.' And to this Bridget answered, 'No dear; whatever your reactions, they were because you felt we were withholding something, whether you were conscious of it or not.'

It was some minutes later when Amy, standing near the table, picked up the envelope that her letter had been in and, pointing to it excitedly, said, 'Look, it's got a Newcastle postmark.'

'So it has,' said Douglas. Then he smiled at her, saying, 'Well, that shows he can't be far away. All we can do now is wait.'

She again turned and looked from one to the other and asked of them both, 'You . . . you think he'll come back on his own?'

Her father nodded at her while Bridget said, 'Yes, I'm sure he will, dear. But just give him a few days, a week, or two at the most. You'll see. You'll see.'

6

It could not possibly be just eight days since he had come into this house; it could have been eight weeks, eight months, eight years, for the Lodge, Meadow House, and that other life seemed to be receding further and further away from him each day.

When he had said to Mr Bright that he could start work on the morrow, he hadn't realised that that day was a Sunday. But he had turned up at half-past seven on that morning, and from the moment he entered the house and left it at fifteen minutes past six to return to the welcoming warmth of Mrs Hanratty, he seemed never to stop running from one end of the house to the other. His route was mostly the same, from the old man's bedroom to the kitchen, back and forth, back and forth, carrying slops down, bringing clean water up, sometimes hot, a large brass-lidded can in each hand: then there were the trays, back and forth, back and forth; and that he had the blessings of the two leg-weary maids did nothing to soothe his feelings or his aching limbs.

But the heaviest part of his duties was the lifting of the almost inert body, the heaving of him up the bed, for the old man's legs were helpless now, and turning him on his side to help clean him up . . . Oh, he had found that a nauseating, disgusting job. And what he felt he would never get used to was the body odour and the smell that pervaded the room. No matter how much lavender water was sprinkled around it or dried mint and other herbs burnt on a shovel and wafted around the room, there still remained that smell. It was so thick at times it seemed to coat the roof of his mouth, and he found he had to hurry through the dressing-room and into the toiletry and there rinse out his mouth with clean water.

There was another thing, the toiletry, so-called, where the jugs of clean water were outmatched by the buckets of effluent. How many times during these first days had he been about to walk out? Perhaps it was only Katie's and Minnie's concern for their old master that made him change his mind. Once they had come upon him standing outside the kitchen door gulping at the fresh air. It had been following his handing over the pails of slops to Ron Yarrow to take to the cesspool. 'He's old. He can't hold it. God help him!' Minnie had said. 'It's awful to be old.'

Those words had set him thinking and determining, with the arrogance of youth, that he would never reach that stage; he would finish it before he would become so dependent on others. He had never thought of the body as disgusting until he had looked on the old man's legs, one so swollen that it was no longer distinguishable as a leg or a foot, while in comparison the other was skin and bone and lifeless.

Mrs Hanratty, too, had said, 'It's a thing you get used to, lad. Except that, for a time after they are gone, the stink stays with you and you can even taste it in your food. Oh, I know, I know. I've had some.'

She was such a comfort, was Mrs Hanratty; yet at times it was questionable, as when she made such statements.

On the third day, the sun was shining, and the windows were open a little. The old man seemed to like the sun for he didn't bawl or shout so much when the sun was shining. And for the first time he spoke quietly to Joseph: 'Let me have a look at you. Stand away from the bed,' he said.

Joseph stood away from the bed, and the old man leaned on his elbow, half turned, as much as he found possible, on to his side and scrutinised him; then he lay back, shook his head and said, 'Where are you from?' And he told him again, 'Beyond Gateshead.'

'Have you always lived there?'

'Yes.'

And so the questions went on until the old man, still looking at him in a quizzical kind of way, said, 'Did your father work here at one time?'

Joseph startled not only the old man but also Bright, who was at the other end of the room arranging the medicine bottles on a side table, when he replied in no small voice, 'No, he didn't work here, and as far as I know, not at any place else.' And it wasn't an afterthought that made him add, 'Sir,' but the look on Bright's face.

Then this poorly-paid major-domo almost thrust him into the dressing-room and there, in a hoarse whisper, he said, 'Don't let me hear you speak to the master in that tone again, or, as badly as I need your assistance, I will show you the door.'

On his fifth day here he was again being hauled over the coals by Bright. He was in the corridor on his way to the far end and the old man's room, out of which Bright had just appeared, when the mistress emerged from her bedroom. On seeing him, she stopped and stared at him. She stared at him so hard that he became embarrassed, and when she didn't speak he felt forced to say something, and what he said was, 'How do you do, ma'am?'

And to this, after a moment's hesitation, she answered, 'I am quite well, thank you;' then turned and, passing Bright, she went towards her father-in-law's room.

Bright almost hauled him back into the dressing-room, and there he closed the communicating door to the bedroom and in a low growl said, 'Don't you know anything? You should never address your betters in that way? . . . How do you do? That is for them to say.' Then he had taken a step back from him and with narrowed eyes he had looked him up and down before adding, 'I'm worried about you. I don't think you are what you appear to be. Have you been up to some mischief? I mean, have you taken this position to hide away from . . . from the police or . . . ?'

'No, I have not. And why shouldn't I say, how do you do? to the mistress of the house? Being polite isn't an offence, yet it seems to be in this establishment.'

'Now, young man' – the finger was wagging at him – 'that, too, is the wrong attitude to take with me or any of the staff; you're just starting in this business, and if you want to go on, you must adjust to our ways.'

'I may not want to go on. In fact I don't want to go on . . . I've no wish to . . .' His voice trailed away, and Bright, who stared at him in silence, seemingly nonplussed, said more quietly, 'Well, that, to me, is a pity.'

A bellow from the next room made Bright turn swiftly to open the door and to go into the bedroom, leaving Joseph standing with his teeth grinding audibly. Then he turned to listen when he heard the old man's voice saying, 'Don't you worry, my dear; just keep him out of her way. Can't you keep her in her room today?'

The answer came, 'Yes; I could for one day but not for any length of time. She would just get out of the window and climb down. She has done it before.'

'What makes you think he is going to stay home now?'

'He's been here two days and he has taken to riding again in the morning.'

'Has he left you your allowance?'

There was no immediate response: when it came, the voice was very low, saying, 'He left some, not what I am due, and no explanation. But then I didn't expect any.'

'Can you manage?'

'Just, as regard the eatables. But the fare may have to be plainer than usual.'

'Damn and blast him! . . . Bright! hand me my purse.'

It astounded Joseph to realise that Bright was still in the room and while an intimate conversation was going on. The next he heard was the mistress's voice, saying, 'But where did you get this from?'

'Never you mind, my dear. Oh, well, I'm a very devious fellow; I kept a bit back from the last sale of land.'

'But that was last year.'

'Yes, I know it was last year, but, my dear, money doesn't melt, does it? Now, be a good woman and go and rest on your bed and I'll tell you what to do with Etta. When she's not out in the garden send her in here. We'll see to her, or she'll see to us, won't she, Bright?'

'Yes, indeed, sir, she will, especially when you're playing cribbage with her.'

There was another pause before the mistress's voice said, 'You are very kind, Father-in-law, and you, too, Bright. Thank you.'

The rustle of the housegown came to him as she passed the dressing-room door; then he knew she had left the room when he heard the old man say, 'When did that lot come?'

'Last week, sir.'

'Odd, you know, Bright: I ask for my purse thinking there was only half a sovereign in it. Did I show any surprise?'

'No, sir, none at all.'

'Odd woman that, can't fathom her. How much did she send you last time?'

'Twenty pounds, sir.'

'Twenty pounds? My! My! It seems like a fortune now, Bright, and at one time I would bet it on a fly crawling up the window . . . Oh, dear. Damn and blast it! I think I need attention again, Bright.'

It was at this Bright shouted, 'Carter!' And as Joseph entered the room the old man barked at him, 'Do you play cribbage?'

'No, sir.'

'What do you play?'

'Whist and mahjong.'

'Mahjong? That's a Chinese game. Where did you learn that?'

'From a friend, sir.'

'Was he Chinese?'

'No, sir.'

During this interchange Bright had turned the bed-clothes back and Joseph, as he had been instructed to do, put his hands on the old man's shoulder and gently brought him onto his side, and Bright did what was necessary in the way of cleaning the wasted limbs. Then, as always, Bright called, 'Hold steady!' and whipped up another draw sheet from a pile standing on a low chest of drawers. It was already rolled up, and he pushed it against his master's legs and hips.

During this part of the proceedings, the old man's face was within a couple of feet of Joseph's, and always at this point the pale blue eyes seemed to pierce him from the sunken sockets, and it was as much as Joseph could do to keep his gaze steady and not to turn his head away, not only from the wrinkled and deep-jowled face, but in what he knew to be a hopeless effort to evade the stench that age and decrepitude were emitting from the body, and the thought saddened him; while at the same time he was amazed that the old man's mind could still remain keen and that therefore he must be aware of the indignity to which he was being subjected.

Now Bright had his hands on his master's shoulders

drawing him towards him, and Joseph, as he had been instructed, eased the remainder of the rolled sheet under the body and over the waterproofed sheeting that covered the mattress.

This part completed, Bright on one side and Joseph on the other hoisted the old man up onto his pillows the while he protested in no small voice: 'That's it! bang my head against the wall.'

Smiling wryly, Bright said, 'As I've told you countless times, sir, your head is more than a foot away from the bed head, let alone the wall . . . Now are you comfortable?'

'Yes, Bright, yes. Thank you.'

The numerous times the old man changed his tone during the day had ceased to surprise Joseph. One minute he could be cursing Bright up to the skies, the next speaking to him in a tone that suggested he was a friend. Altogether, it was an odd situation.

He looked at the figure in the bed. The eyes were closed now, the breathing was coming in short gasps, but they were still deep enough to billow the bedclothes.

As if he knew he was being stared at, the eyelids sprang back, and now he was staring at Joseph, saying, 'Carter, you go and find Miss Henrietta. Tell her I want to play a game of cards.'

At this, Bright put in, 'It will tire you, sir, so early in the day. She'll be all right. The weather is fine and she'll be working away in the garden.'

'She doesn't always work away in the garden, Bright. She wanders around. She can't spend her entire life with a shovel and fork in her hand, and she knows that. You found her in the gallery, didn't you, the other day, looking . . . to use her own words, gazing at the portraits? Now, what's going to happen if they should meet up, eh? You know what took place last time and what he threatened. And after all, no matter what we say' – he stopped now, his breath catching in his throat with agitation – 'he's . . . he's got first charge on her. And old Leadman is on his side. It takes two doctors to certify, but Leadman, the sozzled old swine, could get one of his cronies to side with him.'

'He wouldn't do that, sir. He couldn't.'

'Couldn't he, Bright? You weren't in this room the day she let him have it right in his big fat belly. He's never forgiven her. And I'm sure he would have done something before now if it wasn't for that young Doctor Curry, because it is he who has confirmed what I've said all along: that child, or that young woman, as she is now, is no more mad than I am. It is as he said, she was deaf all right, but the other jangling bit was what was left over from the scarlet fever when she was a child. What did he call it again?'

'Chorea, sir, I think.'

'Chorea, yes, that's it, chorea. Never heard of it before, but that's what causes the jangling to her nerves. But it didn't affect her mind, that I know. So, go on, young fellow, you fetch her in.'

Joseph went swiftly from the room, down the broad corridor, across the gallery and down the stairs. And it was as he went out of the front door that he got his first glimpse of the man who was the reason for his being in this house at all, the man he wanted to see. It was only a side profile of him, yet he recognised him. He was mounted on a horse and riding it across the drive towards the stable yard, and he was looking towards his daughter.

Joseph could see her standing on the low balcony to the left of him; her body looked stretched, her head was straining upwards; and then he witnessed something that sent a chill down his spine: the man on the horse, a whip in his hand, now brought it down in a slashing movement, not on the horse but to the side of it as if he were striking out viciously at something, or someone, and at this the girl's body became distorted. The arms waved widely in the air, the head wagged, she swayed from the waist and her feet left the ground as if she were going into a dance. And what was more she was emitting sounds like someone yelling in a foreign language.

The horse had disappeared round the corner and into the yard by the time Joseph reached her. Catching hold of her arms, he gripped them tightly; and he began to mouth words, his head bobbing all the time, 'It's . . . it's all . . . right. Don't worry . . . . your grandfather . . . wishes . . . to . . . see . . . you.'

'Ip . . . ip.'

'What?'

The jangling was easing off. He felt her body becoming limp under his hands. But she was repeating that word, 'Ip . . . ip.'

'What? Come . . . along, your grandfather wants . . . to see . . . you.'

'Ate . . . ad.'

He couldn't make out what she meant but he again said, 'Come along.' And with this he kept one hand on her arm and led her towards the front door, while she continued every few steps to turn and look back in the direction her father had disappeared . . .

Once in the bedroom, Joseph was amazed at the volubility of the sounds she was making; and when she demonstrated with her hand up and down it was the same action as her father had used with the whip in his hand.

The old man now pulled her gently down on to the side of the bed, saying, 'No, my dear, never. He'd never dare use that whip on you.'

She began to talk rapidly again, and definitely her grandfather could understand what she was saying, because now he replied, 'All right, all right, you hate him. I know, I know you do, but enough, enough.' He then turned to Joseph and asked him: 'What did he actually do with the whip?'

'Just what she said, sir. He gave the impression he was hitting out at someone.'

William nodded slowly now, and lifting his head from the pillow he looked at Bright and muttered, 'If that starts again, we're in for trouble, and it can't go on, can it, Bright?'

It was some little time before Bright said, 'No, sir, not indefinitely.'

'As you say, not indefinitely.' And William Filmore turned to his granddaughter and said brightly, 'We will play cribbage.'

But the young girl shook her head.

'Yes, we shall. I . . . I want to be entertained, and Carter there' – he thumbed towards Joseph – 'he can't play cribbage. Says he plays whist. That's an idea . . . Have you ever played whist, Bright?'

'No, sir; I haven't played whist.'

'Well, you're never too old to learn. Bring a table round here and . . .'

'Do you think it wise, sir?'

'Bright –' And there followed a silence before the old man said, 'We've been together for a long time, but can you tell me when I've done anything that you would consider wise?' and his tone rising quite sharply, and as if he would brook no further denial, he said, 'Bring a table round;' then looked at his granddaughter and explained: 'We . . . play . . . whist. A new . . . card . . . game. Carter, here' – again he thumbed towards Joseph – 'he's . . . he's . . . going . . . to show us, at least you and Bright here. . . .'

The dream stage was back again, for here he was sitting pressed close to the side of a four-poster bed and the man who didn't know he was his grandfather was propped up above him. Next to him sat his half-sister, and the manservant, seated on a high dressing-table stool, was sitting next to her, and as he dealt the cards he had a great desire to laugh. But it wouldn't have been ordinary laughter, it would have been touching on hysteria, for he knew he would have laughed like some women laugh before they burst out crying. The only person missing from this scene, he thought, was Mrs Hanratty. She should be seated on the bed. Although there would be no place for her in the four-handed game, she would have been chatting away, homilies tripping from her tongue.

The dream deepened when, showing the girl sitting next to him how to arrange the cards into suits in her hand, their faces had come close when her eyes had looked into his while she smiled, and there had come into his being a feeling such as he had never experienced before, not even when he first realised he loved Amy, not as a playmate, not as a pal, not as a boy, but as a man, and just as he had thought then he could do nothing about it, so he could do nothing about this either, could he? this feeling of kinship, this feeling that he belonged and that someone belonged to him.

But of a sudden there also entered into him the knowledge from where they had both sprung; and the beauty of that moment, and the tie, faded.

'You look tired, lad.'

'I am tired, Mrs Hanratty.'

'Finding it too hard down there, are you?'

'No, not really, because it isn't hard work, it's just the constant trotting up and down stairs all day.'

'What have you actually got to do?'

So as he worked his way through a large meat pudding, which she termed a potpie, he gave her a rough outline of his duties, and at the end she said, 'Well, it strikes me it needs two of you or three of you on that job. And what you should have had before you had your dinner was a hot wash down. It would help you to get the smell out of your nose. Anyway, I'll see to it the morrow night.'

'Oh, don't trouble yourself, Mrs Hanratty.'

'No trouble at all, lad, no trouble at all. How long d'you think you'll stay there, anyway?'

'I don't know. Perhaps till the old man dies. Bright says the doctor gave him six months to live and that was a year ago. One of his legs is in a dreadful state and he has lost the use of both of them.'

'Is he paralyzed?'

'I don't really know. He can use his upper body quite well.'

'What are the others really like?'

'Oh, the mistress seems very nice, reserved, but very nice.'

'And her daughter?'

'Well, she's a beautiful girl, really beautiful, but afflicted in a way. Yet, she's sensible.'

'Sensible but afflicted.'

'Oh yes, she's perfectly all right in her mind. It's because of her deafness that she cannot speak properly.'

''Tis said roundabout that she fights like a wild beast at times.'

Yes, he could imagine she would, and with reason. Yes, with reason. He now had a vivid mental picture of the man on the horse whipping an imaginary object which the girl knew wasn't imaginary at all. But what he had to acknowledge was that if that girl was his half-sister and the old bedridden man his grandfather, then that man who, given the chance, would have wielded that whip on his daughter, was his father.

7

As Joseph made his way from Mrs Hanratty's along the darkening road in the mornings and returned there along the darkening road at night, the period with the kind old woman and the sound sleep in the feather tick was but a slight interlude away from the house; in fact, once he entered it it was as if he had never left it.

The cook, eyes still blinking from sleep, would push a mug of strong tea towards him, and Katie and Minnie, usually in the same manner, would say, 'By! it's a snifter out there.' At times Ron and Jimmy would be in the kitchen, each with a mug of tea, and they would nod at him as if he had passed through just a moment ago.

Then there was Mr Bright. On this morning he greeted him with, 'The master's had a bad night, with a great deal of pain. I was about to send for the doctor at one stage, but he's easier now. So, be gentle when you're handling him,' only immediately to excuse any insinuation in his words that Joseph had been rough in his handling by adding, 'But I must admit you are less rough than some others have been.'

After donning the white overall which since the first day he had been given to wear, he went into the bedroom and, approaching the bed, he said, 'Good-morning, sir.'

'Oh, Carter . . . what kind . . . of a morning . . . is it?'

'It's very fresh, sir, nippy.'

'Well . . . soon be into November.' There was a long pause now and then he said, 'She enjoyed the game yesterday.'

'I am pleased, sir.'

'She's . . . she's very quick . . . don't you think?'

'Yes, indeed, sir, she's very quick to learn.'

'No . . . no dead hay . . . in the . . . loft, eh?'

Joseph smiled, then said, 'No, sir; no dead hay in the loft.'

And then the routine began: the changing of the bed, the washing of the face and upper body, the shaving of the bristles. Bright did this on his own, gently lifting one piece of jowled flesh after the other, the razor gliding smoothly over it, and this always brought a look of admiration from Joseph.

Then followed breakfast: first, the master's to be brought up and given help to eat it, which business, more than any other in the day, seemed to annoy him. Then Bright would go downstairs for his first meal, and when he returned at nine o'clock, Joseph would be allowed to go for his.

But this morning it was almost half-past nine when he left the room, and immediately his step slowed as he saw, approaching from the other end of the corridor . . . the man.

He was dressed in his riding habit, but without his hat. His figure was tall and straight; there was only a slight bulge to his stomach, and his thick fair hair was a little grizzled above the ears. His face looked red, as if in a continual flush, and the skin below the eyes was puffed. Yet, altogether he presented a very handsome man.

They were almost abreast when Lionel suddenly stopped and, his eyes narrowing, he stared at the young man, first into his face, then over the length of him, before his gaze once more rested on his face. His head then moved slightly back and to the side and the action was one of inquiry, as were the words, 'Who are you?'

What could he say to this? 'I am your son?' Yet he did not want to claim kinship with this man.

'My name is Joseph Carter.'

The tone bore no deference, and this wasn't lost on Lionel Filmore, for now he cried, 'Say sir, when you address me! Do you understand?'

'Yes, I understand.'

'Don't you dare use that tone to me, you insolent pup. Where do you come from?'

'That's my business.' He had backed a step from the man now, and Lionel Filmore's voice was at its loudest as he cried, 'Your business, indeed! Well, it won't be your business much longer in this house.' And now at the top of his voice he yelled, 'Bright! Bright!'

When the bedroom door opened and Bright appeared in the corridor Lionel Filmore marched towards him, commanding, 'Get rid of that man!'

'What, sir?'

'You heard what I said, get rid of him! He's insolent.' He turned and glanced back at the figure who was still standing in the corridor and glaring at him now. Then he cried, 'Why do you take such scum on?' and leaving Bright to do his supposed duty, he marched into his father's bedroom.

Immediately, Bright hurried towards Joseph and gripped his arm and as he shook it he said, 'Take no notice.' Now they were both made to turn and look back towards the open door for the old man was yelling, 'This is still my house! I shall engage whom I like and if there is any dismissing to be done, I will do it.'

'The fellow was insolent, I tell you. His tone, his manner, everything about him; he refused to address me correctly.'

'Oh. Oh, did he? And what would you call correctly, Lionel, eh? Address you correctly? I know how I would address you. I know what I would say if —' There was a gasping for breath here; then the voice, still loud, went on, 'As I said, I know what I would say if I were addressing you correctly. You understand me, man? You understand me? Anyway, why the honour of this visit so early in the morning?'

There was a pause before Lionel Filmore's voice came, saying, 'I want to impress some sense into you.'

'Oh, is that it? Is that it?'

'You know what I mean, sir. You have got to sell the rest of the bottom land. We're in straits.'

There was the sound of a weird throaty laugh in the old man's voice coming to them now: 'In straits?' he was saying sarcastically. 'Dear, dear! we're in straits and you have just found that out, when you've spent your time sitting on your backside, or hopping from one inferior post to another for years, and you tell me we're in straits. Get out! Now I say to you, get out!'

'You've got to come to reason, Father. Look, I hate to put pressure on you but I hold the trump card and you know what it is. I'll have her encased.'

A longer silence ensued; then the old man's voice, lower now, came to them, saying, 'You try that. You make a final bid for that, Lionel, and it'll be the last bid you'll make, I promise you. You should know me: it is I who hold the trump card. And then there is Douglas; he holds a bigger trump even than I do. Have you forgotten that? Do you think that if I can be pushed off tomorrow you'll be safe? You're a fool. There's always Douglas. And the hate that you have for so many of us is nothing compared to the hate he has for you.'

'Huh!' Lionel's voice, too, was low now. 'That doesn't frighten me. You could do nothing now, either of you. Have you ever thought that I could turn the tables on him? Yes; just think of it. He put up such a good act it was too good to be true. Think of that, Father. And I would, too, I'd fight him to my last breath.'

Joseph and Bright were standing close together staring now towards the far door, and when Lionel Filmore stormed out into the corridor, whatever they expected, it wasn't that he would pass them without a glance.

Now Bright was hurrying back into the room with Joseph behind him. The old man was lying back on his pillows, his head deep in them. Bright just glanced at him, then hurried to the table and, pouring out a measure of brown liquid from a bottle into a glass, he carried it to the bed, raised his master's head, put the glass to his lips and tipped it up. Then he stood by the bed waiting. It was some minutes before the old man's breath became easy and he could say to Bright, 'Where . . . where is your mistress?'

'I . . . I think she's still in her room, sir.'

'Well, go to her, explain . . . You heard, didn't you?'

'Yes, sir.'

'Well, tell her . . . keep the child close. Tell her . . . he means business.'

'Yes, sir.'

Bright moved back from the bed, made a pretence of placing the glass on the table and called Joseph to him; then under his breath, he said, 'Stay with him. Sit . . . sit by the bed. I won't be a minute or so.'

Joseph hadn't been seated for more than a minute when the old man, turning his head towards him, said, 'Carter.'

'Yes, sir?'

'Go into the dressing-room . . . bottom drawer under . . . under riding togs . . . long box, fetch it. Quick!'

Joseph went quickly. He pulled open the drawer, pushed aside the riding suits that had probably not been worn for a good many years, and disclosed a long mahogany box. He whipped it up and was back to the bed within seconds;

then was surprised when the old man said, 'Go . . . go into the dressing-room. I'll . . . I'll call you.'

William Filmore made an effort to sit up and his bony fingers fumbled at the two catches on the box, and when he lifted the lid it was to disclose two revolvers. Without hesitation he took one out, looked to ascertain if it was loaded, then released the safety catch. Lifting his arm above his head, he wedged the pistol into a deep fold of the heavy brocade curtain where it was drawn together with a thick, silk rope-like cord that was looped over a brass hook protruding from the wall, its ends weighed down with two heavily braided and lead-weighted tassels.

Now, pressing his head well back into the pillows, he held it there for a moment; then again lifting a hand, he adjusted a fold of the curtain so that it covered the dark object. Now he closed the lid of the case, calling as he did so, 'Carter! Carter!'

When Joseph appeared he thrust the case at him, saying, 'Put it back quick! Don't look at it. Do you hear? Don't look at it. Quick! Quick!' And as Joseph hurried into the dressing-room the voice followed him, saying, 'Then come back here.'

Hurriedly now, Joseph thrust the box into the place from where he had taken it, pushed the drawer closed, then almost at a run he returned to the room and to the old man's side. Immediately the old man grabbed at his hand and quietly and huskily said, 'Don't say a word to Bright. Understand?'

'Yes, sir.'

'Not a word.'

'I understand, sir.'

The old man let go of Joseph's hand, lay back on his pillows and closed his eyes for a moment. Then, his voice still low, he said, 'What do you think was in that case?'

'I have no idea, sir.'

The eyes were open again staring at him. 'Is that the truth?'

'That is the truth, sir.'

'No idea at all?'

'Well' – Joseph was flustered for a moment; then he said what he had at first actually thought, 'I imagined, sir, that it might be a bottle; then I realised the case wasn't quite deep enough.'

'A bottle?' A sound now like a laugh came from the old man's throat before he added, 'If that had been a bottle it would never have survived all this long in that drawer . . . in spite of Bright. Carter.'

'Yes, sir?'

'I . . . I am not sure of you . . . you worry me . . . I don't know why. I . . . I thought perhaps . . . it . . . could be because you are so different from the other types that Bright brought in to help. But . . . but I'm not sure. Sometimes I think you could be a young gentleman; then at others . . . no, no; because there is an earthiness about you that attaches you to people.'

Joseph turned his head now as the door opened and was thankful to see Bright coming back, and when Bright said to him, 'You had better go down and get your breakfast now, Carter,' he immediately left the room. But outside in the corridor he did not hurry towards the gallery and the stairs but, turning about, he went to the top end of the corridor where the closet was.

It was a large room holding three compartments and in each was a toilet pail and also a long shelf attached to the wall on which stood a basin and jug, and underneath it a rack on which were hung two towels. In the room itself there was a large dressing table on which were a number of toiletries, together with a silver-backed hand mirror and a number of brushes. There was a long padded stool in front of the dressing table and on this he sat down and, leaning forward, rested his elbows on his knees and held his head in his hands for a moment as he allowed his mind to roam over what had taken place during the last half hour. He did not at first try to recollect what had passed between the father and son in that room, although he knew it was of great significance, but his mind dwelt on the strange request from the old man. What had been in that case? And he had been so secretive about it. If he had taken anything out of it, where could he hope to hide it? His bed was stripped as many as three times in the day. Perhaps they were papers, a late will or something, though surely that would be at his solicitor's. Oh! He rose to his feet, went out and down the stairs.

Minnie was coming from the drawing-room, carrying a scuttleful of ashes in one hand and a basket holding hearth brushes in the other. She paused and, looking at him, she said, 'This all used to be done, had to be done, afore seven in the mornin's, but what can you expect in this mad house? They went at it again, didn't they?'

When he held out his hand to take a heavy pail from her, she said, 'It's all right, lad, but ta all the same;' then added as she walked on, 'What was it all about?'

He was tactful in saying, 'I was in the corridor at the time with Mr Bright.'

He pushed open the kitchen door for her and as she passed through she nodded at him, saying, 'He'll kill the missis one of these days; she'll have another heart attack, you'll see.' Then lowering her voice as she went up the kitchen, she added, 'That's if Miss Henrietta doesn't do for him afore that. By! lad, you haven't seen anything yet. As cook says, she's like a tiger going for an elephant. Like the picture in one of the old books up in the nursery.' She had reached the table and as she put the bucket down she looked across at cook and said, 'You remember that picture, don't you, cook, about the tiger and the elephant?

And the next picture showed you where the tiger was hanging on to the elephant's throat?'

'Yes' – cook nodded at her – 'but what about it?'

'I was only saying to Carter here, if he ever sees Miss Henrietta in action she'd be like that.'

'God forbid! Oh, aye, God forbid! Because if that happened again it would be the finish of her.' Then turning to Joseph, she added, 'Your breakfast'll be kizzened up to cork, lad. You're late.'

'I'm not very hungry.'

'You're never very hungry. I've never seen anybody at your age eat less.' She had gone to the oven and taken out a covered plate. 'Anyway, the egg'll be as tough as the top of your boots; the bacon, though, an' the bread should be all right. Come on, lad.'

Joseph sat at the corner of the table and ate most of what his mother would have termed a kizzened-up disgrace.

The rest of the day was comparatively quiet. In the afternoon the mistress brought her daughter into the bedroom, and they sat close together near the head of the bed and there was little ensuing talk, and certainly no suggestion of playing whist today; at least Joseph did not hear of it, for Bright had ordered him into the dressing-room and he himself had followed and closed the door.

The dressing-room was as large as an ordinary bedroom. Along two walls were wardrobes reaching almost to the ceiling, and also mahogany tallboys, the drawers of which Joseph soon discovered were amazingly full of different sets of underwear, all neatly arranged. Each tallboy also had a pull-out flap or table on which could be arranged cuff-links, studs, garters and such like accoutrements that were necessary for the dressing of a gentleman.

A long table in the middle of the room was used for

pressing clothes. At one end of this was a smaller table on which stood a spirit stove and, resting on top of it, a flatiron. The window at the far end of the room overlooked the drive, and Bright was standing near it now, saying to Joseph as he pointed to a drawer to the side of him: 'I'll have you clear that. It's full of shirts. A lot of them haven't been used for years; they'll be stained, likely, with age. I'll have to see the mistress about them; they could be given away. Then I think we'll bring some more sheets up from the linen cupboard.' He suddenly turned and glanced at the window; then going close to it, he looked down, saying under his breath, 'Pheasants. He's been enjoying himself.'

Joseph, standing to his side now, could see the rider nearing the yard, and there were a number of birds hanging from his saddle. Bright glanced at him: 'I wonder what it's like to be ostracised,' he said. 'The hunt's got too hot for him. At times I have felt I could be sorry for him, but only at times, and then the time was short. You know, from boy to man he was selfish, and I found him out to be a liar even as a child. The servants were blamed for things they never did. There was only one period during which he seemed to be different, and that was when he was courting the mistress. Then of a sudden that ended. We had an old coachman here, and he always said Mr Lionel was a sprig of his grandfather, who had been a rake.'

Bright sighed, and was about to turn away but swung back to Joseph and, his finger wagging in his admonitory manner, he said, 'Your ears were as open as mine this morning and you'll be asking yourself questions about what you heard. Now I advise you to forget that episode and don't repeat any of it.'

'Why?'

'Why?' Bright drew himself upwards now and actually

bristled as he repeated again, 'Why? Because, young man, it's none of your business.'

'How do you know it isn't?'

Bright's eyes widened. He poked his head forward; then his face screwed up, and now he was peering at Joseph, and the words came from under his breath, saying, 'Who are you, anyway? I've always had my doubts about you. Do you mean mischief? You are not the usual type who does work like this. I've known it from the beginning. Now I ask you, why have you come here? Who are you?'

Joseph stared back at him for a moment. 'I am Joseph Carter,' he said. 'I told you, and I came here because I wanted a job, a different kind of job. Perhaps just to see how the other half lived, as the saying goes.'

Bright stepped back from him, his face still holding a look of puzzled enquiry. But then he drew in a long deep breath and, pointing to the drawer again, said, 'Well, get on with it;' then he went out of the room but not into the bedroom.

Joseph did not immediately get on with it, as bidden, but returned to the window and looked down on to the drive. He could picture the man on the horse, a gun slung across his shoulder, the pheasants hanging from the pommel. Then, as if the thought had probed him with a sharp instrument, he turned and looked towards the closed bedroom door. That case. His gaze swung back to the bottom drawer from where he had taken the case . . . a gun case? A pistol case? A revolver case? He recalled seeing something like it in a magic lantern slide dealing with a pirate story. But a gun. Where could he hide a gun? That was an impossibility. He made a movement towards the drawer; then stopped. What excuse could he give to Bright should he come upon him handling that case? Bright would certainly know all about its presence there. He looked towards the door again. Should he play safe and tell Bright? No, no; he had promised. But what he must do was get his hands underneath that feather tick, because if there was any place for a gun it would be there, and that would be the only place. He couldn't, though, do anything until tomorrow.

But what if he meant to use it tonight?

8

Tomorrow was here, and he put his hand under the feather tick and groped, but could find nothing. He even, supposedly by accident, pulled the bolster away and was rewarded for his stupidity by a reprimand from Bright and a growl from the master, saying, 'Do you both intend to keep me stuck up here like a wooden dolly?'

So another day passed; and more days passed, and he had to come to the conclusion that the old man couldn't have taken anything out of that case. Then there came a Friday, a certain Friday, when he found out differently.

It had been raining for the past twenty-four hours. Part of the drive was flooded; it was impossible to work in the garden, even in the greenhouses; and so Henrietta had, for the past two days, been confined almost entirely to her room, which was situated next to her mother's bedroom.

She stood now looking through the bleared window pane in the direction of the garden, which she couldn't make out through the slanting, wind-driven rain, and after a while, sighing, she turned once more to the easy chair that was set close to a small fireplace, in which a fire dully glowed. She was wearing a shawl over her woollen dress and she pulled it tightly around her neck as she sat down; then she took up a book from a table to the side of her and idly flicked the pages, because she knew the story by heart. It was about a princess who was so sensitive that she could detect a pea while lying on top of a number of mattresses, and it ended that because of her sensitivity she was chosen to be the wife of the prince, and so lived happily ever after . . . What could happy ever after mean when one wasn't happy now?

What was happy? What did happy mean? The feeling that she had when sitting near her mama? or when she was digging in the garden? Oh, yes, yes, when she was digging in the garden, not just picking out seedlings but actually digging. Her hands now left the book and took on the position of holding a spade, and when she dug it to the side of her, she told herself, yes, when she was holding the spade, pushing it into the ground, pushing, pushing hard . . . Yes, hard. Again she made the movements with her hands as if digging.

Her grandfather was nice, but he was very old. When would she be old?

She liked whist. And that young man. Yes, yes; he was kind. She liked his eyes. He was kind, and his hand was gentle. Yes, she liked him.

But she didn't like . . . Her thoughts stopped suddenly and she put her hands to her head and rocked from side to side now. There were noises in there. Why were there always noises in there? When she thought of her father they grew louder, screeching, screaming. She hated him. Her hands came from her head now and she was digging once more to the side of her, thrusting the spade into the imaginary ground.

Abruptly she rose to her feet. She felt ill, not nice, when she thought of him. He was bad. He was going to send her away from her mama. He always said that . . . His mouth was big and wide when he said he would lock her up. When had he first said he would lock her up? From the day he called her by her new name: not Henrietta but idiot.

Idiot!

417

She didn't like that, the way his lips stretched when they said idiot. It was bad. Was she bad?

Oh, she would have to walk. She could not go into her mama, for her mama was resting. She was very tired again. She would go and look at the pictures in the gallery. No. No. Better not, not that way. No, she would go along the corridor to her grandpapa's room and they would play cribbage. But if he was too tired as well, the young man would play with her. They would be quiet and sit in the far corner; they had done that the other day.

She pulled the shawl around her, opened the door, went into the corridor, then turned and closed the door quietly. But she had taken only two steps when, at the far end, coming out of her grandpapa's room, was the man.

Her first instinct was to run back into the room; but then the noise in her head became louder, so loud that it seemed to affect her eyes and for a moment the man seemed to be blotted from her sight. Then she was moving forward; and he, too, was moving.

She did not hug the wall as she sometimes did, but she forced her jangling body to walk up the middle. When he was within touching distance, his arm came out bent from the elbow and, the hand, horizontal and stiff, caught her across the chin; then, with a great cry erupting from the exploding noises in her head, she sprang. Her hands went for his face, her nails clawing so deeply into it that he staggered back, one fist beating her while the other gripped a wrist. But it was as he was dragging her hand from his that her teeth dug deep into his thumb.

The corridor was full of screams from them both, for no matter what he did he could not rid himself of her clawing hands until, at last, other hands came on her, and as Bright pulled her away, Joseph thrust the man back against the wall, only to receive a punch in the chest that sent him reeling and, in his turn, he almost knocked the mistress over. It was her hands that steadied him before she rushed to her daughter to help Bright guide the flailing body along the corridor and into the master's bedroom.

Joseph was left with the man, and for a moment they stood glaring at each other; but seeing that the man was about to make for the bedroom, Joseph ran ahead of him.

Bright and the mistress were trying to control the writhing girl, while the old man had pulled himself up from the pillows and was yelling, 'In the name of God! What's this now!' only to become silent when there appeared in the doorway the bloodstained figure of his son.

Lionel Filmore walked slowly up to his father's bed, while his hand kept wiping away the blood that was running down his face, spilling over his mouth and dripping from his chin. Halfway up the side of the bed he stopped and looked towards Joseph, who was now standing near the head of the bed, and the look said, Get out of my way! and so fearsome did the man appear that Joseph stepped back towards the wardrobe.

Now father and son were gazing at each other, and it was Lionel who spoke first. 'She's sane, you said? Look!' He drew his hand first down one blood-covered cheek then down the other, and again he said, 'Look!' and held up his thumb from where the blood was running down into the cuff of his shirt. 'What do you say to this, Father ... she's sane? If I wanted final proof I've got it. Before, her attacks were mere flea bites to this. Now I'm not going to do a thing to myself, not even to put a handkerchief to my face, but I'm going to ride in and present myself to Doctor Leadman and his disbelieving associate, and, Father, you can do what the hell you like about the other business. But you will not stop me in this, because I'll have her in a strait-jacket if it's the last thing I do.' He looked across the bed now to where his daughter was still writing, but it was on his wife his eyes came to rest as he ended, 'And it's a great pity her mother couldn't accompany her.'

'Don't do this, Lionel.' The old man's voice was quiet. 'I beg of you, don't do this.'

'Father,' — Lionel's voice, too, was low — 'if you could go on your gouty knees to me, it wouldn't make the slightest difference. I've stood all I'm going to stand. I was going to wait until you were gone and then nothing would have stopped me: but I can't wait for that now, not with the evidence I've got.'

The old man nodded at him and his voice came deep and steady as he said, 'That's the answer I would have expected from you. Yes, that's the answer. You are my son but you are rotten to the core. Now Lionel, what I am going to do is something that you did years ago, only in a different way. You murdered a man because he was going to expose you for giving a factory girl a bastard. You cut his throat and left him in a wood and you let his brother hang for your crime. Yes, you can wag your head and look at your wife and Bright and the young fellow to your side, they're all witnesses to what I'm saying, but if they don't believe me they must go to your brother, because he has the evidence. Now, even having been exposed, Lionel, nothing will stop you wreaking your vengeance on the innocent child that you begot, for you can't bear the thought that anything that came out of you could be deformed in any way. No. Well, I'm going to stop you, Lionel. I haven't much longer to go, it might be hours, it might be days. But they can do nothing to me for what I'm going to do now.' And at this the old man's hand, with alacrity that defied his age, swung up to the curtain and pulled from its folds a gun. For a moment there was a deadly silence in the room; then the old man, levelling the gun at his son, said, 'It's been cocked, it's all ready. If I miss with the first I'll get you with the second;' and he fired.

Whether Joseph had been going to dive at the bed to prevent the old man carrying out his intention, or Lionel Filmore's arm had come out and pulled him in front of him, the bullet hit Joseph.

There was a concerted gasping now in the room as the young fellow seemed to spring from the floor then stand rigid for a moment before looking down at the blood oozing through the white overall from somewhere below his shoulder. Then, before anything could be done to help him, the second shot came from the gun, and this time the old man did not miss his aim. The bullet caught Lionel Filmore in the exact spot where his cravat was tied, and he, too, stood for a moment rigid, staring as in amazement at his father, before slowly crumpling onto the floor.

Joseph hadn't fallen but had staggered back and was leaning against the wardrobe door as questions raced through his mind: Why had the old man shot Lionel? Why? He must be in the dream again. It couldn't happen: he didn't want to die. What he wanted was to get away from this house. He had wanted to see the man who was his father. Now he knew and he wished he didn't, because he was a murderer. And why was he lying there? He looked dreadful, dreadful.

What was the matter with him? Why was he floating? This was ridiculous. Yet it wasn't, it was fact: the old man had shot him. He hadn't meant to but that's what he had done. And why was the mistress laughing? She was standing somewhere near and she was laughing, and she was talking loudly about how she had longed to shoot her husband. Well, he had been shot. And he himself had been shot. Why had the old man shot him? He was covered in blood; he felt odd, faint.

He was lying on the floor now. Oh, he hoped he wasn't

lying against him. Yet he was his father. It didn't matter, it didn't matter. He shook his head definitely against the idea of lying against that man, because he was not only cruel to his daughter, he had murdered his stepfather's brother, and his poor stepfather had been hanged for it. *Oh, his mother.* If only his mother had known; perhaps she wouldn't have been so sad.

What were they doing to him? And why was the mistress bending over him? He spoke to her now, saying, 'Tell Mr Douglas and Miss Bridget . . . you know, Mrs Filmore. Mam used to always call her Miss Bridget. Am I going to die? He was my father. They won't take her away, will they? . . . Hello, Ron.'

It was as they lifted him from the floor that he passed into unconsciousness.

9

The doctors had been and gone. Lionel Filmore was pronounced dead. The young man known as Joseph Carter, according to Doctor Curry, had had a lucky escape, for the bullet had lodged itself just below the shoulder blade and he had removed the offending article, under the eyes of the cook, on her kitchen table.

The police, too, had been and had questioned the master of the house in the presence of two doctors. They both confirmed that, although he had admitted to the shooting, it was impossible to move him, and that in any case his time was running out fast.

This had been followed by a consultation around the bed between the old man, Victoria, and Bright, when it was conveyed to the master of the house that the young man who had helped to tend him over the last few weeks was his grandson, the son of the man whom he had shot, and to this he had answered, 'I know.' And when Victoria had said, 'But how, Father-in-law?' he had answered, 'Instinct. From the moment I saw him. He was like Lionel as a boy on the outside, but thanks be to God, I don't think he's got a fragment of him inside.'

It was then that Bright said, 'I think Mr Douglas should be informed.'

'Yes. Yes, of course. Oh, of course.' The old man's head wagged. 'I want to see Douglas. I've been longing to see Douglas. Will you see to it, Bright, please?'

'Yes, sir, right away.'

When Bright had left the room, the old man took hold

of Victoria's hand: 'If I'm sorry for anyone in all this dire business,' he said, 'it is you, my dear, for you've had a dirty deal right from the word go. The only thing I can say against you is that you've been too hard on your cousin, for she's a good woman, you know.'

'Yes, I know, Father-in-law.'

'But you don't know to what extent, my dear.'

'I think I do, Father-in-law. I know that we couldn't have existed all these years without some outward help. I have never questioned how Bright came by such odd amounts of money in times of necessity; but I knew there could be only one source from where he would have received it.'

'Dear! Dear! You are a very strange girl, because you know, that's what you still are underneath that stiff exterior, you are still a girl. And to think, knowing that, you have refused to see her; and she could have been a great comfort to you all these years.'

Victoria now bowed her head, saying, 'Yes, it does seem strange, doesn't it? But you see, I was young and empty-headed when this happened to me and I had the feeling that she had paid the man, who was called my husband, money in order to be free from the responsibility of me.'

Her voice had taken on a sad note now. 'I imagined she had become tired of my prattle, my vanity, my taking everything and giving nothing. Because that's what I did. And then there was the fact that Lionel wouldn't have even dreamed of coming within an arm's length of me if he had known I had no money, whereas I, all the while, was imagining that it was because of my so-called beauty and my charm that he was marrying me, knowing that I hadn't a penny. Can you imagine the shock when I found out otherwise? I grew up overnight. Yes, indeed; from a gullible young girl I became an embittered woman, and remained so for a long time. When I did begin to see things differently it was too late. I then felt I couldn't make a move towards her, yet all the while I wanted to. I longed to. I longed for someone to talk to.'

'And you had only me.'

Her other hand came on top of his now and she said, 'I had to change my opinion of you, too, before I appreciated your worth, and I've always valued you since. And now' – she patted his hand – 'both our times are running out . . .' But at this he pulled his hand away from hers, saying with gasping firmness, 'Don't you . . . talk . . . so. Mine . . . could be . . . hours away, perhaps a few . . . days, but you . . . you are still young.'

'I am forty, Father-in-law. I have lost what looks I ever had and, what is more, my heart is in such a condition that I know it could stop beating within the next minute or so.'

'*Nonsense. Nonsense.* Your heart is in the state it is because of all the worry you've had and the treatment you've had from that man who was my son.' Then he looked away from her and stared over the foot of the bed; and from there he turned his gaze to the window, where a weak wintry sun was doing its best to lighten the room, and he said, 'Imagine killing your son, murdering him and not feeling a trace of regret.' Slowly he turned his head to look at her again and said,'I wonder how God will deal with me? Because I believe in Him, you know. While ignoring Him for years I somehow got to know Him when I had to lie here day after day, month after month, year after year. When I've talked to Him in the middle of the night He would answer me quite frankly. And some of His answers were very hard, condemning. Yet I think He will weigh this business up and see it as something I just had to do, if for nothing else, to save a child from being incarcerated in an asylum.'

She was again holding his hand between hers as she said softly, 'Whatever God does or says about your action, I thank you for it, and from the bottom of my heart. You did what I have longed to do for years, and as I stood over him there' — she turned her head and motioned towards the floor — 'and I laughed, I became terrified that he had won, that from even being dead he had won and that I was going to go mad, because, as you know, I couldn't stop that laughter for a long time. But now I don't think I shall ever laugh again, not really. Smile, yes, but never laugh, because laughter is a terrifying thing when it is humourless.'

He now asked, 'How is the boy? I think of him as a boy, although he must be close on twenty; yet he is a boy, and my grandson. A bastard grandson. Huh! I . . . I wouldn't care if he was a bastard ten times over . . . he . . . is my grandson. I . . . I wonder what Doug will make of it.' He again said, 'Huh! He's known who he is all the time . . . But do you think he knows he's here?'

'I shouldn't think so because, before he became unconscious, in a rambling way he asked me to tell him.'

'Why do you think he came here?'

'Oh, I don't know. Very likely he just wanted to find out to whom he belonged, really belonged.'

'Yes. Yes, likely you're right, dear. Where . . . where have you put him?'

'Just along the corridor.'

'Do you think he'll be well enough to come and see me before . . . ?'

'Yes, yes,' she interrupted him; 'I'm sure he will; and I'm sure he'd want to.'

'Victoria.'

'Yes, Father-in-law?'

'Do you think I could have a port . . . a double, before Bright returns?'

Her smile was soft and her voice, too, as she assured him, 'I'll see what I can do.'

As she rose from the bed he asked hesitantly, 'Tell me, Victoria, do you think that one could have a feeling almost akin to love for a servant?' and, looking down on him, she answered simply, 'Yes, I do.'

'But it would be very hard to speak of it, wouldn't it?'

'Yes, perhaps; yet I imagine that it would be the best way to pay a debt through speaking of it, or a gesture by the hand that indicates it.'

He nodded his head slowly before allowing it to fall back on the pillow; then he closed his eyes and said softly, 'Thank you, Victoria.'

10

Five days later, after an inquest, they buried Lionel Fil-more, and it was noticeable that few people attended his funeral; that, in fact, his brother was the only relative present. Nine days later they buried his father, William James Filmore.

Perhaps it was the clear frosty day which accounted for the very large cortège that followed the family coaches to the cemetery.

Following a short service in the little church, they stood round the grave watching the coffin being lowered into the earth. As the newspapers later briefly reported, his relatives were the younger son Douglas, with his wife and daughter, and next to her the new-found cousin Joseph Skinner, the illegitimate son of the man who had been killed by his father during a family feud.

It wasn't the first time that the papers had referred to Joseph's parentage; in fact, they'd had a field day with regard to the murder and of himself having been shot at the same time as his natural father.

Joseph's arm was still in a sling; his coat was buttoned over it. He stood now, bareheaded, his hat in his hand, as he watched the first clods of earth being shovelled on to the coffin, the while he recalled the final meeting with his grandfather: he could see the tears raining from the bleared eyes, and feel again the swelling in his own chest and the restriction in his throat which prevented words from passing through his lips. He heard again the old man saying, 'Bend down, my boy,' and when he did so the arms came about him; and he returned the embrace, tightly, hungrily, and, as now, his heart was full. But his eyes were dry; yet it was a burning dryness. But not so Bright, who was standing at his side: Bright's head was bowed low and the tears were dripping off the end of his nose and his chin; and when he went to take the older man's arm, he muttered, 'Leave me, sir, just for a while;' and Joseph, after a moment's hesitation, turned slowly and walked to where Amy was waiting for him.

Douglas first helped his wife into the carriage and then his daughter, and lastly he went to assist Joseph; but Joseph, turning to him, said, 'I . . . I won't be coming back with you.'

'*What!*' It was as if Douglas hadn't heard aright.

Now Bridget and Amy were leaning from the carriage and they both said, 'What do you mean?'

'I'm . . . I'm going to stay with Mrs Hanratty for a few days.'

'*You can't.*'

He looked at Amy and said quietly, 'I can. I want to.'

'Why?' Douglas's voice too was low but the word was hard-sounding.

'Because I . . . I want to sort myself out. And anyway I'm all right now . . . and' – he gave a tight smile – 'I'm no longer working there.'

'Don't be silly. You're being awkward again. Don't be silly.'

'Amy, please! Look, I'm going to stay with Mrs Hanratty, I've told you.' And now he looked from one to the other.

'This is ridiculous. Who's going to look after you?' It was Amy again, and he turned to her, saying, 'There's nobody better than Mrs Hanratty.'

'But how are you going to get there? Will we drop you off?'

He turned to answer Bridget: 'No, thank you. There's a cab waiting. Mrs Hanratty saw to it.'

'Dear! Dear! Dear! You have been busy.' Douglas's head was nodding now and he looked anything but pleased as he muttered, 'You are an awkward cuss, you know. It's as Amy says.'

'Yes, I know that. I know that, but I'll likely grow out of it.'

'Please' – Bridget was extending her hand towards him – 'come back with us. Please.'

'Mrs Filmore,' he said, 'please see my side of it: they'll all be waiting; I'm a curio. It's been awkward in the house these last few days: I was a worker, the lowest in the small staff, and now who am I? They are having a job to find out how to treat me, even Bright. And then you are expecting half this crowd to go back to the house, aren't you? It's amazing' – he smiled quizzically now – 'how many friends the old fellow has suddenly accumulated. He has lain there for years, I should imagine, and not one of them looked in on him. If, for nothing else, I should feel too cynical to face them today.'

Douglas looked at this tall young man whom he had seen grow from a boy into a youth and had now jumped from a young man into maturity. It wasn't two full months since he had last seen him yet he seemed to have put on years. He placed his hand on his shoulder, saying, 'Have it the way you want it. We'll come along there tomorrow; we've got a lot to talk about.'

Joseph let the carriage bowl away before he turned and walked to where a solitary cab was waiting. He did not even address the driver, but got into the cab and lay back in a corner of it and closed his eyes . . .

Bertha Hanratty was waiting for him. Her face was bright, her hands outstretched in welcome, and they were gentle as they helped him off with his coat, then practically led him, as if he were an invalid, up to the fire and to the basket chair; and not until then did she speak, saying, 'Well, you got it over?'

'Yes, Mrs Hanratty, I got it over.'

'You know something?'

'No. What should I know?'

'I'd rather you called me Bertha.'

'That would be nice, Bertha. Yes, I'll call you Bertha.'

He looked round the room, sighed and said, 'It's good to be back.'

'Aw, lad.' Her hands one on each side of the chair, she bent over him, her face close to his and said, 'You've got no idea how good it is for me an' all. You know, from the minute you came to that door' – she jerked her head back – 'as wet as a duck that forgot to oil its wings, me whole life has been different, changed. And yours has an' all . . . I mean, changed, hasn't it?'

She straightened up now, adding, 'And to think you belong to that lot down there. Eeh! it's like somethin' that you read about.'

'I don't really belong, Bertha. I'm an offshoot that shouldn't have happened.'

'You belong all right, signed paper or no signed paper.' Her voice had hardened somewhat. 'Half the royalty were got on the wrong side of the blanket and they belong all right. And you belong.' And her tone becoming lighter, she said, 'Now, what are you goin' to have? Let's get down to eatin', eh?' only to add with some concern, 'Don't you feel like anything?'

'Nothing to eat for a while, but I tell you what I would like: a good big glass of your elderberry wine, the oldest stuff.'

'That you'll have in two shakes of a lamb's tail.'

He watched her hurry from the room to the scullery and again his gaze wandered about him. How was it he felt so at home here? How was it he had ever come here in the first place? Just because he was as wet as a duck that hadn't oiled its wings, she had said. He smiled to himself. She came out with some funny things. The old man would have liked her. Oh, yes, he would have liked little Bertha. They would have got on like a house on fire. Funny, but he couldn't get him out of his mind for very long. And then there was his father . . . A murderer.

That part hadn't reached the papers. No, it was too complicated, and the fact that the younger brother had kept silent about it all these years would have made greater headlines still: and would they have believed that he was unaware of his brother's guilt until after the innocent man had been hanged? No; as Douglas had said to him, nobody would have believed it. What was more, he would have been termed an accessory after the fact.

As for the episode that had ended it all, all he could recall vividly was the hate that had swept through him as he tore Henrietta from her father's grasp, and from her grasp on him. In the split second before the bullet had struck him, had his father pulled him forward to protect himself? He would never know for sure, but the suspicion would always remain in his mind. And had the hate of him died? No. No, it hadn't; it was still there. He could only hope that time would dim it. And that's what he wanted, in all ways . . . time. Time to know what he was going to do with his life. Would he go up to Cambridge? No; he didn't think so. Then what would he do? Well, he didn't know, did he? That's why he was here, for if there was any place he would find himself, it would be in the company of Bertha Hanratty.

It was after he had eaten, some two hours or more later, and they were sitting before the fire, that she brought the subject up by saying to him, 'What d'you intend to do

432

with your life, lad?' and he had answered, 'To tell you the truth, Bertha, I don't know.'

'Will you go to the university?'

'No; I've already made up my mind about that.'

She was looking into the fire now as she said, 'Well, whatever you intend to do, don't waste it, lad. You've only got one life. But, you know, you never realise this until you are halfway through it, that's if you get the chance to reach that stage. Often life is taken from people before they realise that they value it. I used to be always sorry when I heard of life being snatched from the young. But then again, it might have been better that way for them, for it may have saved them suppin' sorrow. You know, Joseph, I'm a very healthy woman. I've never known a day's illness in me life and yet I've known such unhappiness that at times I would have swapped it for the peace which some chronic invalids seem to have inside themselves. D'you know what I mean?'

He didn't answer her, not even with a nod, and she went on, 'You've heard me talk about me son in Australia an' that I hear from him every Christmas and that I hope he'll just pop in the door one day. Well, that's all bunkum, lad, all bunkum. Our Jimmy, who's now, I should say, forty-three, come the twentieth of next month, never gave a thought to anybody in his life. I've never heard from him in fifteen years. No Christmas card.' She slanted her gaze towards him now. 'I heard from him when he married and the wife wrote to me when each of the children were born, just a short note. Now I don't know whether any of them are alive or dead. I wrote to them at the last address they gave me but I got no reply. And our Lena, she's forty, has two children. I told you she lived in Jersey. She sends me a Christmas card and I send the bairns something every Christmas. From what I understand she's married decently off, quite warm in fact. But none of the warmth ever came this end. Why didn't they take after my Willie? Very odd, you know, about families, Joseph, very odd. And so, now you know why I nearly ate you up the day you landed on the doorstep in the rain. I was lonely. I look back an' I know I've been lonely every day since Willie died. But from the minute you stepped into the kitchen, as I told you, me life seemed to change. Lad, if you walked out the morrow and I never saw you again, the memory of these last few weeks, waitin' for you comin' in at night, seein' you out in the mornin', the memory of that'll last me.'

'Oh, Bertha.' He leant forward and caught her hand, and she lifted it up and pressed it against her cheek, and at the contact he asked himself, how many kinds of love were there? because here he was telling himself that he loved this little woman in a way that he had never loved his mother, because he had never been able to talk to his mother, at least his mother had never been able to talk to him, as Bertha had. Looking back, he thought that his mother had buried herself in the quicklime that had covered his stepfather. She had only been half-alive all those years, living only because she had to bring him up. It had been a sad life and the sadness had impregnated him. Yet, with Bertha here, it was different. For him, there was a glowing warmth emanating from this little woman, and, although he couldn't tell her, he knew that for the rest of his life he would feel that wherever she was, he must be near her, at least within visiting distance, and that often. 'What about another glass of your lifesaver?' he said.

And this brought her to her feet with a laugh, saying, 'At your service, sir! At your service. And you know somethin'?' She poked her head forward. 'If you hadn't been to a funeral the day I'd put the phonograph on.'

'Why not?' he said. 'Why not?'

'Do you think the old man would have enjoyed it?'

'Yes, he would, I'm sure he would, and this kitchen . . . and you.'

'Well, that bein' so I'll go and get it. It's in a cupboard in the front room.'

He lay back in the chair, his head moving from side to side: he had just buried his grandfather and now they were going to have the phonograph on. He must be back in the dream, he must. Life was crazy, but sort of happy at this moment.

11

They were sitting side by side in the drawing-room. Victoria was lying back on the couch with her feet on a high foot-stool; Bridget was holding her hand and saying, 'Do you think she understands all that has happened? I mean, the relationships, that Joseph is her half-brother, and Douglas her uncle, and Amy her cousin?'

'Oh yes, she understands, although –' Victoria paused here, then said, 'she may not have understood how it all came about because I have not told her about her father's connection with Joseph.' She again paused and made a movement with her head as if dismissing something before ending, 'And Lily's part in all this.' Then turning to look fully at Bridget, she asked quietly, 'When are we leaving?'

'Any time, my dear. Everything is ready for you down at the house. It could be this afternoon.'

Victoria now raised her head from the couch and looked round the room, saying as she did so, 'Once I step out of this house I'll never enter it again, but not a day will pass of those I've got left but I'll be walking its corridors, its rooms, wishing for something to happen, something drastic, something terrible that would wipe him out of my life and leave Henrietta safe. You know, Bridget, if I could have got my hand on a gun, I would have shot him years ago. I've wondered since if it was because he sensed this as much as his need for money that he sold the contents of the gun room, only keeping one or two in his own room ... and under lock and key. You know, at the height of my hate I would turn to the Bible for help, and every character I read of there had some redeeming feature. But I could find none in him, at least I don't think so, except that perhaps he might have had a love for his mistress, judging by the letters and a photograph I found in his drawer. She looked to be an elderly woman, too, which was surprising. Well, all I can hope is that she perhaps found some redeeming feature in him, because I never did.'

Bridget patted Victoria's hand, saying, 'You will forget, and it will be like old times when we were young . . .'

What a stupid thing to say. Nothing would be like old times, and what had happened in the past twenty years would obliterate even the thoughts of those far-gone days. Victoria had said that every day she had left she would recall the time spent in this house. And that was likely, because, if she were to believe the young doctor, her condition was such that her days might spread into a few months, and perhaps with special care and attention, a little longer.

When Amy appeared quite suddenly, dressed for outdoors, Bridget looked at her in some surprise, saying, 'Are you going for a walk in the garden, dear?'

'No, Mammy; I'm going for a walk outside. I'm going to see Joseph.'

'Oh, my dear.' Bridget drew herself to the edge of the couch now, saying, 'Well, we are all going along to see him shortly; your father wants to have a talk with him. I told you last night that your father's got some suggestion . . .'

'I know, Mammy; but there's no reason why I can't visit Joseph on my own, is there?'

'No; but it's a very long walk, and it's a lonely road.'

'I'm used to walking, Mammy; and I'll have to get used to walking lonely roads before I'm finished, don't you think?'

Bridget looked at this daughter of hers who took after herself in so many ways, mostly in her mind, and she didn't think she liked it. She loved her dearly, so very, very dearly, but she wished that she wasn't such a replica of herself and had more of her father's traits. But she had come to realise of late that when one faced oneself, one found some displeasing facets, and one of them was a strong will, which became wilfulness when displayed at Amy's age. She said now, 'Does Daddy know where you're going?'

'Yes; I told him. He's up in the schoolroom with Henrietta.' Then turning, she looked down at her new aunt, as she thought of her, and she said with a smile, 'She said my name quite plainly.'

'Oh, I'm so glad.' Victoria answered her smile, and when Amy said, 'There's a very good school for deaf children in Newcastle, perhaps she could attend there,' Victoria drew herself from the back of the couch, saying, 'Oh, that would be excellent. Oh yes,' and turned to look at Bridget, who said, 'Yes, indeed it would. We'll see into it.' And now she smiled broadly at her daughter, saying, as though assenting to her wishes, 'Be careful how you go. We'll be along very shortly, because we all may be going home this afternoon.'

'Oh; this afternoon?'

'Yes, dear, this afternoon.'

The smile had slid from Amy's face, and she turned quickly and went out without further words. Within minutes she was hurrying along what her mother had termed the lonely road, jumping the ice-capped puddles here and there and even sliding on one of them. And then she was knocking on the door of the cottage.

She had to wait some seconds before it was opened and by Joseph, and his greeting was one that showed a little surprise. 'You're early,' he said; then looking to the side, he asked, 'Are you on your own?'

'Yes. Yes, sir, I'm on my own. May I come in?'

He stood aside, and when she entered the room she did as he had done on his first sight of the kitchen; she stood and stared about her. Then her eyes focussed on the end of the room, and the fire and the chair to the side of it, and the books lying on the mat at its foot.

'Give me your coat.'

As he helped her off with her coat, she said, 'How's your arm feeling?'

'Fine, all right, but I'll be glad when it's out of this sling. Come up by the fire; Bertha's out in the garden feeding her feathered friends.'

'Bertha? You call her Bertha?'

'Yes. Yes, I call her Bertha . . . Sit down.'

As she went to sit in the basket-chair a voice from somewhere behind her shouted, 'Nuff to cut the nose off you out there! I'll soon have to put drawers on Lizzie else her backside will be frozen; they've got her pecked to bits. I think I'll bring her in later . . .' Bertha's voice trailed away; then as she entered the room she exclaimed on a high note, 'Well! Well! And where did you spring from? Did you come down the chimney? I didn't hear a carriage.'

'Amy, this is Mrs Hanratty. Bertha, this is Amy, and apparently, yes, she did come down the chimney.'

'Sit down, lass, sit down. Eeh! look at the sight of me!' She now rubbed her hands down the old black coat she was wearing. 'I must look like a witch to you.'

'She is a witch.' He was smiling at Amy now. 'She makes things happen, turns people inside out. And that's not the half of it.'

Amy sat down and stared from the little dumpling of a woman to this tall young man, this young man whom she loved, and in such a way that it was a constant pain. But she saw immediately that he wasn't the same person who had lived in the Lodge, nor yet the one she had seen during the past few days in the house down the road. He looked different; his long body wasn't stiff any more, and his manner was entirely changed; it was . . . She couldn't find the words readily to explain it, for he appeared not only relaxed, but free . . . free and easy. Yes, that was the term. His manner towards this little woman and hers towards him were as if they had known each other for years. And, too, there seemed something more than that between them. And yet, from what he had said, he had lived in this place only a matter of weeks while attending his grandfather at the house. Yes, and wasn't it strange that he had to help nurse his grandfather? That surely couldn't have made the change in him, could it? But perhaps the change was all for the better; there would be no more barriers to get through.

The little woman had taken her coat off now and had pulled what looked like a man's cap from her head and she was saying, 'I'll just spruce meself up a bit, then I'll make you a drink. But in the meantime get yourself into the front room. Now wasn't it funny –' She was looking at Joseph now. 'Don't you think it's funny that I should light that fire in there this mornin'? I said to you, didn't I, I was lighting it because I felt the room might get a bit damp? But that place is as dry as a bone.' She now turned a beaming face on Amy, ending, 'I must have known you were coming, lass. Well, go on, the pair of you, and leave me to get on in me kitchen and get Charlie singing.'

Somewhat bewildered, Amy allowed herself to be led down the kitchen and into the front room, and here she stopped again as she took in the horsehair suite, the wallpaper with cabbage roses shouting out from it, the dresser holding bits of china, and on a table to the side of the small window a large horn phonograph.

He laughed at her bewilderment, saying, 'You'll get used to it; it isn't the furniture that matters here. Come, sit down on that nice soft seat.' He bent over and thumbed the hard horsehair sofa.

When seated she looked up at him, and said, 'You like it here?'

'Yes. Yes, I like it here.'

'You're changed.'

'How d'you mean, changed?'

'Your manner, everything about you.'

'Oh that. Yes. Yes, I suppose, at least when I'm here.'

'Because . . . because of that funny little woman?'

'She's not a funny little woman.' His tone was one that she recognised now. 'She's a dear, kind, and understanding woman, and wise. Yes, that's the word, wise . . . and lonely.'

She had turned her head away from him as he was speaking, but now she was looking at him again and repeating, 'Lonely?'

'Yes, lonely. She grabbed at me and I grabbed at her for different reasons. We both needed each other badly when we met.' He now sat down beside her and, looking intently at her, he said, 'I was in a state the day I left the Lodge. All I wanted to do at that time was to have a glimpse of the house in which my father lived. From the moment my mother told me as much as she wanted me to know, I became consumed with finding out more. You know, Amy, I'd always felt that I didn't belong anywhere. I knew I had a stepfather, I also knew there was something being kept back from me, something that was shared between my mother and yours, and your father. Well, we've been all through that, haven't we, during the last few days? But it seems to me now that I was drawn here to this very house, to this very cottage, to this very woman, because without her I would have never gone as a helper to an old bedridden man; I'm sure if I'd had to stay in that house twenty-four hours a day I don't think I could have stood it. Coming back here was like coming back into sanity.'

'You didn't think about me, though, when you left?'

'Oh, yes, I did, Amy. I thought very much about you.'

'And now?'

'Well, I can't think more about you than I did then, and always have.'

She moistened her lips, and her eyelids blinked rapidly before she said, 'Are you going to marry me?'

He had been leaning towards her, but he did not straighten up nor did his expression alter as he said, 'No; at least not yet, not until I can find a position of some sort in which I'll be able to . . . Well, not keep you in the spoilt way in which you have been used to, miss, but to provide decently for you, perhaps in a cottage like this.' He waved his hand now.

'You wouldn't need much to provide for me in a cottage like this and I wouldn't mind, horsehair sofa an' all.' She patted the seat to the side of her, and his whole manner now changing, he put out his good hand and touched her cheek, saying, 'It must be sufficient for the time being that I love you. But one day *I* will ask you to marry *me*, and I hope it won't be too far off. But you understand I must find a position of some kind first.' And now he pulled a face at her. 'Have you forgotten there's still your dear mama and papa . . . eh? And also, don't forget, my impetuous Amy, that we are full cousins.'

'It wouldn't matter to me if we were brother and . . .' Her head drooped now. 'Oh, really! The things you make me say.'

His voice was very low as he whispered, 'It wouldn't matter to me either, dear.' Then, bending quickly, he kissed her on the lips, and when her arms went swiftly round his neck he winced, and she withdrew them for a moment, saying, 'Oh, I'm sorry . . . Is it still painful?'

'Well, let's say I know it's there. But also let's say that I'm lucky. Half an inch further, they tell me, and it would have been, Goodbye, Mr Skinner . . . or Mr Carter.'

She shook her head. 'Daddy did get a shock when he saw who Mr Carter was. It was the last place on earth, he said, he expected to find you.'

'Yes; and it was the last place on earth I expected to be that day I left the Lodge.'

As his hand went out to draw her to him again there came the neigh of a horse and she turned and looked over the back of the couch towards the window, saying, 'Oh, there's the carriage. They've come.' And her voice now dropping to an even sad note, she said, 'I don't seem to be able to escape for very long.'

He drew her quickly to her feet and, holding her close, he said, 'You will. Just have a little patience, you will. I'll see to it, I promise you, because I love you. I love you more than I'll ever be able to tell you. Unlike you, I cannot express my feelings as they really are. I suppose that was my mother's doing. Things near the heart were never talked about. And I can understand why now. But then, it became a pattern.' He bent and kissed her swiftly, then said, 'Doubtless, as always, you'll get your own way; and you'll change that through time, and then I'll become a pest.'

'Oh, I hope so, Joseph, I hope so.' She now placed her mouth hard on his, only for them to spring apart when they heard Bertha's high shrill tone, saying, 'Come away in! Come away in! They're in the front room there, an' I've just made a pot of tea. Sit yourself down.'

When they both entered the kitchen walking apart, Bridget greeted Amy with, 'How on earth did you manage

443

to walk along that road! It's like ice; the wheels were slipping.'

'I had a slide here and there,' she said. Then looking at Bertha, she added, 'Mrs Hanratty, these are my parents, Mr and Mrs Filmore.'

'Well, it didn't take me three guesses to come to that conclusion, lass. But come on, all of you, an' sit up an' let's have a cup of tea. I said, sit up, but there's only two chairs at the table. But plant yourself where you like.' Then turning towards the fire, she said, 'The tea's brewed and I've popped some scones in the oven to warm up. I baked them yesterday, but they come up as fresh as ever with a bit of heat.'

Exchanging a quick glance, Bridget and Douglas seated themselves on the two kitchen chairs near the table, but where there was amusement in Douglas's eyes there was slight bewilderment in Bridget's, and this was mixed with some amazement during the next few minutes as she listened to the cross talk between the little woman and Joseph. He was talking as she had never heard him talk to Lily; it was as if they were acquaintances of long standing; in fact, as if they were closely related.

At the first lull in the conversation Bridget looked at Joseph and said tentatively, 'We . . . we would like to discuss something with you. It . . . well, it concerns your future and . . . and the house.' And at this, Bertha got quickly up from the basket chair, saying, 'Well, then, if it's private, I'll leave you to it. I'm goin' to finish lookin' after me livestock.'

'I thought you were finished out there?'

Bertha looked at Joseph, saying, 'Well, you've been here long enough, lad, to know you're never finished with livestock.' And without more ado she took her old black coat from the door, put it on, then pulled a peaked cap onto her grey hair, nodded towards Joseph and went out.

There was a moment's silence before Douglas, his tone brisk now, said, 'Well, I'll put it in a nutshell, if that's possible, Joseph. As you know, the house and land, what is left of it, has come to me. If it had been entailed, it would have gone to Henrietta. Even if it hadn't, she may have had some claim should her mother have taken the matter up, but apparently some time ago my father made a new will . . . Oh, this being so, God only knows what would have happened if Lionel had been alive when Father died; he likely would have aimed to finish me. Indeed, yes. Anyway the place is mortgaged up to the hilt, but I can clear that out of my own business, as well as the smaller debts that have accrued over the years. Now the point is this. The house was going downhill when I last saw it, but twenty years makes a difference and I'm shocked at the sight of it now, both inside and out, and I would like to be able to say that I have enough money to renovate it back to how I recall it in my very young days, because it was then a beautiful house, with an equally beautiful garden; but that isn't possible. Yet my wife here seems only too pleased to throw her money about . . .'

'Our money.'

'Just as you say, my dear, as you wish, our money.'

He smiled tolerantly at her, then went on, 'So she proposes to have it refurbished completely inside, and attention paid to the roof and what is necessary outside; then restore the garden, and even get the little farm working again. But whilst this was being done we would have to live there, and –' Again he looked at Bridget, saying quietly now, 'she has no desire to live there. What is more, Victoria's, that is Mrs Filmore's, only wish is to return to what was her home in her young days, which is of course Meadow House. And so it has been arranged that we take her and Henrietta back with us today. But to return to the business of the house. No matter how good a staff is, it needs a head. Bright has been marvellous all these years. I don't know any other person in the world who would have worked for my father as he has, but he is getting on and, because of his labours, he is tired now and his duties should be light. So, the inside of the house needs guidance. As for the outside, I know from experience that things would tend to slack off not only in the yard and grounds, but also on the farm, if there was not a guiding hand. And so, Joseph, I come to the vital point and it is this: if everyone had their due and there was justice in this world, you, as the son of the elder son, would have inherited that place. But even as it is, we both consider it to be rightfully yours . . .'

'What! *Mine! That place, mine? Never!* Anyway, the law is the law and I have no more right to it than Bertha has.' He jerked his head back towards the door leading into the scullery.

Douglas's voice was still level as he replied, 'I know. Yes, I know that perfectly well. Under law you have no claim to the estate; but that isn't the point I'm trying to put over to you. As it stands the place is mine, and I could sell it tomorrow to a developer, and he would probably pull it down and build rows and rows of pseudo villas on the forty acres or so left. But as I said, I like that house and I want to see it as it once was, and so, therefore, I'm asking you to take on what will be . . . well, a job, for the next few years. And it will take a few years to bring it into order.'

Joseph was sitting apart from Amy on the settle. He turned and looked at her, then from her to her parents. This was a turn of events he had never dreamed of. He, too, had thought that Mr Douglas, as he still thought of him, would surely sell the place, although he hadn't thought, even vaguely, about a developer. But now he could see one jumping at the opportunity.

His mind swam into the dream again. He could see the old man, his grandfather, lying in that huge bed; he could feel his arms about him, and he was telling him something, that at first had no real meaning for him.

When understanding sprang at him, the force of it made him suddenly edge further along the settle, and he heard a voice speaking. It sounded like the old man's to his ears, yet it was his own, and he was saying to Douglas, 'Thank you for the offer. Yes, I will take it on, but only on one condition.'

'Condition?'

'Yes, condition, and that is I marry, take a wife.'

He now groped for Amy's hand and held it; but he was looking at Bridget the while he said, 'I've long loved Amy, and you know that; but it didn't meet with your favour, and I can understand why. Oh yes, I can understand why. But now things have been straightened out in that quarter there has been only one thing in the present situation that has stopped me from asking her to be my wife, and that is I was in no position to support her. But you yourselves have made that way clear.' Now looking directly at Douglas, he said, 'I ask your permission, sir, to marry Amy.'

When Douglas looked at Bridget their glances dropped away from each other, and Douglas said, with a smile, 'Well, I think there'd only be a civil war if I made any objection.' Bridget did not speak, but her silence went unnoticed because Amy, jumping up, ran to them and, standing behind them, put her arms around their shoulders and kissed first one then the other and, almost gabbling, she cried, 'It's wonderful! Wonderful! I never thought of that. And I'll love the place. Oh! Daddy; you will have to tell me what it was like, and I'll see to all the inside, and Joseph will see to the outside. Oh!' – she was kissing them again – 'I love you both very much.'

When Joseph heard Bertha's cough coming from the scullery, he called to her, 'Bertha! Bertha! Come here a minute.' And she came into the room, saying, 'Well, what is it? By! you look cheerful.' And he went to her and put his arm around her waist and said, 'We are going to be married.'

'Oh, lad' – she flapped a hand at him – 'this is so sudden.' And at this he laughed out loud and pushed her from him, and she, looking at Amy who was coming towards them, said, 'Well, I guessed as much. It was as plain as the nose on your face,' and holding out her hand she took Amy's and shook it as she said, 'You're pickin' a good lad, and if good wishes can make you happy, you have mine.'

'Thank you, Mrs Hanratty. Thank you.'

Both Douglas and Bridget had risen to their feet and, speaking for the first time, Bridget said, 'Well, we must be off. We've got a long journey before us.'

Amy now glanced at Joseph; then, looking at her parents, she said softly, 'I'd like to stay.'

'But, my dear, it's all arranged and your Aunt Victoria will be all ready to leave when we get back.'

'I . . . I could find my way. I could get a cab to the station and . . .'

'There's another bed up above goin' beggin'.' They had turned to Bertha, and she nodded ceilingwards before adding, ''Tisn't fancy: 'tis a bedroom but the bed's as dry as a bone. She's welcome and she'll come to no harm.'

Neither Douglas nor Bridget gave any answer to the old woman but they looked at each other and they both knew what the other was thinking. They were going back to a similar situation, a certain New Year's morning when she hadn't returned to her own bed, the morning when the glowing girl standing opposite had been conceived. The fact that there was this old woman in the house with them would make little difference, and she seemed the type, at least to Bridget, that would condone the outcome of suppressed passion. And in both her daughter and Lionel Filmore's son there was suppressed passion at this moment. Yes, there was a snag to this union, at least in her mind, for he could not cease to be the son of Lionel Filmore, that cruel man, the adulterer and murderer.

Well, she could do nothing more about it. She who had begun the series of events was helpless now in the face of the present situation.

She heard herself say, 'If that's what you would like to do, dear, I'll get Minnie to pack up some nightclothes for you and Ron could slip along with the case.'

'Oh, thank you, Mammy. Thank you, and you, too, Daddy.' She was once more kissing them.

Following the goodbyes, they went out and got into the carriage, and as they drove away Bridget looked back at the figures posed in the doorway, Joseph, his arm around Amy, and the little woman standing to his other side, that strange little woman who seemed to have taken him over, and, by the look of it, not only him, but also Amy. She had lost her daughter. Within the last half hour she seemed to have gone from her entirely, and the loss was already weighing on her.

She was lying back in the half-circle of Douglas's arm. He was talking soothingly to her but she was only half listening. She loved Douglas. Oh, yes, she adored him; but there was in her a need for her daughter.

She had long ago realised that a woman needed not only male companionship, she needed female companionship, too. It started with one's mother, she supposed, and then perhaps a sister, followed by a friend, just one friend. You could never have two women friends, not really. But what were friends compared to a daughter? Your mother had bred you but you had nothing to do with that; the sister was connected by blood, a friend by affection; but a daughter was something you had created. You had fostered the seed; then you had thrust it from the shell and tended its growth. At times even the feeling for it had outdone that for the sower. Such was your love for it that you planned its life: not only was it to be impregnated with love but it was to be surrounded with it; and yet you even saw the day when you might have to relinquish your hold on it to another. You saw it as painful but compensated for by the uprighteousness in the character of the man into whose hands you were allowing your beloved flesh to pass.

But it hadn't turned out like that. No. She hadn't taken into account Lily's son . . . Lily's bastard son who, in spite of his appeal, must hold within him all the traits of his father.

Her daughter was from a different line of blood, so she told herself; in fact, at times so opposite did she imagine Douglas to be from his brother that she came to wonder if there was any tie there at all. His mother, she understood, had been a very bright and gay lady at one time. In fact she had almost made herself believe this as the years had unfolded and revealed to her her husband's inner nature, which was that of a good man.

Yet being who she was, she was again forced to face up to the fact that she had been the instigator of all that had happened over the past twenty years, even to the hanging of Joe Skinner. For if she had not in her determined way ensured what she imagined to be Victoria's happiness and allowed her to face life and its inevitable disappointments, Joe Skinner would likely have been alive today. The whole pattern would have been changed and she would not have now lost her daughter . . . But then she had to ask herself, would she ever have had a daughter?

But now it was as if she had never possessed a daughter.

Amy had gone. The thing she had dreaded had come upon her . . .

She was brought out of her dismal thinking by the sound of Douglas's voice. He seemed to have been speaking for some time.

'What did you say, my dear?' she said.

'I said, with good nursing and care and a different atmosphere, Victoria could have a long spell before her. But long or short there will still be Henrietta. Oh yes, there will still be Henrietta.'

She could not tell by his tone if he was glad or sorry there would still be Henrietta. But now into her cold being crept a little warmth at the thought, Yes, there would still be Henrietta, for no matter how far she advanced she would still have to be cared for . . . and moulded.

Yes, there was still Henrietta. God, she supposed, had a way of dealing out compensations.

PART FIVE

The Inheritance
1923

1

Joseph smiled at Henrietta. She was standing in front of
him, her hands spelling out her words and her voice high
and fuddled, yet in part clearly articulate. She was saying,
'I can come on my own. I don't need to be fetched.' And
to this he answered, 'All right; but I like to fetch you.'
Dear! dear! How easy it was to lie. He now turned and
smiled at Douglas and Bridget, who were standing a little
to the side; and she, taking up a position so that she could
face Henrietta, spelt out on her hands, 'Joseph is a busy
man; he has to work.'

The big heavily-built woman, whose beauty had seemed
to fade as her body had developed and who was now
thirty-eight years old, flung her arms in the air and made
a motion with one foot as if she were stamping it, and,
her voice now coming as a gabble, she cried, 'Know . . . I
know . . . I'm not an . . . infant . . . child . . . nor a . . .
girl. He has been . . . working for . . . years . . . years . . .
years.'

Just as suddenly as she had flung up her arms so she
now flopped them down by her side, her head drooped
and she swung round and walked out of the hall and up
the stairs.

'She'll be all right,' Bridget said as though assuring
Joseph, although Douglas, walking towards the door with
Joseph, said, 'She wears one out; she's so demanding. I
suppose, though, I'm lucky; I'm out of the way most of
the day. But I know that when she's up at the house she
never gives you a minute. I can understand Amy's attitude.'

'And I, dear, can understand Henrietta's.' They both turned and looked at Bridget, and she, nodding at them, added, 'She's so frustrated by this affliction, it's understandable.'

'Well, all I can say, dear,' replied Douglas, 'is she should be used to it now; but how you've put up with it all these years I'll never know. But then' — he stepped back and put his arm around her shoulders — 'there's lots of things I'll never know about you, I being a simple man.'

'Yes, poor soul, and I pity your simplicity too.'

Douglas laughed, then said, 'That's funny. You know the hymn with that line in it "Pity my simplicity", I always sang "Pity my simple city" when in church, and the servants did too.'

Joseph looked from one to the other, thinking now, as he had done so often before, how amazing it was that after all these years they were still in love. There was Douglas at sixty-six and Bridget at sixty-three, and they always seemed to act like young lovers. Why didn't Amy take after her mother, or her father? These two loved, and yet they each gave the other their freedom. Bridget still saw to her business, and Douglas still chipped away at his stone; and that was big business now, too, although nothing like Bridget's. And he was part of that. Or was he?

It had taken him fully six years to put the house, garden, and farm back to what Douglas felt it should be, and he had gained a lot of experience during those six years, so much so that Bridget, seeing another branch to her little empire, had acquired an estate and land agency and let him run it. He had enjoyed that. Oh, yes, he had grabbed at it. At the time he did not realise it was a form of escape from the house and . . . other things.

When Bridget said, 'Wrap up well,' Douglas put in,

'Never mind wrapping up well; he doesn't need that in the car. By the way, how are you finding it?'

'Wonderful.'

'Better than the Austin two-seater?'

'Oh yes, miles ahead, and more comfortable.'

'Yes' – Douglas nodded – 'I found that too when I changed over.'

'Mind how you drive. You're a bit reckless, you know. Amy was on the phone yesterday and she said you scared her. Thirty miles an hour! That's far too fast. Now be careful.'

'Very well, ma'am.' He touched his forelock, and Bridget immediately slapped him on the arm.

'Are you going straight home?'

'Yes, but on my way I'll stop at Gateshead and look at that property. It's a very fine house, you know, with four acres. That's unusual in that quarter of the town. It had been attached to a farm at one time, I suppose.'

'Well, give my love to Amy and the children,' said Bridget, 'and we'll see you all on Christmas Eve, weather permitting. But if it's snowing I'm not coming by car.'

'Trains have been known to slip off the rails.'

As Douglas closed the door against the bitter wind Bridget shivered for a moment before she said, 'Have you noticed any change in Joseph?'

'Change? What do you mean?'

'Just what I say, dear, change.' They were near the drawing-room now and she added, 'There are times when I see him going back into the boy he used to be.'

'Well, you had better tell him, dear, and he'll be pleased about that, being thirty-nine now. That's what he is, isn't he, thirty-nine?'

'If you're not exactly blind I think you close your eyes to a lot, Douglas Filmore.'

'Yes, you're right, Mrs Filmore, I think I do, and it makes for happier living. Come and sit down.'

Once seated, he said, 'I'll tell you what does worry me, though, and it's Etta's obsession with him. If it wasn't for Amy's firmness in saying she can only stay there a week at a time, you wouldn't get her away.'

'Yes, I think you're right, dear, but what I find odd is that she doesn't like Amy.'

'You think it's odd?' Douglas drew his brows together as he spoke. 'My dear, I think it's you who are blind in that direction, because from the very first Amy has always made it plain she doesn't care for poor . . . Cousin Henrietta. Perhaps it was the way Henrietta, finding a new brother, or half-brother or whatever, tried to monopolise him.' He laughed as he added, 'And our dear Amy didn't want an opponent in that line, did she, if you remember? That was always her aim, and still is, I think.' He now lay back on the couch before saying musingly, 'He must get a little tired of it all.'

But Bridget did not lie back beside him as she usually did, she bounced to the edge of the couch, saying, 'Douglas! What do you mean?'

'Just what I say, dear. He must get a bit tired, because our daughter, you must admit, has eaten him up since first she set eyes on him, and she had never known any opposition until Henrietta came on the scene; and then of course the six children, and she's always been jealous of them, one after the other, their clamouring for his attention; and mind, I think he's enjoyed that sort of monopolizing.'

'Are you meaning to say, Douglas Filmore, or do you know what you are saying? You're inferring that Amy's love has tired him, or is tiring him as much as Henrietta's.'

He looked at her for a long time before he gave her an answer: 'I didn't actually think of it in that way, but as you put it so plainly, yes, I think it might. You see, you and I love each other. We know we can't love each other more than we do, it's impossible, we're never happy when we're apart, yet you give me my freedom and I give you yours. We both have a hobby, as it were. Our businesses are our hobbies. If I had wanted to paw over you and hold your hand for twenty-four hours a day you, being who you are, would have tired of me . . .'

'Don't talk so . . .' She rose to her feet and went towards the fire and looked down on it for a moment, before turning towards him again and, her gaze soft on him, she said, 'How is it you are always so right?'

'Oh' – he preened himself – 'I suppose it's because, as Ron up at the house would say, "I'm a clever bugger." '

'Be serious, dear, please . . . because this is a serious business, one we seemingly can do nothing about. For instance, I can't go to my daughter and in any kind of a motherly way say, stop loving your husband so much.'

'We are not talking about love, dear; we are talking about possession.'

'Possession?'

'Yes, possession. There are people who cannot live unless they possess something or someone. With some it's money. Lots and lots of money and the power it gives them. With others it's a person. I think that's the worst kind when it's applied to a human being.'

'Oh, don't say that, dear. Now I've got something to worry about.'

'Oh, well, you should have started worrying about this when Lily lived in the Lodge and worked in the kitchen here, and the two children were scampering through the wood together, never separated . . . It's too late to start worrying about them now. But come on, sit down. I want to possess you.'

She pulled a prim face and tried to stop herself from

laughing, and when she was encircled by his arms, their faces only inches apart, she said, 'You're the one to talk about possession.'

He had parked his car in the nearest garage to the house, about five minutes walk away. When he had last looked at the house three days ago, he found a number of boys playing in the deserted garden, and after walking around the house he had come back to find one of them sitting in the driving seat. The boy did not scamper away on his appearance, but peppered him with questions; and when later he had reached home he found a name chalked on the back of the car. Tommy Trotter, it said; and this had caused Ron Yarrow to laugh and say, 'I used to play that; there's a game called Tommy Trotter.'

Well, he didn't want any more Tommy Trotters on the back of his new car; hence his leaving it in the safety of the garage.

But after leaving the garage he found he had to thread his way carefully through a number of side streets, for there was a thin drizzle of rain falling and this on top of the already slush-covered streets, made for careful walking. He had turned up what he imagined to be a short-cut, a plaque on the wall naming it Downey's Passage. He had noticed it before when he had been driving the car slowly, looking for Bradford Villa.

One side of the broad passage was a blank stone wall which, he assumed, would be the back of the scrapyard he had just passed. Opposite were two or three shops: the first was a second-hand clothes shop; the second had opaque windows, a bill in one of them stating the premises to be the office of a printing company; the next single shop window brought him to a halt and there, across the top of the window in large-lettered print, was the word 'Agency'. Well, as he was a land and estate agent himself, he stopped, then read with amazement a section headed: 'Lodging-house keepers', and underneath this a long list of names and addresses. Under the heading 'Dressmakers' was another list. But what brought his eyes wide were the words printed in large letters: LUNATIC ASYLUM — PRIVATE, and printed underneath:

William Garbutt, Proprietor;
W. Marsh Taylor, M. A., Medical Supt.,
Dunstan Lodge, Dunstan.

Well! Well! He had seen everything now. And there were more; the window was stacked full of them. And finally he read the statement which said the owners of the shop were Land Agents; and underneath this, 'Enquire Within'.

So they were Land Agents, too, were they? As one would expect, many businesses were advertised in the newspapers, but he had never seen so many 'stacked' in a shop window. This would amuse Bridget. Oh yes.

The next premises were obviously an off-licence, or outdoor beer shop, as such were usually called, and this business, in comparison with the rest in the short street, appeared spruce. It had bottled spirits, including whisky, brandy and gin arranged as the centrepiece to an array of wines in one window, with bottles of beer from pint size to an enormous decorative flagon in the smaller window beyond the entrance door. He thought that the shop might be out of the way for the sale of such commodities, but then realised that at certain times the area would be alive with workers of one kind or another. Then there was the scrapyard behind that wall opposite.

Beyond the shop the passage turned right, but then petered out between the boundary wall of the shop premises and, opposite, a field edged by a railing. For a moment he wondered if this was the fence of the grounds belonging to the house he was on his way to visit with the intention of buying; but as he wasn't sure, he thought he'd better not cross it. Anyway, he didn't want to get up to his knees in mud, and hearing shouting and running back in the passage, he decided to retrace his steps.

He was turning the beer shop corner again when he was met head-on by what seemed to be a swarm of youngsters. He was bowled over and just as his head hit the pavement a bottle burst near his shoulder and he was splattered with broken glass, and for a moment a voice in his head yelled, I've been shot again.

He slowly became aware of voices all around him, one exclaiming, 'Bloody maniacs! kids these days. They've scattered. Aye. If I could get a hold of one I'd scud his arse for him meself . . . Are you all right, mister?'

'Help him up.'

He put his hands out now to push the helpers away, but it was as he went to place his feet once again firmly on the pavement that he groaned aloud and would have fallen, but for a woman's arms that were thrust out to support him.

'Can you limp, I mean hop?' This was from another woman. He didn't answer her, but with the aid of a man on one side, the woman on the other, he hopped into the shop, then leant against the counter while one of the women, lifting the flap up, said, 'You'll have to go in sidewards, sir; there's not room for two. And you Billy, get in first and give him a hand through.'

It seemed a long way from the counter to the room where he finally dropped down into a chair, and as he lay back and his head began to swim he heard the man's voice say, 'It's a wonder that broken bottle didn't cut him to bits . . . Are you all right, sir?'

He forced himself to open his eyes; then he said, 'I . . . I feel a bit dizzy. Could I have a drink of water?'

'No, not water' – a woman's voice came to him – 'it's no good. It's a strong cup of tea he needs.'

'What about a drop of the hard?'

'Don't be daft, Billy, that's the worst thing you can give anybody with shock.'

'It's never shocked me.'

'Shut up! It could be serious; he's hit his head.'

'D'you think we should get a doctor, Mother?'

'I don't know, lass. One thing, he can't stand; wherever he's for, he's got to be taken there.'

He was in that dream state again: he was in his grandfather's bedroom and the old man was yelling about having his head knocked against the wall, and Bright, on the other side of the bed was smiling. Bright had been dead these five years. He missed Bright. He had become like a father to him and he had told him so. Before he died, Bright, like his master, had put his arms about him and held him close . . . There were all kinds of love. And then there was Bertha. But was this Bertha here with him? Had he dropped in on Bertha? No, he hadn't. But he must go and see Bertha. He must see Amy first, though, and have it out with her. Bertha was getting on, and she was in that isolated place all by herself. He wanted her brought to the house. He had said to Amy he would get a nurse specially to look after her if she ever needed one. Amy was jealous of Bertha. It was ridiculous, wasn't it? . . . There were all kinds of love. And now here he was in a strange land . . . no, just a strange house; and his head was aching, and he was dizzy and . . .

'Could you drink this cup of tea, sir?'

'Oh. Oh, thank you, thank you.'

He drank the tea. It was hot, strong and sweet, and he didn't take sugar; but he liked this, it was a change. He said to the woman standing by his side, 'I . . . I'm sorry I'm . . . putting you to . . . to trouble.'

'No trouble at all, sir. We were just closing for dinner, any rate. Is your head aching?'

'It . . . it seems a bit strange. I must have bumped it.'

'Yes, indeed, you must have bumped it. You were flat out. Those scalliwags must have knocked you flyin'. They walk in when they're sent for a bottle of beer but they come in on wings when they're bringin' back the empties. They get a ha'penny on the bottle, you see, sir.'

'Oh, yes, yes.'

She didn't look like Bertha, but in a way she sounded like Bertha; and the other one, she hadn't spoken. He looked at her. She was a young girl; no, a young woman. She had a lot of hair, brownish, and her eyes were large and her mouth was laughing. And now she spoke: 'Lyin' prone outside an outdoor beer shop is surely a case for the police,' she said; 'but we could prove you never drank on the premises, sir, couldn't we?'

He should laugh; well, he was laughing; then he let out a sound as near a scream as ever he had emitted even when he was shot, and the older woman exclaimed, 'Oh my! Oh my! I should have told you: I was just lifting your bad foot onto the cracket 'cos it was danglin' there. You'll have to get your shoe and sock off for the doctor.'

'I'm sorry.'

'Oh, don't be sorry. Seems to me it's broken.'

'Oh, no, I hope not.'

'Why, have you to walk a lot? Well, we all have to walk, I know that, but I mean, is that your job?'

'Yes, sometimes' – he hesitated – 'in a way, but I have a car that's garaged just a short way off.'

'Oh, at Ridley's. But you'll never be able to drive a car with that foot, whether it's broken or not.'

'No, I doubt if I will.'

'Would you like another cup of tea?'

He hesitated before he said, 'Yes. Yes, I think I would, but could I have it without sugar, please?'

'Yes. Yes. Oh, I stick sugar in everything.'

She disappeared from his view and there was only the younger woman standing to his side now, and she wasn't smiling as she said, 'It's her aim in life to sweeten everything and everybody up.'

'Well' – he had to make himself think of his next words because his head was buzzing badly – 'it's a good aim I should imagine.'

'Yes, very good . . . Where d'you live?'

'On . . . on the outskirts of the town.'

'Oh, well then, you'll be able to get a taxicab. Are you on the telephone?'

'Yes, we're on the telephone.'

'Oh then, we'll be able to telephone and tell your people . . . You're married?'

'Oh, yes.'

'And a family?'

'Six. Three boys and three girls.'

'That's nice. Are they all small?'

'Not really. The youngest is fourteen and the eldest, twins, they're eighteen, nearly nineteen.'

'Oh, practically all grown up?'

'Yes, nearly.'

His eyelids were heavy. He closed them, and her voice came to him as if from a distance, saying, 'You're still feeling dizzy, aren't you? You've likely got a little concussion. Anyway, I'll take that pillow away from your head, you'll be able to lean back further.'

He felt her lifting his head up, then gently laying it back again. That was better, he could go to sleep now . . . What was he thinking? He mustn't go to sleep here; he must get home. He'd have to phone Amy. But he'd better not yet, not until just before he got in that taxicab, else she'd be

465

over here, fussing, fussing, fussing. Why was it she paid so much attention to some things and not to others? She saw to all his needs, she was always stating. That was funny, and he had told her so. That was indeed funny.

He heard the young woman saying, 'I think he's going to sleep, Mother. I wouldn't press him to have the tea . . .'

He was awakened by a man's voice: it was saying, 'Well, well! what have we here? Drunk and disorderly outside an outdoor beer shop. Why do you allow it, Janet? I'll have to report you to the police . . . Hello, sir. I hear you've had a spill. Well now, let's have a look. Does that hurt? Oh yes, I see it does, doesn't it?'

And the doctor's probing fingers caused him further pain before his diagnosis came: 'Well, sir, good report: nothing I can see broken, but a very bad sprain. You'll need to keep it up for some time; but I don't think it'll need plaster, that's if you're sensible and don't put any weight on it. Now about your head. You feel dizzy, I understand?'

'Yes. Yes, a little.'

'And sleepy?'

'Yes, that, too.'

'Ah, well, when you hit the pavement in any way you expect results. Try not to do it the next time you fall.'

He closed his eyes. There were a lot of jokers around here.

'What is your name?'

'Joseph Skinner.'

'And you live where?'

'Grove House, Woodland Road.'

The chubby-face doctor straightened up, nipped his chin between a finger and thumb and nodded as he said, 'Grove House. I know it; the Filmores' place?'

'Yes. Yes, the Filmores' place.'

'Oh, yes, yes.' The man was still nodding. 'You married Douglas Filmore's daughter, didn't you?'

'Yes, I married the daughter.'

The doctor stood back from the chair, then turned and looked first at one woman then at the other and said, 'It's a lovely place, beautiful gardens.' And, bending towards Jospeh again, he added, 'I know the history of that place. And you brought it back to life, made a very good job of it. Your doctor is Frank Mellow, isn't he? I know him; we went through college together. It's a small world, a small world. Well now, sir, what we must do is to get you home. You have a telephone here, Janet, haven't you? Well, you'll first ring up a taxicab and then – ' He now looked at Joseph, asking, 'Your number, sir?'

'Two eight five.' What a fussy man! He didn't care for fussy people. He had lived with fuss too long. Fussy people always wanted to probe into your life, into your inner being . . . nothing was left, nothing, nothing. Bertha, too, was fussy. But she was fussy in a different way: there was no command behind Bertha's fussiness . . . 'What did you say, sir?'

'I said, the sooner you get into bed the better, and I'll telephone Doctor Mellow. But for the present, if you, Liz, will get that taxicab and inform the gentleman's home, I'd be obliged.'

'Yes, I'll do that, doctor.'

'Well, now, I must be off.' He was bending over Joseph now. 'I'm glad to have made your acquaintance, sir. I wish it had been under better circumstances. But there's always a future, isn't there?'

'Yes, there's always a future.'

The little man stood back as if he were waiting for some words of thanks, then said, 'Ah. Ah well, a pleasant journey,' and he went from the room, and Joseph repeated to himself, 'Oh, I know the history of that place. You brought it back to life . . .'

He was hazy about what had followed, except that he shook the elder woman's hand and then that of the younger, who smiled at him and said, 'Take more water with it next time.' He recalled smiling back at her and saying, 'I'll try; but strong liquor is a great temptation,' at which she had laughed . . . laughed outright. It was a laugh that he hadn't heard before. It was clear and had a happy ring to it . . . Take more water with it.

2

He was lying on a couch, placed opposite the fire, in the bedroom where his grandfather had lain in the four-poster bed and had died there. Now there was no four-poster in the room; it had been replaced by a large brass-knobbed bed. There was nothing at all left in the room to remind him of what it had been like at that time, except for the wardrobe and the dressing-table; the former, taking up practically the length of one wall, was really too large to move, and the dressing-table being such a handsome matching piece, Amy, at her father's request, had left it where it always had stood between the large double windows. The carpet was a warm beige colour, and the curtains of dull pink satin brocade, which was repeated in the upholstered easy chairs.

The room at the moment was high with the voices and laughter of six young people, and it was seventeen-year-old Alice who cried, 'Go on! Jonathan; read it to Daddy.'

But eighteen-year-old Malcolm, the elder of the twins, said, 'It's childish, mediocre, and doesn't scan.'

'Oh! listen to the big-headed university type.' This was from fifteen-year-old Kitty, pushing at her brother and adding, 'Your head's getting too big for your hat.' Then, 'Go on! Jonathan, read it to Daddy;' and turning to the man on the couch, she said, 'It's funny. It really is, Daddy. Listen.'

Jonathan, almost a replica of what Douglas had been at sixteen, grinned; then standing up and assuming a pose, one hand laid across his chest, the other holding a sheet of paper chin-high, he read:

> Don't tell me, sir, your tale of woe
> When to Gateshead you did go
> Supposedly a property to view,
> When in your heart you certainly knew
> 'Twas after beer you were intent
> And into an outdoor beer shop you went
> And spent all your money in that place,
> Then landed . . . flat upon your face.
> Result, concussion and an ankle bent.
> You, Mr Skinner, are a disgrace,
> And I ask you to your face,
> Are you sorry that you went?

There was more laughter now and Joseph, reaching from the couch, punched at his son, saying, 'I'll have you up for slander, sir. I was neither drunk nor daft. Well, perhaps a little daft, but no liquor had passed my lips; it was empty bottles that caused my slips.'

'Oh! Oh!' The groans came from all quarters. 'Don't Daddy, don't, please!' This came from Alice. 'Rhyming isn't your forte.'

'And it certainly isn't Master Jonathan's either.'

They all turned on Malcolm again, fourteen-year-old Bertha punching at her big brother as she cried, 'Then let's hear you do better,' before turning to her sister and saying, 'Kitty, let's rag him. You get his hair . . .'

'You'll do nothing of the kind. You can be heard all over the house.'

They all turned and looked towards the door they hadn't heard open, and, all silent now, they watched their mother walk towards the couch where, looking down on Joseph, she said, 'Why do you encourage them? You're supposed to rest. As for you lot, there are jobs downstairs for everyone of you.'

Now the voices assailed her:

'We got the holly in.'

'And we've done the chains.'

'I brought all the stuff down from the attics.'

'Yes, yes, yes.' Amy put up her hands, silencing them. 'But the tree has got to be decorated, the holly has got to be put up. You cannot expect the maids to do everything: they've got enough on their hands. Cook wants extra help in the kitchen, and Linda's there, and Rene's got her own work to see to. And you boys' – she pointed to William and Malcolm – 'you can carry the baskets of washing over from the laundry, and be careful! Florrie and May are ironing over there, and what's more they all want their own hall decorated for their party on Christmas night. That leaves plenty for everyone to do, so get about it, sharp!' Her arm was flung wide as if in command, and amid different forms of protest they all went from the room, and their going left a strained silence behind them.

Lifting a glove from where it hung on a hook to the side of the fireplace, Amy put it on; then, taking up a pair of tongs, she transferred some pieces of coal to the fire, after which she replaced the glove, then wiped her hands one against the other as if getting rid of the dust, and now looking to where Joseph was surveying her, she said, 'You encourage them; the house is like a fairground at times.' She sat down on the side of the couch and took hold of his hand, saying, 'How do you feel?'

'Fine; there's nothing wrong with me.'

'You've been suffering from concussion, besides having a sprained ankle, and you say there's nothing wrong with you. But how you can put up with that noise, I don't know.'

'Why don't you like your family, Amy?'

471

'What?' She jerked herself some inches along the couch from him, then repeated, 'What?'

'You heard what I said: why don't you like your family?'

'What a thing for you to say to me! And you have said some wicked things in your time, at least lately; but that is cruel.'

'It's the truth, Amy. You should never have had children; you should have only had me. Isn't that right?'

Her eyelids were blinky rapidly, her mouth had formed a tight line; then in a trembling voice, she said, 'You don't appreciate being loved. Never have.'

'Oh, I appreciate being loved all right, Amy, always have done, but as I see it there's room in life for all kinds of love, and that extends to one's children.'

'One's children!' Her voice had a bitter note in it now as she repeated, 'One's children! I gave you six children in five years. I became worn out.'

'Not so much worn out, Amy, as determined not to have any more, so much so that you took to a separate room for a time, even after I had promised you faithfully there'd be no more. But you didn't believe me, while all the time professing this great love for me.'

'It was great, it still is. You . . . you don't know anything about real love. Your kind of love is mixed up with . . .'

'Go on, say the word. It's that dreadful, dreadful word, lust. Go on, say it.'

She got to her feet now and said, 'All right! yes, lust.'

'Amy, I'm going to tell you something. You may not understand it but I hope you will; you must work it out for yourself. I think you should have been a nun. Your kind of love would have satisfied God; although, on second thoughts, He, too, wouldn't want to be possessed; and then, on the other hand, like many a frustrated nun, I'm sure you dreamed of caresses; in your case you sought them, you demanded them, you liked to be petted and kissed, but when it came to what usually leads from the petting and the kissing, you became like a frustrated virgin. That's something I could never understand, cold, stiff, no response; it all had to come from me. You're a queer mixture, Amy. At times I've been sorry for you, while at others – ' He now pulled himself up on the couch and, leaning towards her, muttered vehemently, 'At other times I've wanted to thrust you out of my life, because ever since I can remember you've been in it, chasing me, grabbing at me, holding me to you, yet at the same time giving nothing, nothing of yourself. All you wanted was for yourself to have and to hold, like the song says, but never, take me, all of me, my body, my mind, all that is me. That is love, real love. But you have never known it. You are, although you don't recognise it, a selfish woman, Amy, and because I love my children and because they love me, you have tried to push a wedge between us more and more. Oh, don't shake your head like that, I know you; I've had nineteen years of close contact with your whims, your possessiveness, your demands. Almost at the moment you were born, thirty-seven years ago, you stretched out your hand and clutched at me and you've never let go since. I'm tired of it, Amy. Do you hear? tired of it.'

He watched the colour drain from her face before, lips trembling and her head wagging, she said, 'Well, there's a remedy, isn't there? Why don't you go along to your dear Bertha, or that half-uncle of yours in Birtley that you've suddenly taken to calling on. You should set up an old people's home, not forgetting your dear Henrietta. And I'm telling you something now that I'm on, I'm not having her stay here again.'

'Well, that's up to you. You tell your mother and father that, not me; they'll be here tomorrow; but better still, put it to Henrietta herself that she mustn't come here, or near me. That's the point, isn't it? she mustn't come near me. But there's another thing that you haven't faced up to: Henrietta and you are very much alike . . .'

'Oh, how dare you! How dare you!'

'I . . . I dare, but you didn't let me finish. I was going to add: in one way, you've both got a passion for possessing an individual, sucking them dry. Well, Amy, before I'm really frizzled to cork, left dry and spineless, I'm determined to make a stand against it. It might mean leaving here; but I'd have to leave here in any case, wouldn't I? for you have already seen this place passing to Malcolm when your father dies. On that point though, you know, you haven't asked yourself where you'd come in, because, of all our brood, Malcolm is the most unthinking. Now, if it was going to William, he would look after you till the end, not give you a back seat when he brought his wife in to rule the roost. Or there's Jonathan; he too would consider you; but Malcolm is for number one. Do you know who my eldest son is like? He's like my father, my real father, Lionel Filmore.'

'Never! Never!'

'All right; have it your own way, time will tell. He is nearly nineteen years old and he is of the kind, if he takes a fancy to a girl, he'll have her, and he could be married by next year.'

'You've thought it all out, haven't you?'

'Oh yes, I've had plenty of time, nineteen years in fact, ever since your father gave me the job of restoring this house to what it once was. Well, I've done that; but I've also created a business for myself. Leaving here tomorrow wouldn't alter things much; I'd be able to support myself very well. Your father has always paid for the staff, and seen to everything else, whereas I've been but a caretaker, and you, I may say, the caretaker's wife; but you're also their daughter, so they'll see to you all right, in fact take you back into their fold.'

474

'You're an ungrateful swine.'

'A swine perhaps, but never ungrateful. Yet at times I do ask myself what I have to be grateful for. I worked like ten men to restore this place, and I've done a good job on it . . .'

'Yes, and you love it. More than anybody else you love it, because you think it should have been yours.'

'If everyone had their rights, Amy, it would have been mine . . . it should be mine. And I heard the other day, it's just a whisper, that they're thinking about passing a law that will give an illegitimate the right to inherit, or at least to fight for his inheritance. Wouldn't that be funny?'

Again the silence descended on the room; and then she was walking towards the door. But she didn't open it until after she had turned and said, 'There have been times over the past few years, Joseph Skinner, when there has arisen in me a feeling akin to hate. Love you I might, but, let me tell you, I could hate you equally so.'

And he called towards her back, 'I'm quite well aware of that, Amy, because you're a woman with a one-track mind. Some of us could love and hate at the same time, but never you.'

As the door banged he added to himself, 'Because you're an unintelligent woman, Amy.'

3

John Calder had been in Joseph's service now for eleven
years. He was eighteen when he had started as an under-
study to Bright, and six years under that experienced man
had moulded him into an almost exact replica of his
teacher, and, as there had grown up between Bright and
his master, William Filmore, an association that could
only be called friendship, at least over their last years
together, so there had developed between Joseph and John
Calder a relationship in which they spoke almost as equals,
at least from Joseph's side. But John Calder, being the
pupil of Bright, never made the mistake of overstepping
the mark.

Half an hour earlier he had served Joseph's dinner on
a trolley set against the couch, and now he had just cleared
the used dishes onto a tray and was handing it to the
parlourmaid, Rene Bristow, saying, 'I'll bring the tureens
down with the rest.' And to this she answered in a low
voice, 'Thank you, Mr Calder.'

Her tone was deferential; and the sound of it caused
Joseph to smile to himself, for it was well known in the
household that Rene was keen on the butler, but also that
the butler wasn't keen on Rene. Perhaps, it was said,
because he was still carrying his earlier sorrow: before he
had taken up his post here, he had become engaged to a
young girl, and he was still engaged to her when four
years later, she died of consumption. That, however, was
seven years ago, and so it was to be thought he had got

over it; but Joseph surmised he very likely used this loss as a shield against pressing females like Rene.

That the house was run by a happy staff was due, Joseph knew, much more to John's efficient control than to Amy's position as mistress, for Amy had, over the years, become finicky and demanding. He also knew that this had developed because of the tension between themselves; she had to take it out on someone. He recalled the incident of some years ago when young Bertha's nursemaid had stamped out of the house. It was after this that he himself had had a talk with Bridget and had asked her to speak to her daughter. It was that incident, too, that had seemed to point forcibly to the fact that Douglas and Bridget were the rightful owners of this house and he merely a caretaker; the thought, crush it as he would, hurt him . . .

John was pouring out a glass of port when Joseph looked up at him and said, 'Will you do something for me on the quiet, John?'

'Yes, sir. You don't need to ask. Whatever it is, you know you don't need to ask.' They smiled at each other; then on a little laugh, Joseph said, 'I want to send a present or two on the quiet. You see, the lady in the off-licence, as much as I can recall of that incident, was very kind to me; and her daughter, too. So, I'd like to send them a little present without any fuss, you know?'

John nodded, saying, 'I understand, sir.'

'Well, tomorrow, you could take the car. You'll like that, won't you?'

Again they smiled at each other, and John said, 'That's a very exciting duty, sir, and I thank you for providing me with it.'

'Well then, I'd like you to go into town tomorrow and take a gift to Mrs Dunn at the off-licence. It's in a place called Downey's Passage . . . very odd name that, isn't it? . . . and it's in a very odd little street, too. As I remember, there are only four or five shops in it and the off-licence is the last one. I thought I was taking a short cut to a house called Bradford Villa, it being up for sale, when the empty bottle hit me.'

'Well, better empty than full, sir, I would say. Yet it's a wonder you weren't cut by that broken glass.'

'Yes, I myself thought I was lucky there. Well now, as to what I would like you to get: first, a box of good chocolates; then go to a good greengrocer, there's one in the market, Wilson's, and get them to send some fruits and a bouquet of flowers.' He paused before saying, 'And as you'll be delivering the chocolates, you could also take the fruit and the flowers.'

'Yes, of course, sir.'

'Then we have got to have an excuse for your going. I've already bought the girls' presents, but extra sweets are always acceptable, so you can get me three pound boxes of chocolates. They can be wrapped up and put around the tree.'

'Of course, sir.' John went to the side table and lifted up the tray holding the soup and vegetable tureens, and as Joseph watched him ease himself dexterously out of the door, while balancing the tray on one hand, he knew he had no need to explain why his sending a thank-you gift to the woman in the off-licence had to be done on the quiet, for John, he knew, had weighed up the situation in the house some long time ago. And the significance of the fact that his mistress had no women friends.

It was Christmas Eve morning and with the aid of a stick he had hobbled around the room and was now standing near the window when Amy came in; and on the sight of him she said immediately, 'Now look, don't try to be too clever. The doctor said a fortnight.'

As though dismissing the remark, he pointed to the window, saying, 'It's snowing again.'

478

'Yes, I know.'

'Then I think Bertha should be brought along because, if it keeps on, the road could be blocked by tomorrow.'

'Joseph, please have a little consideration. I've had to have two more bedrooms prepared for Mother, Father, and Henrietta . . . nine bedrooms to be seen to.'

'Yes, nine bedrooms; but I understand from your father that in his young days he knew twenty bedrooms being occupied at this time of the year, and coal fires to be attended to. Now you only need to switch on and there you are; all except in this room, and the dining and sitting room.'

'Those other rooms haven't been aired.'

He limped towards her and in a deceptively low voice, he said, 'Of the seven female indoor servants, you could perhaps order one to put some bottles in the bed and switch on the fire. Now couldn't you do that, Amy?'

Her voice, too, was low as she replied. 'You've said yourself that she never wants to sleep here.'

'No; because she knows you don't want her to sleep here. But she's never spent a Christmas Day alone in the last twenty years and this is not going to be the first. She's an old woman, Amy.'

'Yes, except for her tongue; that's never aged.'

'No, thank God; and I hope it remains young and wise to her end.'

She stepped back from him, saying, 'You're odd, Joseph Skinner, that's what you are, odd.'

'Well, we both stem from the same branch, don't we? And my oddities undoubtedly match your own.'

There was that small wagging movement of her head that he had come to know so well over the years and which seemed to return her to the girl that she had once been, and in a way still was, for now she jumped from one subject to another, saying, 'And you have sent John out and you never consulted me. When I enquired what he was up to . . . Going on an errand for the master, he said. So, may I know what errand?'

'Oh yes; there's no secret about that. It was for some odds and ends for the girls. On thinking it over, lying here,' he pointed to the couch, 'I realised I hadn't got them much for their stockings. Presents round the tree, yes, but little for their stockings.'

'Well, if the errand's as simple as that, why couldn't you have consulted me?'

'Oh, you are too busy, Amy: you have so much to see to, you are run off your feet.'

She drew her lips tightly between her teeth for a moment before she said, 'Sometimes, Joseph Skinner, I could slap your face for you.'

'I've no doubt about that, Amy. But tell me, why do you always give me my full title when you're in one of your moods? Why don't you just say emphatically, *you*, instead of Joseph . . . Skinner? By the way' – he now made himself smile at her – 'if that law ever comes into force about inheritance that I mentioned to you earlier, I'll apply to have my name changed to its rightful source of Filmore. Now what do you think of that? Mrs Filmore, the third, fourth, fifth or sixth or seventh? I don't know how many there were before you. Have you ever counted them on the gallery and the staircase and in the hall passage? But you would like to be called Mrs Filmore, wouldn't you? Skinner's a nasty-sounding name, don't you think?'

Seeing her lips tremble, he had the sudden urge to put his arm out and draw her to him and say, 'I'm sorry. I'm sorry. Let's go back to the beginning.'

But what was the beginning? When was the beginning? Just those few weeks prior to his finding her sitting on the edge of the bed there, tears streaming down her face. And why? Because she had discovered she was going to have a baby and, as she had said bluntly even then, she didn't want a baby, she only wanted him.

He let her go out, the door banging again; then he hobbled to the sofa and sat down, and as he stared into the fire, the only coal-fed bedroom fire in the house, he asked himself where they were heading. Was life to go on like this? No, no; it was unthinkable. He was only thirty-nine years old. If he was of his grandfather's stock then he was only halfway through his life. Within a few years the children would be married and be gone, and where would that leave him? Alone with Amy. She would like that. Oh, yes, she would like that. But what about him?

He pulled himself to his feet again, and as if his thoughts were dragging open the closed door of a cage, he said aloud, 'Oh no! No!' Then again louder, *'No!'*

He was lying on the couch again. Douglas was sitting at the foot, and near the head sat Henrietta, in a position that enabled her to look straight at Joseph; she watched his mouth as he said, 'Did Bridget like it?'

She now turned her head towards Douglas as he answered, 'Yes. Yes, very much. But, being Bridget, she thought they were asking far too much for it, seven-hundred and fifty. After all there's only three bedrooms on the first floor and three attic rooms above. But the ground floor is surprisingly spacious. Well, you saw it, didn't you?'

'No, not inside. I just walked round about. There was no board up and I didn't know who was selling it.'

'Oh, it's an old lady in her seventies who still has her wits about her, so Bridget says, and who, to use her own words, "wants no truck with them blokes that charge a lot". She's living in a flat in Newcastle now, I understand, and she is well into her seventies. Talking of seventies, I hear that Bertha refused to come and stay overnight. She's a tough old girl.'

Joseph's response to this was cut off by Henrietta, mouthing now, '*Good! Good!*'

'What do you mean, "good, good"?'

Henrietta's hands moved swiftly and Joseph read them: 'She's not coming . . . Bertha. Glad.'

'She'll be here tomorrow.'

The high, crackling, unnatural voice now came at him, the words spaced, 'But . . . she . . . won't . . . be . . . staying . . . never . . . leaves . . . you . . . alone.'

When Douglas gave vent to a loud laugh she reached out and slapped his knee; and he mouthed at her: 'You're . . . the . . . one . . . to talk, Etta. Who is it that gets in a temper . . . when she can't come and see Joseph?'

To Joseph, it was as if Douglas were talking to a little girl, and the big, almost hefty woman sitting close to him took up the childish pattern by looking at him and saying, 'But . . . Joseph . . . likes . . . me . . . near . . . him, don't you, Joseph?' and she went to grab his hand, but he moved his arm quickly away, for of a sudden he was repelled by her. For some time now she had aroused a similar feeling in him, but only now did he put a name to it. Immediately he recalled when she had first been made aware that they were half-brother and sister. She was then a young, slim, beautiful eighteen-year-old girl; and she seemed to remain so for the next two years until Victoria died, when she came under the full supervision of Bridget. From then, there were no more days spent digging in the garden; she attended school, not part-time as she had been doing, but full-time. And it seemed to be from then that her free time was given over to lazing about and eating. Whether eating assuaged the frustrations, or the frustrations caused her to eat was a question no one could answer.

Although at school she learned to speak volubly on

her hands and there was even some improvement in her speech, there was little in the controlling of her limbs, and her mental prowess remained stationary and she was still given to fits of wild temper. In fact, one such bout ended her schooling, when she floored another pupil and it took two men and a teacher to restrain her.

He recalled his thoughts when he had imagined being alone in this house with Amy once their family had all gone. But now he knew he wouldn't just be alone with Amy; there would be Henrietta, too, to guard him. Three times, lately, she had taken the train and the bus to come here to see him, and he remembered Amy's reaction when she had called her mother and demanded that someone should come and take Henrietta immediately back to Shields, only to be told by an irate Bridget that it wouldn't do her daughter any harm to put up with Henrietta for a week, in order to give her a rest.

Strange how people changed. After Bridget had lost her daughter to him her whole interest became centred on Henrietta: it was Henrietta this and Henrietta that; Henrietta was doing marvellously at school, and on one parent's night she had danced with Douglas and there had been great fun in the school hall . . . And Henrietta had so enjoyed her holiday in the Lake District . . . And Henrietta had a sense of humour; she came out with very funny things at times. Henrietta. Henrietta.

But the applause had dwindled away as Henrietta's body developed, and was heard of no more after Henrietta had attacked a pupil, tearing at her face before felling her to the ground. There had been talk of the parents bringing charges for damages, but the matter had been settled privately. He never did know how much Bridget had paid for that particular tantrum.

For a long time now, this obsession to be near him had embarrassed him, to say the least, for she had taken to pawing him. Although he admitted it was a childlike gesture, as if she were stroking a favourite doll or a puppy, nevertheless the attention was coming from a grown woman, and a very large grown woman at that.

'What's . . . the . . . matter . . . with . . . you? Got . . . a pain?'

'Yes, yes,' Joseph answered, looking towards his foot, while Douglas rose from the end of the couch and, taking hold of Henrietta's arm, he said, 'Come on . . . Joseph's tired . . . Anyway, it'll soon be dinner time . . . Go down and see . . . what the girls . . . are doing . . . They are still decorating the tree.'

Like a petulant child she now shook off Douglas's hand and stamped towards the door and went out, leaving it open.

Douglas slowly walked towards it, closed it, then returned to the couch and, after sitting down again, he looked at Joseph, saying, 'She's becoming a handful.'

'Becoming? She's been that for a long time now, Douglas. I don't know how you and Bridget put up with her.'

'I don't. It's Bridget who has her most of the time. And she's glad, I know, to get out to business these days and leave her to Nellie. What we'd do without her, I don't know. She can handle her. She's almost as big as Henrietta, and she stands no nonsense. It's odd, but it's always on Nellie's day off, or at the weekend, that she makes tracks here for you.' He sighed again; then, leaning forward and resting his elbows on his knees, he allowed his hands to hang slackly between them, and from this position which, to Joseph, appeared to touch on despair, he said, 'I don't know where it's going to end. I used to look forward to when I could retire and spend long peaceful days with Bridget, but now' – he turned his head towards Joseph – 'now there is Henrietta, the great intrusion. You know,

484

Joseph, I'm like my daughter or she's like me; we are a pair in that we only want to be with the person who belongs to us. What's happened between you two, Joseph?'

Joseph was startled. He hadn't thought that the tension, or, to give it its real name, the rift, that had arisen between Amy and him had been detected at all by her parents, because they didn't visit them that often.

However, he didn't give the usual and stupid answer by asking a question, such as, 'What do you mean?' but said, 'I've never felt I belonged to anyone, Douglas. Right from a child I sensed there was a mystery about me, and so I accepted the feeling as part of my nature. Yet, right from when she was a child, Amy tried to possess me — that is the word, possess — and in a way I accepted it, right up till when we were married, because then I hadn't thought about it as possession, I just gave it the name of love. But from shortly after we were married I knew that I had something to contend with, and it became more evident after each child was born, because she became jealous of her children.'

'*Oh! Joseph*. What are you saying?'

'I am saying . . . I am telling you the truth, Douglas, because I've always spoken the truth to you. I've always felt that you understood me and I you. Inside we think alike; we could be brothers, not uncle and nephew, and I repeat what I said: Amy is jealous of her family because they take up my time, they take up my attention, and they take up the love that she thinks should be entirely hers. And when she finally said no more children and — ' he now looked towards the fire as he ended, 'no more of *that*, because *that*, in spite of what I promised, would in the end lead to children, the rift began.

'You see, Douglas, and I must say this to you, your daughter's idea of love is not like yours or Bridget's. Your love for each other is so patent that neither of you has been able to hide the passion of it, not even to this day. But there is no passion in Amy. There is what she terms love, but her love doesn't include the essence that should exist between a husband and wife. Do I need explain further?'

'Dear God! Dear God!' Douglas rose to his feet and went to the fireplace, where he stood looking down on the blazing coals, and like that he muttered, 'I'm grieved, Joseph. I'm grieved to the heart for both of you. She's my daughter and I love her, but I have an equal affection for you, not as a brother, as you said, but as if you were my son, for you came into our household as a baby and my interest in you grew with the years; but I had to keep it under cover, and you know the reason why.'

'What was the reason?' The sharp question caused them both to look towards the door to see Bridget entering; and Douglas realised that he couldn't have shut the door properly or they would have heard it open. But he answered her, saying quickly, 'The reason why the prices of houses are shooting up.'

'Well, what do you imagine the reason to be?'

When he rose but then stood as if thinking up an answer, Joseph put in, 'Profiteers, those people who made a mint during the war and bought up good-class houses for a song.'

'Well, well! Don't forget we bought a number; but of course not large ones, and we paid a fair price. Anyway, how are you feeling?'

'Pretty much the same. I think I like being a semi-invalid and being made a fuss of.'

'Oh, yes, I can imagine how you like being a semi-invalid.' She did not, however, add, 'And being made a fuss of,' but said to Douglas, 'The bell will be going for dinner shortly; you'd better come and tidy up.'

'I don't need to tidy up; I've got a shirt and collar on, woman.'

'And a suit that you wore in the workshop this morning. So, come along.' And she caught hold of his arm, casting a glance back at Joseph as she said, 'Do you think you'll be downstairs tomorrow?'

'Yes, definitely; even if I have to slide down the banister.'

'That's an idea. That's an idea.' Douglas laughed as he allowed Bridget to lead him from the room.

When the sneck clicked, so indicating that the door was closed this time, Joseph leant back on the couch, closed his eyes and asked himself if Douglas would tell Bridget what had really passed between them. He doubted it, for if Douglas could keep the knowledge to himself for twenty years that his brother was a murderer in order to prevent others being hurt, then he wasn't going to hurt his wife by telling her that her daughter was actually a failure as a wife. Anyway, he also doubted if she would believe him . . .

It was quite late the same evening before he had the chance to have a private word with John, who spoke first: 'It's been a very busy day, sir,' he said, 'but I must tell you the ladies were delighted and not a little astonished at the gifts. The box of fruit looked beautiful and the flowers equally so, and I chose a large box of assorted chocolates. I have rarely seen so much pleasure expressed over gifts. I think it was the surprise as much as anything. They sent their very kind enquiries to you. And a very interesting point, sir, which was put over by the daughter in quite a humorous way, but one which I'm sorry I can't emulate for you. Anyway, she told me that the boys who caused your fall came the following day to enquire if you had been really hurt, but that her mother had scared them to death by saying you had died in hospital and they would have the policemen after them shortly. She herself had

had to reassure them, and the way in which she had done so was expressed by the mother in mock sternness; her silly daughter, she said, had then to reward them for causing your distress by giving them an orange and a handful of nuts each. She seems of a very pleasant disposition, the daughter, sir.'

Joseph laughed as he said, 'Poor little beggars. I bet they were scared.'

'Yes, I understand one burst out crying and said his ma would skelp the lugs off him.'

Their laughter joined now, and John ended the conversation by saying more soberly, 'I enjoyed my visit, sir. I felt indeed like Father Christmas, and they both looked like children who had opened their Christmas stockings . . .'

'That's nice,' said Joseph soberly. 'That's nice.'

Christmas Day started early, the girls running from one room to another, saying, 'Thank you, thank you,' for what were merely trivial items, such as articles for their toilet, books, and of course boxes of chocolates. The real presents wouldn't be given out until mid-morning, when the family, together with the staff, would gather round the tree.

It was about half-past ten when Kitty and Bertha dashed into his room, only to come to a dead stop, their hands across their mouths for a moment as they saw their father getting into his shirt. 'Why can't you knock? you hare-brained individuals,' he cried at them as his head appeared through the shirt opening. 'And what do you want?'

It was Kitty who ran towards him and, grabbing the tail of his shirt, said, 'We've come to tuck you in;' and when Bertha joined her sister in tucking his shirt into his trousers, he turned to see John standing at the dressing-room door, his mouth wide with laughter and calling to him, 'You won't need any assistance from me, sir.'

'I'd be glad, John, if you'd help me to get rid of these pests.'

'John wouldn't get rid of us, he's too fond of us,' Bertha shouted and, nodding towards John, informed her father, 'I'm going to marry him when I grow up, aren't I, John?'

'Well, miss, it's something we'll have to go into; and I'm afraid it would have to be a long, long, engagement.'

'How long?'

'Oh, say twenty years at least.'

At this Bertha wagged her hand, saying, 'You'll be an old man then, as old as Daddy,' which brought forth a helpless remonstrance from Joseph: 'Huh! Huh! Get yourselves out, both of you!' he commanded.

'We've come to help you downstairs.'

He turned Kitty about and thrust her towards the door, saying, 'I don't need your help, miss. Get away with you.'

As the door banged behind them he looked towards it and for a moment he knew a feeling of deep happiness. He had a loving family, right from Malcolm down to Bertha . . . And yes; yes, there was good in Malcolm. He might be selfish, but then he had shown himself to be capable of caring. He recalled two years ago when his son was sixteen and Rover, their fourteen-year-old dog, was dying. It had been Malcolm who had sat up two nights in the stable with him, and that dog had died with his head on Malcolm's thigh. And then what had happened? The boy himself had buried the dog, and afterwards had disappeared for a whole day; and when he did return, he had a furious row with his twin, because Willie had said to him he wasn't the only one who cared for Rover. Yes, there was good in Malcolm. His mind suddenly giving him lines from Shakespeare, he muttered:

Finds tongues in trees,
Books in the running brooks,
Sermons in stones,
And good in everything.

Well, he would question that last bit, good in everything
or everyone . . . for there had been very little good in his
father. And yet — he was again questioning, as he had just
done with regard to Malcolm — what about his mistress?
He had loved her, a woman much older than himself and
of no particular attraction, so he understood. Life was
strange.

There had been a great deal of hilarity round the tree:
first, the indoor servants were given their Christmas boxes,
and whether they were gloves, stockings, handkerchiefs
or ties, there was an envelope with each, and in it a gift
of money according to their rank in the household. Add
to these the six outside men, Ron Yarrow, the head
yardman, the gardeners Harry Talbot and James Lom-
bard, the apprentice boy Ben Wallace, then the farmhand
Sam Jones and his assistant Davey Pollard. These latter
two worked under William, who had plumped for farming
rather than, like his brother, university. Without exception, they would declare that the Skinners were a very
good family to work for, even though they all knew that
behind the master stood the wealthy Mr and Mrs Filmore,
and that it was Mr Filmore who really owned the place.
Nevertheless they worked for the Skinners.

Then came the family presents. There was much
laughter from the young people when their father had
given their mother a gold fob watch and in return she had
given him a gold wrist watch; they had all yelled, 'Surprise!
Surprise!' Bridget received a diamond brooch from
Douglas, and she gave him a ruby-studded tiepin and a

number of books, mostly pictorial, showing the works of famous painters and sculptors.

The girls' presents ranged through hats, dresses, skin coats, slippers, and lingerie and lots of accessories; but Henrietta's seemed to fall within the latter category only, and this did not please her, so that she showed how she was feeling when Bertha opened her present from Joseph and in delight held up a winter coat, fur hat and gloves to match: she retreated to a corner where she sat sulking.

When Jonathan unpacked the long box to discover a much used violin case with a violin inside, his eyes filled with tears. He had already shown promise of becoming an exceptionally good instrumentalist, and although this was not, of course, a Stradivarius, he knew instantly it was of great value, and before he even picked it up he went and threw his arms around first Bridget, and then Douglas.

Towards the end of the present-giving, however, it was noted that the twins had had no exceptional gift, no gold watches, no tiepins; socks, ties, and handkerchiefs, yes, but nothing exciting.

It was when there had come a slight lull on the gathering that Douglas, looking at his grandsons, said, 'Well, you two, your presents are outside. You wouldn't expect us to bring them in, would you?'

At this there was a stir: although the twins remained quiet while looking questioningly at their parents and then at their grandparents, the girls were already running down the drawing-room, crying, 'What are they? What are they?'

A minute later all the youngsters were outside, with the elders gathering around the doorway and the servants at the long windows, there to see Malcolm standing beside a two-seater car, while William stood gazing at the horse that John, with a wide grin on his face, was holding.

As if of one mind they both turned towards the house now and slowly shook their heads from side to side. It was in this movement that they showed, as they seldom did, that they were from the same seed, for their actions were simultaneous; even the expression on their faces held the same look of surprise and gratitude.

The girls were now shouting to each of them in turn, 'Get in!' or 'Get on it!' And in answer, William put his foot in the stirrup and hoisted himself onto the saddle, while Malcolm jumped into the car; but when he switched on the ignition, the roar of the engine made the horse toss its head nervously and stamp forward and William to swing round on the saddle, crying, 'Turn that damn thing off, you idiot!'

When order was restored the twins, again as if of one mind, left their respective Christmas boxes and hurried towards the groups standing in the doorway and, as if the car and the horse were of the same sex, expressed their thanks: 'Oh, thank you, thank you, Grandpa. She's wonderful. She's wonderful!' only for Douglas to say, 'Don't thank me, it was your father.'

'*Really! Oh, Dad!*'

When they both grabbed his hand, Joseph shouted, 'Watch out! you pair of idiots, you'll have me on my back again.'

And so ended the Christmas present-giving.

There was more chaffing when Malcolm, pushing his brother, exclaimed, 'You go and put your nag in the stable; I want to try out my baby,' and the diversion created by their pushing at each other and running from the hall seemed itself to create a new one, for Henrietta, who was now standing to the side of Joseph, exclaimed in her loudest form of articulation, 'I ... would ... like ... a ... car!' And when, amid soothing remarks from Bridget and laughing exclamations from the girls, she happened to look towards Bertha, who too was laughing, and she read her lips as she said to Kitty, 'As you say, lass, that would be the day, Henrietta in a car,' her body seemed to leap past Bridget, and when she grabbed the little woman by the shoulders she almost lifted her from the floor as she screeched, 'Yes! Me . . . in . . . a . . . car . . . in . . . a . . . car! I could . . . You old ha . . . ha . . . hag.'

As Douglas grabbed hold of Henrietta's arms, Joseph's hands came out and slapped her face so hard that the force of it sent her staggering back, her body jangling and a hand clasping at her cheek like a child who had been chastised.

There was a momentary silence before Joseph, turning his back on Henrietta, put out his arm and guided the definitely startled old woman towards the drawing-room, to be followed by the rest, except Bridget who, standing in front of Henrietta, said quietly, 'Come upstairs and rest. The excitement's been too much for you.'

'No! No!'

Bridget's voice and expression now changing, she said emphatically, *'Yes! Yes!* And this minute!'

Again like a chastised child, Henrietta did as she was bidden, but definitely under protest, for her arms, legs and head were now all in a highly agitated state.

In the drawing room Alice was saying to Bertha, 'Did she hurt you?'

'No, no, lass; and it was my own fault, I should have watched my tongue.'

'What did you say?'

Before she could answer Kitty said, 'She only repeated what I said: That'll be the day when she drives a car.'

'Is that all? And that's why she went for you?'

'Now, now, Alice,' said Douglas. 'Let's forget about her.'

'That'll take some doing.' It was the first comment Amy had made, and Douglas turned and looked at his daughter, and agreed solemnly, saying, 'Yes, dear, you're right. But it's Christmas Day; come on, come on, all of you. By! weren't the boys amazed. I've never seen such genuine pleasure on anyone's face for a long time.'

'Oh! Grandpa; then you didn't look at my face when I saw my violin.' Jonathan sounded so disappointed. 'Of all the things in the world I've hoped for, that's always been the top, a good violin. Not that' – he was nodding now towards his father – 'the one that you bought me wasn't good, but . . . well, you know what I mean.'

'Yes. Yes, indeed, Jonathan, I know what you mean. You mean that the one I bought you didn't cost a quarter as much as that one.' Joseph now nodded to where the violin case lay on a side table.

'Oh! Dad.'

'Never mind oh dadding me.' Joseph made a gesture of flapping his son aside; but then smiled at him and said, 'Well, you want to get some practice in for the jig tonight. And you, too, Alice, get at that piano. How many are coming?' and he turned questioningly towards Amy; and she, after thinking a moment, said, 'Well, there'll be Malcolm's two friends,' which brought a quick retort from Jonathan who, lifting his chin as far as it would go, said, 'The sons of Sir Arnold and Lady Fordyce, Masters James and Percy.'

'They're not half as stuck up as you are.'

'Now, now, Kitty,' said Amy; then went on, 'Then there's William's friends, the Robsons, Arthur and Hazel. And yours, Alice, Winnie and her two brothers.'

'Oh, yes, don't forget the Barnett brothers,' put in Jonathan now.

'No!' Alice retaliated sharply to her brother; 'nor your friends Sam McBane and his Irish cousin begorra, Patrick.'

494

'Well, there's one thing to be said for begorra Patrick,' Joseph said, trying to calm the situation, 'if anybody can get you laughing it's him. In the end he'll likely turn out to be a Catholic priest, because he's always laughing at himself and his religion.'

'Anyway,' said Kitty now, 'with the Robsons, to my reckoning that's seven males and three females, and counting us there's an extra male. Well, that's as it should be, I suppose.'

Joseph had quietly gone to Bertha, and he asked her, 'How you feeling?'

'I'm all right, fine.'

'Would you like to go and lie down?'

'Lie down? No! of course not. Anyway I'm looking forward to that dance tonight.' She now looked past him and spoke to the girls, saying, 'I'll dance you off your legs, you'll see. I can still do the clog dance, you know. I had a real dancing pair of feet for it at one time. You'll see, you'll have to look out for your lads else you'll lose 'em.'

Almost as though it were an invitation, William approached Bertha, made a deep obeisance towards her and in a high-toned voice said, 'May I have the pleasure of this dance, Miss Bertha?' only for her to come back at him, she, too, adopting a high-falutin' voice, saying, 'No, sir; I'm afraid you can't; me programme's full.' And she held out her hand as if presenting the programme to him. 'What's more, I understand that you are in the band providing the music, and I have always made it a point never to dance with bandsmen. They can never be trusted; they're worse than sailors.'

Amid the general laughter Amy rose and went from the room unnoticed, except apparently by Joseph. That was another thing that irked him: she could never stand or appreciate Bertha's humour. She had never really taken to her right from the beginning. He felt he knew why, and it didn't come into the heading of possessiveness.

The partition between the drawing-room and dining-room had been pushed back and Alice at the piano and Jonathan on his violin had provided music for a number of dances. At first, the visiting guests had shown decorum by their politeness, but after a couple of games of musical chairs and winkey, the decorum seemed to have been pushed into the background, and when Bertha actually demonstrated that she could still do the clog dance, even in a pair of soft leather shoes, she was applauded uproariously.

It was now time for refreshments and the old and the young were scattered about the room, plates on their knees, cups and glasses held carefully away from their dresses or suits. A couple sitting at the end of the conservatory on a slatted form had lain their plates and wine glasses to the side of them, and Alice, nibbling politely on a sandwich, gazed at her partner, while her heart was pumping at more than its usual rate, the exertion being not due to her dancing but to the effect that this young man was having on her. It was not a new effect, for she had first experienced it nearly a year ago at a school friend's birthday party.

He was saying to her, 'You have left school for good? I mean, you are not going on to another?'

'No. No . . . well, not to school as such; I'm going to study under a very good music teacher.'

'You play beautifully.'

'Thank you.'

The young man looked along the length of the conservatory, then glanced sidewards through the open doors into the drawing-room and said, 'This is a beautiful house.'

'Yes. Yes, it is; and . . . and you know something? This seat here' — she patted it — 'it was really here, right just here, that my grandparents first met. There used to be a big palm tree' – she pointed – 'cutting off the view of the drawing-room, and two men were quarrelling behind the palm and it almost fell on grandmother ... And what happened that night was to set off a train of events' – she shook her head – 'which you certainly wouldn't believe.'

'Oh yes, I would. I ... I know quite a bit about the history of your family.'

Her face became straight, her tone a little defensive now as she said, 'Well, then, I ... I suppose you were shocked.'

'Shocked?' He laughed. 'Shocked, because you had a rake of a grandfather? I'll tell you something.' He leant towards her and looked into her eyes as he said, 'You and I are close in more ways than one. Well, what I mean is, we are associated through our family because my grandmother, Daisy, was the mistress of your notorious grandfather. Their association, I understand, went on for a long time, years, ten years or more.'

'Really?' She was biting on her lip now, her face wide with suppressed laughter, and when he nodded at her and said, 'Yes, really. They were very naughty, a disgrace to both families. But if your grandfather was a bit of a roué, my grandmother was a devious woman, if all tales were true. In fact she even played the dirty on her lover. I'm the youngest of a family of ten; I'm what you might call an overspill. It was never intended that I should be born, and my father always became enraged, I understand, when ... the disgrace was mentioned. But from my eldest brother, who was eighteen years older than me, right down to my sister, who was seven years my senior, and there are twins in our family, too, well, we all enjoyed the story and – ' He paused now and, taking her hand and in a low voice, he said, 'When I first met you, Alice, I thought how strange, how very strange that I should fall in love with the granddaughter of that man.' And now there was a plea in his voice: 'Alice, tell me: Do you like me?' She could only mutter, 'Oh! Oh! Roger, more than like, more than like . . .'

Just as years before a couple had been distracted by the noise and gaiety from the ballroom, so now the scraping of a chair, likely the very one that Bridget had vacated all those years ago for the seat behind the palm, was also blotted out; but not Kitty's face, as she appeared in the doorway and grinned at them before turning away.

Kitty now looked around the room and sighting her father hobbling past the partition that divided the rooms, she ran towards him and, taking his arm and her face full of glee, she said, 'Daddy! Daddy! You'll never guess. Roger . . . Roger Barnett is making love to Alice in the conservatory. And you know what he said, and who he is?'

She was surprised when he suddenly growled at her, 'Shut up! Come this way.' He now caught hold of her arm and, hobbling, he drew her to the far end of the corridor to his study and pushed her in, saying, 'Well, now you may spill the rest.'

'Oh, Daddy. Well, I didn't mean . . .'

'Never mind what you meant, just tell me what you were going to say.'

'Well . . . well . . . I didn't mean to listen.'

'You're always listening, Kitty; but that's no fault, except when you repeat what you hear. In this case though, repeat it to me exactly.'

'Well, he said that his father, I mean his grandmother, was the mistress of our grandfather.'

Barnett? Barnett? Daisy Barnett? Yes, he knew all about Daisy Barnett.

'Had our grandfather a mistress? or was he making it up or . . .?'

He limped forward to his seat behind the desk, then

beckoned her to him, and when she was standing by his knee he took her hand and said, 'Now, on no account, do you hear me? on no account, must you repeat this to anybody. There has been a great deal of scandal in this family. You know nothing about it yet. Your grandmother has gone through a great deal of trouble, as have I, and one day you will likely hear the whole story and from the horse's mouth, and that will be mine, or if not mine, your grandfather's. Your grandmother's version might be biased, and she would certainly be biased in this case if she knew Alice was becoming involved with a young man whose grandmother had caused her beloved cousin, Victoria, that is, or was, Henrietta's mother, a great deal of grief. Now you understand what I mean? I know it's puzzling you, but listen: I want you to promise me you'll say nothing about what you overheard tonight passing between Alice and that young man. Now, your solemn promise?'

'Yes, Daddy. I'm ... and I'm sorry. I just ... well I thought it was ... funny, especially about the woman being the mistress ...'

'Do you know what a mistress in that sense means?'

She stared at him blankly for a moment; then, a small smile on her face, she said, 'Well, it doesn't mean a schoolmistress, it means a woman who is wicked and entices a gentleman from his wife and family.'

'Yes, I suppose that's what it means; but the woman need not be wicked, and in some cases neither is the man. But in the case we're talking about neither of them were very nice people; at least, I can speak for one of the parties. But now go back and join the company, and when you see Alice, don't give her that look you sometimes do which says, I know something that you don't know.'

'Do I look like that, Daddy?'

'Yes, you do.' He rose to his feet. 'Remember when

Malcolm was smoking and he set fire to the hay in the loft but he and Willie managed to put it out? And what did little Kitty do? Came to me and said, Daddy, I know something that you don't know. Do you remember?'

Kitty's head drooped, then she looked up at him under her eyebrows and said, 'Well, I know something else that you don't know, Daddy; I'd had a puff at a cigarette, too, that day.'

'What!'

As she went to scamper from him his hand caught her across the bottom, and she ran out squealing merrily, leaving him standing and shaking his head.

He sat down again and placed his elbows on the table and dropped his chin into his hand, and he nodded to himself as he said, 'What is a mistress?' There was indeed a funny side to this: Daisy's grandson and Bridget's granddaughter. But he couldn't laugh about it because the moment it came into the open, Lionel Filmore would rise again from the dead. Bridget would see to that.

4

'You did well to get it for six-eighty.'

'Well, I pointed out to her that it would take a few hundreds to put it into order before we could let it. It's a real mess inside, and there's a bit of dry rot in the basement; and anyway, she's not without a penny: she's pretty warm, I should imagine, and she doesn't really need money.'

'A lot of people don't' — Bridget pursed her lips at him — 'but they'll still beat you down to the last farthing if they can. By the way, Douglas and I were talking last night: we think it's only fair that you should be working under your own name. What do you say to that?'

What Joseph wanted to say was, 'You mean Filmore?' But that would get her back up. Yet strangely, if he were to say it to Douglas he wouldn't mind in the least. In fact, he would say what he had said before: If everyone had their due, that would be your name. So he said, 'That's nice of you.'

His tone was not exactly one of kindly acceptance, and she sensed this and moved some papers on her desk before looking at him again: 'It would please Amy, too, don't you think?' she said.

Now he was unable to hedge, and so he said, 'I don't think she is interested one way or another in what name I work under.'

'*What is the matter with you these days, Joseph?*'

Before answering, he leant towards her across the desk and, looking her straight in the face, he said, 'You should put that to your daughter, Bridget. And you know as well as I do what's the matter with me, only you've closed your eyes to it. But being her mother, you have likely spoken to her woman to woman about this matter.'

He slowly drew himself backwards as he saw her face flushing scarlet, and she snapped, 'I don't go into my daughter's private life.'

'Well then, without going into it, you've been married long enough to know what oils a marriage.'

'*Really! Really! Joseph.*' She had risen to her feet, but he laughed now as he said, 'Oh, don't pretend you're shocked, Bridget, not you. Anyway, to get back to the question that led up to this matter, what will my new status entail?'

Her voice was stiff as she replied, 'It would entail that what business you get in future will be your own; and don't say, not before time, because that, I know, is what you think. But don't forget, over all these years, it is we who have kept The Grove going.'

'No. No, I don't forget that, Bridget; nor do I forget that it isn't my home. It belongs to Douglas and, therefore, you, and when anything happens to Douglas it will go to my eldest son, although not of necessity because the place isn't entailed, but because my eldest son is also the son of your daughter. Oh, I know all that, but when I'm told not to forget certain things, I would remind you, Bridget, that I worked the first six years on that house for practically nothing, but I looked upon it as payment for my schooling at your expense. Yet, at the same time, I considered you were getting good interest on it. We're speaking plainly now, aren't we? And for the last fourteen years I've worked in your business. Oh, yes, I've been well paid, but that was on percentage, too. So, I feel that what you're offering now is somewhat overdue. Yes, overdue. So, I'll say good day to you, Bridget, and go about . . . your business, or what in future is going to be mine.'

Bridget sank back into her chair and looked at the door that had just banged closed and she told herself that there indeed went the son of Lionel Filmore. Oh yes, indeed.

In the street, Joseph got into his car and he drove straight to Bradford Villa. He opened the door and passed into the musty hall; and there he stood, leaning with his back against the wall, feeling that he had just stepped out of Bridget's office, for he could still see the look on her face.

Well – he stepped back from the wall – she wouldn't go back on her word. From now on he'd be in business on his own, but he felt sure that the change had come about through Douglas's suggestion and not hers.

He walked slowly through the house, seeing immediately the work that needed to be done: a wall down here, a bathroom there. It could be made into a really nice house.

The garden, he saw, didn't take up more than half an acre of the land, and there was all that field beyond. He stood at the corner of the outbuildings looking across the field. He reckoned that if he added another half acre to the garden, or even a bit more, there would be sufficient land left to build four good houses right up to the wall of Mrs Dunn's off-licence.

Mrs Dunn's off-licence? He should call in and thank them personally. He had thought about them a number of times during the past few weeks.

He turned quickly, locked up the house, got into his car and drove down the main road until he came to Downey's Passage, then drove up to the shop . . . past it, parked his car, then got out.

He stood for a moment looking in the shop window at

the display of spirit bottles before going in. There was no one in the shop, but the door bell had rung.

When the woman appeared behind the counter she began by saying, 'Yes, sir? An' what can I do . . .?' Then on a high note she exclaimed, 'Why! Mr Skinner. Why! Come along in. Come along in, sir.' She whipped up the counter flap and he passed through, saying, 'I just thought I would like to come and thank you personally . . .'

'Go on through. Liz has just made a cup of coffee.' Her voice rose: 'Liz! see who's here?'

There was no one in the sitting-room, but her daughter's voice came from the kitchen apparently, saying, 'Oh, has Nibbles come back?'

At this Mrs Dunn let out a roar of laughter and, looking at Joseph, she explained, 'That's the cat, Nibbles. Sit yourself down.'

He was smiling as he sat down in the chair he recalled sitting in before, and he also recalled now the cheery atmosphere of this room and the two women.

He heard the daughter's voice saying, 'Two nights on the tiles is one too many.' Then she appeared in the far doorway, bearing a tray on which were two cups of coffee and a plate of biscuits.

She stopped dead for a moment before exclaiming, 'Good lord! You said it was the cat.' She looked at her mother, then back to Joseph; and now she said, 'Hello, there.'

'Hello,' he replied. 'I . . . I thought it was about time I came and said thank you in person.'

'Oh, I think you said it well enough on Christmas Eve. It's we who've got to thank you. Look' – she put down the tray – 'I'll make another cup of coffee. You'd like a cup of coffee?'

'Yes, please. Yes, I would like a cup of coffee,' he said, nodding at her, and she nodded back and said, 'Well, your wish is my command,' and disappeared into the kitchen again on a laugh; and he looked at the older woman and smiled. The atmosphere in this house, or room, was relaxing. That was the only way he could put a name to his feeling at this moment.

'Was it a bad do, I mean, your foot?'

'Well, it took longer than I thought before I was able to walk.'

'Yes; your man told us about it.' And her voice dropping, she said, 'He's your butler, isn't he?'

'Well, that's the name he goes under, but he's a bit of everything. He runs the house and he's a very good fellow altogether.'

'Yes, he seems a nice man. Thinks a lot of you.' Her head was bobbing at him. She turned as her daughter was entering the room and said, 'The butler man, he thinks a lot of his master, doesn't he, by what he said to us?'

Liz handed Joseph the cup of coffee and said, 'My mother has a great respect for family retainers,' stressing the last two words.

He smiled up into her face, saying, 'And you haven't?' And she answered him, 'Not much. But she' – she thumbed towards her mother – 'was brought up on an estate. Her father, my grandfather, was groom to a . . . Scottish Laird' – she again stressed the last two words – 'but then an awful Englishman comes riding by and whips her away to this God-forsaken country.' She laughed. 'That's what my grandfather used to call England, but I say thank God for it. And my grandfather's still bending his knee to his Scottish Laird.'

'You're glad enough to spend your holidays up there, madam, and run wild on a pony and chat with the master.'

'Ah! Ah!' Liz now pointed her finger at Joseph, saying, 'That's the word. It always niggles me, "the master". The very word conjures up slavery.'

'Get out of me way. Just listen to her. Will you have a biscuit, sir?'

'No; thank you, Mrs Dunn.'

'Don't take any notice to what she says, sir. She talks like a communist at times, and she says she doesn't vote Labour or Conservative. You know, to this day I don't know who she votes for. But I know what I vote for.' And she let out a loud laugh before she added, 'A good dinner, a drop of the hard, and a good night's rest. What more could you want?'

'What more indeed!'

He seemed to be smiling all the time.

Mrs Dunn now said, 'Were you on business round this way, sir?'

'Yes, you could say that. I've . . . I've just bought the villa.' He pointed towards the wall. 'I'm in the land and estate business, you know.'

'Oh. Oh, are you? And the villa. Oh my! what are you going to do with it?'

'Well, renovate it I hope; then it'll be for letting.'

'Oh, the old girl who lived there was a caution.'

The shop bell rang loudly, so saying, 'Oh, dear, here we go! A woman's work is never done,' Mrs Dunn trotted out of the room. Taking a seat on the other side of the fireplace and looking straight at Joseph, Liz explained, 'That last exchange with mother may have sounded very class-conscious, but I'm always teasing her about Sir Gilbert, because she's proud of her association with that house.'

He leaned towards her and there was a quirk to his lips as he said, 'But at rock bottom you are not, are you?'

She laid her head back against the top of the tall chair and gave a little chuckle before she gave her answer: 'Perhaps. Then again, I'm not against having to work for someone; we're all working for someone really. We here, in this business, have our masters, but we do seem to have a greater amount of freedom allowed us than in some others, and I've always been against the hold one human being has over another, whether it's in employment or in the family.'

'What about marriage?'

He hadn't meant to say that, but it had come out.

'Yes, you've got a point there. But mine didn't last long enough to test it. I was married a fortnight when he went to France. It was in the middle of nineteen-eighteen, and he was killed within a month.'

The statement sounded unemotional, but he said, 'Oh, I'm sorry. That must have been awful for you. You've got to ask the reason why these . . .'

'I'm sorry,' she cut in sharply now, 'but I think that is a stupid question, that "why"? I myself asked it at the time, but the answer I got was, why should I be asking it? when John was one of a million or more who died. That particular "why" has never been answered and never will be.'

He sat staring at her. The jocular, funny-retort daughter was gone: here was a thinking young woman. She was asking a question now: 'Were you in the war?'

'No. They wouldn't have me; I must have been quite rotten. I tried three or four times, but from my eyes to the soles of my feet they seemed to find something wrong with me.'

And how he had tried to get into that war, not because he wanted to serve King and country, but simply to get away from the war that was brewing around him.

He said, 'Your name isn't Dunn then?' And she answered, 'No, it's Lilburn.'

'Oh, I know a number of Lilburns. Well . . . I mean, they're on the books.'

'Yes, no doubt, because we're a common lot.'

She was smiling again; and when he stated, 'Well, I'm glad you said that, not me, else likely I would be taking my leave through the let-in counter by now,' she laughed loudly as she agreed, 'No doubt. No doubt.'

After a short silence he asked, 'Have you lived here long?'

'Well, they tell me I was born upstairs some twenty-nine years ago. There! my age is out,' and she pulled a face at him now before going on, 'My father owned the house, and the business, too. It was a free house. Well, you know what that means, we can buy where we like.'

'Your father's dead then?'

'Yes, about six years ago. He was elderly, being twenty-two years older than mother, and — ' She now shook her head before going on, 'It's unbelievable, but that was thought terrible in those days. Baby-snatching, they called it. Yet they were very happy together. But then, my mother is a very easy-going woman. I don't think I would have been very happy if I had been married to a man like my father.'

'The master, was he?' He poked his head towards her.

'Yes. Yes. Very possessive.'

There was that word again, possessive. 'You don't like possessive people then?'

'It isn't that I don't like them, I cannot understand what motivates them, unless it is an inadequacy in themselves, some deep want, and in order to alleviate it in some way, they hang on to another human being. It's a sort of desire for power. Those who run businesses are possessed in a similar way. They have power over people; and very often, on their whims depends a man's livelihood.'

He nodded slowly in agreement, and said, 'Have you ever thought of getting on the council?'

'Me! on the council?' She pulled herself forward on the chair. 'The only thing I would want to get on the council for is to tell them what I think about their stupidity. Do you know, they're going to pull Coin Street down. Those beautiful old houses. Do you know the street?'

'Yes. Yes, I do.'

'Well, have you looked at the fanlights and the railed balconies?' She shook her head. 'They're really beautiful, and that cotton wool-brained lot want to pull them down; to build more shops, I suppose.'

'Then why, if you feel so strongly, don't you do something about it? As I said, get on the council.'

She pursed her lips. 'I have no desire to put the world straight and I wouldn't be so presumptuous,' she said. 'Anyway, I have enough trouble keeping my own life in order. I'm like many another, I suppose, I sit back and criticise, knowing that if I got the chance to do something definite I'd be afraid to take it.'

He sat looking at her. Here was a young woman who knew herself. He was amazed at her viewpoint, and at her level-headedness, and when he asked her, 'Have you been in any other business?' he was even more surprised at her answer.

'Oh, yes; I was secretary to a Mr Blythe, of Bayards Engineering Works, from when I was nineteen. But when Father died I left because Mother was in rather a state at that time, and very lonely.'

He knew Arthur Blythe of Bayards. He had met him through Douglas. He said, 'Did you enjoy that kind of work?'

'Yes, very much.'

'But ah' — his finger was wagging at her now — 'you were working under a master.'

'Yes, I suppose so; but he was a very benevolent one and he made no demands upon me. He left me free to run the office.' She preened herself now as she said, 'I suppose I should be flattered. But I had a letter from him last week asking me if I would think about returning. I imagine his secretaries have come and gone rather speedily over the past five years, because, as I remember him, he couldn't suffer fools gladly . . . I sound big-headed, don't I? But that was one job I knew, the only job. And I certainly would have been a dud-head if I hadn't carried it out with some efficiency, because after leaving school at sixteen I went for three years to a Secretarial College. Anyway, why am I giving you the story of my life? You called in just to say thank you, and now you are being burdened, and bored . . .'

'I am certainly not being either burdened or bored. Now I'm going to tell you something. I've never felt so relaxed or at ease anywhere for a long time. The day I found myself in this room things were hazy, yet during the week or so that followed they seemed to clarify themselves, and I've often found myself thinking about it and the two kind ladies who saw to me. And there was a gentleman, too, wasn't there?'

'Yes, Bill. He was a friend of my father's and has remained my mother's friend since.'

At this point Mrs Dunn entered the kitchen, saying, 'That was a shipping order, a packet of Woodbines, a packet of Player's Weights, and five empties brought back, with a pound's worth of gossip from Mrs Chaytors,' and without seeming even to draw breath she was addressing Joseph directly: 'Will you stay and have a bite? Liz has got a hot-pot on and although some of her cooking I wouldn't give to a dog, I can vouch for her hot-pot.'

Laughing, he rose to his feet, the cup still in his hand, and he handed it to the older woman, saying, 'She also makes a good cup of coffee; I'll vouch for that. Thank you for the invitation, but I must be off. I, too, have got to earn a living, you know.' He was glancing at the young woman now, and her reply was, 'And I'm sure you are worked to death.'

'Eeh! She's a cheeky monkey, is my daughter. And I must apologise for her. But there you are; you are welcome any time you are passing.'

'Well, I can assure you now, Mrs Dunn, I'll take up your invitation whenever I'm this way, and that will be quite often, I should imagine, when I'm seeing to the alterations of the villa. But now I'll say again, the reason for this particular visit was to thank you for your kindness, both of you.' And at this, saying, 'Good-bye, Mrs Lilburn,' he turned and, accompanied by Mrs Dunn, went from the room . . .

A minute or so later Janet Dunn had returned to the kitchen and said to her daughter, 'By! isn't he a nice man.'

'Mother!'

'All right, all right, girl. I was just saying, isn't he a nice man.'

'Yes, and I've heard you say that before. Well, don't forget that this one is married and has *six* children.'

'Well, lass, the Bible's a good book and in it it says, Solomon had quite a number of wives.'

When her daughter pushed at her none too gently, then had to steady her against falling, their laughter joined . . .

Out in the street Joseph walked slowly to his car, but it was odd that he should feel reluctant to get into it. He had the desire to walk, even back across the fields towards the villa, for he had the impression that the iron gates of The Grove had opened and he had passed through into freedom. It was an odd feeling like that which overcame him at times, as if he were in a dream, yet knowing that it was no dream, and often that had been the frightening part of it. But not this time.

5

'It's scandalous! It shouldn't be allowed.'

'Oh, Bridget, Bridget, my dear.'

'Don't use that tone to me, as if I was a narrow-minded woman. Don't you realise that that young man is the grandson of your brother's mistress, and was for ten years or more, and must have cost poor Victoria real heartache?'

'My dear Bridget, if I'm to go by what Bright told me, Victoria was thankful that he had such a diversion, for it kept him out of the house and out of her sight, and she was certainly more than thankful that it kept him out of Henrietta's way. Anyway, my dear, Joseph is her father, and he likes the young man and he's given his consent, and Amy can do nothing whatever about it. Anyway, what's it to do with her? These outraged feelings are simply another way of expressing her frustration or whatever's happening to her at this time. She had no real knowledge of Victoria; in fact, I realised it, whether you did or not, my dear, that during the short time Victoria was with us before she died, Amy had taken a dislike to her. Perhaps it was because you were then showering your affection upon her and Henrietta. In a way, you were making up for the loss of Amy in your life, and our dear daughter was quick to recognise that she was being easily replaced.'

'Oh, Douglas, you file everything down to a hair's breadth.'

He bent forward and took her hand, saying, 'But you know inside that logical head of yours that I'm right; and I can tell you this much, and I can see it happening, our dear granddaughter, Alice, though a very sweet girl, has a strong streak in her that she may have inherited from' – he pulled a face now – 'her grandmother, and should her mother lead her hell – oh yes, my dear Bridget, that's what Amy's doing at the present moment – well, I can see our granddaughter, who is verging on eighteen, just picking up her skirts and walking out, if not actually running out. Apparently she said as much to her father.'

'Has . . . has Joseph been talking about this to you?'

'Of course, my dear, he's been talking about this to me. Who else would he discuss it with? Amy is up in arms at the very thought of it. By the way, as we are mentioning Joseph, I think my . . . our . . . your decision to give him a free hand was a very good move, at least for him, because he's changed, hasn't he? He's not so cool or taciturn as he has been of late, more free and easy. Has Amy said anything to you? Oh, come on, come on, she talks to you, as Joseph talks to me.'

'Yes, she talks to me but about nothing of importance with regard to Joseph, except that since he has taken up the business on his own, he is hardly ever at home.'

'Well, why don't you point out to her, dear, that he would stay at home if there was . . . well, less quarrelling.'

'It takes two to make a quarrel, Douglas.'

'Yes, I suppose so. Anyway, there's more news, good and bad, that I can tell you. I saw Joseph this morning. I ran across him as I was going to pick you up, but there was plenty of time, so we had a coffee together, and he told me rather gleefully that there was another courting in the offing. Malcolm has apparently been introduced to James Fordyce's cousin Delia. She is, by the way, Lady Delia, the only daughter of Lord Breck. So, of course, that would please Amy, wouldn't it? But the bad news is, Amy says if he doesn't do something to stop Henrietta coming over to the house, evidently just to see him, then the next time she appears she will lock the doors on her. Now, it was natural for Joseph at this stage to ask me what I was going to do about it, and now I ask you, dear, what are we going to do about it? She slipped Nell's coils last week and we thought that was impossible . . . Bridget – ' He took hold of both her hands and looking fully into her face he said, 'I'll soon be sixty-seven years old, and you are sixty-three, so have you thought what will happen to her when we go, as go we must, sooner or later? And she's likely to go on living for many more years yet. So, I ask you, what will happen to her? She'll have to be put under some restraint.'

'Yes, I know, Douglas. I've thought of that; in fact I've thought about it a lot.'

'Oh, I'm glad to hear that, dear. I know how fond you are of her.'

She smiled at him now as she said, 'Not as fond as I once was. I suppose it's age, but I find her a trial at times. At the same time, though, I cannot bear to think of her incarcerated in any asylum, not as I know them to be.'

'There are private places, dear.'

'Yes, I have thought of that, too.'

'Well now, dear' – he gripped her hands more tightly – 'when we are on these serious subjects I must tell you what has been in my mind for some time, too, and that is, I think the house . . . The Grove, should be left entirely to Joseph. I've always thought it to be his by rights, and so . . .'

'*Oh, no! Douglas*. What about Amy?'

'She is his wife, dear, and naturally her son would inherit.'

'But she expects him to inherit in any case, I mean . . .'

'Dearest' – he let go of her hands – 'I know what you mean, but Joseph is a strong-willed man; I wouldn't like to come up against him in a Court of Justice. And there is something afoot in Parliament. I think it's merely at the discussion stage, but . . . but there are, I surmise, a number of men up there, you know, with offspring in the same position as Joseph, and they are men of some honour who want to see justice done, and so it is they who will be putting this bill forward, which will allow an illegitimate son the right to inherit, at least, where an estate is entailed, give the owner of that estate the power to will it in specific words to his illegitimate son. But, in the case of Joseph, should he take it into his head to press his claim, then I would be the only one standing in his way. And just think, dear, if my ancestors hadn't willed it that the estate should pass to the male line, it could have gone to Henrietta, God forbid.'

'Would you have said "God forbid" if it was to pass to your own daughter?'

'No, I wouldn't.'

'Well, in that case it should pass to her son.'

'It will in time, dear.'

'I don't agree with you in this, Douglas, so let us think it over. Shall we?'

'Yes, dear, just as you wish.' He dare not say at this point, I've already put the wheels in motion, because he knew she was definitely playing for time to talk him round to her way of thinking, which she usually managed to do . . . But not this time.

She was sitting now with her hands tightly clasped on her knees as she said, 'I hate age. I hate getting old. It changes so many things. I never thought, for instance, we would sell the factories. I miss going there, you know.'

He nodded at her, and was saying, 'Yes, I know, dear,' when the door was thrust open and in the framework a tall woman stood silently looking at them, and this brought Bridget swiftly to her feet, saying, 'Oh, no! Nell. No!'

'We were near the bus station, madam. I had turned to

515

the flower stall and said, "Wouldn't it be nice to take your aunt some flowers back?" and when she didn't answer I looked round and' – the woman now shook her head – 'the bus was moving off and I saw her jumping on to it. She'll be making for the house again. I'm so sorry, madam, but at times I think she's really getting beyond me.'

Bridget was hurrying from the room now, saying, 'I must phone Amy,' but Douglas stopped her, calling, 'No! No, don't. Amy will do as she said, she won't let her in. I'll go and get her, don't worry. I'll likely get there as quick as the bus, that's if she hasn't taken the through one. Did you see what bus she took, Nell?'

'No, sir. I was so taken aback. It was too far away.'

'I'll come with you,' Bridget said, and he did nothing to stop her.

They were standing in the hall. Amy was facing Henrietta, and she was mouthing in no small voice, 'I've . . . told . . . you, he . . . won't . . . be in . . . till . . . late. He works late in his office. I . . . keep . . . telling . . . you.'

'I . . . want . . . to stay. I can . . . go . . . back . . . tomorrow.'

'You are not staying here, Henrietta. I've told you before.'

Henrietta looked about her, to one side where stood Malcolm, then to the other towards the green-baized door that led into the kitchen and where John was standing, and her words seemed to embrace them all as she cried, 'This was . . . my home . . . before . . . it was . . . yours. I . . . I have . . . a right here . . . I can stay . . . as long as . . . I like. It was . . . my grandfather's . . . house. It should . . . have been . . . mine.' She had not mentioned her father. 'It . . . is . . . mine.'

Amy came back at her, crying, 'It never was yours! It is my house and I say you can't stay here.' Amy now

516

turned and looked at Malcolm and, lowering her voice, she said, 'Get your car out and take her back.'

'No, Mother. No.' His voice too was low, scarcely audible, but he forgot at the moment that the large objectionable creature, as he viewed her, was standing near him and could lip read, and he went on, 'I've promised to meet . . . well, I'm going to Delia's for tea. As for having her in the car with her bulk, no! Mother. She shouldn't be at large anyway; she should be locked up. You've said all this, but if I had my way . . .'

His voice trailed off as he saw his mother put her hand tightly over her mouth and John move swiftly from his position near the kitchen door. But it was too late.

Henrietta had taken in only bits of what Malcolm had said, because he hadn't been facing her directly. But when she moved so that she was able to read his last words, she was lifted back into the past, and she saw the young man immediately change: he was taller and broader, but his face remained the same. It was that of her father and he was going to put her away, lock her up, take her from her mama. Her body jangling, she sprang: it became the continuation of the day she had encountered her father on the landing.

As her nails tore down Malcolm's cheek she screamed, and so did he, and they were locked together for a while before John and Amy managed to drag her from him. John had gripped her throat and so had almost checked her breathing. This had loosened her hold, but in the ensuing struggle she slipped and fell on the floor; and as if handling a big bale, John rolled her onto her face, then put one knee on her back while he yelled at the two maids, who had made their startled appearance on the stairs, 'Get the men! Ron, and one of the others.'

Amy had pressed Malcolm onto a hall chair and was now wiping his face with a handkerchief, repeating as she

517

did so, 'It's all right. It's all right;' but when he muttered, 'My eye,' she said, 'It's the blood running from your brow. Don't worry. Don't worry, dear. Oh, my God! My God! I knew this would happen. She's a maniac, she's mad. Always has been. When I get to that telephone I'll make my mother see that this is the final straw.'

But there was no need for her to get to the telephone to her mother, for almost at that instant, through the open door came both Bridget and Douglas, and Douglas, taking in the scene, muttered, 'Oh, dear God! not again.'

He went straight to where John still had his knee on the broad back and was now holding on to one of Henrietta's arms and when Douglas said, 'I'll see to her. I'll see to her,' reluctantly, it would seem, John released his hold on the big groaning form, then straightened up, pulled his tunic straight, stroked his hair back and dusted his hands, the while he watched Douglas raise the woman to her feet.

Henrietta's body was still jangling but all the fury had gone out of her, and she was the young girl again, whimpering, 'He said . . . I . . . was mad. He . . . he was . . . going to . . . put me away, Douglas.'

'Don't be silly, Henrietta. He said no such thing.'

'He did! He did!' The childishness had gone out of her tone now and she was yelling and looking towards where Malcolm was being led from the hall by Amy, and she cried out, 'He . . . said it . . . to . . . Amy. He did! He did!'

'Stop that!' It was Bridget now standing before her. 'You have been warned, haven't you, what would happen if you let go of your temper again? Well now, you've brought this on yourself.'

The big face crumpled, the tears came into the eyes and she spelled out on her hands now, 'I just wanted to see Joseph. I've never seen him for a long time.'

'He's very busy. He told you. Come along.'

As Bridget led the jangling woman through the now small crowd of workers round the doorway, Douglas, seeing his daughter emerging from the passage, made his way towards her, saying, 'I'm sorry, dear, I'm . . .'

He got no further for, hissing at him now, Amy said, 'Get her locked up! Do you hear? If it wasn't for who she is, I would have called the police.'

'What has she actually done?'

'What has she actually done! She's clawed Malcolm's face. She went for his eyes. She's mad, I tell you.'

'No, not mad, Amy, just frustrated. She only wanted to see Joseph, and if you had let her stay . . .'

'Daddy.' She now gripped his arm and pulled him into the corridor, away from the sight and sounds in the hall, and still speaking sharply, she said, 'She could have waited a long time because Joseph hardly lives here any more. He goes out in the morning and I don't see him until seven or eight at night, and then only a glimpse before he goes into his office.'

'He's working up a business, dear, you know that; and twice he has taken Kitty and Bertha either to a concert or a play. Apparently you didn't want to accompany them.'

'I've got no taste for blaring bands and comedy strips, and what is more I consider them too young for that kind of thing. Anyway, that isn't the point. She is the point.' Her finger now stabbed along the corridor. 'Put her away before she kills somebody,' she demanded, swinging angrily away from him.

Angry himself now, Douglas hurried across the hall and outside to Bridget and Henrietta, who were already in the car, and when Henrietta whined from the back seat, 'It . . . was what . . . he said . . .' he snapped at her: 'Shut up you! Shut up! Not one more word. I'll deal with you when we get home.'

Henrietta shut up, and Bridget, who had been on the

point of saying something, remained quiet. It wasn't often her beloved Douglas lost his temper, but the few times she had heard him use this tone, she knew there was some plain speaking to be done.

6

The shop was closed. They had the sitting-room to themselves; Janet had gone to the pictures. It was the first time they had actually been alone during all his visits. And now there was a feeling of slight embarrassment between them, but he broke it by coming to the fore, saying, 'Your mother's gone out on purpose in order to leave us alone, hasn't she?'

'Yes. Yes.' She nodded at him from where she was sitting at the end of a small couch placed at right angles to the fire, and she repeated, 'Yes, that's her motive. But . . . but, Joseph, I . . . well, to put it plainly, I know how you feel, and . . . and I know how I feel, but I couldn't live with myself if I were to be the means of breaking up a family . . . separating a man and wife.'

He jerked himself up from his chair and, sitting beside her, he caught her hand as he said, 'You'll certainly not be breaking up the latter. Amy and I are living in the same house, but we haven't been sharing the same bed for some long time now.'

She shook her head. 'That makes no difference, Joseph. You are still a family and I don't want anything to start that we'll both regret.'

'There'll be no regret on my part, Liz, I can assure you. It's very strange, you know, but I can recall the first time I saw you when I was sitting in that chair.' He pointed. 'There was something hit me then that I'd never experienced before. I didn't recognise it until I had called that first time to thank you, but from then I knew. You see,

521

I'd been hemmed in all my life with so-called love, and what love I had to give was, in a way, dragged from me. But this feeling for you was spontaneous. And you, what did you feel?'

She drew in a long breath before she said, 'I'm not going to tell you. I'm not going to go into it, because, as I see it, nothing can come of it.'

'If . . . if I were to get a divorce?'

When she made to spring up he gripped her hands and held her firmly down as she said to him, 'You'll get no divorce through me. If . . . if there'd only been her, your wife, but you've got six of a family, and your youngest is only fifteen now.'

'Yes, but my eldest two are settled, at least they know where they are going. William's definitely a farmer, Malcolm's at university in his second year; he is on twenty now and I think his bent is teaching; he's good at languages. Alice, she is determined to marry and soon. My wife is not for the match, but I am, and it should happen that her young man has a cousin in the British Embassy in Paris and has offered him a post there. But I think they prefer married couples, so he's pressing his suit and Alice is pressing her mother. But even if Amy doesn't give her consent she has mine, and she'll go ahead. That's three settled. Jonathan is nearly seventeen and he has passed for the Royal College of Music. That just leaves Kitty and Bertha. Well, they are two bright girls and I'm very fond of them, and they of me. They're both intelligent and I'm sure would understand the situation. Anyway, I am forty years old, Liz, and the thought of spending the rest of my life in that house with Amy, oh no. *No. No!*' He closed his eyes and shook his head and repeated, 'No! Because I'm determined, once the two girls are settled, and I may say' – he was pointing at her now – 'I had this all worked out in my mind before I met you. Once they were settled in a career whichever way they wanted to go, I was to make the break. And you know, truthfully, I wasn't concerned so much about the effect it would have on my wife, but what it would have on her parents; and again not so much on her mother, but on her father, Douglas, for he is a splendid man, an honest man and kindly with it. So there you have it, Liz. Are we going to say, hello, and ta-ra, everytime I come? Am I not to touch you? Do you know something? We've never kissed, have we? Oh, my dear, my dear.' His arms went about her now and she leant against him, her head on his shoulder, and he stroked her hair, saying, 'There, there. Please. The last thing in the world I want to do is to upset you. We'll have it your way. If it's the family you're worried about, I'll wait; another year or two won't make all that difference as long as you promise me that I can look to the rest of my life being spent with you.'

He now stroked the thick brown hair back from her brow; then lifting up her face, he brought his fingers around her wet cheeks and into her trembling lips, and when she said, 'I've refused two offers of marriage within the last two years and I've asked myself why, and what of my future when Mam dies? What am I waiting for? Yet, the day when I helped to lift you from the pavement outside, and then saw you sitting in that chair, I knew . . . well, like you, perhaps not exactly then. It was when I heard your voice: there was something about your voice, the way you spoke, the look in your eyes. You were different. I knew then why I was waiting, and on Christmas Eve when you sent the fruit and the flowers I cried myself to sleep.'

Gently he took her face between his hands and as gently he placed his lips on hers, and when her arms went round him he held her close, then said quietly, 'Oh, Liz, Liz, as long as I can hold you it will be enough for the time being.'

7

'You must have been mistaken.'

'How could I have been mistaken after going into all those details?'

William turned now and kicked a log further into the blazing fire as he muttered, 'I can't believe it. Dad and a woman?'

They both turned and looked towards the dining-room door now as it opened and Malcolm came in, and he, glancing from one to the other, said, 'Have you seen Mam? I thought she was in here.'

When Jonathan shook his head, Malcolm looked at him and said, 'What's wrong? What's up?'

It was William now who, pointing to his brother, said, 'You tell him. See what he thinks.'

So Jonathan again related his news. He started by saying, 'Father . . . Father's got a woman.'

'Father's got a woman! What do you mean?'

'Just what I say.' Jonathan now pushed his head forward, and in a lowered voice said, 'I told Willie here about it. I was walking from the station looking for Mr Bradley's house, the new master who's taking me during the holidays. Well, I recognised Father's car as it passed me, and of course I recognised him, too, and I thought it was too late to attract his attention, when just a little way on he turned up an alleyway; and as I passed it I saw it was a narrow street with some shops in it and he had stopped the car at the top. I walked up and realised he must have gone into the off-licence shop, so I went in thinking to speak to him, but he wasn't there. A little woman was behind the counter, and I was stumped for a moment; then I asked for ... well, a bottle of beer. Beyond the counter was a glass door, at least the top half was glass, and I could see Father as plain as if he were standing before me now.' He now lowered his head. 'He had his arm around the shoulder of a girl. Well, she looked like a girl, but she could have been a woman; and they were laughing together, and — ' He paused, then muttered, 'I saw him put his face down to hers and then they moved out of sight.'

Malcolm was looking at William and William was nodding at him, saying, 'Well, what d'you make of it? What d'you think?'

There was a longish pause before Malcolm said, 'I can't imagine it of Father ... yet, we all know things haven't been very good between him and Mother for some time, have they? and that's likely why he's out at nights most of the time now.'

'He could be at the office, he's got a lot of work on ...'

'Don't be naive! Willie.' Malcolm turned away disdainfully, and even Jonathan raised his eyebrows.

'What if Mother found out?' said William now.

'Oh, then the fat would be in the frying pan,' said Jonathan, and the other two simultaneously repeated the same words: 'Yes, the fat would be in the frying pan then, all right.'

'Should you tackle Father?'

Malcolm reared now as he looked at his twin and exclaimed, 'Why me? What would I say? But why me?'

'Because,' said William tersely, 'you're always putting it forward that you're the eldest and that, because of those seven minutes, what's coming to you and what isn't coming to me. Oh yes, you've stopped saying openly that this house will be yours one day; but it's still in your mind,

I'll bet. So, that's why you should approach Father.'

'Well, I'm not going to be bawled out and told to mind my own bloody business. Anyway, lots of men of his age have mistresses; and Mam . . . well, as we all know, she isn't too easy to put up with at times.'

'Yes, you're right there,' said William, 'and I think that's because she only has one person on her mind all the time and that's Dad. As Grandpa once told us, she trailed him from the minute she could walk, and was always determined to have him. He said it in fun but . . . well, I should imagine that it can become a bit wearing at times.'

'Do you think he'll ask her for a divorce?'

At this William turned on Jonathan, hissing, 'Shut up! Divorce? No, of course not.'

'Don't be too sure.'

The three of them now looked at each other questioning; then turned quickly towards the archway that led into the serving room, and it was William who darted there. But when he found it empty he looked back at his brothers, saying, 'I thought I heard the door click, didn't you?'

'Look in the corridor.'

At this Jonathan ran to the far door of the dining-room, pulled it open and looked into the corridor. But seeing no one there, he sighed with relief and then joined his brothers again . . .

Amy had reached her bedroom almost at the same time as William opened the dining-room door, and when she got inside, she turned her face to the door and pressed her doubled fists to the panels, but didn't beat up on them. She was gasping as if after a long and heavy run and she brought out her words between gasps: 'I knew it . . . I knew it . . . I hate him! Hate him! Hate him! Divorce, they said. Never! Never! Never in this world. Love him or hate him I'm his wife and he'll never be free. Never!'

She turned now from the door and stumbled to the bed; but there she stiffened and muttered aloud, 'No! No!' and turning swiftly, she went to the dressing-table, sat down and, taking up a comb, she began to run it rapidly through the top of her hair. She would act as if she knew nothing. It would have to come from him, and when it did she would make herself say calmly, 'Divorce, Joseph? I may be a widow one day and let's hope it won't be long, but a divorced wife, never!'

But now the comb dropped to the dressing-table and she covered her face with her hands and moaned, 'Oh, no, no! He wouldn't ask me for that. He wouldn't! He wouldn't!' After a moment she looked at her reflection in the mirror and said to it, 'But apparently he already has. How long has he had her? A year? Two years? And who is she?' Well, she would make it her business quietly to find out.

Again she was covering her face with her hands and, muttering aloud, 'Oh, Mammy! Mammy!' she had the urge now to fly to Bridget and pour out the indignity she was being made to suffer, and to feel the comforting arms about her and perhaps hear her say, 'There, there, my dear. It's all right: your father will see to it. He will have a talk with him.'

Yes; but what would her father talk to Joseph about?

She got to her feet now. Her father liked Joseph. He liked him more as a man than he did as a boy, and this thought led her to Joseph's beginnings and to his mother, who had been a maid in the house. And her hands were joined tightly at her waist as she exclaimed aloud, 'After all that's been done for him! That's gratitude.'

Joseph stopped the car outside Bertha's cottage, and accompanied by young Bertha, he walked up the path to the front door, which he pushed open. And when there was no sight of her, he called, 'Hello! there, Bertha.'

There was no reply, so they walked through to the scullery and out of the back door and saw her clearing muck from the pigsties at the bottom of her land.

He shouted to her over the distance, 'We're not coming down there over all that clarts.'

As she walked towards them, wiping her hands on a coarse apron, she said, 'You could have cleaned your boots, or I could, I've done them afore. You in a hurry? Hello, deary.'

'Not particularly.'

'Well, take off your hat then.'

'I'm going to see Mabel and Nancy, Aunt Bertha.' As his daughter sped away, Joseph followed Bertha into the scullery, where she pulled off her apron and her cap, then washed her hands in the stone sink, while looking over her shoulder at him and asking, 'Tell me, is this a flyin' visit or can you stay for a cup of tea and a meal?'

'I never pay flying visits. And yes, of course, I can stay for both. What's the matter with you? Is it because I've never looked in for a week? I've been very busy.'

'Lad' – she was going into the kitchen now – 'if you didn't turn up for a year I wouldn't question it, because I would know you would be about your own business. You know me.' She nodded up at him, and he said, 'Yes, I know you and your old maxim you were always quoting: Let him go and you'll lose him. Not let him go and you keep him. Yes, you did. Anyway, how are you feeling?'

'As you see me, the fittest woman in the county, or beyond.'

'You'll brag once too often. Why didn't you wear a coat out there?'

'I have no need of coats; me sweat keeps me warm. Anyway, sit yourself down. Charlie's glad to see you.' She ground the kettle into the fire, then turned and grinned at him, before sitting herself down on the edge of the settle. 'Well, have you any news?' she said. 'Anything to tell me? Anything fresh?'

When he didn't answer she looked towards the fire and quietly she said, 'You're up to somethin', aren't you, Joe?'

'Put like that, yes.'

'Aye, well, everybody knows their own business best, and I'm not goin' to ask you what yours is, but I'm just goin' to tell you that I'm not the only one who seems to know you've got somethin' afoot.'

'What do you mean by that, Bertha?'

'Oh, just that I had a visit, an unusual visit from somebody the other day.'

He waited while she leaned forward and gave the kettle a further push into the flames, before she explained: 'Your wife called to see me.'

'Amy came to . . .?'

'Yes.' She was sitting back on the settle now, her hands folded across her stomach. 'Me namesake was with her. Your wife said they were out for a walk, which in itself I thought strange, as I've never known Amy to do any walking outside your grounds, at least from what you've said. Anyway, there she was, sitting exactly where you are now, while Bertha was outside. You know where she makes for when she comes: she seems to have an affinity with the goats; and she's a bit of a goat herself, with the antics she gets up to.'

'What did Amy want? What was she after? I mean, what reason did she give for calling?'

'Just that she was out for a walk, I've told you. But what I gathered from our guarded conversation was that she thought I was in the know. You were very busy these days. She supposed I missed your visits, too, et cetera, et cetera, along those lines. She had a job to keep her voice level, and her face was strained. She looked as white as a sheet. What are you up to? Now *I* am probing.'

He got to his feet, walked up the room to the table, laid his hand on it, and his fingers beat out a quick tattoo as he said, 'I have a friend. That's all she is; at least she is at present, because she wants it that way, but I don't.' He swung round and walked back to the fireplace and, looking into Bertha's upturned face, he said, 'I've fallen in love . . .'

Before he could go on, she had lifted both her hands as if appealing to the ceiling as she cried, 'Oh, my God! I never expected in my life to hear you say anythin' so childish. You, a man of forty.'

'Yes, me a man of forty, and I mean what I say. I've been loved all my life, Bertha, crushed, pressed down with it, but I've never really known what it was to fall in love, to love somebody, really, and I love Liz . . . That's her name. But she happens to be a very good young woman and she's against breaking up a family. That's why I'm still here, or at least living along the road, for I'd go and live with her tomorrow if she would agree. So, there you have it. Yes, I've fallen in love.'

Bertha pushed him aside as she stood up and took the kettle from the stove. She then went into the scullery, mashed the tea, and when she returned with a tray in her hand he was standing, his elbow on the low mantelpiece, staring down into the fire. No words passed between them until she had handed him the cup of tea and had seated herself on the settle again when, in a quiet voice, she said, 'I think it has been said afore, there are all kinds of love, lad. Now I've never had much room for Amy, not since the night she took advantage of my invitation to sleep up there,' she lifted her head upwards, 'and she went to you. If you had gone to her, well, that would have been a different kettle of fish. But there she was the next morning, coming out of your room and we met on the landing, me with the tray of tea in me hand, and we looked at each other and have never cared for each other since. But having said that, she has a side. She loved you. She bore you six children.'

'Yes' – his head snapped upwards now – 'and each one under protest. Do you know something, Bertha? I've always thought it was unjust that if a man had a big family he was thought to be sex-ridden, when he need only have been with his wife once a year. She might only allow him to go with her once a year ... it happens, yet there are other men who don't only have their wives, but anybody who's willing to jump into bed with them. But they're wise, they take precautions. Oh, I've always felt like blowing my mouth off at sniggers in the club when a fellow's going to be the father of the seventh, eighth or the tenth. I tell you, Bertha, I know what I'm talking about. And as you said, there's all kinds of love, and Amy's love has always been like an iron band round me. She's possessive to the point of fanaticism yet she doesn't know how to love ... Do you get what I mean?'

'Yes, I get what you mean, but, laddie, from what you tell me, you're in between two stools now, between the one that loves you too much in her own way and one that doesn't love you enough to give herself to you.'

'She does. Liz does. But she doesn't want to be the means of breaking up a family. If there were just Amy, well that would be different.'

'Ah!' Bertha's voice changed. 'Here's the goatherd.'

Young Bertha came in, saying, 'Oh, isn't the new kid beautiful, Daddy!' She pulled at his arm. 'I'm going to demand ... do you hear? demand that Willie keeps some goats, at least one.'

'No, you mustn't just have one,' said Bertha; 'they want company. Animals, like individuals, hate to be lonely.'

And on this, she turned to Joseph, but her voice was addressing the young girl as she went on, 'An animal, you know, Bertha, is just like us humans: it can be in a crowd of others, like cows, hens, ducks, geese, and the rest, but if it hasn't got one of its own sort, then it's miserable. Loneliness is an awful thing.'

'Well, he'll have to have two then,' said Bertha, 'and that would be better still.'

'Will you have a cup of tea, lass?'

'You know I don't like tea, Aunty Bertha. I'll have a drink of goat's milk.'

When Bertha left the kitchen to go into the scullery to get the milk, her namesake, going to her father, put her arm around his shoulders and whispered to him, 'Do you think Aunty Bertha's lonely?' And he, patting her cheek, answered, 'No, not when she has us.' As he looked down on her he was made to wonder at the power of a name, because he had named his last daughter Bertha . . . and that under protest, but here she was, not only small of stature and always would be, but she even had the look of Bertha about her, and definitely inside she had Bertha's warm heart and thoughtfulness for others.

He was whispering, too, as, his face close to hers, he said, 'Did you ask Mammy to come here with you the other day?'

'No, Daddy; she came to me and said she would like to go for a walk.' And now staring into her father's eyes, and in scarcely a whisper, she made a knowledgeable statement: 'Mammy is not very happy these days, is she, Daddy?'

8

John ran up the stairs and across the landing, rapped sharply on Amy's door, and when he heard, 'Yes?' he called, 'It's the phone, madam; Mrs Filmore.'

When Amy lifted the phone it was to hear Bridget crying, 'It's Daddy! Amy. He's . . . he's had a heart attack. The doctor's been. He's . . . rather ill.'

'Is he in hospital?'

'No; the doctor thought it was best not to move him. Can you come?'

'Of course, of course. I'll come straightaway.'

'Is Joseph there?'

'He's just gone, or at least . . . wait a moment.' She now turned to where John was standing near her and she said, 'Has . . . has the master gone?'

'He may not, madam; he was just on his way out to the car. I'll see.'

She returned to the phone and said, 'John's just gone to see if he's left or not. If he hasn't, we'll come straight through; if not I'll call a taxi.'

She looked to the side now; then speaking into the phone again she said, 'It's all right, he's here. We'll be there shortly. Try not to worry.' She put the phone down and looked at Joseph, saying, 'It's Daddy; he's had a heart attack.'

'Oh, good lord! Is it bad?'

'I don't really know.'

'Well, get your coat on; I'll bring the car round.'

She dashed upstairs again, got into her coat and hat,

533

and when she came down John was standing holding the door open and Joseph was already seated at the wheel of the car; there was no time for courtesy. The passenger door was open and she got in and, as they drove off, he asked, 'Is he in hospital?'

'No. Mammy says the doctor thought it best not to move him. . . .'

They reached the house within half an hour, having touched up to thirty miles an hour on some roads, and they were greeted in the hall by Ada Flannigan who, in a mournful voice, said that the mistress was upstairs with the master and he was ever so poorly.

When they entered the bedroom, Bridget rose from the side of the bed to greet them, saying quietly, 'Oh, I am pleased to see you. He . . . he seems a lot better. It was such a shock. It happened right there.' She pointed to the bottom of the bed. 'He was getting dressed. He was quite cheery; in fact, he was insisting we go away for a holiday.'

A low murmur coming from the bed caused Bridget to turn and hurry back to it, and they followed her, and when Douglas lifted a weary hand towards them and in an equally weary voice said, 'Nonsense; just a dizzy spell,' Amy, taking the hand, said, 'Of course, Daddy. All you would ever have is a dizzy spell.'

He smiled wearily at her; then looked over her shoulder and said to Joseph, 'Fuss, fuss,' and Joseph merely nodded at him.

Bridget said to her daughter, 'Can you stay?' and Amy immediately answered, 'Yes. Oh, yes, of course. I'm not needed back there.' But then, her tone softening, she said, 'As long as you like, Mammy.' And when Bridget turned to Joseph, he simply answered the question in her eyes, saying quietly, 'My time is yours, Bridget. Tell me if there's anything I can do.'

'Well' – she gave a tight smile – 'you can stay with

Douglas for a little while until I get Amy settled in.' It was as if she were talking to a guest; and now she took her daughter's arm and led her from the room, no doubt, Joseph thought, to enquire if there had been any change in the household atmosphere since they had last talked.

Joseph took the seat beside the bed and, taking hold of Douglas's hand, he asked quietly, 'Was it bad?'

Douglas's eyebrows went up slightly as he answered, 'More like a surprise, but it was soon over. Pills and rest, he said . . . the doctor, and I'll be myself again in no time. Joseph.'

'Yes, Douglas?'

'This is not my first attack, but the first she's seen. I took the others to be merely cramps, neuritis, you know, or rheumatism or something like that down the arm.'

'Didn't you go to the doctor?'

'Yes; but when he examined me, I was all right. He said something about my blood pressure mounting and that I had to give up playing with stone, which I did do some time ago, if you remember. Anyway, I wanted a minute alone with you, Joseph, because quite candidly one never knows the moment, does one?'

When Joseph made no response Douglas said, 'I wanted to tell you that I've seen you all right.'

'Oh, please, please, Douglas; we have been through this before. You've done more than enough for me . . .'

'We have done really nothing for you, Joseph. I think, as you once stated to me, or was it to my daughter, that you had been and still were nothing but a manager or a caretaker. And that was quite true. It hurt me to think that you felt like that but, nevertheless, you were right. Now they'll be back in a moment, Joseph, and I don't know whether we'll have time together again but . . . you may have opposition from a certain quarter, a dear, dear quarter, but she knows what I've always thought. Yet she

535

doesn't know exactly what I have done, and I have asked myself, would I have taken that step, that final step if I had known when I put my signature to that will what I know now? And the answer is, yes. Yes, I would have still done it because I think it is your right. But the knowledge that you are keeping a woman . . .'

Joseph put his hand to his brow and pressed his head back as he muttered, 'I am not keeping a woman, Douglas. She is a working girl. I have never given her a penny in my life and I am not sleeping with her. Believe me, I am not sleeping with her. We are friends. Will you believe me?' He was looking into Douglas's eyes and Douglas said, 'Yes. Yes, Joseph, yes, I believe you, and that is good news. But why a friend?'

'Because . . . because I needed a friend, someone undemanding.'

'Do . . . do you care for this woman?'

'Yes. Yes, Douglas, I care for her.'

'Enough to leave Amy?'

Joseph lowered his eyes now, then said, 'I've always given you the truth, Douglas, and yes, I would leave Amy for her, but not until the family are all settled. The boys are all right, but there's the girls to see to.'

Douglas's head sank back into the pillow and he repeated, 'The boys, it was they who came and told me.'

'*The boys?*'

'Yes, your three sons, and they told me how they had come by this information. It was through Jonathan seeing your car outside the off-licence, and he went to find you and spotted you inside talking to a woman. Well, have they made any difference in their manner towards you?'

'No, not at all.'

'No, I didn't think they would. They are very fond of you and they are three good fellows.'

When Douglas began to gasp for breath, Joseph rose

from the chair, saying, 'I'll get Bridget,' but Douglas's hand waved him down; then he muttered, 'A pill,' and pointed to a side table.

Quickly, Joseph took a pill out of a bottle and, holding a glass of water to Douglas's lips, watched him swallow, and when he muttered, 'I'll be all right now,' Joseph said, 'No more talk unless it's from me.' He placed the glass back on the table; then, having taken his seat again, he took hold of Douglas's hand and, very quietly, he said, 'I must tell you, Douglas, that you've been the only real friend I've had in my life. Legally or otherwise you are my uncle, but to me you have been like a father, the father I would have wanted, not the other one. I know there are traits of him in me, but there are also yours in me too, and I promise you in the future I'll try to follow their lead.'

There came a pressure from Douglas's fingers within his hold, then his breathing became easier, and he said, 'Keep an eye on Malcolm, Joseph. He is the spit of Lionel, but I don't know how much is inside.'

'Yes, I'll do that. Yes, I promise I'll do that.'

'And promise me something else?'

Joseph waited, and then Douglas said, 'Whatever you feel bound to do to Amy, try to do it in a kindly fashion. Unfortunately, she's only ever had one aim in life, and that is to have you. Possess you, as you said, but nevertheless, that was her aim, and when she's deprived of it, well, God knows then how she'll cope.'

They sat in silence for all of three minutes; then Douglas slowly turned his head towards the window, saying, 'It's a nice day,' and at that moment the door opened and Bridget entered, and when she came to the bedside and Joseph stood up to give her the seat, Douglas, holding out his hand to her, said, 'I was just remarking to Joseph that it is a very nice day.'

'Yes. Yes, it is, dear.' Then, looking up at Joseph, she said, 'Amy's having her cup of coffee in the breakfast room,' and he answered, 'Well, I'll join her. Then I'll slip through to the office and set things moving; but I'll be back by dinner time.'

'Good. Good.' She nodded at him, and he, bending now towards Douglas, said, 'I'll see you later. Behave yourself.'

When he had gone from the room Bridget looked at her beloved Douglas, but she didn't ask him what had transpired between him and Joseph because she felt that he was really too ill to talk; had she thought otherwise she would have never left them together.

9

'But, Joseph, we've never had a walk along the pier for a long time.'

'I've told you, Henrietta, I'm very, very busy.' He now took her hands away from the lapels of his coat and went to press them gently back, but she snapped them from his hold, crying, 'You . . . are . . . always . . . making excuses. You . . . never . . . even talk to me. What's the matter? You don't . . . like me. You . . . don't . . . like me . . . any more.'

'Now don't be silly, Henrietta.'

'Well, do you . . . like me?'

He had to force himself to say, 'Of course I like you. You know that.'

'You're . . . not the same. You've . . . changed. Everybody's . . . been against me; and now . . . you. You've changed.' Her voice was rising higher and he looked past to where Nell was standing waiting for a signal, and he gave it to her, saying, 'There's Nell waiting. Now she wants to take you for a walk.'

'I don't . . . want to go.' Now the hands were moving rapidly and he read, 'I don't want to go with Nell. I don't need Nell. She treats me as if I'm a prisoner, as if I didn't know what I was doing . . . Why don't you take me out any more?'

His tone changed too, as he wagged his finger at her, saying, 'I've got a business to run, Henrietta; everybody has to work. And what you want to do is to practise your speech . . . therapy. Nell will help you.'

'Damn speech! ... Damn Nell! ... Damn everybody ... ! Take me for a ride ... now!'

Nell came forward and caught Henrietta's flailing arms, allowing Joseph to make a quick retreat, and as he went out of the door Bridget came down the stairs, crying, 'Stop that! this minute. All that noise! You know your uncle is very ill. Go to your room and dress.'

When Henrietta swung pettishly round from her, Bridget looked at Nell and did a pantomime of putting something into her mouth, at which Nell nodded . . .

Henrietta had, long ago, known how to pretend to swallow a pill. It was simple: you tucked it under your tongue; you gulped once or twice in your throat as the water passed down; then you sat quiet, and after a while you pretended to be drowsy and to go to sleep. But she had also learned not to let the pill lie too long under the tongue, else it would melt, and so she sometimes had a bout of coughing or went to the toilet and deposited the offending pill in the pan.

Today the ploy had worked. She knew that when she pretended sleep Nell would go down and get her own dinner, and the others would be in the kitchen, too. Usually, Aunt Bridget would be sitting in the drawing-room with Uncle, but today she would be upstairs beside his bed. There was a special way she could go out. She would go down the back stairs. She wouldn't cross the yard, though, because the men would see her, but she could take the passage that led from the staff quarters into the far end of the conservatory: it was the way the men used to take out the plants so they wouldn't have to go through the house or round about it.

And this is what she did. She put on her hat and coat, picked up the bag in which she jealously kept her allotted pocket money, together with any presents of money she might have been given, and she went down the attic stairs, along the passage and was just about to open the door leading into the conservatory when she caught sight of her Aunt Bridget already there and talking to Amy. She eased back and pressed herself tightly against the wall. The passage was dark; the sunlight didn't penetrate it, but it was filling the conservatory and she could see enough of her Aunt Bridget's face to read her lips. They were saying, 'Never! Never!'

Amy was not fully within her vision and so she was unable to read her further words. But then Bridget's lips were moving again and she was saying, 'The woman in the off-licence? Oh no!' Then she was nodding, saying, 'Yes. Yes, I knew there was a daughter, and you mean to say she is whom he is consorting with?'

There was more talk from Amy now, and then Bridget's lips were saying, 'Oh, you didn't! my dear. You didn't!'

Amy was talking again and she had moved her position slightly so that more of her profile was visible to Henrietta, although not enough for her to distinguish what Amy was saying. Cunningly, she slithered back along the wall of the passage, then crossed to the opposite one and slithered back to the door. She could now see Amy more clearly and what she read was, 'An outdoor beer shop, off-licence, they call them, and in an awful little street. It isn't even a street, it is a passage in the lower quarter called Downeys or some such, and there was his car outside. I saw it. I don't know how I stopped myself from going in and confronting them.'

Henrietta could now not see what Bridget was saying, but Amy's reply was, 'Oh, a couple of weeks ago. I . . . I feel I cannot bear to look at him. What am I going to do, Mammy? I'm . . . I'm just waiting for him to come . . . and tell me he's leaving, or . . . or he wants a divorce, because I know now this has been going on for some time. And you know Bradford Villa, the house he bought last year and had done up? Well, that's just near. And you know what I'm wondering? I'm wondering if they are living there. You remember, he was very keen to have that place, and it was supposed to be let to some very old people, theatrical people, and they left without paying last quarter's rent. You remember? He told you the strange letter the man left, saying they had taken some of the furniture but the rest could stand in lieu of what was owing. That was some weeks ago, but I haven't heard him mention it since. I recall he used to tell the boys about the couple and the weird colours they had painted the rooms and spoiled the nice decorations he'd had done. But for some weeks now he hasn't spoken of it.'

When Henrietta saw Amy fall into her mother's arms, and realising they would now probably move from the conservatory, she made her way back along the passage and ran half way up the back stairs again to where it curved towards the upper landing, and from where she could see if they were to come through the passage; otherwise they would go into the morning room.

After some minutes, and there being no movement in the passage below, she went cautiously down the stairs again, and looking through the glass door and seeing that the conservatory was clear, she opened the door, then hurried through to the opposite one that led to the back lawn. From here, she went into an ungainly, shambling run along a path that would lead onto the drive and then to the bridle path, and she didn't stop running until she had reached the main road.

Liz gazed around the room at the great splashes of coloured paint worked into weird shapes; then turning from looking at the two men who were busily scraping the paper off the walls, she said to Joseph, 'I can't believe it. You had it done so beautifully. It looks crazy.'

'It's a new form of art.'

The two men now turned their laughing faces towards them and one said, 'I have another name for it, sir, but there's a lady present.'

Joseph smiled as he remarked, 'No doubt, no doubt.' Then taking Liz by the arm, he led her into the hall, saying, 'That room's nothing, you should have seen the sitting-room.' He pushed open the door and as he did so a woman got off her knees, exclaiming, 'Oh! Hello there, sir. I've almost finished this one.'

'Thank you, Mrs Adams.' He looked up the room. 'You've made a good job of it. But there's a number yet facing you upstairs.'

'Oh, I don't mind that, sir; it's just work.' She grinned at them, and as they went out to go up the stairs Liz remarked, 'Just work, and on her knees all day. Is she the woman who cleans all the houses for you?'

'Yes; and apparently glad of the job. When she came after it I remember saying to her, 'Don't you think it's a bit too heavy for you?' And she said, "Are you meaning to say, I'm too old for the job? I've been on me knees most of me life. I've got caps on them as thick as horse's saddles." '

They were laughing when they reached the landing; then as Joseph led her from one room to the other, she exclaimed in dismay, 'Oh, it's a scandal. They must have been real cranks. Weren't you mad when you saw it first?'

'Yes and no. It was one of those days when other things were pressing on my mind and I think I must have gone a bit hysterical because when I entered the main bedroom, that was supposed to be this one, I sat on the window-sill over there and I began to laugh. I think I really was a bit hysterical.'

'Yes, I remember: you were still laughing when you

came to us. And that was the day . . . ' She stopped abruptly, and when she lowered her head he put his hands on her shoulders, saying, 'Yes, that was the day I asked you, if it was put to rights again, like it was before, sometime in the future, would you live here with me, and your answer was, you didn't know. Now' – he spread his hand around the bare room – 'seeing how beautiful it is, have you changed your mind?'

'Oh, Joe.' She now put her arms around him. 'I've got to say it. I could live here with you from this minute, in this room as it is now. All my moralizing seems to have gone by the board. I love you. That's all about it. If we can keep the matter quiet and it's not going to hurt your family then . . . well, so be it.'

They were holding close now, their lips tight. The kiss was long and hard and hungry and when it ended he looked into her eyes and said, 'I had a feeling about this house the first day I saw it, the same as I had the feeling about you. Now' – he gripped her chin and wagged it as he said, 'I'll put another two men on tomorrow and they'll have this place scalped within a week, and within another week it'll be back to what it was.'

They kissed again, long and lovingly, before making for the door. Their arms about each other, they were laughing as they stepped on to the landing; but there he froze . . . He was aware of two things: the telephone bell was ringing downstairs, and Henrietta was standing at the top of the stairhead.

After swallowing, he cleared his throat and put his hand over his mouth as he muttered, 'Henrietta. I'll introduce you. Just smile.'

They walked slowly along the landing and as they neared her Joseph said, 'How did you get here, Henrietta?' But Henrietta didn't answer, she was staring at Liz.

They were within an arm's length of her when they

stopped and Joseph, mouthing the words slowly, said, 'This is . . . Elizabeth . . . a friend . . . of mine.'

'No! No! No!' Her voice came out high, almost like a screech, and her eyes held an almost maniacal glare as she cried at Liz, 'Mine! Mine!' and saying this, she put out a hand to grab Joseph's arm, but he slapped it sharply away. This caused her to be still for a moment, but then, her body jangling, she screamed, 'Joseph's mine! Joseph's mine!'

The next instant Joseph was just too late to stop her attack, but luckily Liz had leant backwards to avoid the impact and Henrietta's hands just missed her face but clutched her shoulders, and as she swung Liz round Joseph brought his fist into the side of her head. It seemed that instantly there was a concerted cry: as Henrietta released her hold she thrust Liz from her, and Liz's scream as she tumbled down the stairs was joined by Henrietta's high gabble and the yell that came from Joseph.

When he reached the bottom of the stairs there was no movement from Liz. Her legs were twisted under her, her arms were outspread. The two men were bending over her and Mrs Adams was screaming as she looked up the stairs, crying, 'She's mad! that one. She knocked me over, an' me pail, an' the telephone's been ringin'. It was her mam from the off-licence; she said she was comin', her up there.'

Nobody took any notice of what Mrs Adams was saying because the men were looking down on Joseph, where he was kneeling on the floor holding the inert figure of Liz to him; and, without looking up at them, he muttered, 'Phone for a doctor, will you?'

'I'll do it. I'll do it. An' the polis. An' the polis.'

As Mrs Adams ran out of the hallway Joseph, glancing up the stairs, saw that Henrietta was about to descend, and so he gently laid Liz's head back on the floor; then, rising quickly, said to the men, 'Help me to lift her to one side;' and it was just as they did so that Henrietta reached the hall. Her arms were flailing, her head was wagging and she was yelling again as she made for the door but Joseph, springing towards her, grabbed her. Thrusting her against the wall, he cried, 'For two pins I would do for you this very minute! You mad, crazy, vicious bitch!'

Henrietta now no longer saw the man before her as her dear Joseph, the one person she felt who belonged to her: he was Malcolm; he was Amy; but most of all he was her father; and he had a woman; and she was lying on the floor.

Her hands clawed at him, and as they did so he brought one of his own across her face. But it seemingly had little effect. And when the two men came to his assistance, there was a mêlée for she kicked and flailed while screaming at them, until they managed to bear her to the floor, and there, bundling her onto her face, one of the men knelt on her legs while he shouted to his mate, 'Get some rope; it's in the cart outside!'

Joseph was actually holding her down by the neck, so that all her hands could do now was to claw at the floor. A minute later, the man returned with some pieces of rope and they tied her legs together and her arms behind her; yet still her body writhed . . .

It was still writhing when the police arrived, and they not only immediately telephoned for an ambulance but also for a police van.

The police van happened to arrive first and the policeman asked of Joseph the address of the woman whom they had now pulled to her feet, and who was gabbling in a high screeching tone, and he gave it to them. Then he was asked if he knew the woman. Was he any relation to her? He did not answer that she was his half-sister but said, 'Distantly. She lives with her aunt and uncle.'

546

The policeman now asked quietly, 'Has she been in an asylum, sir?'

'No.' He did not keep his voice low as he answered the policeman. 'But she should have been and she will be from now on.'

They had naturally removed the rope from Henrietta's legs and as the two policemen went to lead her to the door she kicked out at them, causing one of them to react by pushing her none too gently forward and through the doorway.

When the sound of her screeching voice had died away, Joseph said to Mrs Adams, 'Will you run down the road to Mrs Dunn, in the off-licence, you know, and tell her what's happened? Tell her to close the shop and come up here straightaway.'

'Aye, I'll do that. I'll do that. By, I'm shaken to the core. D'you think she'll be all right?' She was backing away as she spoke; and then she looked at one of the men and said, 'Talk about things happening. By, your face is in a mess;' then to the other, 'Look at your hands, Sydney. By, she had nails like talons.'

The two men stood awkwardly looking down on Joseph, who had his hand on Liz's chest, and one of them said, 'How's it going?' And in reply Joseph simply muttered, 'It's all right.'

It was at this moment that Liz opened her eyes and Joseph found himself unable to speak, until she said, 'Joe.'

'Yes, dear. You'll be all right.'

'Mam?'

'Yes. I've sent for her, dear . . . Are you in pain . . . do you feel your legs or . . .?'

'No. No.'

'Oh, well, that's good.'

What a damn silly thing to say. It was when the back

547

was broken that they didn't feel any pain. Oh God! No! Don't let that happen!

'Joe.' It was a whisper, and he whispered back, 'Yes, dear? What is it?'

'It hadn't to be, had it?'

10

Something had gone wrong with the delivery of the papers for the past two days, they had told him; they had sent a different paper. But on the third day his own had arrived and Douglas had scanned the headlines dealing with the trouble in Parliament, the state of the unemployed, officers and men still tramping the country for work. He had smiled at that heading and remarked quizzically to himself that in the search for work, all the officers would have merely returned to men.

He turned the front page and read bits here and there; then his gaze became riveted on a column down the side of page three. It was headed, 'Woman's back broken in attack by mad woman'. His glance might have passed over the rest except that he caught sight of a name in smaller print just below the heading, which read: 'The attack by Henrietta Filmore on Mrs Elizabeth Lilburn has resulted in the latter being paralyzed from the waist down. The attacker is the half-sister of the estate agent Mr Joseph Skinner, who was showing his client, the above-mentioned Mrs Lilburn, around the house in Botany Drive, Gateshead. It has also become known that this is not the first attack made by the woman Filmore, and it is being questioned why her guardians have not had her under strong detention. She is now confined to the asylum'.

Douglas rang the bell beside his chair, and when Bridget appeared he did not speak but handed her the paper, his finger pointing to the column.

After merely glancing at the heading, Bridget said

quietly, 'I . . . I didn't want you disturbed further. The papers had a field day.'

'It says she's in the asylum. Which asylum?'

'The private one.'

'That's no good. When we discussed this before I told you so. They are right to criticise why she wasn't put away.'

'She is not mad, Douglas.'

'Don't be silly, Bridget: you, who have so much common sense, to keep believing that she isn't mad. Like all such, she doesn't appear mad all the time, and they are the worst. She's always been dangerous . . . And the woman, have you heard anything about her, who she is?'

'Yes. Yes, I've heard who she is. She's the woman in question.'

'Well, how did *you* find out about her? And how did Henrietta know where to go?'

'I don't really know. The only thing I can imagine is when Amy was telling me about . . . about the woman, we were in the conservatory. She could have been looking through that glass door – it's the only place – because if she had been in the drawing-room she wouldn't have seen us speaking. Because, as usual, she would have been careful.'

'Which proves that she's so wily. When they're in that mentally affected state they're always wily. And what is Amy going to do now?'

'Oh, please, Douglas. Don't agitate yourself. You've got to rest. You know what the doctor said . . .'

'Damn rest! Tell me what Amy is going to do.'

'She . . . she doesn't know herself. She is terribly upset.'

'Well, that's her own damn fault!'

'Oh, Douglas, Douglas.'

'I repeat, Bridget, it's her own damn fault.'

'All right. All right, dear; but please don't get agitated.'

'Have you seen Joseph since?'

'No, I haven't.'

'And by the sound of you, you don't want to. Well, I would like to have a word with him. So, if you'll be kind enough, dear, you'll get that message to him. And don't look like that, dear; he's not to blame . . . well, not all to blame.'

Bridget went out without answering him; but on the landing she stood and gripped her hands together while she repeated, 'Not to blame, not all to blame.' He's been to blame since the day he was born, and before that. If it hadn't been for him. Oh! She tossed her head as she went down the stairs, forgetting for the moment that it was she herself who had held the whip of fate, from the time she allowed her girlish emotions to dwell on a working man in a blacking factory.

It was three weeks later and Liz had become merely another patient in the end bed of a hospital ward; even the fact that Mr Skinner took up every minute of visiting hours with her and he a married man, and not an ordinary married man, but one connected with the Filmores, was hardly mentioned.

During the first week, memories of the strange Filmore family had been revived, but during the past two they seemed to have receded, so that now little notice was taken of Joseph and his visits, except the fact that he was very concerned for the patient.

He was now sitting by the bedside holding Liz's hand and saying, 'It's all ready, dear, it's all arranged. The house looks as it did in the first place, except that I've had the sitting-room turned into a bedroom, and it's all furnished' – he pulled a face at her – 'your mother has done the choosing. She's excited about it. I think she's glad she's going to sell the business. As she said, she's stood on her pins long enough behind that counter and put up with chatter of little cheeky monkeys with their empty bottles.'

Liz turned her pale, large-eyed face away from him and looked across the ward to the bed opposite and near which two visitors were seated, and she said, 'And where will you live, Joe?'

'Why! with you, at least most of the time.'

'Have you talked this over?'

'No; but there's nothing to talk about, it's understood.'

She brought her gaze back on him and said gently, 'It's understood.' Then softly and wearily she added, 'Joseph, you're tearing yourself and your family apart.'

'Now be quiet. I'm doing no such thing. This would have happened . . . I mean, we would have gone there to live in any case. You know we would. Have I to remind you again of what you said in the bedroom that day?'

'No. No.' She moved her head on the pillow. 'You haven't got to remind me of anything that happened that day, Joseph.'

At this he turned his gaze away from her, thinking, Yes; why had he to bring up the happenings of that day, or the harassment that followed, including that business of one of Janet's customers suggesting her daughter had a case that would skin that mad woman's guardians of every penny they had? And she had immediately threatened him with a bottle. At one time, this would have caused much laughter, but not now . . . And Liz had just said he would have to talk the matter over. Yes, he knew that was to come, and part of that would have to be an explanation to his whole family. Their overall manner towards him hadn't changed but always he seemed to detect the question in all their eyes, asking him why, and to explain. John was the only one he could talk to, come clean with, and it was strange what he had said to him only yesterday: 'Hang on here, sir. Don't leave altogether,' he had urged him; 'I understand your predicament, but I would still keep a hold here, if I were you. But then, of course, sir, it's your business.'

And when he had asked, 'What about the rest of the staff?' John's answer had been, 'Surprise and disbelief in some quarters, but at bottom they're all for you, sir. Without exception, they are all for you.'

Liz was saying now, 'I'm to have exercise, they tell me.'

'Oh, good.'

'And there is the suggestion of an operation some time in the future. It all depends on' – she pulled a face – 'so many things. As the doctor says, they'll see how things go. Oh, Joe' – her hand jerked in his – 'I get bored lying here. I want to get up and . . .' Her voice trailed away and he murmured, 'I know, dear, I know. Look, dear.' He leaned closer to her and very quietly said, 'I've put this to you before, but wouldn't you like to go into a private room?'

'And I've put this to *you* before, too, dear. I'd go daft on my own most of the day. Here, everything is busy, busy. I get bored, as I said, but I think it's mostly during the night when I can't sleep. But that's my own fault. I refuse the pills. But during the day it's sometimes like going to the pictures, there's so much happening. Don't worry, my dear.' She squeezed his hand now. 'The time will soon pass. And talking of worrying, it's you whom I worry about. You must be running from one end of the town to the other most of the time.'

'Oh, yes, I'm run off my feet in the car. Speaking of the car, I'm going to bring Bertha in to see you for a minute or so on Sunday. She's asked once or twice. You've never met Bertha yet. You'll like her. She could be your mother's twin sister: they talk the same language; they'll get on famously together.'

'I like Bertha already. She must be a sort of foster-mother to you.'

'Yes, that's a good name for her, foster-mother. I'm very fond of Bertha.'

'Do you know, Joseph Skinner, you're in the habit of using that word fond? and it's misplaced. You say you're very fond of young Bertha, Kitty, Jonathan, Alice, and the twins. You see, I know the order they go in. But what you mean is, you love them.'

He looked into her soft brown eyes as he said, 'Yes, I suppose you're right, I love them; but I can add to that, I am *very, very* fond of you.'

When the bell rang he looked at his watch, saying, 'It can't be: not an hour, surely!'

'Well, there's always tomorrow. Odd about Sundays here. You can always tell it's Sunday, everything in the ward seems to change. There's not so much noise, or so much bustle. I find that very odd. But until tomorrow, dear.'

He put his lips on hers and she put her arms around his neck; then she watched him step back from the bed. But when, at the end of the ward, he turned and waved, she could only just make him out through the mist in her eyes, and her mother's words came back at her, not in malice, but as a statement of fact, 'If that fellow hadn't slipped outside the shop that day, you wouldn't be lying there now. God has a funny way of working, I must say.'

He sensed the trouble as soon as he entered the house. It was written on John's face as he hurried across the hall towards him, and he didn't speak until he had taken his hat and coat from him, when he said, 'Would you come into the study a minute, sir?'

In some alarm Joseph followed him. Once in the room, John said, 'The mistress had a phone call this afternoon.

Mr Filmore died suddenly after another heart attack.'

Joseph said nothing, but remained still, and after a moment while he stared at John, he closed his eyes and his mind murmured again and again, Oh, Douglas. No, no! not quick, like that. And he recalled their last conversation together when his last words to him were, 'You must do what you think you must, but, at the same time, think about those who are going to be hurt by any decision you might make.' He knew at this moment that he would never again meet up with such an understanding man, such a good man, as Douglas Filmore. He wanted to sit down, put his head on his arms and cry, but he'd have to go down to the house.

'He was such a good man.'

He looked at John and nodded and said, 'Yes. He was a good man, John, a good man.'

'Can I get you a drink before you leave, sir?'

'Yes. Yes, you could, please.'

After John had left the room he did sit down, but he didn't drop his face onto his arms; he reverted to an action he would use as a boy: in the attic bedroom of the Lodge, when things were troubling him, he would bite on the first knuckle of his thumb quite hard until it hurt . . .

It was turned nine o'clock when he reached the house. The blinds were all drawn but he could see there were lights in most of the windows. He was greeted in the hall by Ada Flannigan. Her face was red and swollen, and she said immediately, 'The mistress and Mrs Skinner are in the study, sir.'

He nodded at her; then he took off his hat and coat, and brushed his hair back with his hand, before going along the passage. He tapped on the study door before opening it, to be greeted by the hard stares of his wife and her mother.

On the sight of him, Amy had risen from where she had

555

been sitting beside her mother on the sofa, but she didn't speak to him, she just held his gaze as he approached. Then, when he reached the couch she walked past him and out of the room.

He wasn't surprised at her attitude, but he was by Bridget's tone as she said, 'Well, you've managed to come.'

'I hadn't heard the news, Bridget, until I returned home.'

'Oh, you return home sometimes, then.'

'Oh, Bridget, please.'

'Oh, you can change your tone of "please understand me and my situation". Well, I can say this to you: do you understand me and my situation at this moment? I have lost my beloved husband, my beloved Douglas. My life is finished and you have helped to precipitate it.'

'*What do you mean?* What are you talking about?'

'What I am talking about is your actions, your infidelity. If you hadn't been with your woman, that last incident wouldn't have happened.'

'Now, now, Bridget. I must come back on you about that. If you had done your duty, your real duty, by Henrietta, she would have been under restraint years ago, and you know it. Douglas tried, he advised you, but no, you had to have something to control. Oh . . . Oh' – he raised his hand – 'I know this is not the time to say these things. I don't want to retaliate, but your attitude leaves me nothing but to try to defend myself, and I must say this: when you lost hold on your daughter you grabbed at Henrietta, because Douglas never wanted her in the house.'

'Don't you dare say that! Don't you dare suggest I went against Douglas's wishes.'

'I am saying it.' His voice was quiet. 'I am saying it very plainly, because Douglas loved you so much, not only loved, he worshipped you and would put up with anything in order to please you.'

He watched her eyelids blinking, her mouth trembling, but no tears came, and her voice was still vibrant as she said, 'Yes. Yes, he adored me. And I repeat what I said first, you have been the means of my losing him before his time. If it hadn't been for your last escapade he would have had nothing to excite or aggravate him. But a second heart attack was too much . . .'

'It wasn't a second heart attack, Bridget. What you don't know, what you closed your eyes to, which is another point, is that Douglas had had a number, I don't know how many, but a number of slight attacks over the past two years. He said as much to me.'

'No! No!'

'But yes, Bridget, yes. He didn't want to upset you. Anyway, you can confirm it by speaking to his doctor.'

'Well, whichever way, I still blame you for aggravating his situation. He always trusted you . . .'

'While you mistrusted me, Bridget.' He saw her swallow deeply before she said, 'Unfortunately, you always made me aware of the branch from where you sprang.'

'Thank you. But what you seem to forget, Bridget, is that a tree has many branches, and Douglas was an off-shoot of that particular tree, and his off-shoot was Amy, and we're all linked. You, in a way, are an outsider, always have been, so you cannot really speak of the feelings and workings of the members of the so-called tree. And I would say that you have been lucky in having the love of Douglas, because, in a way, he showed none of the vices of the main body as my father did, like I do, and my son Malcolm does, and' – he now poked his head towards her – 'his mother does, too.' Then, lowering his voice, he said, 'I'm . . . I'm sorry, Bridget, that we're talking like this and at this particular time, because you have lost your husband and I have lost the only real man friend I've ever had. Douglas meant a great deal to me and I imagined, unlike some other people, he did not hold me in bad esteem.'

'And there, I think he was mistaken.'

'Doubtless you do, Bridget; but it could be better all round if for the next few days we could bury our differences. I would like to help you to see to the affairs of . . .'

She broke in sharply, saying, 'Thank you! But all the affairs have already been dealt with; I do not need any assistance. I have arranged for the funeral to be on Wednesday, and I don't wish to see you until then, when there will be business to attend to. As from then, I shall no longer be maintaining your household, and it will be up to you if you decide to stay on and act for your son, as you did in the beginning for Douglas and me.'

The anger that rose in him formed a wave of hate that swelled in his throat. His face turned a deep dark red and for a moment he thought he was going to choke. Then, strangely, it was Douglas's voice he heard. It was loud in his head, saying, 'Get away now. Say nothing more. Nothing. Do you hear? Get away.'

He wasn't conscious of leaving the room, not of going along the passage to the hall, but he became very conscious of glaring at Amy as she stood within the drawing-room door looking towards him. And he kept his gaze on her as he got into his coat and thrust on his hat. When he imagined she was going to take a step towards him he turned swiftly and opened the door and rushed out, because he knew if she had started on him he wouldn't have been able to keep his hands off her.

As he got into the car, there flashed through his mind the description of the tree and its branches. His father had murdered a man and he had used physical force on his own daughter; his daughter had used more physical force on a number of people, and she had almost killed one; his grandfather had shot his own son. There was a dangerous vein running through them all and it was strong in him this moment, for he wanted to hit out at something . . . someone. Looking back, at least over the last twenty years, he could see himself having been used and manipulated, and now that woman had planned that he would go on being caretaker of his son's inheritance. Well, be damned if he would! Be damned if he would!

11

The funeral was over and he'd had no intention of returning to the house; but at the cemetery gates Mr Richard Kemp, who was now an elderly man, had approached him, saying, 'You will be coming back to the house, Mr Skinner?' And to this Joseph had said, 'No, I don't think there is any need.' But Richard Kemp had smiled and said, 'I think you'll find there is a need, Mr Skinner. The will is to be read today, and you should be there.' They had looked hard at each other for a moment, then Joseph had said, 'Very well. Very well.'

So now, here he was sitting in one of the two seats placed near the door. To the side of him was the small staff, and old Sam Benson and his son; in front of him, in two rows of chairs, sat his six children, and in front of them were seated Bridget and Amy. A sofa table fronted them all, and behind it Mr Kemp was seated.

There were two open folders lying on the table and from one Mr Kemp took up a sheet of parchment paper and began to read. The words were the usual, 'I, Douglas Filmore, of the — . . .' Then came the address and the fact that Douglas was in a sound state of mind; after which followed the details of the will. But before actually beginning to read these, Mr Kemp looked at the assembled company, gave a little smile, then began.

'I leave to each of my six grandchildren the sum of five hundred pounds, and to Sam Benson, who has been as my partner and friend for over twenty years, I leave my stonemasonry business, together with the deeds of the stone buildings where we have worked and the farmhouse attached, the whole originally known as Patens Farm, on condition that on his decease he passes the said business and house on to his son, Henry. Included in this are all the implements appertaining to the business, and the money due from customers.'

When Mr Kemp had spoken of the five-hundred pounds left to the grandchildren, there had been no turning of heads, no murmurs. But now came gasps from the two men, and they turned and looked at each other and almost imperceptibly the younger man's hand went out and gripped his father's arm.

Mr Kemp nodded at the two recipients as if expressing his pleasure, too. And now he went on:

'I leave to Joseph Skinner, whom I consider to be my nephew, the sum of two thousand pounds. And now I would like Mr Kemp to read the letter to my wife explaining the reason for my further actions.'

It was now that Mr Kemp lifted up the other sheet of parchment and, looking towards Bridget, he began:

'My dearest wife,
    There is no need for me to tell you how sorry I am that I've had to leave you, and again how sorry I am I have gone against what I know to be your wishes, although they have never actually been voiced. But you know I have always considered that, if everyone had their rights, Joseph, whether illegitimate or legitimate, should have inherited Grove House and the estate. I had hoped that I would have been spared a little longer to witness a new law that is in the offing to the effect

that a man born out of wedlock shall have the legal right to inherit. But as I don't think I shall live to see the time when justice prevails, I am leaving the estate as it stands, the house, all it contains, the farm and the adjoining land, to the man I've already said I consider to be my nephew, Joseph Skinner. Please, Bridget, do not be angry with me for this decision. I would never have rested easy if he had been deprived of his right, for we both know that, when my father died and the house became mine, we would have never lived there and I would likely have sold it. But it is Joseph who, over the years has brought it to its present state, and, just as I loved the place, so does he. The other matters appertaining to Joseph, I am sure, will resolve themselves. Have patience, my dearest, dear, Bridget, and know that in due time it will be passed on to his son, and I hope his son, my grandson Malcolm, will be as worthy of it as I consider his father to be.

I am always and forever, wherever I may be, your devoted husband. Douglas Filmore.'

There were different sounds and murmurs in the room. Both Bridget and Amy had their heads bent; no one could see their expressions; but the tears were running down the faces of the three girls, and William had his hand tight across his mouth, while Jonathan was covering his eyes with his hand; only Malcolm sat staring at the bent heads of his mother and grandmother. But Joseph sat in the back seat, staring over the heads of them all. He really couldn't believe what he had just heard; he felt slightly numb. Strangely, he did not feel elated but he was experiencing a depth of gratitude he could put no name to, and the love for the dead man that was now filling his throat was almost unbearable. He had to get out, get away.

Rising swiftly, he turned to the door at his side, opened

it, then almost blindly groped his way along the passage to the study, and there he dropped down into a leather chair.

It was his. His. How he was going to keep it hadn't yet entered his head. Anyway, it was of no consequence at the moment. The only thing he was aware of was that Douglas had gone against Bridget's wishes, and that must have taken some doing.

He was sitting holding his head in his hands when the door was thrust open and his family came in, or at least five of them, and the girls, in different ways, said, 'It's wonderful, Daddy.' And they hugged him and he kissed them but said nothing, until William, after biting on his lip, nodded at him, saying, 'I never thought it would happen, Father.' And to this Jonathan added, 'Nor I, because he gave us to understand, I mean, Malcolm, that it was all cut and dried. Apparently he got that from mother. He's . . . he's not very pleased, Father.'

And now, for the first time, Joseph forced himself to speak: quietly, he said, 'No, I wouldn't expect him to be.'

It was Alice who now put in, 'And there was that bit that grandpa said about him being worthy of inheriting. Well, as he's left it to you, Daddy, you could leave it to anybody you liked who was worthy of inheriting.'

'Are you coming straight home now, Daddy?'

He looked at Kitty and shook his head, saying, 'Not straightaway. I've . . . I've got to go to the office; and I have one or two other things to see to.'

They all stood silent for a moment, their heads moving, until Bertha said, 'I know who'll be pleased about this;' and William, looking at her, said, 'Who?'

'John, of course, and the staff; won't they, Daddy?'

He did not answer, but he thought, Yes, they might. Yes. But then, what would they think when he had to reduce their numbers? Anyway, that was in the future;

563

now he must get to the hospital. 'Go on and join your mother and grandma,' he said to them. 'They'll both be needing you.'

As they trooped out of the door he heard Alice say, 'I can't understand Grandma.' And William replied, 'I can. Oh, yes, I can.'

Yes, William would understand his grandmother because, in a way, he took after his grandfather.

He let some minutes elapse before he left the room, and then it was to run straight into Bridget, who must have been making for the study. They stared at each other hard for a moment until Bridget muttered, 'I'll never be able to forgive you, Joseph Skinner, for coming between me and my husband. In all our years together he never went against my wishes, *never*.'

To this he could have answered, 'No, no, of course he didn't; he let you have your own way in everything. He was an easy-going man, and that was the best policy to take; and moreover, he had that inordinate love for you. But you can't bear that a sense of justice should override it.'

It was the look on her face, almost of hate, that made him voice his last thoughts: 'You can't bear, Bridget, to think that his sense of justice would override your dominance, can you?' And with that he left her; and as it happened they were the last words they were to exchange.

As he went from the house Mr Kemp was about to get into his car and he stopped and turned towards him and, when he offered his hand, Joseph took it and it was shaken firmly.

'I'm glad things have turned out as they have for you. You've worked for that place if anybody has, much more so, I would say, than any of your ancestors, because it was given to them on a plate. You know what I mean? I couldn't imagine one of them doing a good day's work in his life, except, of course, Mr Douglas. But my father, before he died, God rest his soul, told me quite a bit of the history of the house. In fact, he had documents going way back, and very interesting they were too. They'll be passed on to you when you come to the office, which I would like you to do at your pleasure, but soon. As I said before, you have really worked for that house, but it's going to take some keeping up, isn't it? because, as you can gather, Mrs Filmore will no longer be supporting the staff now that Mr Douglas has gone. We'll have to put our thinking caps on, won't we?'

'Yes, I suppose we shall, Mr Kemp; and if it's convenient to you, I'll look in tomorrow around three.'

'Yes, that will be quite convenient. Well, good day to you, Mr Skinner, or is it going to be Mr Filmore? But we'll go into that too, I mean about getting your name changed. And, as your uncle said, there is a law in the offing that will give you the right to claim the name. But of course, laws take time to get from the offing and on to the statute books. But it will come, it will come. So, until tomorrow, good day, good day to you.'

'Good day, Mr Kemp; and thank you . . .'

From the drawing-room window, where the shades were still half drawn, Amy watched the men part, Joseph to go to his car and drive off. Malcolm, who was by her side, said, 'Didn't you have an inkling of this, Mother?'

'No. No, of course not. I went by what your grandma said. I knew there had been discussion about it with your grandfather, but I understood, as always, he would have acceded to her wishes. Well, you see what happened.'

'Yes, I see what's happened, and I feel I've been let down. This business about being worthy of inheriting. He could leave it to whom he likes if he doesn't think I'm fit; and so I'll have to behave myself like a good little boy. God! I shall hate going back to the house.'

'Well, you have no need to, dear, you may stay here.'

He looked at her sharply. Stay here! with his grandmother in the mournful state she was in and his mother in an equally mournful state? No. And anyway this house wasn't run like the other one; there was no real scope. He turned from her now, saying, 'Oh, I'll have to go back; he's paying my college fees. I'm under that obligation; but it shouldn't be an obligation if everybody had their rights. All this talk about rights. But anyway, this has decided me on something. The Barnett's have an uncle in the British Embassy in Paris. That's where Roger is going when Alice and he marry, and he says his uncle's got a lot of influence there. Last month, there was a post going for a university man. But then they are always going, they're always being moved around the place, he says. So that's where I'll head for.'

'But you haven't finished your second year. Why don't you stay and get your degree?'

He seemed to be thinking, then said, 'Well, he mightn't have the money to keep me there by the sound of things, because Grandma certainly won't fork out for any of the maintenance, will she? And what's more, by the sound of her, she wouldn't give a penny towards my education, because she considers that it's his duty. And what money have you, Mother? Nothing really, at least not until Grandma dies. Then of course' – he smiled now – 'you will be a very wealthy lady, because she must be rolling in it.' When she didn't answer he said, 'Are you coming back home now?'

'No; I can't leave Mother. She's here all alone and she's really in a very odd state. I know she hasn't shed a tear since your grandfather died.'

He drew in a long breath before he said, 'Well, I suppose things will go on as usual. The wonderful John will rule the roost. He, of course, will be over the moon at the news. Father's right hand; he takes too much on himself, I think. Anyway, I'll go and say goodbye to Grandma, and I'll come down tomorrow again before I leave for Oxford.' He bent and kissed her cheek, then went out.

Standing alone in the room, Amy thought. No, her mother hadn't cried, and she had lost her husband; and she herself had lost a husband, but she wanted to cry, almost scream, and for many reasons, not the least of them being that she was never going to return to that house again.

12

It was a fortnight later. Joseph was at home in his office. He was sitting at one side of the desk and John was seated at the other, and Joseph was saying, 'Well, John, I've worked it all out. Now I'll put it to you plainly. There are eight indoor servants, and three men and a boy in the yard and the garden. I'm not counting the farm, because William gives himself a small wage and sees to his man and the boy there out of the profit from the market. But as I see it, my responsibilities for the wages alone come to about three hundred and seventy pounds a year, that is not counting their insurance, or the buying of the food and the renewing of uniforms. Now to cover that, I would need at least six hundred a year. Up till now that has been met by Mr. Filmore. I can see no way of my paying that amount out of what I have in resources. I was left, as I think you know, two thousand by my uncle, and I had less than a thousand saved of my own. The money that comes from the business I have to use for the education of the family. I've always seen to that myself, and that will have to go on, and my earnings barely cover it because, as you know, with the exception of William who, as I said, sees to himself, and Alice who is shortly to be married, there are four still to be met: and Jonathan, as far as I can see now, is going to need supporting for some long time. From his present college he hopes to go on to yet another. But we can forget about the needs of the family; it's the needs of the staff that is forcing me to say what I must, John, and that is, I've got to cut down drastically. Anyway, with Kitty and Bertha at boarding school, Alice soon to be gone, Malcolm at college, it leaves only Willie and me in the house. Now, I've no need to say to you that seven indoor servants is a little more than is required for two people, even taking in the holidays when the girls come back. So, who is to go and who is to stay? It's an awful decision and you've got to help me in this. Outside, Ron will be pensioned off, the boy will do the yard work, but only one gardener can remain.'

'Sir,' said John now, 'it would be impossible for me to say who has to stay and who has to go, because we have been as one family for years; the cook and the girls have practically grown old here, well, if not old, elderly. As for a man getting a post, there seem to be fifty applicants for one job, no matter what kind. As you know, there are men still walking the road from the war, begging even for work that they would have considered degrading before they went to fight for King and country. It is all very sad. But, sir, there's something I want to tell you. We've been expecting something like this, knowing of your circumstances. So, I called a meeting of all the staff a few days ago and there's one thing they all agreed to: that this was a very large house with fifteen main bedrooms besides the attics, and counting the rooms on the ground floor, and excluding servants' quarters, and the basement which runs the length of the house, the cellars and the annexe, not counting these, there are thirty-four main rooms altogether and all could be put to use. The idea came through something you said to me a week ago, sir. You said you intended to bring your friend, who will be an invalid, here, and also her mother to look after her. We discussed which room would be appropriate for a bedroom and we decided that the games room could be turned into such because it has French windows leading on to the side terrace and the gardens. Isn't that so, sir?'

'Yes, John, that is so.'

'Well, then, as I put it to the others, and they all agreed, that what you could do for one invalid you could do for another. It could be a thriving business, sir. And I know of two such in Newcastle which house retired ladies or gentlemen who are past the age of seeing to themselves. In one particular home they have their own room and quite a bit of their own furniture, I understand, around them. I have a friend who is a gardener at Lady Harris's establishment on the outskirts of Newcastle, and Lady Harris's father is in such a home and apparently is very happy. I had a talk with my friend about it.'

Joseph did not speak, but gnawed on his bottom lip for a few seconds; and then he laughed, and when John laughed with him, saying, 'It could be done, sir,' Joseph said, 'Yes, yes indeed, John, it could be done, but . . . but at the moment I'm amazed at your suggestion. It would never have crossed my mind, and yet it should, because I sold a house last year not half the size of this for exactly the same purpose.'

'Well, what do you say, sir?'

'What do I say, John? What do I say? I just don't know. The only thing that strikes me at the moment is that it would keep us all together and that we couldn't lose much by it. There would have to be alterations, I suppose.'

'No, sir, but there would have to be an addition, and that would be a lift up to the first floor. But that could be in an alcove to the side of the stairs where the clothes closet is now. It would be a simple job, sir.'

Joseph started to laugh again and was about to say something when John put in, 'If you only had two or three clients, sir, it would cover expenses. And the people who can afford to take up residence in places like this can afford to pay well, and if things improved you could have at least ten bedrooms occupied, even more if you wanted.

But as I said, the idea stemmed from you in the first place, sir, and your talking of bringing your friend here. By the way, when will that be, sir?'

'I'm not sure now. I thought it might have been next week, but they are talking about another operation.'

'Will she eventually be able to walk, sir?'

'I'm not sure, John; nor are the doctors. I think this business of operations is just trial and error. But one good thing, she is much brighter in herself and is looking forward to getting out of hospital. So she'll submit to anything that's going to happen.'

'We will look forward to her arrival, sir.'

'That is good of you, John. Knowing the circumstances, that is very good, very good of you all.'

'May I be bold enough, sir, to enquire if the mistress has decided to live with her mother?'

'As far as I can gather, John, that's her decision. Otherwise I wouldn't have thought about bringing my friend here. And I may tell you now, I'm going to ask my wife for a divorce.'

'I'm sorry, sir . . . well, what I mean is, that all this had to happen.'

'So am I, John, so am I. But there's one thing that I'm glad about and that is, in the main . . . I say, in the main, my family understand the situation; and as I've pointed out before, there will be only Willie and I in the house. Well, that's just as it is at present, isn't it, as Alice is staying with her mother for the time being and the rest have returned to school. Anyway, you can tell the staff, if we can work out this new plan, things will remain as they were.'

'They will be delighted to hear it, sir, delighted. And thank you.'

As John rose to his feet, so did Joseph, and he, too, said, *Thank you*. Thank you, John. And let me say straightaway, I am very grateful, not only for your loyalty but also for your caring.'

And to this John answered, 'It's always been a pleasure to serve you, sir, and I hope it will continue for a long time.' And on this, with a small inclination of his head, he went out.

Slowly Joseph walked towards the window and looked out onto the garden where the trees were turning to russet, and he thought, An old people's home; and immediately his mind went to Bertha.

13

'Well, that's final: you'll never go back there again. How dare he! Just how dare he openly flaunt public censure and talk of bringing his woman into the house! And then turning it into a boarding house.'

'Apparently, Mother, as Malcolm says, it's for elderly people, monied people.'

'What else did he say? You were long enough on the telephone.'

'Just that he was angry, Mother; that he couldn't go into details because he didn't know them. He had just had a letter from Willie.'

'Well!' Bridget, seated on the couch, looked at her daughter's back, where she was standing before the fire, her head bent apparently staring down at it, and she said, 'That's final. Oh, yes, that's final. You must put in for a divorce immediately. You have the grounds staring you in the face.'

After a moment, and Amy having made no response, her mother demanded, 'Well, why don't you say something? Surely you have an opinion on the matter.'

Amy did not immediately turn round but when she did her slow movement was so different from her usual self-assertive manner, and her voice, too, was without force as she said, 'Yes, Mammy, I have an opinion, a number of opinions.'

'Well, what are you going to do about it?'

'I'm going to think about it.'

'Think!' Bridget's fingers were drumming on the side of

the chair. 'Girl, the time has passed for thinking, it's for acting.'

'Yes, as you say, Mammy, it's a time for acting.' And at this she walked out of the room and took the familiar stairs to her bedroom.

She had been born in this house, she had been brought up in this house, but oh, how she had come to hate it over the past weeks. The monotony, the dullness, her mother buried in her sorrow. It was odd, but the only time she had shown any evidence of her old self was when she had told her the details of the phone conversation between herself and Malcolm. She could go the whole day and hardly speak. As for having nothing to do, it was as if she hadn't any properties at all to see to.

She sat down now on the side of her bed and, like a child, she rocked herself. He was cruel, cruel. He could have taken that woman to the other house . . . anywhere. But to bring her back into Grove House! It was an insult. But she wouldn't divorce him. She wouldn't divorce him.

Her rocking stopped, and now her joined hands were gripped tightly between her knees. He was all she had in life, all she wanted, had ever wanted, that was the pity of it. If she had only turned her thoughts to other things, people. If she had even concentrated on the children. But he had been right about the children, for each one of them had seemed to take him further away from her. She should have had sense, she should have played a game; other women did. But she could see nothing but him; he was a kind of madness with her. She felt at times she would go mad, like that awful Henrietta. What was she to do? There was nothing she could do, was there? She would be stuck here with her mother until she died.

Oh! The prospect brought her from the bed. And that could be years ahead, during which time her mother would get older and more taciturn. She wouldn't be able to stand it . . .

Bridget, too, had come upstairs to her room, and she was standing holding a silver-framed photograph of Douglas: 'My darling,' she was saying. 'Oh, my darling, how I miss you. And I've forgiven you for deceiving me. But as you thought you were doing something for the best, now you must understand, my dear, that I am about to do something for the best, too. You were mistaken about the character of Joseph Skinner: he is like his father, a bad man, in fact I cannot look at him but I see his father. You always said that Malcolm was more like your brother, but I think you were mistaken there, dear, too. So, please bear with me and try to understand what I'm about to do. I will be with you soon because I cannot bear this life without you.' She now kissed the photograph and laid it back on the bedside table. Following this, she picked up the phone from the same table and dialled Mr Kemp's office in Newcastle, and there made an appointment with him for three o'clock that same day.

'Yes, I know what I'm doing, Mr Kemp. You have known me all these years, and have you ever thought that I didn't know what I was doing?'

'No, Mrs Filmore, I have never thought that; but you have recently suffered a great loss, a heavy bereavement, and I wonder if you might not, after consideration and at a later date . . .'

'I've given you an outline of what I mean to do, Mr Kemp. Now will you please take it down and then you can turn it into your own jargon ready for me to sign at your earliest convenience . . . please. So we will begin.'

. . . And she began:

'On my demise I leave to each of my grandchildren one thousand pounds upon their reaching the age of twenty-one. To my eldest grandson, Malcolm Skinner, I leave ten thousand pounds when he reaches the age of thirty. I leave two hundred pounds to each of my servants . . . you have their names already, Mr Kemp. And to my daughter, if at my demise she has become divorced from her husband, Joseph Skinner, I leave my entire fortune, but on condition only that she in no way spends any of the money to aid Joseph Skinner, nor under any condition does she return to Grove House. If she violates one or other of these conditions then my entire estate goes into a trust fund . . . (which I hope you will set up, Mr Kemp.) The monies to be distributed wisely for the needs of hospitals and the sick situated in this county. However, if my daughter does not conform to my wishes I will still provide for her in that she may have the use of Meadow House as long as she lives, together with a sum of five hundred pounds a year. But this allowance is hers only as long as she occupies the house.'

She had stopped speaking for some minutes before Mr Kemp stopped writing, and when he laid his pen down he looked across at this woman whom, following his father, he had served for years. He had never imagined her being vindictive, but this was the most vindictive epistle that he had ever penned. And it was all against Mr Skinner. If anyone was asking his opinion he would have said that what Mr Douglas Filmore had done was what was due to his nephew, whether in or out of law. But definitely he had known from the first that it was against his wife's wishes. Yet, he could never imagine Mrs Filmore taking this attitude, but taken it she had and so therefore he would have to obey her orders. But it would go so very much against the grain, for in trying to penalise Mr Skinner she was acting against her own daughter. Did she not understand that? He was about to put this to her tactfully, when she said, 'I know what you're thinking,

Mr Kemp, but I'd thank you at this moment if you kept your opinions to yourself. I may add that my faculties are not impaired. I know what I am doing. Right prevails in the end.'

He managed to stop himself from adding a quip to that, as his father might have done: 'And so does spite.'

Apart from this, he was very surprised at the change that had come about in this woman since her husband had died. Perhaps it was because her husband had thwarted her. Women were queer cattle; he hadn't really understood them; and now he knew he never would live long enough to learn; not after taking down words that he must transcribe into legal terms and which would hold down a younger woman for the rest of her life, no matter which way she stepped. And it wasn't likely, being a human being, that she would step away from inheriting a fortune, one such as her mother's.

Dear! Dear! He sometimes wished he had taken up a profession that would have given him the opportunity to view humanity through a misted glass.

14

Joseph stood by the bed and looked down at Liz. She was dressed for the operating theatre and her face was bright as she looked up at him and said, 'You've really got a lift in?'

'Yes, and it works by electricity; and also, near it, a chute to take trays et cetera to the first floor.'

'Really? That's marvellous. It sounds exciting.'

'Well, it certainly is to your mother. She's been up and down it like a sweep's brush.'

Her face lost its smile now as she said, 'It's a pity there have been no applicants for the shop.'

'There's plenty of time.'

'She was telling me how she enjoys Bertha. A kindred spirit, she called her.'

'Oh, yes, they get on like a house on fire. Bertha says she wouldn't mind taking over the outdoor beer shop herself, and your mother says she wouldn't mind doing an exchange tomorrow, because she's always wanted to have a few hens and ducks. And I tell them, all right, they can make the exchange whenever they like, but to stop jabbering about it.'

She pulled back the sleeve of her theatre gown and put out her hand to him, and when he took it between his own, she asked quietly, 'Have you heard anything yet, I mean, from the solicitor?'

'Yes, from mine, but he doesn't seem to be making much headway with hers. I got on to Mr Kemp myself and he said as soon as his client made up her mind, he would let me know. But it doesn't matter, dear. We've accepted the situation; it doesn't matter a fig to me: you're coming home with me, everything's ready for you. The doctor promised me you'll be there for Christmas, and the staff are looking forward to meeting you, as are the family.'

When she closed her eyes he shook the hand within his, saying, 'I am not just saying that.' Although at the bottom of his heart he knew he *was* just saying that, because they all wouldn't have been human if they hadn't raised their eyebrows, or let their tongues wag about the situation. The only one he could really rely on to accept it wholly was John. But he wasn't going to worry; they, the rest, would all fall into place through time, and when they got to know Liz, they would love her; they couldn't help but do so.

She looked at him now, saying, 'You do know, dear, that this is a case of touch and go . . . well, what I mean to say is, I may be able to get some use back into them through time and exercise; on the other hand, it may mean I'll be like this for good?'

He bent over her now and, squeezing her hand further, he said, 'Either way, my love, either way, we'll be together.'

He stood aside as three nurses and a porter came in smiling, and one of the nurses, her voice very hearty, said, 'I'm sick and tired of pushing you down that passage. Well, I've gone on strike so I'm handing over to Percy here. Anyway, you've got all the men running after you, so come on, don't lie there, hoist yourself on to this trolley.'

As the breezy nurse was speaking, the other two and the porter lifted Liz bodily on to the trolley, then put a blanket over her, and now, her head back on the low pillow, she looked up at Joseph and said, 'Until tonight, dear,' and he answered, 'Until tonight. I'll be waiting.'

'By! some folks are lucky,' the talkative nurse said; 'I wonder when my turn'll come,' to which the porter quipped, 'Any minute, dear, any minute. Just say the word.'

Joseph walked some distance behind the trolley until it disappeared into a lift; and there he stood, seemingly lost, for some minutes. Even as he walked away and passed the waiting room, he had the strong desire to go in and sit down and wait until she came out of the theatre. Yet, not knowing how long that would be and also remembering he had an appointment at four o'clock with a client to view a house, he told himself he would phone at about five and hope to have a word with her doctor; then he would go home, have a quick bite to eat and be back for seven o'clock . . .

As it was, he returned to the hospital at a quarter to seven. Generally, there would already be a number of people sitting in the waiting room. He would not join them, but would stand in the corridor together with one or two other men. But tonight he did not reach the corridor, for he was beckoned to the reception desk, and there the nurse on duty, who had come to know him well and always had a cheery word for him, greeted him with, 'Mr Skinner, will you please go' – she pointed across the hall – 'down that corridor. It's the second door. The doctor would like to see you.'

He stared at her, but she was avoiding his gaze; she was writing something in a book. Of a sudden his feet felt as if they were glued to the floor, and he had to make an effort to move away from the desk and the sight of the top of her starched cap.

He knocked on the second door and a voice said, 'Come in.'

When he entered the room he saw the usual doctor and

the surgeon, but the latter was no longer in his white coat, he was dressed as if for the street. They were both standing and must have been in close conversation, but they turned and looked at him. Then Doctor Armitage said, 'Oh. Oh, hello, Mr Skinner. Do come in. Would you like to take a seat?'

'No, thank you. What's the matter?'

The two men exchanged a quick glance; then it was the surgeon who spoke, and he said, 'I'm terribly, terribly sorry about the news I have to give you. We . . . we could do nothing. It was so sudden; yet . . . yet not unexpected.'

'What . . . was . . . unexpected?' He found he had to push one word after another out from his mouth.

'Well, she knew the risk but she didn't want to alarm you or her mother. But strangely, the particular risk we were afraid of didn't happen. What I mean is, the operation went through successfully. We were delighted. But then she began to bleed, her pulmonary system . . . her veins were very thin. She had told me she was subject to frequent nose bleedings, and when this happens it often points to a weakened pulmonary system. Everything possible that could be done was done, I assure you, but we couldn't stop the bleeding. It seemed that a whole length of vein broke down altogether.'

Joseph didn't speak but he took a step to the side and sat down on the seat that had previously been offered to him. If either of these men had asked him what he felt at that moment he could have answered truthfully: nothing, nothing at all; he could have been as dead as she was.

When a hand pushed a small glass towards his face and a voice said as if from a distance, 'Drink this, Mr Skinner,' obediently he took the glass and drank it. It was sweet tasting, that is until it got down his throat and then it seemed to burn like whisky.

He blinked now as he looked from one to the other,

and when Doctor Armitage said, 'What did you say, Mr Skinner?' he said to the face hovering in front of him, 'She always said it wouldn't work.'

'Did she? You mean?' The doctor's voice was cut off abruptly by the surgeon saying, 'She was a very nice woman.' And as Joseph looked up at him he repeated to himself, Yes, she was a very nice woman. She was a lovely woman, a lovely girl. She was or had been someone who could love him and let him go. She had said that to him only last week, 'I love you, but if circumstances were such that you found you must go back, then I could let you go.' But now she was gone. *No! No!* She couldn't be. Life wouldn't do this to him. He wasn't a bad man. He wasn't like his father. Aren't you? Aren't you? There was a voice coming from the back of his head and it kept saying just that: Aren't you? Aren't you? *He* had left his wife and taken a mistress, and what were you intent on doing? You left Amy and took up with Liz.

Now he was yelling back at the voice, But there's all the difference in the world; I never treated Amy badly and she's a difficult person, Amy. Very difficult, and spiteful like her mother has become, for she would rather have seen that house go to Malcolm. Oh, yes, to Malcolm. I didn't count. I was just Joe Skinner, Lily's bastard son.

Now the voice had changed and it was saying, 'Put your head well between your knees. That's it. That's it.' Then another voice said, 'Breathe deeply. Try to take deep breaths.'

Then another voice said, 'Ring for the sister; he should lie down for a time. The mother reacted in the same way; she's in the side ward now.'

Janet was in the side ward, they were saying. What was the matter with him? Pull yourself together. Pull yourself together.

He put his head back and looked from one man to the

other, saying, 'I'm sorry. I'm sorry. I'm all right now. It . . . It was silly.'

'Not silly at all. It's the most natural thing in the world. Shock takes us like that at times. But I think you should rest here for a time before . . . You came by car? Well, I don't think you should drive home. Perhaps you would like to join Mrs Dunn?'

'Yes. Yes, I would.'

At this point the sister entered the room and the doctor asked her to take Mr Skinner along to the side ward where Mrs Dunn was resting.

As if in a slight daze he heard himself thanking the doctors, but at the same time asking himself what he had to thank them for; they had let her die. No! No! Pull yourself together.

He was walking along the corridor now. Sister had taken hold of his arm, yet he felt there was no need for that, he could walk straight enough. Then he was in the side room and there was Janet lying on a narrow bed, her face streaming with tears and at the sight of him she held out her arms to him, saying, 'Oh! Joe. Joe.'

When the door closed on them they had their arms about each other, and now his face was as wet as hers, and when he heard himself sobbing, he told himself it didn't matter, it didn't matter; he had to cry or his head would explode.

When they had released each other Janet said, 'What am I going to do without her? She was my life, Joe, my life. She was all I lived for. And you, you loved her. I know you loved her and you were right for her. From the first minute I saw you, I knew you were right for her. I can't believe it, Joe. I can't believe it.'

'Nor can I, Janet, nor can I.'

'She knew though, didn't she?'

'Knew what, Janet?'

'That no way, no how, it could ever be. Nothing could come of it. She said that to me, more than once. It was as if it was all clear in her mind; and you know something, Joe? She knew in her heart that she would never get to your house, because she knew it wasn't right. What am I going to do without her?'

He didn't answer. Her mother was asking what she was going to do without Liz, and he was asking, too, what he was going to do without Liz? Comparatively speaking he had known her such a short time, yet there had been something about her, something about her character that had deluded him into thinking he had known her all his life. And now he was lost, and that's what Janet was saying.

'I feel so lost already, Joe. The world seems empty.'

'It won't be, Janet, so don't worry; I'll always be there.'

'I'd been looking forward to coming to your house, but not now.'

'Why not?'

'No, no. It wouldn't be right. Anyway, I'll keep on the shop. It will give me something to do till the time comes. It will save me from going mad, I suppose. But it will be the loneliness that I'll have to get used to. Even while she's been in hospital there was always the knowledge that I knew she was there.'

He made no remark on this but he thought, Yes, it's the loneliness that will take some getting used to. He had the house to go back to, his family, and the staff, yet they offered no consolation. He had lost Liz . . . There was that voice from the back of his head speaking at him again, saying, This is how Amy must have felt. Her family, or her parents, had been of no consolation to her when she had first lost him . . . And that was some years ago.

Everything was linked. In a way, Amy was to blame that Liz had died, for if it hadn't been for the closed door

584

across the landing he would not have been so susceptible to the kindness and charm of another woman. Then, because he had, that jealous, mad woman had to cripple Liz, and now she was dead.

Life was a linked chain and he was tied to it. And at this moment he wished to God that he too was dead.

15

'Well, how did it go?'

'Very well, Mammy. As expected, very well.'

Amy stood in the hall taking off her loose grey-silk coat, which she laid over a chair before easing up her bun of fair hair, so as to release the elastic band that was holding her large, flat-rimmed, cream-coloured, leghorn hat in place, before answering her mother's next question. 'Yes, I told them that you were terribly sorry you couldn't get there, because you weren't well enough.'

She now preceded Bridget into the sitting-room and, after sitting down to the side of the fire, she took up the poker and began to rearrange the burning coals in the grate. This had become a habit of hers, but today it irritated Bridget, and she protested: 'Stop that! Amy, will you, and tell me what happened?'

Amy laid the poker down; then, turning slowly, she looked at her mother and said, 'My daughter was married, that's what happened, and all the family were there, and his family, too. It was supposed to be a quiet wedding but there were a lot of spectators around the little church.'

'Well, I expected that; but I mean . . . well, you know what I mean. Don't hedge. What happened when you met up with him?'

'When I met up with him, Mammy, we greeted each other like civilised people. He said, "How are you, Amy?" and I said, "Quite well, thank you." Then we stood together and had our photographs taken with the happy couple, as is usual, you know, at weddings, Mammy.'

'You're annoying me, Amy, you know you are. You've got into the habit of doing that lately.'

Amy bit on her lip and turned to gaze into the fire again. Her mother had said she was annoying her. Dear God! If she only knew how that feeling was reciprocated, for there were times when she felt she would yell at her, scream at her.

'What were his folks like? Were the titled ones there?'

'Yes, I think they were.'

'Weren't you introduced to them?'

'No. I kept in the background, Mammy.'

'Were you asked to go back to the house?'

'Yes, I was pressed to go back to the house. But as I told you before I left, I wasn't going to do that.'

'I should think not, a boarding house!'

'Well, boarding house it may be, but as far as I can gather it's a very profitable boarding house.'

'How do you know that?'

'Oh,' Amy now shrugged her shoulders, 'someone told me, that's all.' She couldn't say she had got it practically from the horse's mouth . . .

She had always been a little jealous of John's authority in the house. Yet, today it had been he who had shown her the most consideration, even more than had her eldest son, for Malcolm seemed to have been taken up with another one of the Barnett tribe, one of a number of laughing, giggling girls. But it was John whom she had been undoubtedly surprised to see at the wedding, thinking that he would be back at the house attending to the refreshments or whatever they were having. But apparently it was at Alice's request he was there, so she had been informed by Bertha. Nevertheless, it was he who had spoken to her most kindly. She had been standing near the end of the church while more photographs were being taken on the green, when he addressed her, at first very formally, saying, 'Good afternoon, Mrs Skinner. It was a lovely service, don't you think?'

'Yes, John,' she had answered; 'it was a lovely service.' And then they had stood in silence looking at one another until he asked in a very ordinary way, 'How are you faring?' and she had replied, 'Quite well, John. Quite well.'

Two small bridesmaids and a page scampering between them caused an interruption; but, their eyes meeting again, he said quietly, 'May I be allowed to say, Mrs Skinner, that we miss you, that I . . . we all miss you,' and she had found herself quite incapable of saying a word and so she had turned her head away, only to see her husband talking to the overdressed woman she had earlier realised was the bridegroom's mother. She noted that he had lost weight; in fact, he looked slightly gaunt, but handsome, very handsome, which apparently wasn't lost on the woman who was ogling him. It was at this point she told herself, There I go again; I'll never learn.

She was brought back to face John's gaze by his saying, 'The house is just the same, madam . . . I mean, in spite of the business. There are four guests in at present and they mostly keep to their rooms, but the master has had a general sitting-room made for them on the first floor. It is all very well arranged and it's all in the west corridor, you know.'

It was still impossible to make any reply to him. Then she was amazed by the liberty he was taking, and yet warmed by it when, his voice very low, he said, 'The house is not the same without you; it needs a mistress,' at which point the words were forced out of her and she said, 'Oh, John! please.' And he replied, 'I'm sorry, madam, if I've overstepped the mark. But I thought I would like you to know.' At this she had said, 'Do you think you can bring my car around to the side gate? I would like to leave now.'

'Of course, madam, of course . . .'

She heard her mother saying, 'There are things you are holding back from me, aren't there, Amy? Did you have a talk with him?'

She sprang to her feet now. 'No, Mammy, I didn't have a talk with him,' she answered vehemently. 'Would you like me to have had a talk with him? If you think I should have said, "Will you take me back, Joseph? Here I am ready and willing," if you think I should have said that, then I will phone him now and carry out your orders.'

'Don't be impertinent! You know what I think.'

'Yes, Mammy; I know only too well what you think.'

'Well, in a way, you are wrong, because I only think what is for your good. I think of nothing else. I don't want you to be used, to be hurt again, because what he has done once he can do a second time. It's over six months and it won't be long before he takes up with somebody else. He is his father's son. I shall go to the grave thinking that. And another thing, when we are talking so plainly, I think it very strange that you haven't heard anything about the divorce. You did put in for it, didn't you? You told me . . .'

'Yes, Mammy, I told you I did, but I was lying, I didn't.'

'Oh, dear God!' Bridget now sat back on the couch slowly shaking her head as she said, 'You think you'll go back to him, don't you?'

'No, Mammy, I don't. I don't think I'll go back to him, for the simple reason he wouldn't have me.' She almost yelled the last few words. 'And now, as you said, that we're speaking plainly, I'll tell you, during this last six months or so, I've had a lot of time to look back at myself, and what Father used to say I've found very true, there are all kinds of love. But I had thought there was only one kind, mine. You say you love me. Well, I can tell you, Mammy, your love for me was of the same type as my

589

love for Joe, and it was that kind of love that drove a wedge between us. But there it is, I can't love any other way, and apparently nor can you. So, because I now realise that, I'm not going to blame him for what he has done or what he might do in the future. That will be up to him.'

As she turned and rushed down the room Bridget cried after her, 'Come back here! this minute. Come here! girl.'

Amy had reached the door. She stopped as if pulled up short in her tracks and, turning and looking up the room towards her mother, she cried, 'I am not a girl, Mammy, I'm a middle-aged woman of forty, and I am a fool. I always have been and I shall likely go on being one.' And with that she went out and banged the door.

Bridget now pressed her hand tightly against her ribs. Her heart was beating loudly in her ears, and she felt a swimming in her head. The feeling wasn't new, but as it came she cried, 'Oh! Douglas, Douglas. Where are you? What a way to come to the end of life, because I *am* near the end. I shall soon be with you, and I want that, the sooner the better. But I can't leave until I know she will see sense.'

Her heart-beats began to slow and as they did so she said to herself, 'She will never see sense, so thank God I am seeing sense for her. Vindictive as it might seem, I wouldn't rest in my grave if I thought The Grove and that man were prospering through a penny of mine. Victoria would understand what I am doing is right. Oh, yes, she would understand.'

There now crept over her a chill feeling, as if a window had been opened and a blast of air had suddenly filled the room. Her eyes were closed but there before her, standing with his back to the fire, was Lionel Filmore, and he was leering at her. His lips were back from his teeth and he was actually leering at her. And when his lips began to move she was reading the words, as she had so often read his daughter's, and he was saying, 'You didn't have a bastard, but you lowered yourself by lusting after a common workman, and you did sell Victoria to me. Two thousand pounds you paid me to take her, do you remember? And I did murder for that two thousand pounds. You started all this. You said so yourself, and now you're going to finish it, aren't you? Well, my bastard has beaten you so far, and there's still the future. Here! Take Joe Skinner to help you on your way.' He was holding out a long black candle towards her, and at this point she almost lifted herself to the front of the couch, her eyes gaping wide now; but there was nothing between her and the fire but the high railed fender.

As she cried, 'No! No! Imagination, impossible. Just imagination,' she got to her feet. Her hand held tightly across her mouth, she whimpered, 'Oh! Douglas, Douglas. Why did you have to go? And why did you have to trick me before you went? That's what's made me feel so bad, your tricking me. You who loved me so much. You adored me, yet you tricked me. Knowing how I felt about him you tricked me.'

She now groped her way to the door, pulled it open, but felt she could go no further, and Rose Grey and Ada Flannigan, crossing the hall together at that moment, turned and saw her. They hurried towards her and each took an arm, and as they helped her up the stairs Ada kept yelling, 'Miss Amy! Miss Amy!'

16

Bridget took to her bed on the day her granddaughter was married, which was the first Wednesday in May, 1925, but she didn't die until the second of January, 1926.

Only four of her grandchildren attended the funeral: Alice was with her husband in Australia, where he was now in a solicitor's firm; Malcolm was teaching French at a school quite near them. He was to return in the spring when he was due to marry his brother-in-law's cousin. The idea of a situation in the Paris Embassy had not materialized.

Joseph had attended the funeral, but naturally he had not returned to the house, and so on this day Mr Kemp had only five of the family seated before him, together with three maids and the two outside men, and it was with evident distaste that he began to read the will. William, Jonathan, Kitty, and Bertha had remained still while hearing what their grandmother had left them, and also about the ten thousand pounds left to Malcolm. But it was when they realised how their grandmother had treated their mother that their heads turned towards her, to see her face as white as that of any corpse, and her fists so tightly clasped at her waist that the knuckles showed white, and they all, at one point, shuffled in their chairs as if moving towards her.

When Mr Kemp was finished there was silence in the sitting-room until, standing up and looking towards the staff, he said, 'Would you kindly leave us for a moment, please?' and his glance included Amy's two sons and daughters. But William said, 'No, we won't leave Mother; and let me say, Mr Kemp, I think it's scandalous, outrageous. She must have been mad, like Henrietta.'

'No, William; I'm afraid she wasn't mad, and, as you know, she's of a different breed from Henrietta. Vindictive, yes, which apparently stems from a cause which originated way back in her life.' He now looked at Amy, who was still sitting rigid in her chair, and he now cried, 'I tried to persuade her otherwise. I did my very best, but she was adamant, and I must admit again, full of vindictiveness. Oh yes, full of vindictiveness. I have never before met anything like it; and I was amazed by her attitude, because she had always been a kind and caring woman. Of course, she was very strong-willed and she had her likes and dislikes; but haven't we all? But that she would do this to you – ' He now bent over Amy and lifted up one of her clenched fists and gently unfolded her fingers, as he said, 'But don't let it floor you. You are still a young woman; there's a lot of life before you. You'll have a home as long as you want to keep it . . .'

'It's scandalous!' Kitty's interruption checked him now; and she went on, 'Couldn't you have told her it was cruel, dreadful? And her only daughter. She needn't have left us anything; that wouldn't have mattered, would it?' She looked at Bertha, and Bertha shook her head. 'Yet she goes and leaves ten thousand to Malcolm, and what has he ever done for anybody but himself? Here's Willie; he works from morning till night, but she didn't leave you ten thousand, did she?'

'Shut up!'

'I won't shut up. I feel mad. I wish she were here, I would . . . Oh!' She ground her teeth, not daring to say what she would like to do, which was to slap her face.

She now went to her mother and put her arms around her neck, saying, 'I know you would lose everything if you came back, Mammy, but oh, Mammy, we do miss you. We really do. The holidays are not the same. I'm glad to get back to school. And Daddy's like a wet blanket . . .' Her voice trailed off.

William said quietly, 'I'll come down tomorrow and we'll have a talk.'

Amy looked up at him. Willie was kind; he was like her father; he used to say that he regretted he had never gone in for farming so that he could work with pigs. Willie too liked working with pigs. Her father used to say they were the most sensible creatures and weren't dirty at all; they smelt, but so did everybody else, if the truth was spoken. And there was Kitty and Bertha. They seemed to love her too. What was the matter with her? A few minutes ago she had been burnt up with hate of her mother; now it had ebbed, pushed back by members of her family. Jonathan was the only one as yet who hadn't said a word to her. She looked towards him, and he came over to her and, dropping on his hunkers before her, he took her hands and said, 'I'll come here and stay with you, Mother. I can learn the violin anywhere. There are good teachers round about . . .'

She took her hand from his and put it on his head, saying, 'Thank you, Jonathan, but that's the last thing I would want, to interrupt your career. But thank you, dear, for your suggestion.'

'Well, there's no reason why the girls can't stay here.' She turned to look at William now, then to the girls who were nodding assent, but she said, 'Now, now. Leave things as they are for a time. Let us all cool down. That's the best way, isn't it, Mr Kemp?'

Mr Kemp had been gathering up his papers and he nodded his assent. 'Yes, my dear, that's the best way. Give things time, something will evolve.'

'Could the case be taken to court?' William asked him,

which caused Mr Kemp to raise one hand as if taking an oath and to say, 'Oh, my dear fellow, now you have posed a question; and the answer to it is, yes, if you are willing to try to prove that your grandmother was of unsound mind at the time she made her will.'

'I think she must have been.'

'Well, as I said, young man, that would have to be proved, and the responsibility would lie with your mother.' He now looked at Amy and she, looking back at him, said, 'Yes. Yes, Mr Kemp, the responsibility lies with me.'

They'd had supper in the breakfast room, and they were still seated round the table, the four of them looking at their father where he sat at the end of the table, his head bowed. He had listened to them interrupting each other, their indignation on their mother's behalf still spurting from them, and he had imbibed their feelings, even to the pity they were expressing for Amy. But he was thinking: The bloody, cold-blooded old bitch. She's tied her up so she can't move. She'll lose at every turn, and if she doesn't divorce me, she's left in such a position she'll hardly be getting more than is doled out to her staff, and not half as much a week as it costs to keep that mad woman in the asylum. God in heaven! I can't believe it. Well, I can do that much for her. I can give her a divorce . . . And this was one thing he could say to them; and so, raising his head slowly, he looked at one after the other and he said, 'Well, the way's open for me to make her path smooth in one way. She can have a divorce and that'll ensure she gets what is rightfully hers.'

'Oh! Daddy, you wouldn't divorce her, would you?'

'Don't be such a dumb female, Kitty.' Jonathan poked his head towards his sister. 'Mother will be the one to get the divorce. Father will just agree to it.'

'I know that, string fingers.' Now Kitty pulled a face at him; then, looking at her father, she said, 'That's how it would be, wouldn't it?'

'Yes, that's how it would be.'

William now asked, 'How much do you think Grandma was worth?'

'Oh, William' — Joseph pulled a face — 'your guess is as good as mine. The factories alone brought in a small fortune; then, scattered around the towns, she has more than fifty houses, some large some small, but all paying rent, and they'll go on paying rent.'

'And if mother doesn't divorce you, she'll only get about ten pounds a week out of all that! It's dreadful, dreadful! Why did she do it?'

'Oh, I can tell you why she did it . . . because your grandfather left me this house. She wouldn't have minded it going to Malcolm; in fact that's what she wanted, because Malcolm was legitimate. But I, being the bastard son of your other grandfather, oh, she couldn't tolerate me because she had hated him, right from the day she first met him, I think. And anyway, you know all the story, all the circumstances that led up to the tragedy, when your great-grandfather shot him . . . and me, too.' He smiled now. 'But there you have the reason why your mother is being made to suffer. To put it simply, because she married me.'

Bertha, who had spoken little during all the conversation, said now in a very small voice, 'I'd kept hoping that . . . well, that Mammy would come back. But now that will never happen.'

Joseph put out a hand and patted his daughter's plump cheek, and as quietly he repeated her words, 'No, dear, that will never happen,' and even as he ended, he rose from the table and went from the room, the feeling of loneliness that had pervaded his being since Liz's going, deepening further.

In his bedroom he went straight to the side table and took up the phone and when the voice on the other end of the line spoke the number he paused for a moment, then said, 'Hello, Amy. It's Joseph here.'

There was another pause before her voice came, saying, 'Oh, hello.'

'I . . . I just want to say, I think it's damnable, I mean the will. I . . . I can't understand her.' Why was he saying that? he understood the old vixen all right; but he went on, 'I'll make it all right for you. You can have the divorce any time you like. They can get it through pretty quickly these days . . . Are you there?'

'Yes. Yes, I'm here.'

He knew by her voice that she was crying and so he said now, 'Don't upset yourself, please. It'll be all right.'

'Joseph.'

'Yes? Yes, Amy?'

'Could . . . could I see you?'

'See me? Of course, of course.'

'Could you come down tomorrow?'

'Yes, any time. What time would suit you?'

'Whatever will suit you.'

'Well then, I've got to be in Hebburn around ten. Say eleven?'

There was another pause before she said, 'Yes. Yes, thank you. That'll be fine.'

'All right. All right, Amy. Good night.'

'Good night, Joseph.'

17

He was held up in Hebburn; the lady wouldn't make up her mind about the house. She didn't know whether it was too big or not big enough, and then she discovered, as if at the last moment, that it was situated on the outskirts of Hebburn and really near Jarrow, but, as she remarked, the best end. Yes, he agreed with her, it was the best end and that it was a very nice house and it had belonged to a doctor. It wasn't until he said to her, 'Why don't you bring your husband and let him decide for you?' that she coyly looked at him and replied, 'I am a widow, Mr Skinner;' and he almost closed his eyes and sighed as he realised that this lady needed a house as much as he needed to jump into the freezing waters of the Tyne at this moment, for the snow was already two inches deep outside.

In no polite voice, he said, 'Mrs Green, I have another appointment. There is a client waiting for me' – he looked at his watch – 'and I'm already late for it. I'm afraid I'll have to shut up the house,' and with these last words he inclined his head towards her.

She stumped out of the front door and as he was turning the key in the lock she cried at him, 'You are no business man, Mr Skinner. You have lost a good customer.'

He faced her squarely. 'It's the third house I have shown you in the last few days, Mrs Green,' he said. 'The other two were furnished and I had to put the people to inconvenience to stay while you made your rambling inspection. Now, if you're really in need of a house then there are other estate agents who will be quite willing to serve you. And I'm sorry I cannot offer you a lift back to the centre of the town, but there is a bus stop over there.' He pointed.

'You mean to leave me here standing in the snow?'

'No, Mrs Green. I've noted that you are a very good walker. As I said, there's the bus stop.'

'I'll report you to your office.'

'Do that, Mrs Green, and I'll be the first one to open your letter.'

After turning the car around, he could see her marching head up in the air towards the bus stop, and he began to laugh; and continued to laugh at intervals until he was passing through Tyne Dock, when it occurred to him that he hadn't laughed like this for a long, long time. Altogether, he thought, he must have spent a full day of his time on Mrs Green, but that after all it had been worth it: for a few minutes he had felt lighter than he had done for months. But now there was the problem of facing Amy. However, there could be no doubt she'd be glad to see him, knowing that he'd be with her all the way in getting a divorce.

Twenty minutes later he rang the bell, and when Ada opened the door she greeted him with, 'Oh! hello, sir. But why do you bring such weather with you? Isn't it awful? Who'd live here, I keep asking myself? Come in. Give me your coat, sir. The mistress went upstairs just about five minutes ago, but I'll tell her. Go on in the sitting-room; there's a lovely fire on.'

He smiled at her but said nothing, then went across the hall and into the sitting-room. He hadn't been in this room for some time and it appeared to him now, as it hadn't before, to be rather shabby and dated.

Standing with his back to the fire, he looked about him, thinking, 'Well, I don't think she'll stay long here. Once she has the money she can do what she likes and I wouldn't blame her for getting away from this place. Yet Bridget had always looked upon it as a kind of palace. Well, modes and tastes change, as in everything else. Look at the fancy little boxes they are sticking up on every piece of spare land they could get their hands on.

He turned now and looked down on the fire and asked himself why he wasn't feeling agitated at meeting Amy? Probably because he was going to do something for her to make up for past hurts. But then, he must remember, in any case she could do it for herself . . . get a divorce naming Liz. Liz being dead, of course, there could be no corroboration of any admission he might make. What he must point out to her, and tactfully of course, was that he would have to give her evidence. There were ways and means. It had to be paid for, but nevertheless, he would do that, lawful or otherwise.

When the door opened he swung round; and he became speechless at the sight of her. He hadn't seen her since Alice's wedding. She had looked very white and drawn then, and he had kept in the background at her mother's funeral, but now she appeared to have hardly any flesh on her. He took a couple of steps towards her, saying, 'I'm terribly sorry I'm late. I had a client, one of those, you know, who want to look under the floorboards. I've shown her three houses in the last ten days and I still don't know what she wants.' Even as he was saying this he told himself he knew exactly what Mrs Green wanted, but Amy would never have appreciated being told the cold facts, such as they were; she could never stand another woman looking at him. Oh, what was he yarping on about to himself? He said to her, 'Aren't you feeling well? Oh, I suppose that's a stupid thing to say at this time.'

'Sit down,' she said.

So he sat down in the armchair to the side of the fire,

and he watched her slowly lower herself into the corner of the couch.

'It's dreadful weather,' she said.

'Yes. Yes, it is that.' He nodded in affirmation.

Her next question surprised him. 'How is your business going?'

'Oh, you mean the estate agency? Oh, that's . . .'

'No, I meant the Grove House business, with your guests.'

He was a little time in answering; then he said, 'Going very well, Amy, surprisingly so. There's seven guests upstairs. But I think before we take in any more, we'll have to get a matron, or someone like that, you know. John's very good; in fact, he's excellent. He runs the show, but he always did, didn't he?' He smiled at her, but she didn't return the smile, she just continued to look at him and wait for him to go on; and so he went on, hesitantly now, saying, 'Well, it was his suggestion. As he put it, men are all right in their place and so are maids, but he seems to think it needs a kind of matron or sister, someone like that, to oversee things. You see, I'm out all day and it's he that runs the show. Now there's generally only Willie and myself at home in the evenings and then that time is taken up discussing the business side connected with the guests; but the girls are expected today . . .'

'How many can you take?'

'Oh, we can take twelve comfortably. They're in the main corridor, you know. It leaves the other one private. We've got a lift in now, and it's a Godsend. It saves a lot of running up and down the stairs with trays, and I know how heavy that can be.' He pursed his lips now. 'I had some weeks of it at one time, you know.'

'Yes. Yes. I can remember. Would . . . would you like a cup of coffee?'

'Yes. Yes, I would, Amy. Thank you.'

She got up, but she didn't pull on the bell near the fireplace. He watched her walk to the door, then listened to her steps going across the parquet floor in the direction of the kitchen, and he turned now and leant his elbow on the arm of the chair and supported his head in his hand, and like that he let out a long slow breath. They were so polite to each other, like strangers meeting on a train; and she looked awful . . . well, not awful, she looked ill. She'd had to nurse her mother for months. However, he had to broach the subject of the divorce, but how would he go about it?

It was some time before she returned, and he was surprised to see her carrying a tray with two cups on it. He rose quickly and took it from her; then when she was seated, he handed her a cup and, taking the other, he sat down.

After sipping at the coffee, he placed the cup back on the side table and, looking at her squarely now, he said, 'Well, we'd better get down to the business of why we are meeting, hadn't we, Amy?'

'Yes. Yes, Joseph, just as you say, we'd better get down to business.'

She, too, had put her cup aside now and she sat looking at him until he said, 'I must say, Amy, I think it is a dastardly thing your mother has done to you, dreadful! And it would seem out of character if I didn't know the reason, and I'm to blame for that.'

She didn't contradict him but sat looking at him. Her eyes looked enormous in her white face, their expression one he hadn't seen there before and he couldn't explain it to himself. She didn't really look like the Amy he knew; she must be ill. He found he was feeling deeply, deeply sorry for her. His voice was very low as he said, 'About the divorce, Amy. I shall make it as easy as possible. I know you could have got it some time ago because of . . .

my association with Mrs Lilburn, but as you know, she died and I don't know whether any admission on my part would be valid as evidence for a divorce. But there are other ways . . . and I will take one so that you don't have to wait to inherit money that is rightfully yours in any case. Again, I say, it is scandalous, but still it is done and I can only make it as easy as possible for you . . .'

'How much do you think my mother was worth, Joseph?'

'Oh – ' He widened his eyes, pursed his lips again, shook his head and said, 'Well, I know she got about sixty thousand for the two factories as they stood. She'd had a lot of new machinery put into the blacking side, hadn't she? and an extension. Then she had bought vans and all kinds of things. Oh, I'm sure it was sixty thousand for both of them, although I wasn't given the full details at the time. In her eyes' – and now he couldn't keep his bitterness from his tone – 'I was merely the caretaker. We both knew that.' His face was straight now and he bit on his lip before going on, 'Then she owned over fifty houses, and if we are talking about properties apart from rents . . . oh, well, I'd have to do some homework. Taking it altogether, I would say, about one hundred and fifty to one hundred and seventy-five thousand, because, you know, her money had been accumulating right back from her father's time.'

She drew in a sharp breath before she said, 'You are over a hundred thousand out. Three hundred thousand is nearer the mark.'

'Really! That's amazing. But I'm not surprised, no, because there were investments and things like that. Now and again she tried the stock market, didn't she?'

'I didn't know about that. I only know I don't want any of it.'

He leaned back, drawing in his chin and looked at her

as if trying to get her into focus; then he said, 'What did you say?'

There was the slightest of smiles on her lips now as she said, 'You were always in the habit, Joseph, of saying to me, "You heard what I said." '

'Yes. Yes, that was a pet phrase of mine, I suppose. But you said you wanted none of it . . . not any of it.'

'That's right.'

'What do you mean by that? You just have to get the divorce and it's yours. And, of course, I understand there was another clause: no part of that money is to come to my assistance. Well, I don't need it, so you needn't worry about that. I don't want a penny that belongs to her, and I might as well tell you I never did. It hurt me when she used to pay my staff; but you didn't understand that.'

'There were lots of things I didn't understand, Joseph. I didn't understand I had become a great trial to you. I didn't understand when to stop holding on, hanging on.'

'Oh, please!' He put up his hand and his fingers wagged tentatively towards her as if to stop her flow; but to no effect, and it was as if she was determined to be heard when she said, 'Let me talk, please, Joseph. I've lost everything I've ever valued, which was when I lost you; but in a strange way it was a good thing. It's like an operation: I was cut open and I saw all my bad bits. But the awful thing is I knew I couldn't do much about them. They were part of me. I had a kind of disease and that disease was you, and it was the means of ruining me. For years, Joseph, I was unhappy living side by side with you in that house, knowing that I had lost your love and that it was through my own fault. But that pain was nothing to what I've endured since I left the house and you, and the fact that you had found love somewhere else almost destroyed me. Yet, at the same time it was strange that I was unable to put the whole blame on you. In fact, no part of it, for I had a lot of time in which to look back on our lives together and I realised that right from the beginning . . . I wanted . . . I wanted; without giving, I wanted; and my mother aided me in this way. Whatever I wanted I got; except she never wanted me to have you, because she had this fixation about your father. And what is so unfortunate, Joseph, is, I'm still wanting. But . . . but I think, in a different way, more understanding. I know what I want and it isn't that money, it's . . . it's . . .' Her voice broke, her head went low and her whole body began to tremble, and when a hard sob came from her throat, he got up swiftly and sat down beside her on the sofa and, taking her hand, he said, 'Oh, don't, Amy. Don't give way. It's all right, I'll do whatever you want in this matter about the divorce or . . .'

'I . . . I don't . . . I don't want a divorce.'

'You don't? But . . . but you stand to lose all that money!'

She lifted her head and turned her tear-stained face towards him. 'Joseph.'

'Yes, Amy?'

'Will . . . will you take me back? I'll . . . I'll be different. I won't demand. I'll do anything you ask: keep in the background or the foreground, anything. I'm so lonely, Joseph, lost. Lost . . . Oh, Joseph.'

When his arms went about her, her head fell on his shoulder and the emotion in her body shook his own, and when she began to gasp for breath and almost choke and her unintelligible words became a wail, he rocked her backwards and forwards as he would have a child, saying, 'There, there, now. There, now. It's all right. It's going to be all right.'

His own eyes were moist now, and his heart was battering against his ribs as his mind told him she would have to come back with him no matter how he felt.

Well, how did he feel? The answer was, lonely. In a way, he was as lonely as she was; and she had changed, she was different. He had never imagined the Amy he knew making a confession of her faults as she had done.

Still gasping, tears still spouting from her eyes, she pulled herself away from him and, her words jerking from her mouth, she said, 'I . . . I didn't mean . . . I . . . I meant to be . . . calm . . . and ask you.'

He took a handkerchief from his pocket, and his voice, too, was thick now as he said, 'Come on. Dry your eyes.' And as he wiped her face her hand covered his and she muttered, 'I . . . I promise, I . . . I . . .'

'No more. No more. There's no need to promise anything. You're going home . . . You're coming home.' He patted first one cheek, then the other, saying, 'John said he wanted a matron to run the place. He always knows what he's doing, that fellow.'

'Oh Joseph! Joseph!'

'Now, now. No more. But do you really know in your own mind what you're throwing away?'

She shook her head slowly now, saying, 'I'm not throwing anything away, because I never had it in the first place.'

He stood up and held out his hands, saying, 'Come on. I'll go and phone the children. They'll be delighted. Now you go upstairs and pack a case, just your necessary things. You can come back later, or what you need can be sent on, and while you're up there I'll go in the kitchen and talk to the others. I'll explain that this house will have to be sold; and two of them are ready for retirement in any case, I should imagine. But the rest, I'll find work for them up at our place or somewhere. You have nothing to worry about. Go on now.'

She didn't move but she stood still before him and, her voice breaking, she said simply, 'Joseph! Oh, Joseph!' And such was the look in her eyes and the pleas in her voice that his heart was stirred as she had never stirred it for years and, bending towards her, he again took her face between his hands and gently he kissed her on the lips.

THE END

THE HARROGATE SECRET
by Catherine Cookson

Born into grinding poverty, ten-year old Freddie Musgrove spent his childhood living by his wits. The shillings he picked up running messages and smuggled goods past the ever-watchful eyes of the customs agents helped to feed his family. But one night a mission took this small runner to the great house at The Towers, where madness had been known to lurk, and there he witnessed a scene of unremiting horror.

Cookson is at the top of her form as she returns to her native Tyneside to tell this spellbinding story of a young boy and the dark secret that will change the course of his life forever.

Coming soon in Corgi paperback